Real Vampires Say Read My Hips

GERRY BARTLETT

REAL VAMPIRES SAY READ MY HIPS

Dragon Lady Publishing. League City, Texas, USA
Cover artist: Christopher Long

ISBN: 0991486013
ISBN-13: 978-0991486014

DEDICATION

For all my loyal readers through eleven books. I hope you enjoy Glory's happily ever after.

December, 2014.

Praise for the Real Vampires Series

"This has got to be the best series I have ever read."—*Night Owl Reviews*

"...fast-paced and funny entertainment expected from the series. Glory is hysterical..." —*Fresh Fiction*

"Glory gives girl power a whole new meaning, especially in the undead way." —**All** ***About Romance***

" I am completely enamored of Glory St. Clair and enjoy seeing what she gets herself into through each new book." —*Once Upon a Romance*

"Real vampires, real fun, real sexy!" —**Kerrelyn Sparks,** *New York Times* bestselling author of the *Love At Stake* series

Titles by Gerry Bartlett

REAL VAMPIRES HAVE CURVES

REAL VAMPIRES LIVE LARGE

REAL VAMPIRES GET LUCKY

REAL VAMPIRES DON'T DIET

REAL VAMPIRES HATE THEIR THIGHS

REAL VAMPIRES HAVE MORE TO LOVE

REAL VAMPIRES DON'T WEAR SIZE SIX

REAL VAMPIRES HATE SKINNY JEANS

REAL VAMPIRES KNOW HIPS HAPPEN

REAL VAMPIRES KNOW SIZE MATTERS

Novella: REAL VAMPIRES TAKE A BITE OUT OF CHRISTMAS

REAL VAMPIRES SAY READ MY HIPS

ONE

Lacy attacked me when I walked into the shop. "Let me see that ring again. Oh my God, it's huge!" She held my hand, her grin wide. "Are you ready for the wedding yet?"

"New Year's Day is way too soon. Of course not." I felt like I was on a runaway train when Lacy squealed and started ranting about details that I hadn't even considered.

"I know. But Jerry's determined to get the knot tied before I change my mind." I sank down on the stool we kept for customers near the cash register. "Wow. Do you realize we've never even lived together for any length of time?" I leaned closer. "And we met hundreds of years ago." I'd resisted that eternal commitment for over four hundred years.

So what had changed? Me. I was finally ready to admit that he was the one. Oh, let me say that again. THE ONE. After centuries of struggling against his domineering warrior nature and worrying that he'd never let me be independent, I'd finally realized we'd worked out a relationship I could live with. Actually, he'd changed too. Miracles do happen.

"Are you insane?" My mother suddenly appeared in the middle of the dress section. Yes, just materialized.

"Mother!" I glanced around, afraid some unsuspecting customer had fainted from shock.

"Give me some credit, Gloriana. None of your mortal customers saw me. Though I am sorely tempted to nip into the dressing room and tell the woman in there that she'll never get her butt into that size ten." My mother is a goddess from Olympus. She has a giant ego and considers mere mortals insignificant. I knew there was little chance she'd bother.

"You will not." I grabbed her arm and dragged her toward the back of the store. "Spandex can do wonders. If she wants to fit into a ten, I'm sure she'll manage it." I waved at Lacy to check. Zippers in the vintage clothes we sell in my shop weren't so forgiving.

"Oh, good. We're going to your back room. We need to have a mother-daughter talk." She was now the one doing the dragging, her fingers clamped on my arm. I gave Lacy a "save me" look but my were-cat manager had already found a size twelve and was halfway to the dressing room. Lacy has a bossy mother too. She did give me a sympathetic finger wave.

When the door finally closed behind me, I jerked my arm free. "I hope you're not here to disturb my wedding, Mother. You have to know I love Jerry. Why wouldn't I eventually marry him?"

"Because you have good sense, of course. He's a vampire, Gloriana." My mother shuddered. She sat in my only chair and crossed her legs. This season's Prada pumps in black lizard. Gorgeous. She always had on the most exquisite clothes. She materialized them with goddess magic which I envied.

"Don't say vampire like it's a bad word. You know what I am, Mother. That makes Jerry and me perfect for each other." I sat on my work table. "It took me a long time to realize it, but I'm ready to commit."

"Commit to an asylum perhaps. We have those on Olympus, darling. They're hell-holes. You should hear the screams. When a god or goddess goes off the deep end, the poor dears throw lightning bolts at anyone and everyone. It's quite annoying." My mother glanced at my concrete floor then kept her Gucci bag in her lap. "Obviously they must be locked away until they come to their senses. The screams are from the handmaidens who must care for them. The gods are stuck in tiny little cells, something like the coffins I've heard your council uses for punishment." Another delicate shudder.

"You sound like you've been there yourself, Mother. I hope this isn't a hint that mental illness runs in the family." I saw that I'd struck a nerve. Mean, maybe, but I was tired of her attitude. She hated what I was so naturally that meant Jerry was worthless too. "Luckily I've never actually seen the coffins. They're for vampires who break council law. I try to follow the rules here."

"I never said I had to be locked up. But I've visited friends there. I know you're angry with me, Gloriana, but please try to understand. It takes a lot to make a god go insane but I've seen it happen. Because Zeus drove the person to madness." She glared at me with eyes the same blue as mine. Hers shot sparks which was pretty and scary at the same time. "He can do that when he's angry. I'm afraid that when he discovers I've lied to him because I kept you a secret all these years, he'll let me have it." She lowered her head and sniffed. "I'm not sure I can handle his worst when he throws it at me."

"Then your best move is to disavow me, Mother. Write me off. Head back to Olympus as if I never existed." I hopped down to kneel in front of her when tears filled her eyes. "Don't get me wrong. It's been wonderful finding out I have a family after all this time and I'd hate to lose you. I've been so… alone in the world. Except for Jerry." I took a breath.

"Darling. We *are* family. You and me, even Zeus." My mother dabbed at her eyes with a hanky she pulled from her purse. "What you feel for that vampire is gratitude. Even *I* am grateful to him. For saving you and keeping you alive for me."

"He certainly didn't do it for you, Mother." I stood and looked down at her. "He loves me. For over four hundred years, he's taken care of me and has always been there for me. Now I'm finally strong enough to commit to him. Before . . ." I looked away from her. "Well, I was insecure. Afraid to use my powers. Not sure I even knew what they were."

"And now?" Her hand was on my shoulder.

"Now I know who I am and what I'm capable of." I turned to face her again and took her hand. "Thank you for that. So I'm confident that I can hold my own with Jerry, as an equal."

"Well, at least you're giving me credit for something." She took a breath. "I blame Achelous for all of this vampire madness." She frowned. "He will pay for tossing you away and forgetting you."

"Well, I hope so. But remember who left me with him in the first place. You lost the right to tell me what to do when you abandoned me in his orphanage, Mother. So accept my decision gracefully, please. I'm marrying Jerry and that's that." I put as much distance between us as the small room allowed and waited to see what she'd do. Toss a lightning bolt? It was one of her favorite tricks. It wasn't smart to stay too close to any of the gods or goddess from Olympus when they were pissed.

"Well." She stared at me, obviously thinking about her next move. "Am I invited to this event? Will there be bridal showers? A rehearsal dinner?" She pulled out a cell phone.

I could only gawk. I had no idea she even owned one. "Of course. Jerry and I have many friends. In fact, Flo is hosting a bridesmaids' dinner for me tomorrow night."

She punched something into her phone. "Surely you were going to have your mother there. What would your friends think if I didn't come? And I will bring an appropriate gift. Where is it? Is there a theme?"

"I, uh, you know Flo, or maybe you don't. Anyway, she's having it at her house. It's lovely. I'll text you directions if you'll give me your number." I heard my own phone, which I kept in my pants pocket, chime.

"There, you have it." She smiled as if we were just the most ordinary bride and her adoring mother. "The theme, Gloriana. And are you registered anywhere?"

I swallowed, not sure this wasn't a ploy of some kind. "Seriously? You're going to come to Flo's party and act like a happy mother of the bride? You won't cause a scene? Throw lightning bolts? Burn her beautiful house down?"

"Well, clearly you don't trust me." Her hand trembled where it held her phone. "I am trying to understand you, Gloriana. You say you love and are grateful to this vampire. You wish to marry him. I want to have a relationship with you so I must not stand in the way of your happiness. Correct?" She moistened her lips with her tongue, as if she were nervous.

"Yes. Thank you, Mother." I hugged her then stepped back again, still not sure this wasn't all for show. "Flo is doing an Arabian nights theme. She wants us to come dressed in harem clothes. She does love costumes. And my shop has plenty of that kind of garb. Leave it to Flo to think of something that will stimulate my business."

"Why, it sounds like fun. I knew Scheherazade. Such a clever girl. And she loved beautiful clothes. I may have something I can conjure that will be perfect." She clapped her hands, suddenly all smiles.

"Flo promises some surprises. I'll text you where I'm registered. Don't know why, but Flo insisted Jerry and I sign up for all the typical newlywed things."

"You are setting up housekeeping, aren't you? It is only proper." She tapped her foot. "I have much to do. A mother of the bride dress. I never thought I'd need such a thing. What are your colors?"

"I'm wearing red, Flo is wearing whatever she wants. We haven't--"

"Oh, dear. You clearly needed a wedding planner. But I suppose it's too late for that." She looked me over. "Yes, red's a good color for you. And lucky, I think. I will ask my astrologer about the date too. You did say New Year's Day. Hmm." Her brow wrinkled. "The party is tomorrow? That doesn't leave me much time. Text me when it starts. I wouldn't want to be late." She brushed my cheek with a light kiss. "I'd better go."

"About Zeus." Probably stupid to bring it up, but I knew she hadn't forgotten about taking me to Olympus. "Seriously. He doesn't need to know I even exist."

"Nonsense. My father will see you and love you on sight. I know it. You are the very image of my mother. That will soften him to me and make him forget my little fabrications." She managed a tremulous smile. "You mustn't worry about that."

"I think hiding an affair with a mortal and the resulting child for more than a thousand years is more than a *little* fabrication." I really, really didn't want to go to Olympus. "And what about the fact that I'm a vampire? How is Zeus going to take that?"

My mother actually bit her fingernail, a sign she was highly disturbed. When she realized she'd chipped her red polish, she frowned and blinked to fix it.

"Oh, he can never know that." She sighed and pasted on a smile. "Trust me to spin this situation to our advantage when the time comes. Now I'm off to check my closet. Mother of the bride. If only you could lose the fangs before the wedding." She dropped her cell into her bag and then disappeared.

Lose the fangs? I was still trying to process my mother's

surprising change in attitude and final remark when the door into the storeroom was flung open. My best friend ran inside to wrap me in a hug. "Glory! Lacy called me and said your mother is here. Is she causing trouble? As Matron of Honor I am ready to protect you. Do I have to send her skinny butt straight back to where she came from?" Florence da Vinci held me against her soft bosom.

The idea of my little friend taking on my mother was so ridiculous that I laughed. But once I started, I couldn't stop. Oh, God. My mother's sudden determination to get involved in my wedding plans scared the hell out of me.

"*Amica*! What did she say? What did she do?" Flo handed me a tissue to wipe my eyes.

"You won't believe it. She's all over the wedding now. She's coming to your party and is looking for a Mother of the Bride dress as we speak." I dabbed at my wet cheeks. "But thanks for the hug, Flo, I needed it."

"Did she do her usual vampire bashing?" Flo sat in the same chair my mother had just vacated. My friend also had on expensive shoes and a designer dress. It reminded me of my new goal—to make a big success of my business so I could afford to buy my own high end clothes. Flo might be content to take things from her rich husband, but I was fighting against the urge to let Jerry turn me into his trophy wife.

"She started in on it, but I shut her down. I'm not going to listen to her disrespect Jerry. I think she got the message." My phone chimed and I pulled it out of my pocket. "She just texted me. Where am I registered? It's been less than five minutes and she's bugging me already." I began to punch in the answers. "Let me send it now so she'll leave me alone."

"*Mio Dio*. Hebe at the party." Flo fanned her face with her hand. "I must order in more blood with alcohol. We'll both need it, eh?"

I hit send then grinned at Flo. "Definitely." I walked over to a rack and pulled out my costume for tomorrow night. "What do you think? Is this too much?" The crop top dipped low in front and was covered in gold sequins. I had matching sheer harem pants.

"It's perfect!" Flo jumped up to examine the fabric. "When Jeremiah sees you in this, he will carry you off to the bedroom so fast, you won't have time to open even one present. Better hide it from him until after the party."

I grinned and held it against me. "It is pretty bold. I've got some gold lame bikini panties to wear under it but that's all. He will love it."

"I hope you are selling plenty of costumes here in your shop for this party. Are you?" Flo sat again.

"Yes, thanks to you and your clever theme, Flo. I know some people will expect me to just marry Jerry and give up this place, but I want to make it even bigger and better."

Flo shook her head, clearly mystified. "You've always had this thing about independence. *Sciocchezza*, if you ask me." Flo opened her purse, a vintage piece that made me want to snatch it up and stick a price tag on it. "You marry a rich man, *amica*, so you should enjoy letting him take care of you."

"Did you just call me crazy?" I knew we didn't have the same philosophy when it came to men but I hoped we weren't going to fight about it.

"No, no. Just a little foolish." She smiled.

"Jerry understands that I like to make my own money. He's even helping me with a business plan."

"Well. I am surprised." Flo glanced at my new tablet and the pile of bills next to it. "He has always seemed a very, how you say, traditional man. He likes to travel, check on his other investments. Don't you think he will want you with him on those trips once you're married?"

"We'll work it out." Though my stomach had gone into free fall. Trust Flo to zero in on my main worry. Traditional? That was a polite way to say Jerry was a throwback to his sixteenth century Highland roots.

Flo frowned. "I have said too much. Now you are worrying. I shut up and go. Come early tomorrow night. Help me with your mother. I don't trust her. Do you?"

"Not at all. She gave up too easily on her plan to take me off to Olympus. Of course she's still plotting." I hugged Flo tight. "Together you and I will handle whatever trouble she starts."

"Of course!" She patted my back. "I'm just glad you finally said yes to Jeremiah. He's been very patient with you."

"Yes, he has. I'm lucky he didn't find another woman." I remembered a real bitch from his past we'd managed to run out of town not long ago. "Or at least the *right* other woman."

"He's yours now. And I sense he's coming. I go out the back." Flo winked. "Take care of him. Do not be too stubborn about some things." She looked around the back room again and gestured at that stack of bills. "Are you really so crazy about this little shop? Jeremiah is a wealthy man. Enjoy what he can give you. We could go shopping together, in Paris, Roma. I have wished for this a long time. Don't be stubborn, Glory. Let him take care of you."

I refused to fight with my best friend. She just didn't understand how different we were. She rushed out the back door just as the one from the shop opened again and Jerry walked in, his smile taking my breath away. I had never seen him happier. I ran up to him and threw my arms around him.

"That's a fine welcome." He leaned down and took my mouth with his. There it was, the perfect kiss that reassured me we were meant to be. I savored his taste, the way we fit. I sighed when he pulled back. We were both smiling and I saw that he was flushed. Of course I hadn't done *that*. He'd obviously found a blood donor in an alley along busy Sixth Street on his way to meet me.

"I'm glad to see you. Flo just left. We were talking about the bridal party. I have a sexy costume to wear. What do you think about the Arabian Nights?" I twined my fingers through his curls. He had let his hair grow almost to his shoulders and it was a look I loved.

"If you're going to be my harem of one, I'm eager to try an Arabian night." He glanced at the rack where my costume was hanging. "Is yours the green number that I can see through? Try it on now and give me a preview." He slid a hand down to my hip to pull me closer.

"Mmm. Tempting, but no." I leaned against him. Flo had raised questions I wanted answered. "Can we talk?"

"If we must." He let me go and sat on the table, patting the space beside him. "What's on your mind? Lacy said your mother was here earlier. Did she upset you?"

"She tried. When that didn't work, she decided to get on the wedding bandwagon. I'm still not sure I believe her act, but she says she's coming to the wedding and all the other festivities." I sat and leaned against him. He was so solid and so reliably mine. I slid my arm around his waist. "But forget her. Flo made me think about our future."

"What about it?" He stiffened under my fingertips. "Damn it,

Gloriana, I will not take that ring back."

"I'm not changing my mind, just trying to work out logistics." I felt him relax again. I'd made my big strong Highlander insecure about our relationship with my hot and cold attitude and my affair with another man. He'd forgiven but he hadn't forgotten. I was going to have to work to make him trust me not to back out of this commitment.

"Logistics. We've settled the living arrangements, of course." He kissed my nose.

"Yes, I love our new apartment." I'd been surprised when Jerry had bought the apartment building that also housed my shop. Then he'd evicted the other tenants on the second floor so we could have a huge apartment. At first I'd seen his taking over the living arrangements as high-handed and manipulative. I'd finally realized that was my kneejerk reaction to almost everything he did when he was simply trying to please me. It wasn't easy for me to accept gifts from Jerry, but I was learning to do it.

"This is turning out to be a good investment. If you ever decide to give up the shop, this space could easily be rented out to someone else. Places on Sixth Street are always in demand. The rents from the apartments upstairs along with the shops down here, including yours and Mugs and Muffins next door, bring in a good income." He set a folder on the table next to him.

"I don't plan to give up the shop." I ignored his hands on my back as he pulled me closer. "You aren't counting on that, are you?"

"Don't get your panties in a twist, Gloriana. I wasn't suggesting such a thing." He smiled and traced my frown line which I knew had appeared between my brows. "In fact, I have a wedding present for you." He reached for the folder and put it in my hands. "Look and see."

"What is it?" I flipped it open then gasped. "Jerry! It's the deed to this building. You, you put it in my name." I scanned the document. There was a lot of legalese but the meaning was clear. Jeremy Blade, the name he was going by in Austin, had deeded this property over to one Gloriana St. Clair for the sum of one dollar.

"No, I sold it to you. You owe me a dollar. I figure you're good for it." He was grinning, entirely pleased with himself.

"This is too much!" I blinked as tears filled my eyes. I'd never owned a piece of property in my life. And I had a feeling the price

Jerry had paid Damian just a month ago had been in the seven figures.

"Nothing is too much for you, my love." He rubbed a tear off my cheek. "Did I surprise you?"

"Surprise? You've blown me away. I don't know what to say." I looked the deed over again. It was real. I owned this entire block. On Austin's Sixth Street. I worried for a minute, thinking about taxes and insurance, and then deliberately put all of that out of my mind. Jerry said the income was good. It would cover such things. And, if I couldn't afford it, I could always sell it.

"You're awfully quiet. *Is* it too much?" He was starting to look worried. "You know I'd give you much more if you'd let me."

"So you've said." I sighed and carefully set the folder on the table next to him. "I was thinking how much I like it here."

"True. We've both lived many places. Austin seems like home, doesn't it?" Jerry pulled me close. "Someday we'll have to move, but not anytime soon."

"No, not anytime soon." I leaned against him. "I'll always remember Austin now. Where we made our home. Where we married. We have such good friends here."

"That we do." He ran a thumb across my cheek and to the back of my neck so that our lips almost touched. "You've built a fine business here. I admire that. Keep it as long as you wish. I'll help any way I can. Or leave you to it. Just tell me what you want, my love. Owning the building will give you options. You can expand if you want. Kick out the tattoo parlor next door if you need that space." He didn't have to pull me close this time as I kissed him with all the love that I had. When I finally leaned back, I rested my head against his shoulder.

"Have I told you how much I love you, Jeremiah Campbell?" I ran my hand over his chest, loving the hard contours of my warrior.

"I never get tired of hearing it, lass." He lifted my chin and kissed me, lying back on the table, until I was stretched out on top of him.

"Wait!" I wrenched out of his arms and rescued my computer, bills and that precious deed, stowing them on a shelf before I ripped off my sweater to fling it across the room. Then I locked the doors.

"Is this *my* wedding present?" He grinned up at me as he reached for the front clasp of my skimpy black lace bra.

"Well, since I can't afford buildings, I guess this will have to do. How can you keep surprising me?" I unbuttoned his cotton shirt so I could smooth my hands over his chest. Bending over him, I licked my way from one nipple to the other, sucking one into my mouth.

"I consider it a constant challenge." He moaned when I dragged a fang along his skin, drawing blood then licking it away.

"Good. I want to keep you on your toes, lover." This man was mine and I wasn't going to let him forget it.

"Gloriana." He groaned and pushed his hands into the back of my jeans. Got to love spandex. I wasn't about to admit the size of mine. In fact, I cut out the tag as soon as I got them. Some things Jerry just didn't need to know.

I sat up and opened my jeans then hopped off the table to wrestle them off. I didn't want to delay things while Jerry tried to pry them off. He'd been busy getting naked himself and kicked his own jeans away then lifted me to the edge of the table where he stood between my legs. He kissed me endlessly while his fingers worked their magic. I ran my hands over his hard body, finding all the places I knew made him groan with pleasure. There's a lot to be said for centuries of history together. The miracle was that we had never tired of each other. That the spark not only still glowed but burst into bright flames at every touch.

He ran his tongue around each of my nipples, his fangs nipping and playing until I pulled on his hair, moaning with pleasure. Then he sank to his knees, breathing in my scent before he pressed his mouth between my thighs. I grasped his ears. There was no need to guide him since he knew just how to make me shriek my release. So soon. I crossed my feet behind his head, rocking into him as he found and plucked the sensitive nub with his lips. My hips arched off that hard table as excitement shivered through me. I was close again. But I wouldn't let him make me come without him. Not this time.

"God, Jerry! I need you inside me! Now." I actually remembered that the door into the shop wasn't soundproof. Of course the clerks out there were paranormals who could hear things mortals couldn't. Still… The music in the shop got louder. I collapsed back on the table, pulling Jerry up until his erection teased me, nudging for entrance. But he wouldn't give me what I wanted. Not yet.

"Say it again, Gloriana. Say you'll marry me on New Year's Day. Nothing will stop us from becoming man and wife. Nothing." He was serious, his muscular arms bulging as he held himself just above me. His face was inches from mine, his eyes dark and serious.

"I love you, Jeremiah Campbell, Jeremy Blade, any name you call yourself. I'll always be yours. Only yours. And on the first day of the New Year, I'll declare it before all of our friends. Now take me before I go mad." I scored his back with my nails, afraid I was about to do something mean with my Olympus powers if he didn't put me out of my misery.

"I love you, Gloriana. And I'm never letting you go." He plunged into me then, the pressure of his cock all it took to make me bite back my scream of release. I shuddered, feeling my completion rocket through me. His mouth on mine swallowed my squeal of pleasure. I pounded on his back, my heels sliding up and down the backs of his strong legs.

But Jerry wasn't finished, not by a long shot. He kept staring into my eyes--trying to read my mind? I wasn't about to let him. I could block my thoughts and did. He was never letting me go? Fine. That worked both ways. I wanted to belong to him now. He was as tied to me as I was to him. Marriage. In the vampire world it was even more difficult to break that bond than it was for mortals. We were a fairly small community and it was inevitable that we'd see each other, run into each other. Only death would part us. And death for a vampire was rare and never natural.

He held my hips and began a slow seduction again. Teasing me, he kept pulling out until I begged him to push deeper, go faster. He stayed in control, his face solemn until I saw him finally lose it. He began to drive into me, finding the perfect angle that he knew would send me over the brink again. Yes, the tension was there, building, tightening inside me until my toes curled. For a moment I resisted. I didn't want… But this was Jerry, my beloved, the man who would do anything for me. Even buy me a damned building.

My second orgasm broke me into a thousand pieces as Jerry shouted his own release. I let him go, my hands landing on the wooden table. He lay on me for a few moments, his lips brushing my throat gently. It was a sweet vampire kiss showing love, not hunger for my blood.

When he finally rolled off of me with a satisfied groan I opened my eyes to stare at the cheap acoustical tiles above my head. I realized my hands were fisted and I opened them finger by finger then ran my hand over his hair-roughened stomach and felt the muscles contract. I loved how masculine he was. I did. I loved *him*.

Jerry's heavy hand landed on my thigh, like he owned it. I turned my head and saw his smile. Satisfaction. Happiness. Not possession. He was glad we'd be together forever. I managed my own smile. If I had doubts I would chalk them up to bridal nerves. Yes, that had to be it. Everything Jerry did for me was out of love, not for any other reason.

"I have an appointment with my lawyer for you to sign that deed in front of a notary, Gloriana. A formality. That will make it yours. Can you come with me now?" Jerry jumped off the table, eager to get to business. He grabbed his jeans and stepped into them.

I wasn't about to lie around naked and exposed under those fluorescent lights. I was right behind him, snapping on my bra, pulling my sweater over my head. I'd just stepped into my panties when he held my jeans just out of reach.

"You're awfully quiet, Gloriana. Is this a bad time?" He was serious, watching me.

I grabbed a belt loop and tugged him close then kissed his lips, wishing he'd smile again. I could see that he wanted to please me and I was going to have to stop imagining control issues that just weren't there.

"You can't know how much I love that you're doing this for me. It's perfect." I slid my hands down his chest then around his waist. "This marriage should be a partnership, Jerry. How can I ever match this kind of generosity?"

"Don't be ridiculous." He jerked me closer. "All I've wanted for centuries is to make you happy." He dropped the jeans and slid his hands down to cup my butt. "You want to give me something? Give me two weeks away from this shop. For a proper honeymoon. Can the girls handle that?" His smile was back, a wicked one this time that promised all kinds of naughty honeymoon delights.

"Hmm. Sure." I ran my fingers through his thick hair. "Where will we go?" Sandy beaches and moonlight. Or maybe a mountain chalet. Someplace far away from Austin and my stupid doubts.

"Anywhere you wish." He kissed me one more time then stepped back. "Now are you coming with me to the lawyer's office?"

"Can you give me half an hour? Lacy needs to take a dinner break then I can meet you there."

"Perfect." He kissed me, pressed the card with the address into my hand then slipped out the back door. I sat in my own chair for a change and realized I probably had a goofy grin on my face. I was beginning to think this was going to work. We could be happy. He was respecting me. My doubts were silly. I struggled into my jeans then just sat there, finally sure I could go through with it. I was going to marry Jeremiah Campbell and have an amazing honeymoon.

"I can see that I will have to take drastic measures."

"Mother? You weren't spying on me, were you?"

"Unfortunately." She was back and glaring at me from beside the back door. "It is not something that I enjoy. Bacchanals in Rome were more entertaining."

"That's disgusting." I was sure my face was as red as her Gucci handbag. "What do you mean by drastic measures?"

"I'm sorry that I have to do this, but you leave me no choice, Gloriana." She raised her hand.

I blinked and the crowded back room in my shop was gone. Instead I was lying on a bed. It was a golden monstrosity and huge, an ornate four poster. The canopy over my head was draped with gold and white silk. Under me I could feel more silk and big fluffy pillows. I struggled to sit up and look around. The bedroom had fancy French furniture, clearly vintage and that must have cost a fortune. Looking down I saw one of those gorgeous rugs that would feel like velvet under my feet. I was still dressed in my jeans and sweater though my feet were bare. My shoes were on the floor next to the bed. Where the hell was I?

"Mother? What have you done?"

"What you forced me to do, daughter." She appeared next to me. There was a woman behind her. A woman in a toga. Oh, God. "Here, enjoy your first meal. I'm sure you've been craving chocolate. And how about some croissants? You won't believe what they do with pastry here." She flicked her wrist and the woman set the tray down on my lap.

My eyes watered as the aroma of fresh hot chocolate wafted from a delicate bone china cup. Next to it sat a pair of flaky pastries and a bowl of glistening strawberry preserves. All of it was laid out to perfection on a tray set with a linen napkin and sterling silver flatware.

"What the hell is this? Are you into torturing me now? You

know I can't eat."

"Yes, you can. Here." My mother smiled. "Welcome to Olympus, darling."

TWO

I ran my tongue over my teeth. Inhaled the woman standing next to the bed after she'd set the tray in my lap. Tested my teeth again.

"Where are my fangs?" I was shaking and the cup rattled against the saucer, sloshing chocolate all over the tray.

"Oh, I got rid of those, darling. Aren't you glad?" Mother gloated, thrilled with her little trick.

I wanted to toss that tray at her but the smell of chocolate was too much for me. I picked up the delicate porcelain and drank. Heaven in a cup. Had anything ever tasted better? Hell, yes! A-B Negative from a live donor. I slammed down the cup and hot liquid splashed my fingers.

"Ouch. Damn." I sucked chocolate off my hand and glared at this woman who claimed to love me. "What the hell have you done? Last I knew you were searching for a dress for my wedding."

Mother gestured and the servant vanished. "I thought I could go along with your plans, Gloriana. Even though they were ridiculous." She paced the carpet next to the bed. "I knew I had to try to reason with you. Make you understand that the marriage could not take place. But when I turned back and you were having sex with that monster? Drawing blood with your fangs as if that gave you pleasure?" Her voice had risen until I wanted to cover my ears. She stopped beside the bed and visibly collected herself. "Well. I cannot describe how disgusting I found that display. No mother worth anything would leave her daughter to such a fate."

"What fate? Happiness with the man I love?" I pushed the tray off my lap and jumped out of bed to face her. "And don't get me started on your worth as a mother. We've been through that, haven't we?" I so wished for my fangs because I couldn't work up a good snarl without them. "Damn it, Mother. I won't stay here. Take me back." I stuck a finger in her face, close enough that she actually took a step back. "Right. Now."

"No." She grabbed my finger and shoved me back against the bed. "Calm down. Give this a chance, Gloriana. You'll love it here once you think about it. I saw the way you drank that chocolate. And you haven't even eaten yet." She picked up the croissant and waved it under my nose. "Come now. You know you want to. Savor the taste of real food, darling. Can you smell it? I'm horrified that you've had to subsist on blood like an animal for hundreds of years."

"Damn it, Mother. You won't win me over with baked goods." I knocked it out of her hands. Of course I could smell it. But it creeped me out that I couldn't tune into the things I normally did. Like the beating of her heart, the smell of her own blood, or that of her servant who had crept back in with a fresh pot of that Devil's brew, the hot chocolate.

"Calm down, Gloriana. Give Olympus a chance. This can be a little visit. Not a permanent arrangement." My mother looked me over. "Just wait until you see the wardrobe I've prepared for you. I don't imagine you'll be in such a hurry to leave then."

"Stop it! I told you Flo is hosting a bridal party for me tomorrow night. Jerry is waiting for me even now." I followed her to double doors near the bed. "Forget bribing me to stay here. Take me home."

"This *is* your home. You're staying. So relax and enjoy the perks of being daughter to a goddess, Gloriana." Mother threw open the doors. I caught a glimpse of colorful clothes, racks of them. Shoes, handbags. I turned my back on them and grabbed her arm. Her servant gasped and scurried out of the room.

"You have to listen to me. I didn't agree to this. What if Zeus finds out I'm here? Do you want to be locked up in one of those little cells? He'll probably lock me up too, if he doesn't fry us both into ashes with lightning bolts as soon as he sees us. Take me back!"

When she just smiled and shook her head, I lost it. I ran to the bed, grabbed the tray, and tossed it at her. I had goddess strength now. It flew. She deflected it with a flick of her wrist but the trajectory was right on. It made an impressive crash landing on that exquisite rug. We both stared at the chocolate and strawberry stained Aubusson and sighed then glared at each other.

"Calm down, Gloriana. I had to do something. You were acting like a love sick teenager. About to make one of the biggest mistakes of your long life. I couldn't let you tie yourself to that fang wearing monster." Mother stamped her foot, filled with righteous indignation. Like she was the wronged party. "Where's your gratitude?"

"Gratitude? For you ruining everything?" I'm sure my face was strawberry red. Damn. I should have tasted… No. "Jerry's not a monster and I love him, Mother. If you were eavesdropping then you know he was buying me a home, planning a dream honeymoon." I looked down and realized Mother had pulled one of her tricks and I was now wearing a toga like hers. My shoes had disappeared and delicate silver sandals sat on the floor next to the bed. "What more do you want from him?"

"I want him to be worthy! I want him to be a god! You are the granddaughter of the greatest god of all. You should have an arranged marriage. Zeus will know who best to have you marry. Let me plan all of this to your advantage, Gloriana." Mother paced the carpet. She frowned and the handmaiden suddenly appeared long enough to collect the broken dishes and tray. The stains magically disappeared.

"You're insane. I will never marry anyone else. I could barely convince myself to marry Jerry and I've loved him for centuries." I stomped around the room. It was filled with collectibles that made my resale shop roots quiver. I could make a fortune from this bedroom alone. Oh, who was I kidding? It would take a miracle to get out of here with my skin whole. I'd certainly never be able to take any trinkets with me. Though that vintage snuff box…

"Gloriana, you are thinking like a shop keeper. I can't tell you how that dismays me." My mother laid her hand on my back. "When I remember how you've had to scramble to earn your own living all these years, it makes me so terribly sad."

"Yeah, well, it made me strong too, Mother. I'm not apologizing for it. I have a nice little business. I wouldn't have to scramble if you'd toss down a few of these goodies once in a while." I heard myself and stopped. Money. I was getting obsessed with it. That had to stop. I was about to ruin another relationship over it. Mine with my mother, mine with Jerry. "Forget it. The main thing is that you don't want me here. It will get you in trouble with your father. Let's go. Back down to Earth. I've come here so you got your wish. I even drank some chocolate. But I feel weird, off kilter. My vampire nature is too much a part of me now. I can't just forget it and become a goddess like you want me to be."

It was the truth. I felt the loss of my fangs constantly, my tongue searching for them and coming up empty. It was uncomfortable. Creepy. Depressing.

"You haven't seen anything, darling. I have two precious boys. Your brothers. You must meet them while you're here. You want that, don't you?" Mother settled into a chair. "And, don't be stubborn, check out the closet. I've picked out a fabulous wardrobe for you. The toga is just for court appearances. I had the best time shopping. Look in the mirror. How do you like your new body? I couldn't decide on a two or a zero. I settled on a two. Zeroes tend to have skinny arms, don't you think?"

I swallowed, suddenly queasy. Look in the mirror. Okay. So a goddess could see her reflection. There was a large full-length hanging on one wall next to that set of double doors. I'd never even glanced at the mirror because I was out of the habit.

"Two? Like a *size* two?" I glanced down. The toga didn't give me much of an idea of my actual size but I could tell I wasn't Glory as usual. I could see my silver painted toenails past my trimmer boobs. Wow. I couldn't remember ever seeing my toes without putting my feet up.

I sat on the side of the bed, dizzy. What the hell had she done? My size twelve and double D's were me. Sure they were bigger than I'd always dreamed of being. But I was comfortable with them. Jerry's exes had tended to run in the size six range. A two? No way I could…

"Relax, darling. If you want something else, you have only to snap your fingers and picture it. It's what goddesses can do, you see. It's a wonderful skill." Mother was in her element. She'd picked up a large wooden box and now sat with it open in her lap. "I have a jewelry collection here as well. I'm very partial to earrings. Large dangly ones because they show up so well when we have long hair, don't you agree?" She held up a pair of pearl and diamond drops. "I think these are sweet."

Sweet? They could have financed a revolution in a third world country. I grabbed my own earlobes, comforted by the feel of the dangling sapphire and diamond drops Flo had given me when Jerry and I had announced our engagement. I got up on wobbly legs to see… A glance in the mirror said they were exactly as Flo had described them and matched my eyes perfectly. I drew closer to that mirror, shocked down to my bare toes. Oh. My. God.

The blond staring at me could not be Gloriana St. Clair. Simply could not be. Sure, I had a computer that let me see myself when I put on makeup, but now… I had the same blue eyes and my face was a similar shape, but hello cheek bones! And look at my pretty sculpted chin and delicate bone structure. My extra pounds had done a good job of disguising what was clearly a petite frame too.

"Mother!" I turned to face her.

"Too much? I can make you a six. Or do it yourself. Go ahead. Think and snap. It's a game you can play. Size yourself." She was busy trying on necklaces. Heavy gold chains draped her neck and she now wore a plain linen sheath in cream to show off the jewelry.

"No! I'm perfect." I blinked when she blurred. Stupid, crying over the way I looked. Jerry didn't care. He loved my curves. I looked down. I bet I was no more than a B cup now, less than a handful, he'd say. I ran my palms down my flat stomach. I could feel my hip bones, wear a bikini. Even—

"So I'm really not vampire up here? I could see the sun?"

"Of course, Gloriana. If you chose to visit Earth in this form. We don't bother with day, night, or weather up here. Except when we're using certain elements as weapons like those lightning bolts you've seen some of the gods toss around, including me when I'm angry." Mother shuddered. "Zeus can make it storm over your head like you wouldn't believe. I've been soaked to the skin more than once when I displeased him."

"I guess a bad temper runs in the family." I couldn't resist saying that.

Mother ignored me and glanced around. "I have us in a safe place here but we must move fast and get you in front of my father. Like I told you, you are the image of my mother. In court dress with your hair down, I'm sure you will melt his heart." She bit her lip. "Of course my parents are not always happy with each other." She shrugged. "No, I just know he will be thrilled to have another child to indulge. Father is very family oriented."

"Think, Mother. You sound unsure. This could be a disaster in the making. For both of us. Take me home." But I couldn't resist stepping through those double doors and into the closet. It stretched before me until it ended in an angled three way mirror. Color coded dresses, skirts, blouses and pants were evenly divided down most of the sides though there was a dazzling array of shelves holding handbags and designer shoes. I was drawn in almost against my will. I had to touch the silks, stroke the fine leathers.

"Not yet. Look at you. This closet alone is worth the trip. I have pleased you. You are crying with joy." She was right behind me, almost breathing down my neck. Not that I could smell her over the scent of new fabric. It had always been like an aphrodisiac to me. A rare and wonderful fragrance that could get me higher than—

I whirled around. "No! I am crying because you are trying to manipulate me. My own mother. Using the very things I love to try to lure me away from everything I ever wanted or needed." I backed up, but she stayed right with me. "Without the man I love and my friends, this is meaningless. I can't be bought!"

"Calm down, Gloriana." Mother nodded toward the shoes. Every name brand I'd ever coveted was well represented. "Try something on."

"No! I won't stay here. I love Jerry. I want my man and my fangs back. My friends. Please, Mother. Let me go." We were nose to nose. Which made me very uncomfortable. Her power pushed me back and I stumbled, landing on a padded bench set in the middle of the massive closet. A place to sit when I slipped on the fabulous Gucci slingback with the double "G"s on the high heels. No, I didn't want to even see them. I stared up at a delicate pink Murano glass chandelier. Maybe it was childish but I was making a point.

"Gloriana, you're not going back. Not until we have arranged the meeting with your grandfather. After that, we will see. You may not want to return to that mundane little life you've created down there." My mother sat beside me. "Listen to me and listen well. Your very existence depends on it. We will be going before Zeus in a few hours. My handmaidens will prepare you. Hair, makeup, the works.

You'll look better than you ever have. I will tutor you. Tell you what to say. You will not mess this up, Daughter."

"I told you--" I froze and it wasn't by choice. She had a silver painted nail pinned on my forehead.

"Enough. You will tell me nothing. This is about my survival too. Obey me. No more questions or complaints." She shook her head. "I cannot believe your stubbornness. It must come from your father."

I really wanted to know more about this mysterious father of mine. She'd claimed once that I was the result of a fling with a mortal male. But knowing her as I did now, I doubted she'd stoop so low. Was it one of the gods here? I saw her eyes narrow, obviously reading my mind. She rose with a swish of her toga. And wasn't that telling? I could move again and stood on shaky legs.

"What now?" I followed her out of the closet.

"You will be bathed, plucked, shampooed and fluffed to within an inch of your life." She clapped her hands and a trio of handmaidens appeared. More double doors were flung open and I could see an ornate bathroom at the other end of the room.

"A spa day in Olympus." I couldn't muster up any enthusiasm. Because I knew at the end of all these treatments I'd have to face the head honcho himself. How would he react to the secret baby scenario? Would he shoot us down on the spot? Or worse—decide to make me his new favorite? Which would make it almost impossible for me to get back where I belonged.

"Gloriana, trust me to make this work out for the best." My mother nodded and the trio of brunette toga-wearing clones grabbed me and tugged me toward the bathroom.

"Trust you. Sure, Mother. While I'm doing this, why don't you check your own closet for that Mother of the Bride dress?" I knew I sounded bitter and rightly so. Those were my last words before I was stripped and gawked at. No worries. My perfect new body was something to be proud of, though apparently it still had a way to go to meet the high standards of Olympus. I was scrubbed, waxed and polished to a high gloss.

I thought of Jerry as I suffered for beauty. He'd love the new Brazilian wax job. And my smooth legs and heels. Yes, vamps didn't age and we had the overnight healing thing, but I'd never been perfect. Now, looking in the mirror as I was draped with the white silk toga, I felt like I was getting there. My hair was a golden cloud around my shoulders and even my eyebrows had been waxed into perfect arches. Makeup had been used with a deft hand and looked natural, giving me a dewy flush on my cheeks.

"Here, wear this." My mother pinned a diamond brooch on my shoulder. I recognized it as one she usually wore on her own toga. Today she had fastened hers with a larger one resembling the sun. Yellow diamonds made up the burst of glittering stones. "I am very pleased."

"I admit I've never felt beautiful, until now." I turned around in front of the mirror. I couldn't get over the novelty of seeing my reflection. I'd never been satisfied with myself. Now? Thanks to my mother's magic, I was perfect.

"You *are* beautiful. Zeus has to love you on sight." My mother took a breath and I swear she was nervous. This was a new look on her.

"And if he doesn't?" I took her hand. It was icy. "What will he do to you? To us?"

"I can't imagine and don't want to. Let's get this over with. Too many people are aware I've brought you here. My handmaidens are sworn to secrecy on pain of death, but that doesn't mean someone hasn't noticed the activity around my chambers." She squeezed my fingers then drew away from me. "Come on. Just follow my lead. Say nothing. If he asks you a direct question, answer briefly. For both our sakes, do not say the 'v' word."

"Deny what I've been?" I stayed on her heels as she led the way across the bedroom to yet another set of double doors. I was finally going to get to see the rest of Olympus. I couldn't say I was eager. The gods and goddesses I'd met so far were volatile and terrifying. What kind of place produced such creatures?

"Of course you'll deny it! He can read your mind but I hope he'll be so dazzled by your resemblance to Mother that he'll forget to do it. Concentrate on your surroundings. On the splendor. On your grandfather's magnificence. Push away any thoughts of your past. It is for the best. Trust me on this." She stopped with her hand on the doorknob, her face pale. "Swear you will do as I ask. On your lover's life."

"God, Mother. You are seriously freaking me out. Are you threatening Jerry?" I swallowed, queasy and sure I was as pale as she was.

"If that's what it takes. This is no time to be jockeying for your ridiculous independence, Gloriana. Zeus considers women vassals, useful for making alliances." She put up her hand when I started to object. "Spare me. I know it's an antiquated notion. It is why he and my mother are always at war. Do you see me acting like an oppressed helpmate to some man? Of course not." Her laugh was more than a little tinged with bitterness. "Even if I saw my husband more than once a decade, I would not bow down to him. It is not in me. Am I not Zeus's daughter? But I'll certainly not flaunt my attitude in front of my father. It would only serve to stir his temper." She shuddered. "We do not want to do that."

"I get it. Zeus mad is a disaster." I squeezed her shoulder. "I'll behave if you promise to leave Jerry alone."

"As long as your behavior pleases me, your vampire lover is safe from my wrath. As for your grandfather..? Keep in mind that Zeus mad is more than a disaster, it's a tsunami, a cataclysm, the annihilation of a planet, Gloriana." She took a breath. "Now we must delay no longer." She flung the door open and we were on a path. Paved with gold. Yep. The real deal. It gleamed beneath our feet. The grout looked like diamonds. The twinkling effect dazzled me. I was tempted to reach down just to feel…

"Look straight ahead. We must act like we are out for a stroll, at ease here." Mother took my arm, guiding me to the right when the path branched. "Oh, look, there's a play going on. As an actress, it might interest you to know that the gods and goddesses enjoy creating their own productions." She waved at someone on the stage. It was a costume drama, the look similar to one from Shakespeare's time. Either it was a dress rehearsal or no one cared that the audience consisted of just a handful of people sitting at tables enjoying a meal and drinking what looked like goblets of wine.

"Everyone here is so, um, beautiful." I couldn't help but stare, especially at the men. They were in skimpy garb, Trojan maybe. Jerry had worn that type of short leather loin cloth for Halloween and it showed off perfect male physiques. "But they seem bored."

"Yes, well, unless there's a fight going on, perfection can get old after a while." My mother hurried me past the audience when someone turned to stare at us. "I'm afraid you've been recognized. We don't have cell phones up here, but mental telepathy is even faster. The word is going out that I have a new friend who looks a lot like me. This isn't helping. Hold on, I'm going to have to take us there another way."

I swallowed. Then everything around us disappeared. I got a strange feeling which I recognized. I'd dematerialized before but only for a second. That had been in an emergency. I guess Mother considered this one. She held onto me as we settled into a new room. I knew as soon as things came into focus that this must be the throne room. There was a large gilded chair set on a dais in front. Mother sighed audibly when we saw that the chair was empty.

"He's late." A man spoke from behind us. "What or who have you brought him, Hebe?"

"Shut up, Dionysus. And get away from me with that wine. You've ruined too many of my togas already." Mother shoved his arm away.

"My, aren't you in a mood. And I can see why." The man who was handsome even though he had bloodshot eyes, snapped his fingers and a man in the crowd around him took his goblet. "Who is this tidbit who looks the image of you? A by-blow? Did you forget to tell dear old Dad about her perhaps?"

"Go away before I tell our father that you are the one who got his favorite mistress with child during your last debauch." Mother whirled to face him. "You want to face his wrath? It would suit me very well to have him spend it on you instead of me."

"Calm down. I don't know where you get your information but the woman isn't expecting anything more than another visit from our father when he finds the time. We shared some wine and a good time. I know how to prevent complications. Unlike you it seems." The man backed away. "You can be such a bitch. Go ahead, introduce your little girl and see what happens. Father has been entertaining one of his other concubines. He's in a good mood, I hear. And your mother is nowhere to be found. Which is another reason for Father's happy state." He looked me over. "If you think this girl's resemblance to your mama will soften him, think again. Hera does her best to make him suffer when he strays from his marriage vows."

I felt my mother's hand shaking as she gripped my arm. That didn't make me feel better. What had she brought me to? It seemed more and more likely that we'd both end up spending the rest of eternity in adjoining tiny cells. Maybe she'd teach me to shoot lightning bolts using poor handmaidens for target practice. I swallowed, sure I was going to throw up or fall down. I gasped when Mother squeezed tighter. Her smile masked her nervousness.

"Oh, give it up, Dionysus. You know our father has a tender spot for *all* of his children and grandchildren." She even managed a carefree laugh. "I am counting on it. Now don't you have somewhere to be, an orgy to organize?"

"Now that you mention it." He gestured to his posse and grabbed his goblet. "Don't say I didn't warn you if this doesn't go as you hoped." He disappeared.

I pulled my mother's hand off of me, sure I'd be bruised. "I knew this was a bad idea. Zeus will kill us both. Take me back down to Earth. Now."

"Too late. He's coming. Don't listen to my brother. He's a drunken pessimist. He does throw a good party however. I will have him arrange things when Zeus accepts you. A celebration." She reached out and fluffed my hair, then pinched my cheeks. "There. You were pale as a ghost. Now I'm looking on the bright side. I insist you do the same." Mother smiled and straightened her shoulders as trumpets blared. "Stand tall, Gloriana. Show him you are not afraid."

"That would be a lie." I couldn't breathe or even swallow. My mouth was so dry I couldn't spit. Not that I would have dared. Oh, God. I actually grabbed my mother's hand, that's how scared I was.

"Nonsense. Mind empty, remember? Just enjoy the show." She smiled and dragged me toward that glittering throne as a giant of a man appeared. He strode in from a side door and looked around the vast hall. Suddenly there were dozens of people in snow white togas crowding around us. We were surrounded.

Okay. That made me feel better. Part of a crowd. Not quite so obvious. Then I felt his eyes on me. They were ice blue. Cold and hard. Intent. I felt them probing my mind and I almost fainted from the way they scanned my every thought. Lucifer had done this to me once. Power, good or evil, hit me hard and I staggered. Mother's hand tightened on mine. Strength flowed into me and I stayed on my feet.

"Come here." The command wasn't spoken aloud, just in my mind. I couldn't stop my feet from moving forward. My mother dropped my hand, as compelled as I was, I assumed. Soon I was

alone at the foot of that massive throne. I stared up at him where he sat now, his elbows on his knees. He was handsome, masculine, with fine features and those light eyes that gleamed with a worldly knowledge and intelligence. They were two different things. Yes, he knew everything and he also knew what to do with it.

I couldn't look away. His hair was dark and wavy, brushed back from his face and falling past his shoulders. He wore the short toga that all the men wore. It was belted at the waist with leather and a gold buckle. His sandals were leather too and he had neatly clipped toenails. Stupid to notice such a detail but I'd lost my nerve and couldn't meet his gaze. Instead I found myself mesmerized by those perfect toes.

"Gloriana. So Hebe has finally brought you to me."

"Yes, sire." I managed to get that out but it was barely a whisper. Sire? Apparently my mother had told me to say that. I couldn't remember.

"You are lovely. Look up here, girl." His voice was kindly but it was a command, no doubt about it.

I raised my chin. He gestured and my mother stood by my side.

"Explain, Daughter."

"It was a mistake, Father. Many, many years ago. I fostered her with Achelous. Then the bastard tired of her and cast her out into the world." She raised her chin. "We should make him pay for that." She was getting wound up but, at a gesture from Zeus, got back to the point. "By your great god's own luck, she was made immortal. I found her again very recently and brought her straight to you. You are right. She is lovely, isn't she?" My mother brushed my hair back behind my shoulders. "I hope you are pleased."

"Pleased?" His voice thundered over our heads and crystal chandeliers that I'd been too freaked out to notice until now shivered and tinkled above us. The stones under my feet cracked. "You think I would be pleased that you hid such a beauty from me? A granddaughter?"

"I was worried. I'd betrayed my husband." Mother bit her lip. I'd glanced at her to see her reaction. Plus she was holding onto me until I was afraid she'd break my hand. I wiggled my fingers and she finally let go. Good thing because she got a lightning bolt just then.

"There's your wakeup call, you stupid girl. Since when do I care about marriage vows?" He was on his feet. He stomped down the steps toward us, stopping inches from me. "You have a child, you claim it. Have I not done so with all of my many offspring?"

"I have heard quite enough." The feminine voice that rang out made Zeus's eyes widen. If I didn't know better, I'd think he was cringing.

"Hera! My love. I didn't mean--"

"To disrespect our marriage vows yet again and in a public forum?" The woman who appeared next to me wore her toga perfectly. I thought my diamond pin was beautiful. Hers had a central stone as big as a robin's egg. She looked me over, then clasped me to her generous bosom. "Darling! You are the image of me." She practically threw me aside to grab my mother. "Precious, how you must have suffered with this secret. You should have come to me immediately." She glared at her husband. "Immediately." She kissed my mother on both cheeks and examined her. "Lightning bolts? On your own precious child, Zeus? Barbarian!" She whirled and I thought she was about to throw one of her own. I backed up a step.

"Hera. We are not alone here." Zeus spoke quietly and I felt sure the four of us were the only ones who could hear him.

"Ah, *now* you are concerned with the audience." She faced the packed room. Clearly gossip had spread because more people had arrived since we'd first come. As a way to conquer boredom, a dustup in the royal family was obviously considered fine entertainment.

"Out! All of you. Leave us. If one word of our conversation goes beyond this room, there will be two weeks in the isolation rooms for the source. No exceptions. Even if it is from one of my children or my husband's offspring." She gave Dionysus a hard look. He'd reappeared in the back of the room. At that look, he hurried out again.

In less than a minute, every person had vanished. I wished I could have gone with them. I had no desire to be in the middle of a domestic dispute. I really should have read up on my mythology. I knew Hera and Zeus were married but that he'd had children by a lot of women. Of course any wife would be unhappy with the situation. I had forgotten that my thoughts were an open book around here when Hera suddenly eyed me, her smile disappearing.

"I, uh, totally relate. Unfaithful men. Disgusting."

"Silence, Gloriana." My mother tugged on my hand. "Mother,

thank you for coming. You have to know how hard this has been for me. I regretted giving Gloriana up as soon as I did so. But her father, well," Mother looked down at her silver painted toenails. "It was an awkward situation. I didn't want to tell him I'd been careless. And I was already married to Hercules, of course. Unhappily. When he discovered the sons I gave him would never grow to manhood, Hercules swore he'd never lie with me again. I didn't want to have more children either and assumed Gloriana would be afflicted as well. You can imagine my joy when I later discovered she grew to full adulthood." She stared at me, her eyes shining. "I consider it a miracle."

She meant it. She truly loved me. Whatever wrong-headed things she did, it was because she wanted me with her. To show me off, bring me into the world she knew. I was going to have to fight hard to get back where I wanted to be, but at least I knew what she did was from an honest effort to make me happy. My eyes filled and I wished for a tissue. The kink in this was that I had to convince her where my true happiness lay.

"Who is her father, Hebe?" Zeus was anxious to get down to what he considered the bottom line. "Does he know her? Has he acknowledged her and supported her since you found her? Where was he when you tossed her into Achelous's hellhole?" His frown was fierce enough to make me shiver. I noticed my mother trembling too. "And, yes, I will deal with that situation. Be sure of it."

"They have met but he didn't know that she was his daughter. I never told him I was with child." My mother glanced at me. "It's Mars, Father. I see his spirit in her. I'm sure that's how she survived living on Earth for four centuries."

"By all the gods. A warrior. Of course." Zeus slapped his thighs then looked me over again. "Remarkable. Yes, that pleases me, Daughter. But how did she become immortal while she was on Earth?"

I was too busy absorbing the fact that Mars, a man my mother had actually fixed me up with on a blind date, was my father. Impossible. Though I did like him. In fact, we'd had an instant connection, though no chemistry, thank God.

"I'd rather not say." My mother had her face down and looked like she wanted to crawl out of the room. I figured she was desperately trying to block her thoughts. I had a feeling no one could block them from Zeus. I was right. Two pairs of eyes, both blue, one of them icier than the other were staring at me. My grandparents.

"You can't be. Say it isn't so, Gloriana." Hera looked truly distressed and held onto my mother for support.

"I'm sorry. Well, I'm not really." I wanted to run from the room but knew all three of these gods could freeze me in my tracks if I made the move. Of course my mother had warned me from the beginning that vampires weren't on the guest list at Olympus functions. My grandparents stared hard at my mouth. Well, might as well get it over with. I smiled, showing them that my teeth were perfectly straight now.

"I'm not one here, of course, Mother changed me to goddess status, she said, when she kidnapped me--" I jumped when Mother pinched me. "Sorry, of course I didn't realize how wonderful it would be to meet you or I'd have come sooner." Babbling. My nerves were getting the best of me.

"Say it, girl." Zeus growled, still hoping I'd deny it, I guess.

"It was how I survived, you know." I lifted my chin. "I became immortal in 1604 when I was turned vampire."

THREE

To say that all hell broke loose would be an understatement. Hera, my grandmother, shrieked and half-dozen handmaidens ran in with everything from a chaise lounge to smelling salts. Zeus's roar brought a dozen warriors into the room from all sides. They wore battle armor and carried spears, ready to annihilate whoever had caused their leader such pain.

I just stood there, waiting for my own lightning bolt. I'd been hit in the past and knew it wouldn't be a treat. At the least it would take off the bottoms of my silver sandals. At its worst? You don't want to know and neither did I.

Lightning popped and sizzled around the top of the room. The chandeliers rained glass until it looked like a crystal hail storm. A vein bulged in Zeus's face and his fists were clenched in front of him. I actually took that as a good sign. At least he wasn't pointing a finger at me.

"Father." My mother sobbed and threw herself on the floor at his feet. "If I'd known…"

"How could you, Daughter? I lay this on Achelous's head. Bring him to me!" The walls shook and five of the warriors disappeared, I guess to go after Achelous. Hera's lounge chair jumped a good foot and she moaned.

"Must you be so loud? I have a headache." Hera closed her eyes and one of the handmaidens laid a cloth across her brow.

"When have you not?" Zeus paced the floor. "Get up, Daughter. Do not debase yourself. We will deal with Achelous together. What punishment would make you happy?"

Mother practically leaped to her feet. "Really? I can name his sentence?" She glanced at me. "I must tell you, Father, that it is only Circe's intervention that saved Gloriana from dying a mortal's death all those years ago. It was the goddess's hand that sent the vampire to our girl and gave her the gift of immortality."

"Indeed." Zeus paced in front of his throne. "Now this bears some thought. Why didn't Circe just come to you or me and tell us the girl was in trouble? I think we must punish this vixen as well. She did not handle the situation as I would have wished." He gestured and two more soldiers vanished.

"What will you do to her?" I didn't like Circe. She'd played a role in having me tortured by Aggie when the siren had been a sea monster in Lake Travis. And I knew Circe hated vampires. So for her to make sure I became one meant she'd been sticking it to someone, even while she was making sure I would live. Zeus was watching me. He nodded.

"I see you understand the complexities here, Gloriana. Circe is forever scheming. Why did she have you made vampire, you wonder. There are other immortals she could have steered to you, or as I said, she could have come straight to me. I will toss her into a cell until she realizes she cannot get away with hurting a member of my family." Zeus smiled and touched my mother's cheek. "Does that please you, Hebe?"

"Yes, Father. Remember that she did finally tell me about my daughter and led me to her. So perhaps make it a short stay? I owe her a debt." Mother knelt in front of him and kissed his hand. "As a favor to me. I would not want her to become a bitter enemy to either of us."

"Wise. Alliances come in handy, do they not? I will be the villain here then and let her know you won her a reprieve from a long stay in the cells." He pulled my mother to her feet and kissed her forehead. "As for Achelous? Do not beg for a lighter sentence for him. He has been a pain in my backside for a long time. I am delighted at the excuse to make him pay."

"Can you make him mortal, Grandfather?" I spoke before I

thought, but realized it would be the worst thing Achelous could imagine. "It's what he did to me and seems a perfect revenge. No powers, getting older day by day. He will be as vulnerable as I was when he cast me out. It would be a joy to imagine him in the real world like that." I smiled when I saw that Zeus liked the idea.

"Ah, you are certainly my blood, Gloriana. It is perfect. And I say we leave him there until he is ready for a mortal's natural death. Then, if I think he has learned his lesson, I might bring him back. He is a god after all. But I won't allow him knowledge of that possibility. Now hush, he is coming." Zeus rubbed his hands together and sparks flew. Mother and I both backed away, afraid our togas would catch fire.

Achelous was carried in by the warriors who'd fetched him. One of them must have had the power to freeze him because he was stiff as a corpse in rigor mortis. They stood him up and Zeus clapped his hands.

"What is the meaning of this, sire?" Achelous looked around but, when he saw me and my mother quickly shut his mouth.

"Ah, I see you have figured it out. Surely you did not mean to leave my granddaughter to die when you cast her out of the Siren harem, did you?" Zeus couldn't have looked more threatening and Achelous tried to back up. The soldiers at his back prodded him with their spears and he stopped.

"I had no idea she was related to you when I did that, sire. You cannot imagine how many immature females I have to watch over in the harem. Hundreds, nay, thousands. Keeping records on their origins is impossible." Achelous waved his hands, growing more agitated as Zeus glared at him. "And the problems they cause. Some are insatiable. Always after my attention. Or they are like this one, refusing to do their jobs." He pointed at me with a shaking finger.

"I have quotas. And needed to set an example. I admit I must have failed to check her parentage. If I'd known she was connected to the great house of Zeus…" He dropped to his knees. "You must understand, sire. All I knew was that she wasn't bringing in the gold. And she had inadequate kill numbers--"

"Silence!" A soprano voice screeched and the crystal chandeliers couldn't take it. One crashed to the stone floor. A dozen handmaidens appeared and quickly swept away the mess.

"Kill numbers? Kill numbers?" Hera brushed aside a velvet

throw and sat up. "If my husband didn't have plans for you, I swear I would strike you dead where you stand." She wiped a tear from her cheek.

Achelous bowed his head and didn't dare say a word. Zeus nodded and moved to stand next to his wife's chaise.

"I cannot bear the thought that my granddaughter was expected to kill for you. You are a disgrace to Olympus." She patted the seat next to her. "Come here, child." She shook her head when my mother moved forward. "Not you, Hebe. I am not happy with you right now. You never should have placed your daughter into that Siren harem. Gloriana, come here."

I glanced at Zeus but he wasn't paying any attention to me. He'd stepped forward again and had started in on Achelous who was getting his first dose of lightning. I hurried over to sit next to Hera.

"How could you bear to be a Siren, child?" Hera waved her hand and a handmaiden gave us each a goblet of sweet wine. I didn't hesitate to take a sip. It tasted wonderful and I took a deeper swallow.

"I don't remember any of it, Grandmother, if I may call you that."

"Yes, of course. You don't remember?" She patted my knee.

I was feeling a nice warmth in my stomach and I figured there was more than just wine in that goblet. "No. Achelous gave me amnesia when he cast me out. I was found wandering the streets of London with no memory and no skills."

She gasped and clutched my knee. "Zeus! Spare him no mercy! It is a miracle our dear girl survived. Cruel and careless bastard." She raised a finger and fire shot out. Achelous screamed with pain, his body enveloped in a blue and white flame.

My eyes widened. I'd seen ruthless people before, plenty of them, but the smell of burning flesh, along with Achelous's agonizing screams turned my stomach.

"Please, Grandmother! I, I didn't suffer long. I was pretty enough to quickly attract a man to take care of me." I focused on her and tried to block out the smells and sounds around me.

"Of course you were. Clever girl." She smiled when I shook my head. "We use what we can to make our way in the world, don't we?" She glanced at Zeus, her look calculating.

"I would have liked to have done it on my own." I sipped more wine. "But at first I had to rely on men for help. The world being the way it was back then." Damn it, I hated to admit that. It was a pattern I'd worked centuries to break.

"Ah, child, don't feel bad about that. You had something to work with and you used it. Of course you were beautiful. It is a family gift. You are the image of me and your dear mother." She smiled and my goblet was full again. I didn't remember draining it.

"It seems this family has many gifts. It took me a while but I finally learned to crave my own power, to not always be dependent on a man." I glanced at Zeus again but he was busily giving Achelous an Olympus hot foot, setting fire to the god's sandals.

"I understand completely. Yes, power is important. But here in Olympus, it is still a man's world. Your grandfather's, I'm afraid. I struggle constantly to hold my own, but his word is law." Hera smiled sadly. "Not that I am overly concerned with some of his dictates. A clever woman can do much here. I am proud that you survived as you did. Despite that bastard Achelous's irresponsibility." She frowned and sent a dart of fire toward Achelous again, this time with a blink of her brilliant blue eyes. It was a neat trick I wouldn't mind learning. She smiled at me and nodded.

"I'm glad that I didn't make a good Siren, Grandmother. That I wasn't good at killing. But I've learned it's important to be able to defend myself." I glanced at Achelous again. I didn't like torture though. They should just go ahead and lock him up. This game of hurting him and making him scream sickened me.

"You obviously have a tender heart. Don't feel sorry for Achelous." Grandmother waved a finger and the goblets disappeared. "Now tell me. What are you good at, Gloriana?"

"She has her own business, Mother. The most adorable little shop." My mother had obviously gotten tired of the "Fry Achelous" show too and stepped closer.

I must have looked shocked because as far as I knew my mother hated my shop.

"Really? You work? In trade?" Grandmother's perfectly arched eyebrows couldn't get any higher.

"She's into beautiful clothing, Mother. Vintage pieces. Jewels too." My mother was spinning as fast as she could. She laughed and patted my shoulder. "And has the same love of shoes and handbags we share."

"Well, I suppose that is acceptable." Grandmother looked thoughtful. I doubted a goddess ever had to earn a living when she could wave a fingertip and produce a new outfit with a thought. I hadn't tried it yet but the very idea made my eyes sting. What a gift.

"It was a way to survive on Earth. To gain my independence. I wanted to be a strong independent woman and I've made a success of my shop." This truth made me straighten my shoulders and I felt better when my mother's hand landed there, support I needed.

"And do you have lovers, Gloriana?" Hera glanced at Zeus. "You will have inherited a lusty nature from your grandfather, all of his children and their children seem to have done so."

"Yes, I've just promised to marry the man who made me vampire all those years ago, Jeremiah Campbell. He is my one true love." My mother's hand tightened painfully on my shoulder. Guess she didn't want me to share that.

"Vampire?" Hera shook her head. "No, that will not do. I'm sure your mother explained things to you. Now that you are here, there will be no more of that vampire nonsense."

"I told you, Gloriana." Mother gasped when I jumped up, grabbing the back of the chaise when the room wobbled.

"It's not nonsense. It's what I am. Vampire." I heard Achelous scream again. He was buried in molten lava. I was glad he was hurting, the sadistic bastard, but I didn't have to stay and watch. "I need to go. I think I'm going to be sick."

"Gloriana." My mother stayed by my side, offering her arm. "You cannot leave until Zeus gives his permission."

"Grandfather. I am unwell. May I go?" I raised my voice so he could hear me over Achelous's pleas for mercy.

"For now. But you must come back tomorrow. Your mother wants a celebration. To introduce you to the court. I like the idea. Dionysus will arrange a party. He has a talent for such things. We will invite everyone. Except this pitiful excuse for a god and Circe." Zeus looked away from Achelous long enough to gesture at me and I went to him and got a kiss on the forehead. He smelled like ozone, acrid and hot. I was afraid for a moment that I was going to sneeze.

Mother squeezed my arm. "Thank you, Father. That will be wonderful. Won't it, Gloriana?"

I managed a nod. "Yes, I, uh, I'm honored." Can. Not. Sneeze. I stepped back, careful to avoid getting close to Achelous.

"Excellent. The highlight of the evening will be when we tell your father about you. Won't that be a fine surprise?" Zeus waved us away and went back to his torture. A ring of warriors surrounded Achelous, preparing to throw their spears at him.

I was pretty sure I was going to hurl and almost ran out of the room.

"Calm down, Gloriana. He was almost finished. I wanted to see Achelous's face when he finds out he's going to become mortal." My mother held onto my arm.

"Fine. Stay and watch the show. Just send a handmaiden with me to show me back to my room." I had had more than enough of the Olympus drama. I wanted to go to bed and sleep for a week. I looked up as soon as the doors closed behind us. Blue sky. No sun but no stars either. No death sleep. I felt strange, not myself. I searched my memory and realized I was… hungry. And not for blood.

"I'll do that. And, Gloriana, I'll order you some supper. You didn't eat your breakfast and then drank Mother's spiced wine. No wonder you are out of sorts. I will send you something delicious and then you can go to bed afterwards." Mother patted my arm, obviously eager to get back inside. "I know it's a bit overwhelming, but this went well, I think."

"Well?" I glanced back at that enormous door, sure I could still hear Achelous's agonized screams. "They won't accept what I am."

"What you were, you mean. Here you are perfect. Just what they love. A goddess." Mother touched my cheek. "Now tomorrow is critical, of course, but we will pull it off. Mother has been wonderful, championing you. But don't go on about your vampire lover. Hera can be pushed too far. I know that. She is happy now but she values wedding vows. Once she thinks on it, the fact that I betrayed Hercules with Mars will make her unhappy. She can take it out on you."

"No vampire talk. After seeing what Zeus is doing to Achelous, I'm not eager to piss off any of the gods. But don't think I am over what you did, setting me up on a date with my own father. He kissed me on the lips, Mother. That's an ick factor I don't think I'll ever get over." I took a breath, relieved that the air was fresh out here.

"Darling. I knew nothing significant would happen between you two. He and I…" she actually flushed and stared down at the stones under our feet, "Well, we have been lovers for thousands of years. He only went on the date with you to tease me. He is in love with me." When she looked up her eyes were wet. "And I with him."

"Mother. You can't ever be together? Isn't there divorce here?" I actually felt sorry for her.

"No. So we must meet in secret. Hide our true feelings in public. Your existence changes things but we will still have to be discreet." She sighed. "Gloriana, I will never regret that you came from our love. And Mars will be so thrilled… Please don't obsess over that one date. If he flirted with you, know that his heart wasn't in it. He told me later that he truly liked you, but there was no passion between you."

"Well, I should hope not!" I couldn't stand here much longer. Between my empty stomach and my reeling mind, I was minutes away from falling to the ground. "Forgetting the entire thing right now." I sighed. "Now go enjoy seeing Achelous get his punishment. Send the handmaiden and supper. See you later. And, thanks."

"Thanks?" She stopped as she was turning away.

"Yes. I may not appreciate everything that's going on up here but you are obviously doing all of this, bringing me to Olympus, showing me off, out of love. And I, um, love you too." I fell back when she slammed into me, hugging me fiercely.

"Darling. You can't know what it means to hear you say that. Thank you! My precious daughter." She dabbed at her eyes. "I will do anything for you, anything."

I bit back all the things I really wanted her to do. Why spoil the moment? But the time would come when I would test that love. Because I wasn't staying here. No way in heaven or hell.

#

The great hall was filled with people. The crystal chandeliers had been restored and polished to a high shine and tables piled high with food and drink lined the walls. Either someone had gone to work with air freshener or magic had made any trace of Achelous and his frying punishment disappear. All I could smell were the delicious aromas of roast beef and fresh pastries.

"Welcome to your first bacchanal, niece." Dionysus stuck a goblet in my hand. He was smiling and looked handsome in a short toga belted at the waist. His sandals were strapped and tied up to his knees. It was a hot look.

"This is quite a turnout." I sipped the wine. More of that spiced stuff that made my tummy warm and my head light. I had on a beautiful toga again too. This was obviously the uniform for formal events when Zeus was going to be present. Too bad. That closet full of designer clothes had been calling my name and I'd tried on a few of the more exciting looks. Size two? Insane. I had a feeling Jerry would have claimed I looked gaunt. He liked my curves fuller and would have hated that I wasn't showing cleavage in this rig.

"Command performance. Everyone not in the cells had to be here." He smiled, his teeth perfect and white. "Not that we needed a command. Who wouldn't be curious about Hebe's bastard daughter?" He laughed. "Now don't look like that. There are more illegitimate children up here than those born in wedlock, myself included."

I guess I'd recoiled when called a bastard. Not that it really mattered to me but it was just not acceptable to uptight families like the Campbells. Or hadn't been when Jerry had first taken me home to the Highlands of Scotland to meet his folks back in the sixteen hundreds. Of course times have changed since then. But his immortal parents hadn't. Jerry's father liked me, his mother? Didn't. I had never been good enough for her boy.

I glanced at the golden thrones at the front of the room. Of course now I was a *royal* bastard. Mag Campbell might even be impressed with that. If she believed it. I hardly believed it myself. I caught people staring at me, assessing me and whispering. I guess word had gotten around. Zeus's granddaughter. These people would be watching closely to see how he treated me. If he accepted me, no one would dare be anything but thrilled to know me.

I wondered if Mars was here yet. I looked for his familiar red plume, the one on top of his helmet. Would he wear his armor to an event like this? Maybe not. The only armor I spied was worn by the warriors standing guard at the doors. I did like Mars, had from the moment we'd met. To think that he was my father… My heart swelled. I'd always wanted a family.

Trumpets blared and a man in a toga with a booming voice announced Zeus and Hera. Everyone bowed low and I followed suit. An aisle had been left down the center of the room and the two walked side by side as they entered from the back of the room. I'd noticed two thrones on the dais tonight. One was noticeably shorter than the other. No surprise that Zeus helped Hera settle herself into the smaller one before he sat in the larger one. You could have heard a laurel leaf drop as the god gazed around the room. Then as one we bowed even lower, practically prostrating ourselves on the floor.

"Please rise, everyone. Hebe, Gloriana, come forward." Zeus smiled as we raised our heads. He held out his hands and I moved toward him. My mother walked from the other side of the room. When we were directly in front of him, he gestured for us to turn and face the crowd. It was so quiet that I shivered, unnerved. There must have been close to five hundred people in the room and every one of them stared at me, sizing me up.

"My daughter Hebe has found a daughter who was lost to her for many years. Allow me to introduce my granddaughter, Gloriana. Treat her with all the respect due her station as beloved of my wife Hera and I. We are happy to have such a beautiful addition to our family. Who, you may ask, is her father?" He gazed around the room. "It is not Hebe's husband, who is still away fighting a war which it seems will never end. One cannot blame my daughter for seeking comfort for her loneliness." His gaze raked the room, as if daring anyone to think ill of my mother.

Hera made a sound and I noticed that she really wanted to say something but kept her mouth closed at a sharp glance from Zeus. He nodded then went on.

"Of course we respect the bonds of matrimony as my wife reminds me. Hebe regrets her lapse and has been adequately punished for that by losing touch with Gloriana for many, many years." He glanced at Hera and was rewarded with a slight smile. "But that will not keep us from now acknowledging this daughter and seeking to bring her into our world here at Olympus. I am sure you will make her welcome. And I am sure Gloriana's father will be happy to learn he has a daughter as well." Zeus paused, for dramatic effect, I was sure.

"Mars, come forward and meet your daughter."

There were gasps and a stir as the crowd parted and Mars strode forward from the back of the room. No armor for him tonight. He was in the same snowy toga as the rest of the men. It was short to show off his muscular legs and he wore it belted. He wore a shiny silver breastplate, small and emblazoned with a crest that marked him as a military man. He stopped just feet from my mother and touched her hand.

"Hebe, is this true? We had a daughter and you never told me?" He looked very solemn, no, furious. "Where has she been all this time?"

I could almost see the crowd leaning forward, eager to get the gossip as my mother nodded, tears streaking down her cheeks. I couldn't stand it.

"Mars? Are you really my father?" I blinked as tears filled my eyes too. "Will you acknowledge me?"

He quit glaring at my mother and turned to me. He looked me up and down and the most beautiful smile broke over his sun-browned face. Before I knew what he was going to do, he stepped forward and grabbed me, picking me up in a tremendous hug.

"By the hand of Zeus, I acknowledge this beautiful girl as my own daughter." He kissed me on each cheek then set me down again. His dark eyes were glittering. "I couldn't be more proud." He looked up at Zeus. "This is an honor I didn't expect, Sire. Thank you for allowing me to claim this perfect child. If I'd known she existed, I would have raised her from a babe, taken full responsibility from the moment of her birth."

Zeus smiled. "I am sure you would have. You and my daughter need to talk. I hope you will resolve your issues and work together to make Gloriana's life here a happy one." He quit smiling. "Now is not the time for such a discussion however. We are here for a celebration. I want to see everyone eating, drinking and," he glanced at Hera, "enjoying themselves. It is my command." And with that he stood and walked down to the crowd, nodding to certain courtiers and kissing some of the women on the cheek. He suddenly had a goblet in his hand and totally ignored his wife, still on her throne.

"Mars." My mother edged closer to me.

"You heard your father, Hebe. Not now. I want to speak to my daughter." Mars reached out and snagged two goblets off a tray being passed by a handmaiden. "We are celebrating. Come, Gloriana, there are people I want you to meet." He put an arm around my waist and led me into the crowd.

I looked back and saw my mother approach Hera. My grandmother was surrounded by handmaidens who were bringing her food and drink. Several courtiers had also come closer and were fawning over her. My mother looked lonely and actually a little scared. Then a handsome man approached her and I saw her light up, turning on the charm like she always did.

"Don't worry about your mother, Gloriana. She can take care of herself." Mars stopped next to a banquet table. "But she obviously didn't take care of you. Tell me what happened. But not here. We need to meet. I want details. I know something of your background because of how we met before." He picked up a perfect apple and tossed it up and down like a baseball. Nerves? I couldn't believe it.

"I think we have to stay here for a while. I've already learned that you don't disobey Zeus or make him mad." I was into the wine again. False courage. I felt someone at my back and turned. Dionysus.

"Put on your happy faces, people. You are the guests of honor, you know. Gloriana, you have many aunts, uncles and cousins to meet. Allow me to do the honors. Mars, quit glowering at me and follow along like a dutiful papa. But first go placate your wife. She has picked up a knife and seems likely to do murder. Can you calm her? Or should we send her to your rooms with a pair of soldiers as escort?" He laughed merrily. "This is one of my best parties yet. Great gossip, perfect food and wine and Hera looks like she could eat ground glass." Dionysus clapped his hands. "Start the music!"

To my surprise an indie rock band began playing on a stage that emerged from one side of the massive marble hall. I guess I'd expected lutes and lyres. But this group had obviously evolved and several couples got the dancing going. One god let loose a few lightning bolts with his extreme dance moves. Obviously he'd hit the wine too hard. He was helped outside by soldiers.

"My wife. Excuse me, Gloriana. I need to do something about this. Zeus has his ways and I know he is our leader, but a warning here might have helped prevent some pain and embarrassment." Mars frowned and hurried over to a woman who had her own group of sympathizers surrounding her while she waved her arms and shouted. Yes, she did seem to have a knife in one hand. The music drowned out their conversation but clearly it was heated. Finally Mars gestured for that pair of soldiers and the woman who must be his wife was led weeping out of the room.

"Don't worry about her, Gloriana." Dionysus led me to a group of people across the room. "Roxanne is unstable at the best of times. No one blames Mars for seeking the comfort of another woman's bed."

I had nothing to say to that and was soon surrounded by dozens of gods, goddesses and nymphs, all eager to meet Hebe's daughter. There were also wizards and other assorted creatures that looked human but obviously weren't. I had goddess radar now and it was buzzing warnings constantly. After three hours Dionysus finally whispered in my ear that I could leave since Zeus had slipped out with one of his many mistresses and Hera had retired with one of her famous headaches.

"Thank goodness. I can't wait to get out of here." I had filled my plate twice with goodies from the buffet but not even the delicious aroma of roasted pig could get the food past my closing throat. Being the center of attention in *this* crowd was too much for me. Plus I'd never keep all the Greek or Roman names straight.

"Let me walk you to your rooms." Mars hadn't left my side for even a moment once his wife was gone.

"Thanks." I headed for the doors. As soon as we were outside, I relaxed. I'd been "on" for hours.

"You were vampire when we met before." Mars said this quietly.

"It was how I managed to stay alive, Mars." I glanced at him. "Would you let me call you Dad?" I braced myself for the vampire talk. He didn't look happy. "Or Father?"

"Call me whatever you wish." He stopped in the middle of the path directly in front of me. "Daughter. I am amazed and delighted. I don't know what your mother told you about our relationship…"

"That you love each other. She's not happy in her marriage. I'm glad she has you." I reached out and took his hand. "Dad. You can't know how I've longed for a family. This is a miracle."

He squeezed my hand then looked away. "A complicated one. Damn Hebe. Why did she hide you from me? It drives me mad to think of you fending for yourself. All the dangers on Earth you had to face. So horrible that you had to rely on a vampire!" He tugged me into his arms. "I'm sorry you weren't here, with me."

"I think Mother did what she thought was best at the time." I couldn't believe I was defending her.

Mars pushed back and shook his head. "She made a mistake. She knows I love all my children. I would have found a way…" He sighed. "Too late to change things of course. Gloriana, you have brothers and sisters now. You should meet them. I will arrange it!"

His eyes lit up.

"Sure, I'll meet them. But I'm not up to it tonight." I blurted out what I needed him to know before he got too excited about this family reunion. "Please, listen to me. I don't plan to stay here. I, I want to go home." There, I'd said it. He got a look on his face, like he was about to go into battle. Determined.

"*This* should be your home. You should take your rightful place here, Gloriana. As a granddaughter of Zeus, it is a powerful one." Mars put his hands on my shoulders. "When I remember how you were a blood sucker, with a dangerous life on Earth…" He shook his head when I started to speak and held onto both my shoulders with an iron grip. "Don't deny it. I was there when you faced a threat from a voodoo priestess. And I'm sure that wasn't the first time you were at risk. Was it?"

"Well, no. But I survived down there for over four hundred years, Dad. And now that I know about my Olympus powers…" I smiled, "Thanks to you and Mother, I will be fine. I have a good life down there and Jerry, my fiancé. We are to be married soon."

"Impossible." His frown was scary and I tried to wiggle away from his grasp. Not happening. "I will not let Hebe off lightly for this. She has much to explain."

"That's between you and my mother." I lifted my chin. "My rightful place is back down there. Being a bloodsucker as you call it is what I am. I *must* go back." Tears choked me. I finally jerked away from him and saw that my bedchamber was just steps away. I still didn't understand this world or how the rooms were set up but I recognized my room and the golden door with my initials painted in the center. A silly detail but at least it helped me now.

"Gloriana, wait!" Mars was right behind me as I wrenched open the door. "We must talk. What is down there that you feel you must return to such a sordid existence?"

"I told you. My lover. Jeremiah Campbell. Jeremy Blade. You met him. Even thought he was a fine warrior, I know you did." I faced him, this man I knew now was my father. His eyes had gone from kind to hard and ruthless. I knew one of his powers included standing as the deity for a voodoo religion. Sure enough, I sensed a wash of dark power around him now. It sent a chill through me but didn't scare me. Had I inherited some of that juju? The thought gave me a kind of twisted satisfaction. I shouldn't rush home without learning what I could about that and any other new things that could help me. I narrowed my eyes at this new father of mine when he smiled.

"Oh, no, you don't. If you're planting thoughts in my mind, stop it now." I shook my head and refused to make eye contact with him before my mind went off the rails entirely.

"I only want what's best for you, Gloriana." He leaned against the door frame but didn't come inside. "That vampire male you think you love? Surely you can't believe you will be going back to him. It's not seemly, Gloriana. No daughter of mine will be with a vampire." He crossed his arms over his massive chest, in full warrior mode now and issuing orders. Clearly he had no idea how to handle me as he'd soon find out.

"It's way too late for you to dictate to me, Mars. I raised myself. I was left on my own for hundreds, no, more than a thousand years and I survived. I'm my own woman and I won't just fall into the goddess line here. I'm a vampire and proud of it. Deal with it." I planted a hand on his shiny breastplate, gave him a firm push then slammed the door in his face.

I leaned against the door, my heart pounding. Had I really just told off the god of war? I waited for an explosion or at least the crackling and smell of fire after a lightning bolt hit the wooden door. The silence and lack of action almost scared me more than if Mars had lost his cool. I looked up and met the frightened gazes of half a dozen handmaidens. Of course they'd heard the whole thing. One of them sucked it up and came forward.

"You'd better lie down, mistress. If we lay the blame on a brain seizure, surely he will forgive your outburst." She led me to the bed and helped me take off my sandals. Another handmaiden pulled back the covers while a third laid a cool cloth on my forehead. They all looked worried, wringing their hands and whispering among themselves.

What would happen if Mars burst into the room and took out his anger on them? I ordered them out of the room, relieved when they scurried away through yet another set of doors I'd never noticed before. Then I closed my eyes and waited. When nothing happened, I guess I fell asleep, thinking maybe I'd won the first round. But when I woke up I was still in Olympus and my parents were standing over me, determined looks on their faces. Somehow I knew I wasn't going to like what they had to say.

FOUR

I was about to throw back the covers and confront them when I realized I wasn't wearing anything. I'd dreamed I was with Jerry last night. It had been pretty hot. Great that I could dream at all—vamps couldn't do that--and now I realized I must be able to change or lose my clothing in my sleep. Freaky.

"Could you give me a minute? I'd like to get dressed, brush my teeth and maybe, I don't know, wake up?" It was clear from the looks on their faces that they were going to try to bully me into staying here. I had to persuade them to let me go home. For a moment I panicked. On the power-o-meter, I was a one and they were off the charts.

"Gloriana, relax. We can certainly read your thoughts." My mother smiled, obviously deciding to try a softer approach. "Mars, let's go into her sitting room and have breakfast while our daughter pulls herself together. Don't make us wait long, darling." She hooked her arm through her lover's, pulling him from the bedside.

"Don't think to make a run for it, Gloriana. There's nowhere to hide up here and no one who will help you." Mars lifted my mother's hand from his arm. Oh, still mad at her. "We'll wait for ten minutes then we'll be back." The commander had issued his orders.

I saluted, refusing to say another word. He scowled, then stomped off toward yet another set of double doors. I guess I did have a sitting room. First I'd heard of it. A handmaiden rushed to me with a robe as soon as they were out of sight and the doors closed behind them.

"Thanks. Guess I don't have time for one of those great soaking tub baths." I did love my new bathroom. I rushed through cleaning up and putting myself into some kind of order. It took me longer to pick out an outfit than it did to slap on makeup. So many designers, so little time. I settled on a wonderful Pucci print sheath and Prada pumps that fit like a dream. I stopped in front of the mirror. I looked like a goddess. Too bad I didn't feel like I had a snowball's chance at winning points in the pissing contest to come.

"Come, sit. Look at these lovely pastries. You can eat whatever you wish and it won't show on your new waistline, Gloriana. Isn't that wonderful?" My mother handed me a piece of brioche slathered in butter when I got to the breakfast table in my sitting room.

I didn't say anything, just savored both the info and the taste. Whoever cooked up here was a genius. But, God, I missed my fangs. I couldn't even smell my parents' blood from across the table, just my mother's delicate perfume and the aroma of all that food. Mars was all man, no flirty perfume for him, but he was clean and reeked of leather and whatever his servants used to polish his silver belt buckle.

After hundreds of years of sizing up people by the pint, I didn't know how to act. So I stuffed my face with food. Next came a raspberry tart. I tried to slow down and take dainty bites, but it was just too delicious. When I reached for another one, Mars had waited long enough.

"Can we get to the point?" He slammed down his coffee cup. An empty plate sat in front of him. Obviously he'd finished *his* breakfast and that was all he cared about.

"And that point is?" I blotted my lips with a snowy napkin. I hadn't been so greedy that I'd forgotten to be careful not to spill on my dress.

"You know the point, Gloriana. You are staying here and we're arranging a proper marriage for you. You're certainly not marrying that fanged monster on Earth!" Mars slapped the table and the silverware rattled.

"Over my dead body." I jumped to my feet. *Would* he strike me dead? No. But he could freeze me in place, hurt me. Let him. I wasn't going to marry anyone but Jerry. I showed him that in my eyes.

"Stubborn wench." He'd jumped to his feet too and I could see his frustration in his scowl and fisted hands. "It's for your own benefit. There are many worthy warriors up here and a good alliance can protect you."

"Sit down, both of you." My mother calmly drank her tea. "This argument is going nowhere, I can see that. You are both too stubborn."

I sat but leaned forward. "Who do you think has protected me since 1604? Jeremiah Campbell." Tears filled my eyes and ran down my cheeks. "The man rescued me from poverty, loved me, kept me from danger and even paid for bodyguards when we took breaks from each other." Hearing it laid out like that made me even more determined to fight them and fight for Jerry.

Mars settled back in his chair and the wood creaked under his weight. He was a big man and, even without his armor, strained the delicate furniture that someone had used to fill my sitting room. He was obviously thinking about what I'd said.

"That's all very well, Gloriana. But here you are not a vampire. You are our daughter. A goddess in your own right and from the house of Zeus. There are many gods who would be honored to call you wife." My mother set down her porcelain cup. "Mars and I would let you choose from among them, of course. A man who would be kind and lusty enough to keep you happy. Give you children!" She leaned forward and clasped my hand before I could stop her. "Can your vampire do that? Give you children?" She stared until I had to look away. "Of course not." She released me and sat back then nodded at Mars. He took up the argument.

"Listen to your mother, Gloriana. This is important. Zeus may take the matter out of our hands, of course." He toyed with a knife at his belt. He wore a leather outfit suitable for a soldier, not a toga, but from an ancient time. "Hebe, I remember this man Gloriana is so fond of. He threw himself in front of her once when she was in danger. He calls himself Blade."

"Yes!" I grabbed my father's arm. Could he be coming around to my way of thinking? "He goes by Jeremy Blade now. Because he's handy with a knife. I've seen him hit a target dead center from yards away. You would enjoy getting to know him better, Dad. I know you would. He's a warrior like you are and has been in many battles. He's the bravest man I know and a leader. Just like you are, Dad." I dropped in the "D" word again, hoping to tease a little fatherly feeling from him. Whatever that meant up here.

"Not just like Mars, Gloriana. Not even close. He's not a god." Mother frowned, obviously not happy with me.

"One more reason that I love him." I lifted my chin. "My dealings with gods haven't exactly made me trust them, have they?" I didn't care if I made these two mad. What else could they do to me? When would I learn not to think like that?

My mother went from irritated to furious in a blink of an eye. "Daughter, you need to learn to curb your tongue!" She lifted her hand as if to toss a lightning bolt and I braced myself.

Mars stood so abruptly the dishes rattled. "Hebe, leave her alone. Gloriana has reason to be in a temper. Look what she's been through."

"Please sit, Mars. I, more than anyone else, know what we've all been through. I'm sorry, Gloriana. This has been a trying time for you of course. But you know I'm only doing what is best for you. Bringing you to the place where you belong to claim your birthright." Mother whipped out a hanky and worked up a tear. "Mars, I thought we agreed . . ." She sighed. "Never mind. Gloriana, we are grateful to this man, Blade. Perhaps a gift is in order." Mother glanced at Mars. "One of your swords would please him no doubt. Especially if you gave it a magical power."

"A true warrior or a man in love would be insulted by the offer." Mars glared at her. "Like we are trying to buy him off."

"He would. He's a rich man, successful and from a highborn family. He has pride, Mother. To try to reward him now would not be wise." I took a breath. I had to find a way out of this. "Send me back. You can come visit me whenever you want. I know you both have spouses here so I'll be nothing but trouble for you. A reminder of an affair that they surely disapprove of. And you already know what Hera thinks about betraying your marriage vows."

"My mother will get over that. She loved you on sight." My mother gazed longingly at Mars. "She understood that I was lonely and never loved my husband. He was cruel to me when he realized our sons were never to grow to manhood. Hercules has quite a temper and took the boys' affliction out on me."

That finally got Mars' attention. "You never told me… What did he do, Hebe? I swear, if he hurt you, I'll make him sorry he was ever born."

"He knew better than to lay a hand on me." Mother reached out and touched Mars' arm. He finally took her hand. "But he can be very cold and cruel. With words. Until you and I finally were together, I was sure that *I* was the reason he got no satisfaction in our marriage bed. He claimed I was frigid and could make any man's," she actually flushed, "cock shrink with just a look."

"We both know how wrong he was about that, don't we?" Mars pulled her hand to his mouth. "But you never should have hidden this child from me. Why did you?" He released her. "I'm sure Gloriana wants to know as well."

"The way Grandmother is accepting me now makes me wonder why you didn't just go to her at the time." I saw Mother shrink in her chair as we both focused on her.

"I was scared, confused. Mother has mellowed over the centuries. I guess Father's many indiscretions have convinced her there is no use wasting her time worrying about fidelity. But back then, she was rabid on the subject. I couldn't count on her support. In fact, I was afraid she'd have made me," Mother stared down at her lap, "rid myself of the pregnancy early on." She looked up. "I couldn't do that. Not a child made from our love, Mars."

"But you could drop it into Achelous's harem of horrors?" I jumped to my feet. "Do you have any idea how he treated his women? I am blessed that I don't remember it but I have heard from the Sirens how it was and still is." I took a breath. The breakfast I'd enjoyed threatened to choke me. "They had to kill whoever they lured with their song, give Achelous the gold they stole then service that pig you call a god as well. At least Circe is in charge there now. I'm sure the Sirens are celebrating. She is bound to be a gentler mistress."

"Gloriana. Will you ever forgive me?" Tears flowed down my mother's cheeks.

"She might but I'm not sure I will. Gloriana is right. The Sirens are nothing but whores and killers, Hebe. This sickens me." Mars stared at me for a long moment, ignoring my mother's sobs. "I just found you. I am certainly not going to send you back to Earth, Gloriana. Even if Zeus would tolerate that, which I'm sure he won't. But I can do something to please you." And he suddenly disappeared.

"Oh, gods, I cannot lose him." My mother buried her face in a napkin, her shoulders shaking. "What have I done?"

"Finally gotten what you deserved?" I knew that was cruel but my father was right. Dooming a child to a life as a murderous whore was a horrible thing to do. "You seem to think it's quite all right to deny me a life with the man I love so excuse me if I don't break down over Mars being mad at you. At least you still live in the same place." I sat at the table again, gesturing for a handmaiden as I'd seen my mother do. Sure enough one appeared and cleared the table. Thank God, because I couldn't take the smell of food for much longer.

"I thought we were coming to an understanding, Gloriana." Mother mopped her eyes with a napkin. "I can't change the past."

"No, that's true. But surely there were other options back then. Adoption to a loving family. A childless woman who would have taken me in?" I leaned forward. I wasn't letting her off easily. This was a big deal to me and to my father.

"I was confused. I knew another woman who had used Achelous in a similar situation and…" She wadded up that napkin. "Gloriana, you can't know how terrified I was. All I knew was that Achelous promised to keep you safe. I had no reason to think you would ever reach puberty. Your brothers certainly never did. So I imagined you living in the Siren nursery, playing with the babies after you stopped growing, never gaining maturity. If you'd stayed in Olympus, word of a child who had never become an adult would have been whispered in certain quarters, eventually reaching the wrong ears. I couldn't take that chance."

"You miscalculated." I couldn't look at her. Had she honestly believed she'd done her best for me? By dooming me to an eternity as a nursemaid to children who'd end up as Sirens killing for Achelous? I shivered, my mind filled with so many horrific pictures that I swayed.

She was suddenly next to me. "Gloriana, please listen to me. I lied a few moments ago. Of course Hercules beat me. I wasn't going to tell Mars that or he would have started a war over it. But my husband is one of the most violent men I know. I had to make sure he didn't find out about the baby. He was off fighting one of his wars when I got pregnant. That's how I was so sure you belonged to Mars." Her hand shook when she touched my shoulder. "It will take

Zeus's own strength to keep Hercules from killing me when he hears about my affair with Mars and your existence now."

"Surely you could have gone to your parents…" In spite of everything, I was beginning to feel sorry for her.

"I tell you I wasn't thinking straight!" She began pacing, beautiful with her cheeks flushed. "In a way, I'm glad it's all out now. My father will protect me and I can stop this pretense of being a faithful wife. No, there's no divorce here, but I'm leaving Hercules' palace now. We are finally done." She managed a strained smile as she paused in front of me. "Gods, but I hate that son of a bitch."

"Well, I'm glad this is working out for you." Clearly dredging up the past was useless. But obviously she'd taken a big chance bringing me up here. Because she loved me. Nursing a grudge wouldn't help me deal with my new reality here either.

"It will only work out for me, Gloriana, if you cooperate." She lost her smile. "You did well with Zeus when you met him. And you've charmed Mars. It's a start."

"Yes, well, I've learned how to deal with whatever life hands me. I've had centuries of practice." I'd also had centuries to learn that honey worked better than a surly attitude. This woman was my key to getting back down to Earth. Time to try a softer approach even though my heart wasn't in it. "Can you tell me what you think Mars is up to? He wants to please me. Could he have gone to Zeus to persuade him to send me home?" I pushed back from the table, pretty sure that idea was a nonstarter. Hopelessness washed over me and not even the sight of my pretty shoes could make me feel better.

"Not that. You're dreaming, darling. But I'm sure it will be something good. Mars has a generous heart. He's a warrior, yes, but not like my husband. Mars is a fair man. He knows when to be gentle and when to be cruel. He would never raise his hand to me." Her eyes welled again. "I'm positive I can get him to forgive me. He just needs time to come to terms with this surprise."

"Time. Yes, he's still reeling." I wandered back into the bedroom and then that fabulous closet. "I intend to get my fangs back, Mother."

My mother was right behind me and ignored that. "While your father is gone, we might as well introduce you to your two brothers. You must look your best for it. Have you tried to change clothes with a thought yet?" She wandered down one side of the closet, brushing the silk blouses with her fingertips. "Try. Pick out an outfit to wear to meet the boys. Picture it then snap your fingers and see what happens."

She wanted to distract me. Okay, I'd play along. What else could I do? I settled on a pair of white skinny jeans that I never would have fit into on Earth and a soft blue cashmere sweater. Then I snapped my fingers. Looking down, I couldn't believe my eyes. I was not only wearing the new outfit, I looked like a model in it.

"This is amazing."

"You look wonderful, darling. Now why would you ever leave here when you have this kind of magic at your fingertips? Up here you are a goddess with awesome powers. Unfortunately, on Earth, you lose many of them. Why, I don't know. Something about gravity, I think. I'm certainly no scientist to explain such things." Mother smiled and led me out of the room. "Lose this fabulous trick for a man? Believe me, I can find you some wonderful, sexy men right here. Give me a chance. I promise to make you forget that vampire."

"Quit pushing me, Mother." I stopped in my tracks.

"Very well. I won't mention it again today. The boys are supposed to be guarding Olympus. That is their assigned task though you will see it doesn't really occupy them. Please, come with me. You will absolutely love them." She leaned close to whisper in my ear. "Remember, they were cursed with eternal youth. My fault. Please do not remark on their short stature or the fact that they never became, um, men. It is a sensitive subject."

"How sad." I took her hand, seeing the deep sorrow in her eyes. "Are you sure it's your fault?"

"I'm the goddess of youth. Of course it is. Why you grew to adulthood is a mystery. I can only think that Mars is just so virile…" She looked dreamy for a moment. "Well, it's something to think about. What a twist of fate if it were somehow to be laid at Hercules' door." She sighed deeply. "But whoever is to blame, it is a fact we deal with daily. The boys are always boys and have been for millennia. Be kind."

"Of course. I hope they accept me. They may resent my very existence." I felt a flutter of nerves in my stomach.

"Yes, they might. I'll be careful to warn them to be on their best behavior. They have their father's own temper." She sighed. "Come. Cheer up. If they have any sense at all they will adore you."

I walked by her side down yet another glittering golden path. Twin brothers. I hoped I wasn't walking toward double trouble.

In moments we arrived at a large field. Teams were playing soccer--one in red shirts, one in blue--and I saw what appeared to be identical twins captaining the opposing teams. Mother and I watched the rough play for a while until a referee finally called a halt. One player lay still on the field, knocked unconscious by a particularly vicious hit.

"Boys, come meet someone." My mother waved a scarf at the field and the twins ran to the sidelines.

"Did you see, Mother? I got a goal on Alex's team just a few moments ago." One of the boys was grinning and kissed Mother on her cheek.

"After you laid out one of my players. Illegal as hell, Anni." The other boy kissed Mother as well. "Who's this?"

"Darlings. I thought you might have heard the gossip. This is your, um, sister." Mother pulled me closer. "Gloriana, these are your brothers, Alexiaares and Anicetus."

"Sister?" Anni looked me over. "This is news indeed. Does Father know you have acknowledged this by-blow as yours?"

"Manners!" Mother tapped him lightly on his uniform shirt. "He will know soon enough. Be aware that Gloriana has already been accepted by Zeus and is under his protection. You know your grandfather's word is law. It will be in your best interests to embrace her as family."

"Of course. Any bastard child of our mother's is a sister of ours." Alex laughed. "Gods, but I can't wait to see Father's reaction to the news."

"This isn't funny, Alex." Mother touched a handkerchief to her eyes. "He will of course be displeased."

"And Father displeased is a world of hurt for whoever crosses him." Anni put his arm around her. "If he tries anything, send for us. Alex and I will stand between you." He glanced at me. "I don't care about this girl, but we love you, Mother, and will protect you from him. Never doubt it. We have felt the lash of his temper too often ourselves."

The hanky was soaked now. "Boys, you cannot know what it means to hear you say that." Mother ignored me as she linked her arms with the twins. "I don't want you brawling with your father. Trust that Zeus will make sure I am safe from Hercules' anger. But do me the kindness of at least pretending to accept Gloriana. Please?"

"Who is her father?" Alex glared at me. "Why is she fully grown and we..?"

"Darling, I don't know why she is the way she is but her father is Mars." She brushed a fingertip across Alex's cheek. "This ties our family to him, does it not? I would say you can use that alliance to your advantage."

"Yes, we can. Mars." Anni gave me a measuring look. "She's the image of you, Mother. I suppose we can pretend to love her, for your sake. And it will be fun to watch Father stew over this new development. At least there's no way his anger can turn to us for this." He and his brother stared at each other, maybe with some silent communication. "I think I'll send a runner to give him the news. Do you mind?"

"Not at all. We might as well get it over with." Mother released them. "Oh, I think the others are ready to resume the game. Good luck. But I know you don't need it. What's the score?"

"We are tied. Aren't we almost always?" Alex grumbled, staring at the scoreboard which I'd just noticed.

"You are perfectly matched, my darling boys." Mother kissed each of them, then watched as they trotted back onto the field.

"They are certainly handsome." I felt compelled to say something, though neither boy had said a thing to me.

"Yes. But they never aged past ten or so. Very bright, of course. Especially Anni. When it comes to court matters, he is always thinking. Their father has been terribly hard on them. They will be very happy to see him taken down a peg by Zeus in this matter with you and Mars." Mother clapped when Alex, whose team wore blue, scored a goal.

"Do you want to stay and watch them play?" I realized there were bleachers but no audience.

"No, they do this sort of sport on almost a daily basis. It is a dead bore but keeps them out of trouble. They are supposed to be guarding Olympus but it is a title, nothing more. They have an army, squads of soldiers, to do the actual duty." She led the way along the path. "Come, I will introduce you to some of my friends. They are dying to meet you."

"I'm sure the gossip has been flying." I braced myself. It didn't seem like there was much to do in Olympus but play and gossip.

"Of course, darling. You were a hot topic, as they say where you've been living." Mother grinned.

"Oh, great." We hadn't gotten far when a soldier ran up to us.

"Your pardon, your highness." He handed a note to my mother then ran away again.

"Well, I wonder what this was about." She tore open the envelope then read the note inside. She didn't say a word but I could tell it bothered her.

"What is it? Zeus? Your husband?" I could tell she was thinking. I wanted to shake it loose from her but just waited. Finally she turned to me.

"No, it seems your father has a surprise for you. He asked us to meet him at his palace." She crumpled the note and it disappeared. "I wish… But he is your father so he does have the right…"

"What is it?" Interesting that she could make the paper and envelope just vanish. I'd like to learn a trick like that. But more importantly, whatever my father had done made her bite her lip.

"Remember I told you once that time moves differently here than it does on Earth?" She faced me and took my hand.

"Yes." My stomach rumbled. I was really going to have to watch what I ate. Now dread was giving me a really queasy feeling. "Why? How long have I been gone from down there? Jerry? My friends? How long have I been missing?"

"It's only been a few days here, you know." Her grip tightened and I jerked away from her.

"Answer me, Mother. How long have I been gone? From my shop? My life?" My voice rose and I was on my way to a full blown meltdown. "What does this have to do with Dad's surprise?"

"I'll not spoil his plans. But you've been gone from Earth about, um, two months."

"No! I'd set a wedding day and now it's past. What is Jerry thinking? He must be frantic." I was sick but refused to give her the satisfaction of crying in front of her. "I missed the bridal party that Flo planned and, God! did Jerry remember to feed my cat?" I wondered what would happen if I slapped my mother across her selfish face. Oh, it was tempting. But she had powers I didn't want to test. So I stared down at my feet. Was that where my home was? Was Olympus in the clouds? A hellish kind of Heaven? I couldn't stand it.

"I need to go. Now!" I stomped my foot. "How could you do this to me, if you love me as you claim?"

"Darling." My mother tried to take me into her arms. I was having none of it.

"Get the hell away from me." I stormed off down the path with no idea where I was going.

She stayed next to me. "Keep walking. Straight ahead. We'll be there soon. Your father's gift will make you feel better. I swear it." She thrust a snowy hanky into my hand. "Pull yourself together. You will want to look your best for this. I promise you."

"Why?" I stopped dead. "What has Mars done?"

"I was beginning to think you'd never get here." Mars appeared in the path in front of us. "So I came to fetch you." He looked me over. I'm sure he wasn't happy with my red nose and wet cheeks. "You're upset. Why?"

"I just found out I've been gone for two months in Earth time. Two freaking months!" I wiped my cheeks and blew my nose. Now I was mad. "How could you do that to me? I have a life down there. The man I love probably thinks I got cold feet. On top of that my cat may have died of neglect!" I took a shuddery breath.

"No, Lacy took Boogie in and has been caring for him. He's fine, Gloriana." The deep voice came from behind Mars.

I actually grabbed my father--the god of war, no less--and shoved him out of the way. Then I threw myself at the one man who could make it okay for me to stay here a while.

"Jerry." I sobbed against his chest for a second then latched on to his mouth. He tasted the same, so dear, so perfect. But then we drew back, both more than horrified.

"Where the hell are your fangs?" He stared down at me. Even shocked he looked wonderful to me, so strong and unbelievably right in the short leather tunic similar to my father's. I guess the Olympus garb had been necessary.

"Yours are gone too, lover." I brushed his lips with my fingertips. "I don't care, kiss me again. I can't believe you're here."

"I'd go to hell itself to be with you, Gloriana."

"I'm afraid that's what you've just done." I smiled when he pushed his hands into my hair then took my mouth with his. The kiss went on for a while as we learned how to deal with the new sensations. No fangs. Strange and exciting.

"You two can do more of that later. Let her go, Blade, and heed me. You too, Gloriana." Mars' voice boomed from only a few feet away.

I dragged myself out of Jerry's arms but held onto his hand. "Okay, this is a wonderful surprise. But I hope you don't expect this to make me content to remain here. Jerry can't stay here either. He's powerless in this land of gods and goddesses."

"Gloriana…" Jerry started to speak but I wasn't about to stop now. He had no idea what rat hole he'd fallen into.

"You've got to see reason, Mars. Please, please take us both back down to Earth where we belong. Now."

The ground shook under our feet and I heard a sword slip from its scabbard right before the world went black.

FIVE

I woke up in one of those cells I'd been warned about. Flashes of lightning played across the ceiling down a hallway I could see through the bars of the door near my feet. I lay on the hard concrete floor, pains hitting me from head to toe.

"Jerry?" My voice came out as a croak. I was desperately thirsty. How long had I been here? I glanced around. No water, just a slop jar that was blessedly empty. For now. I suddenly had an urgent need to pee. Damn. I'd die before I squatted over that thing.

"Jerry!" I sat up, the effort costing me. The worst pain was around my chest. Had I been tortured? What I wouldn't give for my vampire healing sleep right now. Seems a goddess was more like a mortal than I'd realized. My bare feet were filthy and my size two white jeans were now soiled and split down the sides. Well hell. While I'd slept my size had morphed into my usual twelve. I'd popped buttons and the zipper until I looked like a sausage left too long on the grill.

I reached back and managed to open the clasp on my bra. Instantly the searing pain around my chest was relieved when my breasts sprang free. My sweater would have to be peeled off of me but I had nothing else to wear. Misery, thy name is an outfit five sizes too small. I tried the "think thin and snap" trick. Nothing happened. Someone had really done a number on me. Someone? Two guesses. One or both of my parents. Damn them.

I heard a commotion coming from down the hall. Screaming.

Female. A handmaiden ran past, her toga ripped and the ends of her hair on fire. She sobbed as she batted at the flames with a towel. I dragged myself to the barred door.

"Please. Help me. Is Jeremy Blade, a mortal, here?" I coughed as a cloud of black smoke filled the corridor. "Jerry!"

Mars appeared in front of my cell. "He's down the hall next to Achelous. Mortals are usually kept away from the gods. But… Well, your mother didn't like my little surprise." My father frowned toward the place where the smoke was thickest. "Stupid asshole. Achelous is only making it worse for himself. Zeus may end him yet. Our leader is still figuring out where to send the god to spend his mortal time on Earth. Pity the mortals who end up with him. What do you say, Gloriana? Who deserves such a gift? Any suggestions?"

"Send him as far away from Texas as possible." I groaned as I crawled to the iron door and dragged myself to my feet. "Wait. My *mother* sent Jerry and me here??" I really wasn't surprised but it still hurt.

"Hebe *is* Zeus's daughter. She needed to show you her power." Mars frowned when there was another flash of lightning. "And show me too, I suppose. I love her but she has the devil's own temper. She really hates what you were on Earth."

"She's made that very clear." I dragged myself to my feet. "But I can't help what I am, was. Neither can Jerry." I reached toward him, through the bars. "Mars, I mean, Dad, please. Help me. I know I didn't act thrilled that you brought Jerry to me but you clearly meant well. It's just that you have to know we don't belong here. Jerry's a vampire and has to stay on Earth. His family and friends must be frantic."

"Hush, child. Don't use the 'v' word here. You will only make things more difficult for yourself." Mars glanced around. "I don't want to keep you locked up but you must see reason. Your place is here. On Olympus, I mean. You will marry a worthy man and make me proud. Zeus is ready to acknowledge you and find you a fine mate. It's a great honor. Think, Gloriana. Take your destiny in your hands and choose freedom."

"I choose freedom. From this place and the politics that make no sense. I want no part of it." I sank to the floor again, my legs too wobbly to hold me for long. The cell was so small that if I tried to lie down, my head would touch the wall and my feet the door. Jerry wouldn't be able to straighten his body in a cell like this. I sniffed and wiped away a tear. None of that.

"You seemed happy to see your lover." Mars leaned against the bars.

"Of course I was. We're planning to marry." I propped myself up against the wall when I heard another thunderclap.

"I wouldn't count on it. He's right next door to that maniac Achelous." He nodded toward the billowing smoke. "Hebe secretly hopes your lover won't survive, I think. I imagine Blade's having trouble breathing through the smoke. Achelous sets anything flammable within reach on fire so he's kept naked now." Mars shook his head. "Not a pretty sight."

"You can't let him die!" I leaned my head against my knees.

"It's not up to me, Gloriana." Mars stared at me, the message clear. There was only one way to save Jerry. My parents wanted me to give him up and go along with their plans. I shuddered, everything in me refusing to consider it. Yet what choice did I have? Could I doom Jerry to life behind bars? Of course not. I had to send him home where he would forget me. Eventually.

"All right. You win. Let Jerry go and I'll do whatever you want. Just send him home in one piece." I turned my face to the wall, broken. I knew I would never find another man to love. No matter what "arrangements" Zeus made for me. I felt empty, lifeless, as if whatever my parents had in store for me no longer mattered. And it didn't. Life without Jerry was meaningless. Jerry would get over me. He was a handsome man with forever to find a woman to make him happy, a woman far worthier than me. I heard the creak of the iron door opening.

"Gloriana, you have chosen wisely." Mars laid his hand on my back. "Come. Your mother…"

"Don't even say that word to me! I have no mother. A real mother would never have forced me to make this choice." I straightened, looking him in the eye to make sure he knew I meant it. "I will never forgive her for this. If Jerry is mortally wounded I will go after her myself and make her pay."

Mars picked me up before I could stop him. "I see you have your mother's own temper. Both of you are not unlike the great Zeus himself. Hebe can help you here. Declaring war on her will only make us all miserable."

I glanced around my squalid cell. "She started it. Now take me to Jerry. Please? I need to see that he is still alive. He can't go back to Earth until he is okay." I leaned against Mars' solid strength. I'd always wanted a father. If Mars was what I got, I hoped he'd stand with me against whatever else my mother threw at me.

"Very well." He carried me into the hall. "But try to see reason. Hercules is back and eager for a confrontation. Hebe's in a panic. Afraid of what he will do." He lifted my chin so that I stared into his dark eyes. "You will stand by my side and show both me *and* your mother respect, won't you? When we are in public?"

"No promises. I want to see Jerry first. See for myself that he's all right. After being next to Achelous…" I could hardly breathe for the stench of burning flesh and ozone in the air. It made me miss my vampire ways even more. On Earth I'd never had to breathe. Here I was supposedly a goddess but I was so constantly out-gunned in the power department, I felt weak, vulnerable. And without my fangs, helpless. For Jerry it was even worse. He was mortal here, a whisper away from death every moment he stayed.

I shuddered as inhuman howls filled the air. "Mother must pay for this." I raised my voice to make sure Mars heard me.

"Gods, but you are stubborn." Mars strode toward the intermittent lightning bolts and the dissipating smoke.

"What is that?" I asked after a particularly loud shriek.

"Achelous is getting his daily shock treatment." Mars shrugged and I could feel his muscles moving under me. "The bastard deserves far worse. He knows he is to be made mortal now. Zeus is torturing him first. I know you can't appreciate it now, but your grandfather is a family man above all else. Harm one of his own and you will be sorry."

"I'm sorry I ever heard of any of you." I coughed, ignoring Mars warning squeeze.

"We're here. Try to ignore Achelous while we speak to Blade."

"Can't you just release Jerry?" Mars didn't answer me, just kept striding down the hall. I looked around, not sure which cell Jerry could be in. The smoke was thick and black here. I wanted down but was afraid my legs wouldn't hold me. "How long have I been in this hell hole?"

"A few days. It was for the best. Hercules was looking for you. He never thought to check here. He might have killed you before

Zeus could stop him. Hercules knows he is too powerful to be punished severely, especially with the size of the army at his command." Mars stopped in front of a vacant cell.

"Kill me? Why?" I coughed again and my eyes were tearing.

"To hurt your mother, of course." Mars kicked the cell with his sandal. "Here he is. On the right. Brace yourself. Blade didn't sleep the days away like you did. You can thank your mother for the sleeping spell that kept you oblivious. She had second thoughts after she saw what was happening here so she had a sorcerer take care of it. She would have let you go, but by then had heard of Hercules' threats. She had no pity for your lover. Blade's been listening to Achelous rant. It can wear on a man."

"He, he's in here?" I wiggled in Mars' arms. The cell I had thought vacant had a pile of rags in one corner. Surely, surely that couldn't be Jerry. "Let me down. I have to go to him."

"You can try. But, if you fall, I'll catch you." He set me gently on my feet, steadying me when I stumbled. "My brave girl. Are you sure you can manage?"

"Yes, I'm just a little weak. Guess food and water weren't included in that sorcerer's sleep package."

"Guess not." Mars gestured and I walked the few feet to the cage where a lump of humanity lay against the far wall. He was filthy and curled up as far from an overflowing slop jar as he could get. It reeked even from the hallway and I couldn't imagine being closed inside with it. His once fine leather tunic was torn and ragged. Jerry's usually carefully shaved face was covered with a growing beard, his hair was matted. A growl from nearby made me jump.

"Don't even think about it." Mars stretched out a hand and fire flared toward the man in the next cage.

"Word is that you have claimed the bitch Gloriana as your own. I see it must be true. But you obviously don't care much for the bargain. Since you threw her in this prison." Achelous laughed and capered about in his cage. Naked, he wasn't his usual imposing figure. Instead, he looked like a creepy scarecrow, his once handsomely muscled frame having shrunk since I last saw him. He was also covered in bruises, burns and cuts, some healing, some fresh and bleeding. I couldn't stand to look at him.

I turned away and laid my hand on Mars' arm. "I have given you my word. Will you unlock Jerry's cage and let him out now?"

"I'll catch hell from your mother if I do and you go back on your promise, Gloriana." Mars glanced at Achelous, clearly uneasy discussing this in front of the god.

"I swear. Let him go. I just want to say good-bye. But not here. We must take him out, clean him up and help him recover before we send him back." I didn't care who heard me. "Please, Dad."

"Ooo, listen to the bitch. Sounds a bit too much like her mother for my taste. Watch out, Mars. Do as she says and you might be crossing Hebe. The goddess will eat your stones for breakfast, sautéed over an open flame and served with a sauce made from whatever she can whip from your sadly depleted manhood if you go against her. You know that's true." Achelous cackled and moved close to the barred door. "Mars, I can see this one is already twisting you around her dainty fingers." He looked me up and down. "Not so dainty. Been hitting the pastries a little hard up here, Gloriana?"

"Shut up!" I aimed a finger at him. If Mars and my grandmother could shoot fire, maybe I could. I gasped when a flame striped Achelous's chest.

"Zeus's balls! Where'd you learn that trick?" Achelous backed up.

"My dear old dad. Now leave us alone." I glanced up at Mars and got an approving wink.

"Very well, let's get him out of here. Hebe can't be too upset if I allow you to give him a proper send-off. She just wants to be rid of him." Mars gestured and we were suddenly surrounded by a half-dozen soldiers. "Get the mortal out and take him to my quarters. Make him presentable, then bring him to my daughter's rooms. I expect him to be lucid and ready to greet her in an hour. Understood?"

There was a murmur of "Yes, sire." Then the men opened the door and bundled Jerry away before I could do more than touch his filthy cheek. He never opened his eyes.

#

I'd been content to let the handmaidens scrub my back and wash my hair until I finally got the stench of that horrible place out of my nostrils, but now I was swathed in a fluffy robe wondering what next. Of course that was my mother's cue to appear by my side. We were in my massive closet, full of clothes I wouldn't be able to fit into even with the help of a crowbar.

"Go away. I can't believe you did this to me." I sat on the bench in the middle of the room, my back to the mirror. Of course I wasn't talking about my size. "But forget me. I'll never forgive you for what you did to Jerry."

"That man!" Mother stood in front of me, as usual perfection itself. "I would think my own predicament here would teach you something about how making a fool of yourself over a man can lead to nothing but regret."

I jumped to my feet, refusing to look up at her. "Now the truth comes out. Have you told Mars about these 'regrets?'?" I reeled when she slapped my face.

"Guard your tongue." She looked around then sank down on the bench. "I love him but you see how complicated things are now."

I held my hand to my burning cheek. "Ah, so I've gone from a regret to a complication. Thanks a lot, Mother." I let my hand fall to my side. Send Jerry and me home and maybe you can smooth thing out here. I won't--"

"I regret striking you, Gloriana, but won't hesitate to do it again or worse," she raised a finger significantly, "if you don't stop harping on a subject that Mars assures me is closed." She put her hands in her lap. "Or did you lie to your father?"

My legs were about to give out on me. I sat on the bench as far from her as I could get. "No, I gave him my word. I will do anything to spare Jerry, even if it means giving him up." I turned to look at her. "But that doesn't mean I'm going to be a happy and obedient daughter to you now. You threw me in the cells!"

"I thought it would show you the wisdom of accepting who has the power here, Gloriana. Pouting like a child will not help." She was so damned calm I wanted to do something outrageous. Hit her back? I sat on my hands to keep from getting a lightning bolt.

"I'm not pouting, Mother, I'm plotting revenge." I settled for glaring at her. "How could you! Achelous was down the hall doing the most horrific things. I could have been killed. And Jerry…" I didn't see a bit of sympathy in her perfectly made up face. Instead, she just stared at me, haughty, every inch the goddess, daughter of Zeus.

"I knew how you were every moment. You weren't in any real danger. And I, I lost my nerve." Her lips quivered. "I let you sleep through it. A harsher mother would have made you suffer the way your lover did. He didn't sleep a single hour until he lost consciousness."

"How could he? Next to that raving lunatic. It's a miracle he wasn't barbequed." I jumped to my feet. "I love him, Mother. If he'd died, then I would have found a way to kill you myself."

"So dramatic. Do you really think that's possible? That you could hurt me? Physically?" She produced a hanky. This was her way to show she was upset but I doubted she ever felt real emotions. "But you don't hesitate to tear out my heart with your rejection of my plans for you. You will get us both tossed back in the cells forever if you don't stop these willful ways."

"Oh, stop it. I don't believe your father would treat you as badly as you just treated me." I found the strength to jump up and pace the closet.

"Would he not?" My mother paced alongside me. "I spent the better part of a century there when I tried to leave Hercules early in my marriage. Of course Mother had much to do with that. She demanded I honor my vows. Neither of them cared to hear that Hercules beat me. I was to be an obedient wife. The matter was hushed up and most in Olympus think I merely took myself off to a spa for an extended period of rest after the boys were born." The hanky got a workout. "I was only released after I promised to put on a front, claiming all was well with my marriage."

I didn't want to hear this. I couldn't feel sorry for her. Wasn't she trying to make me take on the same kind of loveless marriage she'd been doomed to endure? I stopped in my tracks and started to trot out that argument but one look and I knew she'd read my thoughts.

"It's no use, Gloriana. Zeus will decide your fate now. Even if I wanted to let you go back to your old life with Blade, I could not. My father has sent word that he's picked a man for you. And when Zeus decides to control a matter, it is done. All we can do now is wait to see who he wishes for you to wed."

"But he hasn't met Jerry yet. He may decide *he* is worthy." I looked down, suddenly determined to meet this new challenge on my own terms. I pictured myself as I wanted to be and snapped my fingers. To my astonishment I was a size twelve wearing the kind of designer dress that I loved. It fit perfectly and matched the cobalt blue heels I now wore. I strutted over to the mirror.

"What are you doing?" Mother stood behind me.

"Preparing to have a meeting with my grandfather. If he sees me as I really am, maybe he'll let me go home. To Earth." I wanted to be clear about that.

"But you could be any size now. Why that one?" Mother clearly didn't approve my choice.

"Because it's the size I wore down there for centuries and how Jerry likes me."

"Yes, it is." Jerry stood in the doorway, flanked by a pair of soldiers. "Good to see you survived that hell hole they threw us in. You look amazing." He stepped forward and pulled me into his arms.

"Really, Mars, will you do whatever Gloriana asks of you?" My mother crossed her arms over her chest. "And, trust me, pleasing this man is not on *my* agenda." She snapped her fingers and I was a size two again.

"If I hadn't released him Gloriana wouldn't be speaking to you." Mars dismissed the soldiers and walked into the closet. "You went too far. Our daughter didn't deserve that treatment."

"I saved her life. If Hercules had found her…" Hebe looked defensive.

"I doubt he'd harm Zeus's granddaughter." Mars glanced at me.

"Can Jerry and I have a few minutes alone?" I laid my head on Jerry's broad chest. He had on a short toga this time. Like he was going to court. The thought of him in front of Zeus made me swallow, hard. "Mars, you promised . . ."

"I'm not returning back to Earth without you, Gloriana." Jerry's arms tightened around me.

"As if he has anything to say about it." Hebe pulled at my arm. "I've heard enough of this rebellious talk. Get away from him."

"Leave them alone, Hebe. You and I have much to discuss. Come with me to my palace. Now," Mars said before they both disappeared.

"This is a horrible place, Gloriana. They've got to let you leave with me." Jerry stroked my back. "I was glad to see you looking more like yourself. But you are always beautiful."

"I'm working on getting us out of here but you have to go first. I want--" I couldn't say another word because Jerry kissed me, taking my mouth ferociously as if he couldn't get enough of it. Finally, he pulled back.

"I thought I'd lost you, sweetheart."

"It might be better if you did." I stroked his freshly shaved cheek. "Wanting me is dangerous. Zeus--"

"Forget Zeus. Surely we can get away from all this. Your mother…"

"Is not our ally." I tugged him out of the closet and into my bedroom, dismissing the pair of handmaidens waiting there. "She wants me here. Wants me to make a match with one of the gods. Word is that Zeus has already picked one out for me to marry."

"But you can't go along with that. I'm sure you told them you are promised to me." Jerry sat on the side of the bed and pulled me between his legs. "You wear my ring."

I glanced down at it. I'd refused to take it off and it was one of the few requests my mother had honored, probably because she knew quality jewelry when she saw it.

"They don't care. Well, they do care. The fact that you're a vampire makes you completely unacceptable. You're lucky Mars brought you here to please me. But it was foolish of him. It just delayed the inevitable."

"What the hell do you mean?" His hands tightened on my waist. "What's inevitable?"

"We can't marry, Jerry. I'm stuck here. Even if I get back down to Earth, I will have to please Zeus and marry one of his gods. It's the only way to placate him."

"And if you don't placate this bastard?" Jerry's eyes were hard, like he was thinking of starting a war.

"Hush." I put a hand over his mouth. "Zeus knows everything that goes on here. His power is immense. I've seen him torture other gods and you saw it too. Look at how Achelous was suffering in the cell next to you." I sighed. "I doubt Zeus would bother playing with a mortal. And that's all you are here, Jer. He'll just end you on the spot if you defy him."

"I'm not leaving you here, Gloriana." He pulled me closer, his thighs trapping me.

I pushed him back until he was lying on the bed. "I need you, Jerry. I don't want to send you home. But let's not talk about that now. Make love to me." I slid my hand up to the simple clasp that held his toga together and opened it. The cloth parted and I could see his chest and the smooth skin there. Even after suffering in the cells, he was still strong. I gasped as he wrapped his arms around me and pulled me close.

"My love. You never need to ask twice." His kiss was hungry as he found my zipper and slid it down. His warm hand found my bra clasp and opened it. He shoved my dress off and lifted me so that I could wiggle out of it completely. No vampire strength or tricks this time, just a man who'd been fit enough to survive horrors that would have broken many men. Whatever energy drink Mars' men had used to revive him had certainly worked. He was eager to take me, but determined to make sure I was ready for him. It wouldn't take much since I couldn't wait to feel him inside me.

He rolled me under him to kiss the curve of my breast and suck one of my nipples into the heat of his mouth. Heat. The novelty made my womb contract with longing.

"Jerry!" I held onto his hair when he gently bit down on one breast before moving to the other. No blood this time, just sweet loving. I nibbled on his ear and licked a path to the hollow of his throat. His toga landed on the floor along with the last bits of my clothing and my shoes. I wanted to taste him and pushed him to his back, running my hands down to his shaft and sliding my fingers up and down until he moaned my name. When I took him in my mouth he grabbed my hair, his hips bucking off the bed.

Oh, but I loved the power I had to make him need me. Finally he could take no more and pulled me up to kiss me. I sat on top of him, refusing to think about good-byes or what might come next. This man belonged to me. I sank down on him, so that he filled me until I gasped. Then I rode him, his hands on my hips anchoring me when I got so wild that I screamed his name.

Just when I thought I could take no more, he came. His hot seed inside me shocked me into silence. He was mortal. I was a goddess. Neither of us was now a cold-blooded sterile vampire. What did that mean? I took what he gave me and fell on him, holding him close and thinking about how I never wanted this to end. We were so close it was as if we were one person.

One person. No, two. But we didn't need vows to make us married. I knew, when his arms locked around me as if he'd never let me go, that I was his. That what we had was forever, no matter what others tried to do to tear us apart. I'd just have to be clever. And maybe what had just happened would help. I'd have to wait and see.

SIX

"Time's up." My mother didn't bother knocking. She stood beside the bed while Jerry dragged a sheet over us. "He's going back."

"Not so fast." Mars glowered at her side. "Gloriana loves him. Perhaps Zeus should get a chance to meet him. Size him up."

I clutched Jerry's arm. "No! What chance would he have among those gods?"

"Gloriana, I'm not afraid to meet the man who Mars tells me is your grandfather." Jerry threw back the sheet and got up, reaching for his toga that we'd tossed on the floor. Of course my mother was checking him out.

"Hebe, let these two have time to get dressed." Mars jerked at her arm when she nodded at me, eyebrow raised.

"To say good-bye you mean. Gloriana is right. There's no point in dragging this man in front of my father. He will not approve. Not when he finds out what he was on Earth." Mother frowned. "Don't just lay there staring daggers at us, Daughter. This world is what it is. We didn't make it. We'll leave you to get dressed. Put on your court toga after you wash off the smell of sex. My father does want to see you. We've all been summoned. If Blade doesn't leave now, he will have to go with us." She and Mars left without another word.

I felt sick, terrified. Jerry of course had no idea what he was in for. Though he'd been next to Achelous for the better part of a week so maybe he did.

"Stop." I jumped out of bed as he was about to pick up a pair of daggers. "You heard my mother. We smell like sex. The bathrooms here are decadent. Come into the shower with me." I took his hand and dragged him toward the door.

"We don't want to keep Zeus waiting." Jerry threw off his toga though and picked me up, striding toward the door I indicated. "Don't try to distract me now. We are just to get clean, nothing more."

"Of course not." I skimmed a finger down his jaw. He was worried of course. "You should wait here while I go see him. There's no rush for you to confront--"

"I'm not a coward, Gloriana." He set me down on the cold tile floor and faced me.

"I know that. But Zeus is not like the other men you've faced. He's a god. No, he's *the* god. Head honcho with the power to go with it. Who do you think is torturing Achelous?" I punctuated that with a finger into Jerry's chest. "You've seen him in action. Do you want to be next?" I was too scared to get weepy. "Say one wrong word and you'd be a burnt spot on the ground before I could even try to save you."

"I'll save myself, lass, or I wouldn't be worthy of you." He brushed my hair back from my face and kissed my forehead before staring into my eyes. "It's quite a place you've landed in, isn't it, my girl?"

"Oh, God, Jerry." I wrapped my arms around him and just savored his comfort. "You have no idea." We stood there for a moment but a knock on the door brought reality in on a rush. "What is it?"

"Sorry, mistress, but your mother is insistent. You have ten minutes to present yourself to her for inspection." A handmaiden bustled in with snowy towels. She didn't look at Jerry, just began adjusting the water in the shower and gathering my hair to wrap into one of the towels so it wouldn't get wet, even though I was still pressed against my man.

"Ten minutes?" I turned but stayed close to Jer so she couldn't see what she probably wanted to inspect. Handmaidens acted like they were deaf, dumb and blind, but I knew better. "Then leave us.

We'll be ready. Arrange fresh clothing for both of us on the bench there." I pointed to one next to the door. She nodded then scurried out.

"There's not much in the way of privacy here is there?" Jerry pulled me toward the huge shower stall.

"None at all." I sighed.

"Yet some would say Olympus is paradise. Unless you're stuck in prison here." He stood under the water and I admired the way the many jets hit his body. Even down a few pounds after his stint in that hell hole, he still cut a fine strong figure.

I grabbed a bar of soap, careful to pick one not scented with my favorite floral, and stepped in next to him. When I heard the bathroom door open again, the handmaiden with our clothes, no doubt, I shut the frosted glass doors behind me, closing us inside.

"Are you sure I can't persuade you to go home and wait for me there?" I slid in front of him, dragging the soap across his chest.

"No way in hell. It's clear they want to keep you here. I won't leave without you." He jerked me to him. "You have no idea… I went mad when you disappeared, Gloriana. The night before your bridal party?" He kissed me hard. "I knew it had to have been against your will. Florence, of course, went raving mad, convinced you'd been kidnapped."

"Flo was right. My mother did it." I dropped the soap. "I never wanted to come here. It's crazy. The gods and goddesses. Their powers. They hate vampires, of course. And here we're not." I bit my lip. "We're different."

"You don't have to tell me that. I feel weak and can't smell much of anything. Except you, Gloriana. I'd still know you in the dark. Not your blood, your . . ." He shook his head. "I'm not a damned poet. But what is going on with this new form of yours? How is it possible?" He ran his hand down to my backside, slipping a finger into the crease gently. "Look at you. Hardly any curves at all." He pushed me back a few inches and thumbed on of my nipples. "While I have to say these are pretty bubbies, there's not much of them."

I slapped his shoulder. "Beast." But I had to smile. Of course I'd changed back to a size two when he'd arrived in my bedroom. Trust Jerry to say the right thing. I did love him so. "It's an Olympus trick. One of the more harmless ones. But now we've got to be quick. Pick up the soap and scrub off. We can't make Zeus wait. If you thought Achelous was bad, you should see my grandfather in a temper." I shuddered. "He scared me, Jer."

"Damn it, I should have been here to protect you." Jerry grabbed the soap and quickly ran it between his legs.

"No one can protect me from Zeus." I realized how true that was and took the soap from my lover. It said something about my state of mind that I washed efficiently and neither of us made any kind of sexual advance after that statement. We weren't stupid or so mindless with lust that we forgot how to prioritize.

As soon as we stepped out of the bathroom in our togas, Jerry strapped on a belt and slid the pair of daggers that Mars must have left for him into holsters.

"Gloriana, perhaps your grandfather can be reasoned with. Surely he'd want you to be happy." He frowned and looked me over. "Damn it, you're shaking. No matter what happens to me at this meeting, surely your parents will protect *you*."

"I have no idea how this will turn out. But it's you I'm worried about, Jerry. Mars seems to admire you as a warrior. He already risked a lot just bringing you here to please me. But I can't imagine he'd go up against Zeus and risk his standing here in Olympus for you." I held onto him, leaning against his chest and breathing in his dear, familiar scent. It was different here, earthier, with more heat. Even more seductive. I stepped away and did the snap trick, enjoying his look of astonishment when I added silver sandals and a diamond brooch to my outfit.

"Interesting trick. Anything else you've learned up here that could be of use if Zeus decides to attack me?" That was my man, always interested in defense.

"I can shoot fire out of my fingertips. I'd love to demonstrate but burning down my bedchamber won't win me any points with Grandfather." I kissed his look of astonishment. "I did zap Achelous outside your cell. Sorry you missed it. But I wouldn't dare aim a finger at Zeus. He'd roast and toast me before I could lift a pinky."

"That powerful, huh?" Jerry followed me to the door where I knew my parents waited.

"You have no idea." I stopped and grabbed him one more time. "It's not too late for you to go home, Jer. Believe me when I say you don't want to meet Zeus. Trust me to get back to you somehow."

"I don't run away from a fight, Gloriana." He leaned down to kiss me, a sweet and dangerous claim that I couldn't resist. When he finally raised his head, he seemed even more determined. "You'll belong to no man but me. Mars has made it clear that there is talk of giving you in marriage to a god up here. I won't have it."

I sighed and brushed his firm lips with a fingertip. Yes, it could throw fire but I'd never hurt the man I loved. Too bad I couldn't freeze him in place and leave him here. But I'd promised to never pull that trick on him again and knew he'd never forgive me if I did it, even if it was to save his life. Once a Highland warrior, always a Highland warrior. Of course he fought for his woman. Some primitive part of me loved that.

"Okay. But follow my lead and watch Mars for cues. You have no power and no standing here. But Zeus is a family man and wants to please me. That's the greatest thing we've got going for us." I held his hand and pushed open the door to my sitting room. "The less you say, the better."

"I'll not play the meek and mild suitor, Gloriana. Zeus won't respect that."

"He's right, Gloriana." Mars stood and walked toward us. "If we're to do this, Blade must show he's worthy of you." He clapped Jerry on the shoulder. "A real man wouldn't let his woman do the talking for him."

"Dad, stop it. You'll get Jerry killed." I glanced at Jerry's set face. "He's in a strange place and outmanned. He'd never just walk into an enemy camp and start making demands without backup. Would you, Jerry?"

"Sometimes the bluff works, Gloriana." Jerry touched his knives, clearly not willing to listen to me.

"She has a point, Blade." Mars glanced at my mother who sat at the table, studying her nails with a little smile on her face. "Hebe, you will not try to manipulate this so that Blade here is hurt in any way. Gloriana would never forgive you."

"Did I say a word?" Mother stood and shook out her toga. "I can no more control my father than you can, Mars. We will see what happens when we get there. Which had better be soon. We're running late."

"Mother, Dad is right. You try to hurt Jerry with your little tricks and we are done. I mean it." I let go of Jerry and faced her. "Even if I am stuck here forever you will be dead to me. Invisible if we cross paths. Understand?"

"I certainly do. You wound me with your accusations when I am doing nothing but answering my father's summons. Now let's go. Blame your grandfather if things go awry. Not me, Daughter." And with that she raised a hand and we were suddenly outside Zeus's throne room. The walkway was crowded with courtiers. They all looked us over and started whispering behind their hands. Jerry in particular got a lot of attention.

A soldier stepped outside and everyone got quiet. "His Highness is holding private sessions today. He will only see these people." He held up a scroll and read the names. I wasn't surprised to hear my own, my mother's, Mars and then … "Is there a mortal here called Jeremy Blade?"

"Yes, I am Jeremy Blade." Jerry stepped forward.

"Hand me your weapons, then you are to come with me as well." The soldier took Jerry's knives then actually frisked him before he held one of the double doors for us so we could slip inside. The crowd almost moaned with disappointment. I'm sure they had hoped to witness the drama sure to unfold. The whispers swelled until the door shut. The room echoed with our footsteps as we walked toward those golden thrones.

Zeus and Hera were already sitting, watching us come toward them. No smiles. That didn't encourage me. A tall handsome man stood nearby. Not only wasn't he smiling, he looked ready to strike someone dead. Lucky for us, he was restrained by a half dozen soldiers.

"Hercules," my mother whispered. "Obviously he got here first." She reached the throne and sank down to her knees. It didn't take a tug on my toga to get me down there too. Jerry and Mars knelt behind us.

"Rise and let us discuss the mess you have created, Hebe." Zeus's voice was cold. Obviously whatever Hercules had said before we got here had put my grandfather in a temper.

"Father, I don't consider this beautiful grandchild I have given you a 'mess'." Mother was on her feet, my hand in hers so that I was forced to stand by her side. We were a united front. Mars and Jerry stood at attention like good soldiers.

"Your husband is not happy with you. Flaunting your child like this has opened him to ridicule." Zeus waved a hand and I felt a strong hot breeze hit my face.

"You've made me a laughing stock, you unfaithful bitch." Hercules broke away from the soldiers, sending them to the floor. He leaped in front of us, his face wearing an ugly snarl. "Look at her, grown to adulthood, while all you gave me were little boys who will never father children, never lead men in battle. They are content to play games and--"

"Enough!" Zeus thundered. "Those are my grandsons you malign. They are brilliant, fine young men. I begin to see that it is not Hebe's fault that their growth was stunted. What other children have *you* fathered? How have they fared, Hercules?"

"Are you trying to lay their condition on me? I am not the goddess of eternal youth." Hercules stomped the floor and the vibration almost knocked me off my feet. "I have been laboring in far off lands. I don't have time to take lovers and sow my seed like my faithless wife obviously has done."

"No other children, Hercules? I don't care that you prefer the company of men. It has been a relief to be rid of your clumsy attentions." My mother watched while half-dozen soldiers kept Hercules from hitting her. His curses rang through the chamber but I didn't hear a denial.

Mother stepped forward. "I have stayed silent out of respect for my marriage vows, Mother." She nodded toward Hera. "But this man is brutal. I am glad he is gone most of the time because when he's home, he beats me as if I were the lowest mule in his stable. Clearly he can't abide women, even his own wife."

"Liar!" But Hercules fists were raised and he looked like he was about to take another swing at Mother if he hadn't been held back.

"Coward! Face a real man with your temper!" Mars lunged, barely missing me as he went for Hercules' throat. More soldiers appeared from behind the throne and grabbed both men, forcing them apart.

"Silence!" Zeus's face was red. "I have heard enough. Hera, what think you?"

"That our daughter may leave this man if she so wishes." My grandmother stood and walked over to pull my mother into a hug then kissed both her cheeks. "I'm sorry I didn't believe you all those years ago, darling. He is clearly not the man to make you happy." She glanced at Mars, held by five men. "We will not dissolve the marriage, it is not our way. But you may have separate quarters as you have wished, Hebe. And must no longer answer to Hercules in any fashion." She ignored a shout from behind her.

"This is wrong! She is my wife, my property." Hercules struggled against the men restraining him. "Zeus, my lord, this is a dangerous policy that will cause problems once your people hear of it. Others will want similar arrangements. Alliances that help you control your minions will be shattered."

"Some alliances cannot be sustained. And you are my vassal, Hercules. You will do as you are told." Zeus walked over to face the man. His fury had lit his eyes with a fire so intense that I'd taken a few steps back before I could stop myself. I bumped into Jerry who settled a comforting hand on my shoulder.

"Of course, sire." Hercules suddenly lost his bluster and dropped to his knees.

"You laid a hand on my daughter? You are still alive only because of past deeds that earned you special favor here. Be assured that this matter isn't over. I will give it more thought. Your treatment of a member of my family may yet cause me to mete out a punishment more suitable than banishment from court and freedom for my daughter. Now out of my sight before I forget certain vows and take your head." He flung up his hands and Hercules disappeared.

"Father! Thank you!" My mother fell at his feet once Hera released her. "You cannot know the misery that man has caused me. The boys too. He is a bully, a--"

"Say no more. We are not done here. There is the matter of Gloriana and this person Mars has brought from Earth." Zeus lifted her to her feet and stalked over to face Mars. My father actually fell to his knees again, his face toward the floor. "Yes, you'd better show some contrition. I know what this man was there. And what he did to Gloriana." He gently moved me aside and looked Jerry over then raised his hand.

"Grandfather, wait." I was terrified he was going to make Jerry vanish like he'd done to Hercules. "Remember, please, that this man gave me immortality on Earth. He saved me or I'd have perished centuries ago." I stepped to Jerry's side and held his hand. "I know you don't care for the way he saved me, but what other choice did he have? After Achelous left me to die? I consider Jeremiah Campbell, known to you as Jeremy Blade, a gift from the gods. Many times over the years he risked his life for me." I glanced at Jerry who still stood at attention, following Mars' lead. "Look at him. He's strong in our world down there. A warrior and a leader of men. Many admire him."

"Is this true, Blade?" Zeus finally let his hand fall to his side and stepped closer.

I tried not to cringe. My grandfather's power was like a ripple in the air, invisible yet strong enough to make my hair rise. "Yes, sire. I am a Highlander. Originally from Scotland. We pride ourselves on being able to go into battle and fight side by side with our men. I have the scars to prove I've never run away from a fight."

Zeus looked Jerry up and down. "And would you fight for Gloriana?"

"To the death, sire." Jerry knelt at Zeus's feet. "I am sorry you don't approve of the way I saved Gloriana. I loved her the moment I saw her. Making her what I did," he was careful not to say the "v" word, I'd warned him about that, "was the only way I could be sure that she would be with me forever."

"Yes, I can see that. But you are not a god and I won't make you one. My granddaughter must be married to someone her equal." Zeus tapped Jerry on the shoulder. "Get up. Let me look you in the eye."

"I may not be her equal here, but, on Earth, we are equal partners and she wishes to marry me. She wears my ring. We are promised." Jerry said this while looking straight at Zeus, never flinching. If my grandfather needed proof that Jerry had balls, this should do it.

"I have someone picked out for her. A fine man. I suppose there's one way to see just how worthy you are. I can let you fight for her. Are you willing?" Zeus smiled, obviously relishing an evening's entertainment.

"No! Don't agree, Jerry. Grandfather, you can't pit a god against a mortal. That's all Jerry is here. It will be a slaughter. Please, spare him. I love him." I threw myself at Zeus's feet.

"Oh, get up. I know how to arrange a fair fight." Zeus pulled me up and handed me a handkerchief. "Wipe your eyes, you silly girl." He turned to a soldier. "Send in Kratos."

"That would hardly be an even match, sire." Mars had found his voice and stood next to Jerry.

"Who is he?" I asked while darting worried looks at Jerry. I'd expected a reaction from him. Then I realized someone here had frozen him in place. Not me, of course. But any of the other people in the room could have done it, even one of Zeus's soldiers, to make sure their leader wasn't in danger standing so close to this outsider.

"Kratos is a god of strength and might." Mars fingered his own sword which I knew had magical powers. "If Blade goes up against him unarmed it'll be a slaughter."

"Nonsense. I'll make them both equally matched. I can make Kratos mortal again since I'm the one who turned him into a god after he did me a service." Zeus turned as a pair of soldiers entered the room, flanking yet another handsome man who looked to be in his prime. He had broad shoulders and a shock of dark hair that matched his eyes. He and Jerry looked enough alike to be brothers. He bowed before my grandfather but quickly straightened to stare at me.

"You must be Gloriana. Your grandmother told me you were beautiful. But I didn't expect…" He lost his smile when I did my snap trick and became a size twelve right before his eyes. "This."

"Mother, is this the man you've selected to match with Gloriana?" My mother eyed him critically. She hadn't noticed my change. "What are the terms?"

"Don't trouble yourself, dear. Be assured that Kratos will fill our coffers for a chance to ally himself even further with the house of Zeus." Hera strolled forward. "Child, what have you done to yourself? This will not do." In a flash, I was a size two again. "Rebellious chit. You must not have learned a thing in the cells." She turned to my mother. "It's obvious she wasn't raised here, isn't it? We will have our work cut out for us before she is ready to walk down the aisle with Kratos."

"I'm not marrying this man." I put my hands on my much smaller hips. I remembered to give him a small smile. "I'm not intending an insult. You seem like a fine man, perfect for any woman who is not promised to another." I scooted closer to Jerry and picked up his stiff hand. I hated that he was still frozen and unable to squeeze my fingers. "It's just that I'm already in love with this man and we plan to marry. Good luck finding someone else."

"Gloriana, I'm sorry if your heart is engaged, but this is not your decision to make." Zeus smiled.

"Indeed not. For once, my husband and I are in perfect agreement." Hera pulled me away from Jerry, proving that her powers were too strong to resist. "Sit beside me and keep your mouth shut, Gloriana. Zeus will arrange matters."

I glared at her but my vocal chords no longer worked. Damn her.

"Kratos, are you willing to fight for a chance to claim Gloriana as your bride?"

The god looked me over, a hungry smile on his face. "Now I am. For a moment there… Well, I was afraid she was one of those greedy wenches, always into the sweetmeats. But I see now it was just an illusion. To put me off perhaps?" He winked at me. "You'll get used to me, Gloriana. I'm sure I can make you see that I am the man for you. I'm known for my prowess, on the battlefield and…off." He moved closer, as if to touch me. Hera gave him a look and he stopped a few feet away.

Oh, but I wanted to do something, anything, to stop this. I eyed the short sword my father had hanging from his toga. Kratos had a strong build and probably thought his bragging would impress me. I'd like to impress him with a sword to his manhood.

His eyes widened. "Well, she's a feisty one, sire." He'd obviously read my mind. He laughed and faced Zeus. "Is it a fight to the death? I'm sure once this mortal lover of hers is put down, it won't take long for me to make her forget he ever existed."

"Strong words. I like your attitude. Now here are the terms." Zeus glanced at me and probably saw how distressed I was. Fight to the death? No way in hell would I sit still for that.

"I won't risk you, a most trusted ally in such a way. This won't be a fight to the death. Just until one of you is declared winner to my satisfaction. And you'll both be fighting as mortals. No special skills or powers."

Mars leaned close and whispered in Zeus's ear.

"Ah, it seems our visitor has a special skill. How are you with a knife, Kratos?"

"I'm proud to say more than proficient. Not to brag," He winked at me, "But I can hit the eye of a running deer at sixty paces."

Mars snorted. Since I had no idea if such a feat was even possible, I was afraid that meant Kratos was as good with a knife as

Jerry was. However, clearly the god had a huge ego. If I had to marry him, which I vowed was never going to happen, his bragging would become irritating beyond belief.

Zeus rubbed his hands together and sparks flew. "Kratos, I hope you aren't overstating your ability because I've decided that you will both be armed with two knives and a broad sword. I am given to understand those are the weapons Gloriana's champion is proficient with. Is that correct, granddaughter?"

I was suddenly allowed to stand and even speak. I left Hera's side and ran to Jerry's. "Yes, but I don't want--"

"Gloriana, hush. This seems more than fair. Don't you think I can handle this kind of challenge?" Jerry had been thawed and now put his arm around my shoulders. "This seems more than fair. I thank you, Zeus. What say you, Kratos? Will you meet me in hand-to-hand combat?"

Kratos leaned back his head and laughed out loud. "Ah, listen to the lovesick swain. Willing to fight for his lady. You've not even heard all the terms yet, idiot. Say them now, sire."

"Ah, the terms. Winner gets the hand of the fair Gloriana, of course." He nodded toward me.

"And the loser?" Kratos stared at Jerry, obviously considering him an unworthy opponent. Jerry did look pale, his time in the cells finally showing.

"A century in the cells." Zeus smiled. "Unless one of you accidentally kills the other."

"There must not be such an accident." I realized Jerry's hand had slipped off my shoulder. Then I heard Kratos laugh, a braying sound that got on my last nerve.

"Why I think I've won before even one blow has been delivered." He nodded behind me.

"Jerry!" I turned and saw that my lover had collapsed. He was clearly unconscious.

"Sorry, sire." Mars gestured and a couple of soldiers picked up Jerry and carried him toward the double doors. "If you'll give this man time to recover from his incarceration before the fight, I'm sure he'll give you a fine evening's entertainment."

"Entertainment!" I stayed by Jerry's side. "My entire future rests on this fight." I picked up his limp hand and rubbed it. He was unresponsive. I gestured and the soldiers stopped. I knew we didn't dare leave Zeus's presence without permission. "Sire?"

"Hebe, I heard you threw this man into the cell next to Achelous. A fit of temper, perhaps?" Zeus stared at my mother.

"Yes, Father. I saw no need to have him here. Knowing what he was." She glanced at Mars. "But my daughter is willful and does seem to truly love him."

"Yes, you have my own temper." He smiled, ignoring his wife's humph of agreement. "Very well, we'll hold the fight in a month's time. Make it an event. Take your man away, Gloriana. Send in Dionysus. He can arrange things so that this will be a fine evening's amusement." Zeus laughed and walked over to settle on his throne. "Open the betting books. I can imagine Olympus will be quite lively for the next month."

"A month?" But I looked down at Jerry's pale face and could only nod. He needed to rest, restore his health and practice with his knives and broad sword. I could hear Kratos bragging about his skills as the doors opened to the curious crowd and the soldiers carried Jerry out. God.

"Did Zeus kill him?" Dionysus was suddenly next to me.

"No. Grandfather wants you next. We're to have a party. Go ask him about it." I looked around, refusing to say more in this place with so many listening ears. "Can you send me to my bedchamber with your magic? Or tell me how to do it?"

"Certainly. I assume you want to take your fallen warrior with you?" My uncle ran his gaze over Jerry. "He looks a bit pale but should be all right with your tender loving care." He grabbed my hand and placed it on Jerry's chest. "Now imagine your bedchamber, no, your bed. Think hard and you'll be there in a blink." He rubbed his hands together. "A party! Thank you, Gloriana. You have no idea how dull this place can be." With that he whisked through the double doors which shut behind him.

I did as he said, my hand firm on Jerry, my mind visualizing my bed inside my bedchamber. With a combo of "I think I can" and "Please take me there" I soon found us in the middle of my king sized bed. Unfortunately the soldiers had been holding his head and feet and they were with us too. We were all in a pile on the bed. Oh, well, I guess for a first try, I'd done well.

"You may go now and thank you." I dismissed them after we'd sorted things out.

I gestured for handmaidens who quickly got to work. Apparently the secrets of Olympus were known to them, just not to me. One brought an elixir which she forced down Jerry's throat. Another pried off Jerry's sandals while another seemed determined to take off his toga. At that point, I took over.

"Thanks, but I've got it from here. Go. Leave us." I took a damp cloth from one of them and ran it across his forehead. It soon became obvious that the elixir was working.

"Gloriana." Jerry's eyes fluttered open. "Tell me I didn't pass out in Zeus's chambers."

"Afraid so."

"God, no man there will forget that." He shut his eyes again.

"See it as an advantage. Now they will underestimate you." I kissed his lips. "They've given you a month to recover before the big event."

"That's something." He struggled to sit up. "Where the hell?"

"You're in my bed. I guess no one cares if we cohabitate while you recover. Morals are fairly lax here as long as we don't advertise it. My grandmother is the only one who is strict about marriage vows." I sighed and stuck a pillow behind his head. "You should rest. Your time in the cells was harder on you than we thought."

"Mars' had dosed me with a magic potion before he brought me here. I guess it wore off. I tried to stay upright but then the world went dark and that's all I remember. Is it a fight to the death or not?" Jerry pulled me down next to him and cradled me in his arms.

"Not. Unless Kratos does something shady."

"He won't." Mars suddenly appeared at the end of the bed. "I'll make sure of that. And I have news that should cheer you both."

"I can't imagine what it could be." I sat up and straightened my toga. Jerry had managed to slide his hand inside the bodice.

"Kratos has a man to be his second. Zeus will turn him mortal as well. To make the fight what he considers fair." Mars threw the two knives that had been confiscated from Jerry on the foot of the bed. "So I demanded you have a trusted man as your second. Someone from Earth."

"You're kidding. You're thinking of bringing a man from home to act as my second?" Jerry reached for the knives and tucked them under his pillows. "I hate the idea of any of my friends coming here."

"Too late. He's brought your best man and I wouldn't come

without my wife. So you've got us both for the next month." The voice was accompanied by a squeal before someone landed on the bed on top of me.

"Olympus, *amica*. What an adventure, eh?" Flo hugged me then kissed Jerry on the cheek. "Can you believe Ricardo wouldn't come without me?"

"No, go back! This is crazy." I shoved her off the bed and jumped up to stand beside her. "Mars, what were you thinking?"

"You don't want us?" Flo's eyes filled. "But we came to help you."

"Richard, you have no idea what you are in for here." Jerry started to get out of bed but I put a hand on his shoulder.

"Stay in bed." I smiled as I said it. "Jerry just spent time in the Olympus jail. Did Mars tell you that?" I shook my head. "This place is a fancy version of hell."

"Well, I wouldn't say that." Mars looked offended.

"We're here and we're staying." Richard pulled Flo to his side. "Darling, calm down. Gloriana is just surprised. I'm sure she will love having you here."

I sighed. Of course I'd pined for some company. A true friend to confide in. I opened my arms. "God, come here, Flo. You have no idea how glad I am to see you. And just wait until you see my closet."

SEVEN

There was no way to keep Jerry resting in bed. He and Richard had gone off with Mars to the "armory." Their talk of weapons worried me, but it obviously made the men happy. I let Flo explore my closet then took her to my sitting room so I could catch up on the latest gossip from home.

"Everything in that closet is so beautiful. And I can't fit into even one thing. Not even the shoes!" Flo waved her hands in disgust. "I would like to steal the purses and try on the jewelry but what would your mama do? Throw lightning at me?" She sighed and eyed the tray a handmaiden set in the center of the table. I'd asked the servant to bring in a selection of Italian desserts. Another woman entered with a carafe of pink sparkling wine and two crystal flutes.

"It's possible. I know she won't be happy when she finds out Mars brought you here. He admitted he went behind her back." My father had brought my pal here to please me. He'd definitely scored points. Now I couldn't help but be thrilled that I was smaller than Flo for a change. "Mother insists I stay this size."

"Insists?" Flo looked me over. "You make me crazy. Don't bother pretending to complain. You have always wanted to be little. Now you are and make me feel like a *gigante*." She waved a hand at the table. "What's all this? Another way to torment me?"

"No, not at all. Try something." I picked up a chocolate dipped biscotti and bit off one end. "Mmm. Delicious."

"What are you doing?" Flo leaned forward.

"Eating." I poured us each a glass of wine. "And drinking." I sipped some of the sweet wine and sighed. "Come on. Try it."

"Now you are being mean. You know I cannot..." She did pick up a pastry and sniffed it. "I remember these. My *nonna*..." Her eyes sparkled and I wondered if she was going to cry. "Well, this brings back memories. From centuries ago."

I reached across the table and squeezed her hand. "Flo, honey, haven't you realized yet that you're not a vampire up here?" I said the "v" word quietly. I knew my mother had downplayed my past, and Zeus could probably make everyone up here forget I'd ever been a blood sucker.

"No. I mean, seriously?" She picked up a cookie. "I'm starving. Not the way I can be, when I haven't fed but," she suddenly stuffed the pastry into her mouth and chewed. "*Madre di Dio*!" She said that with her mouth full, her hand already reaching for another one.

I laughed. "Slow down. You don't want to make yourself sick. Drink some wine before you choke." I pressed the wine glass into her hand. For a few moments there wasn't much to say as she ate and drank. Finally, she slowed down, moaning as she rubbed her stomach.

"Did that really happen just now? *Madre di Dio*, I think I am in Heaven. Did someone stake me in my death sleep? Have we met in the afterlife, *amica*?" She wiped her mouth with a napkin then refilled her wine glass, sneezing when the bubbles tickled her nose. "Mortal. How is it possible? I've been vampire for hundreds of years, more than I will admit to anyone even *mio amato* Ricardo."

I got up and hugged her. She had a streak of cream on her cheek, and I wiped it off with my napkin. "No, you're not in Heaven. Just the opposite."

"What do you mean?" Flo filled her plate and began eating again.

. "I can't wait to get out of this place. Everyone here hates me except my parents and even they put conditions on their love. I can't trust anyone, especially not my mother." I sat down and put a pastry on my plate, but I had no appetite. "Flo, she threw me in a cell because I wouldn't go along with her plans. Jerry's still recovering from *his* stay in prison and the horrible conditions there."

"*Cagna*." Flo was going for more wine but the carafe was almost empty. "It is too bad you can't trust your own mother. But with the powers you have and all of this," her gesture included the beautiful room, my closet and the laden table, "I am afraid you won't ever want to come home."

"Remember, Mars brought you and Richard here because Zeus expects me to marry one of his gods. Does that sound like a place I want to stay?" I knew *cagna* meant bitch and I couldn't agree more.

"No, guess not. Jeremiah can best this man in a fight, can't he? Are you worried that he won't?" Flo finished her wine. "Where's the handmaiden? We need more wine and biscotti."

"Maybe not. I don't trust the god to play fair." When Flo giggled, belched, then reached for the last pastry, I also knew I couldn't let my friend keep on eating without a serious warning. "About the food and drink. We may not need more of that either." I looked pointedly at Flo's waist where I noticed she'd unbuttoned. "Pants feeling tight?"

"A little." She grinned. "It is so good, Glory, I can't help myself. Do you have a bell to ring or do you just shout for the girl to serve us?"

"I gesture. Have no idea how it works. But maybe you should slow down on the sweets, pal. Mortal. Remember? You can gain weight. Or lose it. Go check yourself out in the mirror. When you were in my closet earlier, you never looked. Because you didn't think you'd show up, of course. Well, go see yourself now." I laughed when she raced straight for the doors. Her shriek didn't surprise me, and I headed to the three-way mirror to find her turning this way and that, frowning at her reflection.

"Why the hell didn't you tell me never to wear white pants with my big fat ass?"

"One, no way is a size six fat. And two, I'd never dare criticize you when I was sporting a size twelve. I would have killed for a six down there." I grabbed her hand and pulled her back to the table. I did my thing and a handmaiden appeared. "Can we have some fruit and sparkling water?" I turned to Flo. "Should I have her bring more pastries?"

"Are you kidding? Sure. I can lose weight, you said." Flo grinned. "So I find out how to do that. Exercise." She shuddered. "Or get your mother to make me smaller. You think she'll do that for me?"

"I wouldn't count on it." I dreaded the moment when Mother found out my vampire friends were up here. "But let me show you a trick she taught me. You won't believe it."

I stood and snapped my fingers. Suddenly it was *me* wearing white skinny jeans, with a blue silky blouse tucked in and a gold belt at the waist. My gold sandals were designer and had rhinestones across the instep.

"What did you do? I have never seen you tuck in a blouse before. And look at your little butt." She walked around me. "Show off." But she hugged me and wiped a tear from her eye. "You deserve it. Thrown into a prison by your own mama. I hate to think of it. And then trying to marry you off to some horrible man. Is he at least handsome?" Flo settled at the table when the handmaiden entered with a laden tray again.

"Yes. Even has Jerry's coloring. He's a warrior too. That's one reason I'm worried about this fight. He's a self-made man and earned his godly title on the battlefield." I poured water for me, ignoring the fresh carafe of wine the handmaiden had brought. Flo decided to hit the wine again.

"I put my money on Jeremiah. He has had centuries to learn how to fight and he loves you. No one has more reason to win than he does. It will make him fierce." Flo looked wistfully at the fresh tray of cannolis, tortas and pignolos then picked up the crystal glass and downed her wine. "I must thank Mars for bringing us here. At least for a little while I can be a human again. It's fun. A change."

"Think, Flo. There are other drawbacks besides the weight thing. You're weak. With none of the special skills you're used to having. And, be careful, or you could go home with a bun in your oven."

Flo looked confused until I patted my now flat tummy. "No! You're talking crazy. *Impossibile*. You think Ricardo and I could make a *bebè* here? When we make love?"

"I'm counting on the possibility." I smiled and picked up my glass of water.

Flo grabbed my hand, spilling water everywhere. "Have you lost your mind? You're trying to get *pregnante*? Does Jeremiah know?"

"No one knows." I couldn't resist one of the chocolate pastries and nibbled on it. "I think it's one way I can guarantee Zeus will let me come home. He won't tolerate a vampire's child in Olympus and I certainly wouldn't give my child away like my mother did. Jerry's child, Flo! It's something I've only dreamed about." I took a moment to fantasize. A baby. I'd thought I'd come to terms with never having one. Now? Flo made a noise and she was frowning.

"Think, Flo. Zeus's choice for my husband certainly wouldn't want to be saddled with a bride pregnant by another man. It's a perfect plan." I waited for her usual smile. Didn't happen.

"No, it's not." Flo blotted her mouth, clearly struggling to get her arguments in order before she leaned toward me. "A child, Glory. How will that work? Surely you will be vampire when you come back home. So will Jeremiah. You can't carry a child in your body if you are, um, dead."

"I've been thinking about that." I took a sip of cold water. "I can go home as a mortal. Then after the baby is born--"

"What? Take care of it at night after you become vampire again? What happens to it during the day? Or will you wait twenty years, grow old then turn again." Flo refilled her wine glass and took a gulp. "Think this through, Glory. A child has no place among our kind. Certainly not a mortal child who could become someone's food." She shuddered. "And I can't imagine a child who is not mortal. *Capirmi*?"

"I admit it's complicated. I haven't thought about all the logistics yet. But if it helps me get the hell out of here? I'm going for it." I set down my glass with a clink. "I'd hoped you'd be with me on this. Can you understand how desperate I am?"

"You must be to ask for help from this creature." My mother suddenly appeared next to the table. We were both struck dumb as she pulled out a chair and filled my empty wine glass for herself.

How much had she heard? "Mother. You remember Florence da Vinci, don't you? My best friend."

She nodded, Mother's face a study in distaste. "Mars has really done it this time. Bringing your vampire friends here. I can't imagine what Zeus will say."

"I'm sure he's fine with it. Flo's husband is to act as Jerry's second in this fight for my hand in marriage." I sipped more water. I really wished I could numb myself with some of that wine. But I was going to be careful from now on, just in case.

"What are you up to, Gloriana? I see you scheming." Mother selected a grape and popped it into her mouth. "Surely you realize

Kratos will win this battle and you will have to marry him. It is a good match. I thought him very handsome."

"Yes. He's good looking." I glanced at Flo. "I guess you could say he's my type, except that he seemed arrogant."

"It's not arrogance when a man has earned the right to brag a bit." My mother sipped her wine. "He's an accomplished man. On the battlefield and in the bedroom." She smiled, determined to ignore Flo when she made a sound that could have been one of either approval or disgust. It was hard to tell.

"Surely you didn't test him yourself, Mother. Though in Olympus I suppose anything is possible." I caught Flo's eye and shook my head. Better that she stay quiet. I wouldn't put it past my mother to send Flo right back to Earth if my friend pissed her off.

"Don't be crude, Gloriana." My mother drained her glass. "I asked around. Women who have tested his, um, mettle say he is quite the lover."

"Good to know, but I'm sure Jerry will best him in their fight and I won't have to worry about that." I exchanged looks with Flo. "Having a friend here has certainly helped me forget my recent stay in the cells." I sighed, playing the hurt daughter.

"I told you I was sorry for that, Gloriana." Mother toyed with her empty glass.

"Then perhaps you will help me out with a wardrobe for Florence while she's here. I doubt Mars thought of such details." I looked at her with a hint of begging. I knew she wouldn't believe me if I outright pleaded with her.

"Of course he didn't." Mother nodded. If there was anything she enjoyed more than arranging my life it was an excuse to shop, even if it was for a vampire. "Tell me, Florence, what sort of clothes do you enjoy wearing?"

"I am giving up white jeans," Flo said emphatically. "Glory always says black makes a butt look smaller."

I barely listened as Flo and my mother swapped opinions about fashions. The smell of the rich Italian pastries was making my stomach churn. Was that a sign? Time moved differently here so how long would a pregnancy last? I carefully cleared my mind when my mother glanced at me. I certainly didn't want her to get wind of my escape plan.

"That sounds wonderful, Mother. You have such great taste.

Where will Flo and Richard be staying?" I still didn't have a clue how Olympus was laid out, let alone where I was in the grand design.

"There are rooms next door. I will arrange for your friends to stay there. But don't think I'm doing this just to please you." Mother stood and waited until I rose as well. "You must do something for me as well."

Here it came. I knew she'd been too accommodating for the last five minutes. "What is it?"

"You will let Kratos come here and court you." She held up a hand when I started to object. "No, don't say a word. I saw your thoughts a moment ago. You know I could send Florence home this moment. Correct?"

"Yes, I know that." I went to stand next to Flo. "Please don't. I need some company here. The handmaidens are the only people who don't hate me."

"And they don't count." Mother's smile was so condescending I wanted to slap her. "I'm not asking you to sleep with the man, merely to let him get to know you. As you would if you were promised to a man in the normal course of things."

"You mean if this were the Dark Ages." I couldn't help it. What century did these people think this was? "Seriously, Mother. An arranged marriage? Even if I wasn't in love with Jerry and planning to marry him, I'd have never gone along with this crap."

"This crap is how Zeus maintains control of his kingdom." Mother's mouth tightened. "I didn't have a choice when I married and neither will you. It's our way."

"Your way sucks." I sat down with a thump. "But if it will keep my friend here, I'll at least meet with the guy. Let him bring me flowers or whatever you consider the courtship routine here." I sat up straight. "I won't encourage him!"

"But you'll be nice to him. And he'll show you respect or risk the wrath of Zeus himself. Remind him of that if he comes on too strong." Mother drew herself up in her best daughter of Zeus way. "Now, come with me, Florence, and I'll show you where your rooms are." Mother frowned when Flo stuffed yet another biscotti in her mouth then looked my friend up and down. "Gloriana, you did tell your friend when she goes home, she won't magically return to her former size, didn't you? But then perhaps you don't care, Florence."

"*Merda*! She did warn me but I have no will power, no control.

Glory, you cannot sit there and let me stuff my face. Next time, slap my hand." Flo threw down her napkin and grabbed my water glass.

"Flo, relax. A few pastries won't hurt you." I got up and followed them to the door. "I want to see where they will be staying, Mother. You know I still get lost here."

"Yes, I know. Which is as it should be. Don't go wandering around Olympus on your own, either one of you. I mean it." Mother put her hand on my shoulder. "There are many people here who wish you ill, Gloriana. Mars' wife is not happy that he acknowledged you. And you saw how Hercules behaved. He has family and friends who would be glad to arrange an accident for you."

"Thanks for the warning, Mother." I sighed. "You sure I shouldn't just go back home where I am safe?"

"You'll be safe here. Your father will see to it. Just keep bodyguards with you when you go out." She gestured and two soldiers fell in behind us as I followed her to a villa just a few steps down one of the many golden paths. "Olympus is your home now. No more talk of that other place."

I gritted my teeth. "Not if Jerry wins his fight with Kratos. Then we'll surely be allowed to return to our lives in Austin." I stopped beside my mother in front of what must be Flo's door. "I need your promise on that."

Mother didn't answer, just pushed open the door and gestured for Flo and me to enter. "I think you'll find these quarters satisfactory for the next month, Florence. You have a bedroom and sitting room, a luxurious bathroom of course. Merely ring the bell on that table and a handmaiden will bring you whatever you need. Food, wine, books." She frowned when I jumped in front of her.

"Mother, you haven't said anything. What happens after Jerry beats Kratos?"

"I see no point in discussing such impossibility, Gloriana. But after the fight, your friends and your lover will certainly return to their old lives." She smiled at Flo who stood close beside me. "We'll see how you feel then."

"I *know* how I'll feel." I stepped away from her. Clearly I was never going to get the straight answer I wanted. But somehow, some way, I was going to get us *all* back home. No matter what it took.

"We'll see. Now why don't you and Florence enjoy exploring her closet? I must go. Zeus is calling." Mother waved her hand and a servant appeared. "If you decide to go out, be sure to take an armed escort. You are not to go without one. Understand?"

"Yes, I get it." I couldn't wait for her to leave and she did disappear in her usual abrupt fashion.

"Glory, I begin to see what you mean. About this place. There's not much freedom here." Flo glanced at the servant. "Go. When I need you, I ring the bell." The servant bowed and left.

I hated to see Flo frowning, especially when I knew there was nothing she could do about the situation. This was all on me. "What are you waiting for? Let's see what's in your closet."

That got my friend distracted and we enjoyed a happy half hour doing the clothes thing. Finally, though, I knew it was time to take care of an important issue. I gestured for a handmaiden. No need for a bell for me. Goddess magic. She hurried to my side.

"Alesha, right?" I smiled at the woman I recognized from my own home.

"Yes, mistress." She nodded with a smile. "How can I help you?"

I bit my lip. This might get back to my mother but I had to take a chance. "My friend and I have just realized we're mortal here with a mortal's, um, vulnerabilities."

"It is so." Alesha looked at me curiously.

"Well, we both need to do something about, um, birth control."

Flo grabbed my hand. "Yes, we do! I'm so glad you agree, Glory."

I didn't correct her. "Can you arrange for us to get something?"

"I'm afraid only a sorcerer provides such things here in Olympus. There aren't many mortals allowed to stay. And," she bowed her head, "we are at the mercy of those who are of higher station than we are."

"Oh. I'm sorry." I realized the handmaidens must be mortal and little more than slaves. "Can we get a sorcerer to come here?"

"Oh, no, mistress. They are very highly placed. Though so are you. If I invoke your mother's name…"

"Sounds like we'd make a stir then." I thought about it. "And it might take a while. Can you set up an appointment? For both of us?" I nodded at Flo.

"Certainly. I'm sure he will see you immediately." She smiled. "Your men seem very lusty. So I think we must hurry."

"Yes, my Ricardo is always eager to have me." Flo laughed and wagged a finger. "And I am just as eager, *capire*?"

"You are very lucky. To have a man of your own choosing." Alesha sighed then flushed. "I hope it will turn out that way for you, mistress." She smiled at me then hurried to the door. "I will be back in a few minutes."

"*She* hopes. I'm not marrying Kratos and that's that." I looked up at the ornate ceiling.

"I hope you are right. Now your mother said you need an armed guard if we're to go out." Flo patted my shoulder. "Is it really necessary? To go see some witch doctor?"

"A person would have to be insane to attack Zeus's granddaughter. I say we can do without the guards. Where are you going?" I smiled when Flo ran to her closet.

"To change, of course. I wear black, I think. Something loose to hide these extra pounds." She gave me a long look. "You make me look fat now when I stand next to you."

"I'm not listening to that. But I will show off my new trick again." I stood and imagined myself in a cream designer sweater with brown leggings and thigh high leather boots. Snap.

"Oh, I hate you. Zeus's granddaughter. Who knew?" Flo darted into her closet and I heard the sounds of clothes hangers rattling. "But it has advantages. No?" She came out in a black knit dress with boots of her own. "How I look?"

"Cute and skinny." I turned when Alesha appeared in a doorway. "Can we go now?"

"Yes, he'll see you but we must hurry. He has other appointments after you." She gestured for us to follow her. "Self-important male. One word to your mother and she will have him thrown in the cells for impertinence."

"Let's leave my mother out of this." Though I figured she'd be all for this effort at birth control, if she thought I was using it.

"Hopefully it's not far." Flo was right by my side as we headed down one of the golden paths, avoiding the soldiers who were smoking under a tree a few yards away. "What do you think he'll give us? Condoms or something to take? A pill? Some elixir that will taste nasty and do strange things to us?" She did a little hop. "Do you know I'm a little excited about this? It will make our lovemaking, I don't know, dangerous. *Capice*?"

"Don't freak yourself out, Flo. Or me either." I added that when she gave me a suspicious look. I had to pretend like I was going to do whatever this sorcerer suggested too. I just hoped he wouldn't insist we take whatever it was in front of him. That would take some maneuvering.

Soon we were in front of a golden door. It had a moon and stars carved in the center of it which Alesha explained was the symbol for sorcerers. I commanded the handmaiden to wait for us outside then knocked. A deep voice told us to enter and the door swung open on creaking hinges. Flo and I stepped inside where a man in purple velvet robes lay on a pile of pillows stacked on a Persian rug. I recognized him and wasn't happy about it. When he choked on a grape being fed to him by a handmaiden, I knew he remembered me as well. Oh, how I wished for my fangs.

"Waldo!" I turned, ready to head right back out the door. "Come on, Flo. I'm not taking anything *this* guy makes."

"Wait!" The sorcerer stood and straightened his robes. His hat slipped off his head and it was obvious that he was completely bald. When we'd met before he'd been punished by a more competent sorcerer by having his hair and beard singed off. Apparently it had never grown back.

"Why should we?" I turned to face him. "You almost killed Jerry, my lover, with a Hellfire potion. Cornelius is the one who saved him. I want to go see *him*. He's a sorcerer I would trust."

"Maybe so, but he doesn't lower himself to do the kind of ordinary work you're after today." Waldo dismissed his handmaiden and smiled broadly. "But then maybe you don't wish to use birth control after all?" He breathed deeply. "Mortals. Hmm? Well, you can always just take your chances."

"Glory, no!" Flo grabbed my arm. "What did this man do? Explain. I've never seen him before."

"You're the lucky one. I met him at Ian's. My mother had hired him to help with Jerry's amnesia. Instead he almost killed Jer with his stupid potion." I looked him over. "Birth control must be an easy job here for *you* to be trusted with it, Waldo."

"The gods and goddesses rarely have need of my services." Waldo frowned. "They have the ability to do their own thing. Though it sometimes misfires." He nodded at me. "*You* are evidence of that." He swished his robes and walked over to a long table full of the tools of his trade. There were glass beakers, bubbling mixtures over low flames, and several boxes of various leaves and powders. The smell made my eyes burn and my nose itch.

"Be careful how you speak to me, Waldo. I have two very powerful parents and my grandparents…"

"Threatening me, Gloriana? I have a few good connections myself." He stirred a mixture then sniffed and added a few leaves which made it boil and hiss. "Now why don't we get down to business? I have something you want and old grudges shouldn't enter into our current business." He whirled around, his long robe almost catching fire when it brushed too close to a flame.

"Fine. I believe our handmaiden explained what we need." I couldn't get out of here fast enough.

"Ah, yes. I do a brisk business aiding visitors here and helping the handmaidens. The lusty gods don't seem to care if they leave one of the servants in a family way." He picked up a vial of green liquid. "They leave it to the girl to figure out what to do about that." His smile made my skin crawl. "So you see, I provide a very valuable service."

Flo and I exchanged glances. I wasn't surprised that the arrogant gods didn't worry about consequences when they were with mere mortals. But did I trust Waldo's elixirs? I couldn't forget how Jerry had suffered from the Hellfire potion. Jer had been burning from the inside out until Cornelius, Waldo's superior, had arrived with an antidote.

Flo decided to speak up. "Do you sell condoms?"

Waldo laughed. "No. It wouldn't help the handmaidens when they lie with a god. Those men would never wear anything." He shrugged. "And even if a clever girl could persuade them, I'd bet their swimmers would be able to penetrate through any material I could create."

"Too much information, Waldo." I tried not to think about what would happen if Jerry couldn't beat Kratos and I'd have to… Well, there was just no way I'd ever lie with that man. *Not even to save the man you love?* I shook my head and glanced at Flo.

"What *do* you have?" She looked skeptical when checking out his array of beakers and I didn't blame her. It all looked pretty primitive. Dark ages indeed.

"This." He handed the vial to her, uncapping it. "If you want to avoid getting pregnant during your stay here, you must take this elixir, every day or night before you lie with your lover. It will prevent any unwanted consequences."

"And the cost?" Flo was always about the bottom line.

"Hmm. Shall I charge it to your mother, Gloriana? I'm sure she will be happy to cover the expense. For you, anyway. I can pad the bill to cover your friend here." He winked. "It can be our little secret."

Mother would pay of course. I wondered if she even wanted to be a grandmother. Flo would need plenty of the potion. But then I didn't intend to take it myself. Waldo's eyes narrowed as he studied me. Surely he wasn't reading my mind, was he? I didn't like the idea of making a special secret deal with him but what choice did I have?

"Yes, charge it to my mother. All of it. And load up enough of that stuff for both of us for a month. Do you take it every time you make love or just every night no matter how many times you, um, do it?" I smiled at Flo, ignoring Waldo's chuckle of satisfaction.

The sorcerer grinned and winked. "Lusty men, eh? Once a night should take care of it or every four hours. If you enjoy a morning or afternoon delight, take it again."

Flo exclaimed. She'd just sniffed the elixir. "This smell. I don't like it. Here, smell it, Glory." She thrust it under my nose.

I sniffed and fought a grin. "Are you sure this will work, Waldo?" I patted Flo's shoulder when he nodded. "Relax, pal. I had my first hamburger yesterday. This actually smells like dill pickles." I passed it back to her. "Which is weird, especially for birth control."

"I've never eaten a dill pickle in my life." She sniffed again. "You ate a hamburger, Glory? Now I must try one. French fries too. Do the handmaidens take dinner orders?" She screwed on the cap. "Pah. I will go home as big as a house if I'm not careful."

"I have an elixir for that." Waldo rummaged in a cabinet and came out with a vial of pale pink liquid. "Guaranteed to keep you slim and trim. Take a vial before every meal and the calories are magically whisked away." He laughed. "It's one of my greatest inventions. Even Cornelius was impressed when I came up with it."

"Don't take it, Flo. Waldo tends to screw things up. Remember, he almost incinerated Jerry." I tried to snatch it out of her hand. She wasn't letting go.

"No! This smells nice. Like roses." She smiled and slapped my hand. "Please, Glory. *Amica*! Don't deny me this. I want to eat. I *have* to eat. When will I have another chance, I ask you?" Her eyes filled with tears. "If this works--"

"Oh, it does. Money back guarantee." Waldo quickly filled a burlap bag with at least two dozen vials. "Of course if I charge it to your mother, Gloriana…"

"You can't. She'll know I don't need that kind of product." I heard Flo actually sob. Oh, give me a break. I knew a fake one from the real deal. "Stop it. I'll figure out a way to pay for it. We can ask Mars for some cash or whatever currency you use up here."

"Cash works. It has a picture of Zeus on it. Gold coins, of course." Waldo was ecstatic. "Blessings upon you, Gloriana, for being such a kind friend to Flo here."

"Yes, she is." Flo hugged me so hard I had to push her off.

I watched as Waldo loaded the small vials of birth control into two canvas bags. "Any side effects you'd care to share from the birth control, Waldo? A craving for hamburgers, perhaps?"

"Very funny." He frowned. "You made me lose count." He pulled the vials out and started over. "No, you won't breathe fire or see everything in shades of green."

"Flo, Waldo's last elixir had horrendous side effects. Try this one while I watch. Let me know if you feel funny or if anything happens." I smiled and shoved a vial into her hand.

"Wait. Why me?" She tried to shove it back at me. "You first."

"Did I or did I not just agree to do you a tremendous favor? Besides, I'm the granddaughter of Zeus." I cut my eyes at Waldo. "Which you'd better remember, Waldo. So up here I have seniority. Come on, Flo. You are usually up for anything. Not chicken, are you?"

"Is this a dare?" Flo's eyes twinkled. "Yes, you are letting me eat. Side effects. I need to know this too. About both elixirs. And, Mr. Waldo, I know you would not dare hurt our Glory. Her grandfather would make a necklace out of your testicles. Am I right?"

Waldo paled but he just went back to counting the vials. Finally he finished and set two bags on the table. "Of course the elixir is perfectly safe. Ask your handmaidens. The pickle smell is from the combination of ingredients. I could add a scent if it would please you but it would take me another day before I could deliver it to you. Would you wish me to do that?" He pressed his fist to his heart and bowed. "Lady Gloriana?"

"No, no. we need it immediately. And I liked the dill pickles." I eyed Flo. "But we must be assured it has no ill effects. Flo?"

"Fine. Fine. I try." She uncapped the vial and drank the stuff down, wincing as she swallowed. Waldo handed her a glass of water which she took gratefully. "Nasty stuff. I tell them leave the pickles off the hamburger, I think." She looked around. "I feel okay. But it had better work. I don't want any little surprises. You understand me?" She gave Waldo a hard look. "No bunny in my oven to surprise my lover." He just shrugged like he had no idea what she was raving about.

I picked up our sacks and handed one to Flo. "We'll let you know if and when we need more. I assume next time you will deliver."

"Certainly, Lady Gloriana." Waldo bowed again. "I will give your friend the magic weight loss potion on credit. I know you will take care of the bill when I present it." He handed Flo another bag, this one blue velvet.

"Of course. Now I'm glad you're finally remembering how unhappy my mother was the last time I saw you with her." I practiced a haughty look, similar to what my mother used when she was displeased. It worked because Waldo couldn't get us out of there fast enough.

"Wow. You have that granddaughter of Zeus thing working well." Flo skipped along the golden path. "I wonder where Ricardo is. Now that I've taken my little elixir, I want to try it out. Four hours. Time for some fun, I think." Flo stopped at her door. "Alesha, can you send someone to find my husband and tell him I need him? It is an, um, emergency." She laughed. "I think your mother put some sexy nighties in my closet drawers, Glory. I will go get ready. What a surprise for him."

"Certainly, madam." Alesha bowed.

"Sounds like a plan, Flo." I was determined to play this to the hilt. "I'll wait to drink mine until Jerry is with me. But I've got some amazing nightgowns too." I put a hand on Flo's shoulder. "I'm sorry I made you test the elixir. That was a bad thing to do."

"No, you were right. We needed to see if it would make us sprout horns or fall down or whatever." Flo laughed. "See you later." She flushed. "Much later." She fanned her face. "Oh, Ricardo. I need you."

Alesha giggled.

"I didn't know it worked as an aphrodisiac but it seems to." I walked on down the path toward my own door.

"Did someone say aphrodisiac?" Kratos suddenly appeared in front of me. He was flanked by two of his soldiers. "You have just become even more fascinating for me, Gloriana."

"I think you misheard, Kratos." I wracked my brain. "I said that I once worked as an acrobat. In a circus."

"Even better." He laughed and punched one of his men on a muscled bicep. "I love flexible women."

Oh, God. Was there any way to discourage this man? "I was just on my way back to my chambers."

"Allow me to escort you. There are some people in Olympus who might mean you harm." He held out his arm. "You shouldn't be out with a mere handmaiden as company." He snatched my sack of elixirs before I could stop him. "What's this?"

"Nothing. Just doing a little shopping." I slipped my hand around his forearm. "Please hand it to Alesha. She can carry it to my rooms while you show me more of Olympus. I've seen so little of it."

"Certainly." Kratos smiled and passed the sack to the handmaiden. "Have you seen Pan's musical theater? It's quite charming."

"No, I'd love that." I let him lead me down more golden paths. I listened to him drone on about the many battles he'd won and how he'd rescued this god or that goddess from certain death. He'd also found some of the magic musical instruments being played in the ornate theater where Pan held court.

"Your mother tells me you used to be a dancer." Kratos settled me into a velvet chair in front of the stage. "Perhaps you'd like to join the company here once we are married. It will give you something to do when you aren't raising our children."

"You are taking a lot for granted, Kratos. You have to win my hand first." I looked around and saw that we were getting appraising looks from the other people in attendance. Part of the problem was my casual outfit. With a snap I was in a sapphire blue Dior cocktail dress cut low in front. It hit just above my knees. My strappy sandals were designer and I gave myself a clutch that matched. Kratos grinned and suddenly wore an elegant suit by an Italian maker. I couldn't find fault with his taste. Which kind of pissed me off.

Beautiful music began playing and dancers appeared. The audience applauded when one woman took center stage and began a solo performance. Her leaps and twirls made me wish I'd been as graceful. I'd danced in a chorus line. My double Ds had more to do with getting that gig than my grace. It had been in Vegas where they also appreciated my high kicks. No way could I have ever done the elegant moves this woman made.

She worked her way across the stage and down some steps until she stood in front of Kratos. Her dark hair was pulled back into a bun, showing off her huge black eyes. She wore one of those filmy outfits that showed every perfect curve of her lithe body. When she bowed to Kratos, her eyes were luminous with unshed tears. Then she looked at me. If she could have shot lightning bolts, I'd have been fried in my seat. I shifted, ready to run for it. Then she burst into tears and ran away, soon completely out of sight.

"Who was that?" I touched Kratos' clenched fists which he held in his lap.

"No one." He kept staring straight ahead where a new company of dancers had filled the stage.

"Liar."

That got him to look at me. "Excuse me?"

"I called you a liar. Clearly she is someone who cares about you. And I don't think you are indifferent to her." I stood. "Is this plan of Zeus's ruining your life as well as mine?"

"No, of course not." He took my elbow and steered me toward an exit in the opposite direction from the way the woman had run. "I told you the girl is no one. I am not responsible for what she thinks or feels. If I'd known she was performing today, I wouldn't have brought you here."

"But you did." I was relieved when we were outside, away from all those listening ears and avid gazes. We'd obviously been much more entertaining than what had been happening on the stage. "Did you hope to see her again?" I grabbed his arm when he ignored me. "Kratos, please. This is important." If he was in love with someone else, maybe I could talk him into cancelling the fight with Jerry.

He faced me and shook his head. "Stop it, Gloriana. I can see what you're thinking and it will never happen. I am happy we are to be wed. Your old lover is merely a minor obstacle in the way to our bliss. As is mine." He removed my hand from his arm and started walking quickly. I had to skip to keep up.

"Minor? Not to me and certainly not to Jerry. Or to that woman." I thought about grabbing him again but couldn't ignore the curious looks from his men. "Please. At least talk to me. Can we lose the escort?" I gestured at his two soldiers. "If we are to be, um, wed, there are things we need to discuss. Privately."

"Alone time. Yes, I wouldn't mind that myself." He led me to a bench under a large oak tree. I hadn't noticed it before but then Olympus was so full of surprises and magic that for all I knew he'd just made it appear. "Leave us." He gestured and the men stepped away so that we wouldn't be heard. They even turned their backs. I guess we could even make love if their commander got lucky.

"Talk to me, Kratos. Tell me about that woman. She is obviously in love with you. And you weren't unmoved. I saw the way your fists clenched and your jaw tightened when she approached us." I watched for a reaction. But this time he was in control. He picked up my hand and brought it to his mouth.

"I will admit Calista and I had a fling. You will not be my first lover and I know I am not yours." He smiled, then ran his tongue across my knuckles. I shivered in spite of myself. "Experience will make both of us better lovers. Don't you agree?"

I tugged at my hand. "Quit trying to distract me. I'm sure you are quite the lover. And I'm no slouch either." Okay, so I couldn't resist that brag. "But, Kratos, my heart won't belong to you. It will be a loveless alliance. And I'll never forgive you if you kill Jerry during this fight. He has my heart. You never will."

"Never say never, Gloriana. I've learned that's a fool's statement." He dropped my hand. "This alliance is the opportunity I've been waiting for all my life. To be a member of Zeus's family? You cannot know the meaning of such a thing for a man like me. I was made a god, not born to it. It's something that the true gods and goddesses here never let me forget." His mouth tightened. "You haven't lived here very long but just wait. Even you will hear gossip about your parentage, the fact that you are a mistake."

"I don't care about that." I searched his hard features. A warrior. How could I get through to him? "Where I've lived the past centuries, a person makes his or her own way. I didn't know or care who my parents were until recently. Why is this so important? Can't you--"

"Stop it. I will never give you up now that I've been given this chance. So you might as well get used to the idea. We *will* be married." He stood, towering over me, the picture of resolute male. "I'm telling you that I've endured the slights and being treated like little more than a servant for the last time. The gods and goddesses know I'm not their equal and never will be, even though Zeus himself honored me. But if I marry you, my children will be in that inner circle and will take me along with them. It's my dream come true." His eyes shone and I could see this was truly everything for him. "No one will dare disrespect me then."

"Well, I'm sorry, truly. But you can't get your dream with me." I gasped when he grabbed my shoulders and dragged me up to face him.

"Can I not? Hear me now, Gloriana. You will go through with this or I'll make sure your lover doesn't live to fight me for you. Do you understand?" Kratos was no longer the wooing lover. I'd just seen the steely warrior and he scared me to death.

EIGHT

"This isn't the way to win me, Kratos." I jumped up. Did I have any allies here? Where was my father? I thought his name and like a miracle, he appeared.

"Gloriana, I felt your distress. Is this man bothering you?" Mars carried a weapon from another era. I couldn't remember the name, but it was wicked looking, a spiked ball on a chain, that could do some serious damage if he used it on Kratos' head. I liked the idea.

"Sire, we are just getting to know each other." Kratos was on his feet, his soldiers on alert nearby. I was pretty sure they knew better than to attack a god of Mars' standing though.

"Dad! Would you mind escorting me back to my rooms?" I wouldn't look at Kratos. "The more I learn about this man I'm supposed to marry, the more anxious I am for Jerry to beat him to a bloody pulp." I heard swords slip out of their scabbards.

"Relax, men." My father gave them a stern look. "Gloriana, mind your tongue. Your grandfather handpicked Kratos and we must accept Zeus's wisdom."

I heard Kratos laugh behind me and whirled to face him. "Wisdom? Does Zeus know how you speak to me? Threaten to end the fight before it even happens?" I lunged for him and was hauled back by my waist just before I could scratch his eyes out. Damn it. I struggled but Mars had a firm hold on me.

"Daughter, I don't know what Kratos said, but I'm sure he's going to try to make amends and soon. Isn't that right, sir?" Mars kept a grip on me and held me by his side.

"Yes, sire. I'm sorry, Gloriana. I meant no disrespect to you or to your, uh, friend from Earth." Kratos scowled. "We will have a fair fight at the assigned time. I swear it."

"You'd better. If anything happens to Jerry before then, I'll see you in the cells until your manhood withers to nothing." I elbowed my father. "Right, Dad?"

"Certainly. Fair play, Kratos. If you want my daughter's hand, you must make this a fair fight."

"Fine. This goes both ways. Gloriana should be willing to let me woo her fairly." Kratos showed all of his teeth in what might have passed for a smile if it didn't look dangerous. "She speaks endlessly about this lover of hers. What man can endure that?"

"Gloriana? Do you need more time in the cells? Or does Blade?" Mars squeezed my arm and I felt his strength. "If you haven't learned your lesson…"

"The lesson here being blind obedience?" I couldn't do that, no matter how my father's mouth tightened. "How could the fight be fair if Jerry is sent to suffer in the cells and weakened even more than he is?" I tried to wrestle away from my father's firm grip.

"Perhaps I don't care." Mars nodded to Kratos who now looked positively gleeful. "I want your promise, Gloriana, that you'll be cordial to this man and let him court you properly. Neither of us can forget that he's your grandfather's choice. So you'll welcome his attentions. Be seen with him in public and show him some affection." Mars held me with his left hand but swung his weapon with his right. "But not too much affection. Understand me, soldier?"

"Yes, of course. I will respect your daughter, Mars. I also understand the honor Zeus has bestowed on me. I'll not squander this opportunity." Kratos said this directly to me. Obviously poor Calista was going to have to get over him or settle for being his mistress.

"Enough of this. I want to go to my rooms. I hope your presence here, Father, means Jerry is finished training for today and is waiting for me." I smirked at Kratos. "I'm not yours yet, sir."

"Gloriana, you seem determined to end up in the cells. Your attitude shows a clear lack of respect for a man who deserves it."

Mars growled at me, then nodded at Kratos before whisking us both away.

We ended up in front of my door. I felt a little dizzy. Transporting like that always did that to me. But I couldn't let my father's last comment go unanswered.

"Does he? Does Kratos deserve my respect? He's in love with another woman, yet is willing to marry me to improve his position at court." I could see this argument didn't impress Mars, who was examining the chain on his weapon. "Damn it, Father, would you listen to me?"

"All I hear is the noise of a petulant child who wants her way regardless of the consequences." He looked behind him and tossed the flail, I think it was called, to a soldier. "Now listen to me and don't interrupt. You went out without a guard. Dangerous behavior and that will not happen again."

I could feel the heat of his anger and looked away. I didn't want to promise this. "Why not just put one of those electronic ankle bracelets on me? Where's my freedom?"

"It's for your own protection, Gloriana!" He grabbed my chin and forced me to stare into his eyes. Dark eyes. Eyes that could see my thoughts even when I tried to hide them. "I know you want your vampire. I brought him here, didn't I?"

"Was it only to torment me? So I could watch him be hurt, maybe killed by Kratos?" I shuddered. "You've made it clear who you want to win this fight."

"It's not just who I *want* to win, it is who is likely to win." He must have seen the question in my eyes. "And, yes, Kratos will try to kill him because you've made it clear that as long as Blade is alive, Kratos can never hope to win your heart. You've gone about this foolishly and ensured your man is doomed, girl." He sighed and took me into his arms. "I'm sorry, but that's the truth."

"What can I do?" I wailed it against the hard steel of his armor when I really needed a cuddle from my father.

"Kratos is a proper mate. Take Blade as a lover later if you have to. I can arrange something." Mars glanced around and gestured. His soldiers disappeared. "Do this. Take your rightful place here and I will make sure you're allowed visits to Earth. To see Blade and spend time with him after you are married. Give Kratos a child or two and he won't care what you do. He will certainly take his own lover."

"Oh, yes, I'm sure he will. He already has her picked out." I stepped back, refusing to even think about my father's proposition. "But do you really think a proud warrior like my Jerry would be content with such an arrangement?" I didn't have to see my father's face to know he realized it was a non-starter. "And, honestly, Dad, how could I sleep with Kratos, bear his children, and then expect Jerry to wait for me and take the god's leavings? You know that's how a man like my guy would see it."

"If he loves you enough, he will take what he can get." My father sounded bitter. From experience? Of course. Hadn't he and my mother been sneaking around behind her brute of a husband's back for centuries? And I still hadn't heard much about my father's wife. Where was she in the picture?

"I won't ask it of him. You know time moves differently here than on Earth. I can't expect Jerry to spend years, maybe centuries, waiting for me while only a few months pass on Olympus." I shook my head when Mars started to object.

Mars stroked my hair. "I'm sorry you have to deal with this, Gloriana. I will say no more. Just help prepare your lover for his fight." He gestured and his men were back, shuffling their feet and obviously ready to move on. "Your man needs to get his strength back. Send for Cornelius the sorcerer and have him make an elixir that will boost Blade's energy." He snapped his fingers and a velvet sack appeared in his hand. "Pay him with this and let me know if you need more gold."

"Thank you, Dad." I took the bag then kissed Mars' cheek. "But I'm not sure Jerry will take an elixir. You have no idea how one badly affected him before."

"I'm counting on your powers of persuasion, my dear." He smiled. "Now I must go. Wars to be won, you know."

"Sure. Thanks for coming when I called." I hugged him again, armor and all.

"I always will, Gloriana. Remember that." Then he disappeared.

I stepped into my rooms expecting Jerry to be waiting for me. A handmaiden was setting out a meal. The smells were wonderful and I took a moment to make sure it was hearty, with the kinds of dishes good for a man who needed to build up his strength. Then I sent Alesha to see Cornelius to ask for a strengthening elixir for Jerry. I thought it would be better to just slip it into his wine instead of getting into a big debate about it.

Could I really deceive him like that? With a sigh, I headed for our luxurious bathroom. Jerry was stretched out in the enormous tub, all the jets bubbling away. He had his eyes closed, a cheroot in his mouth and a snifter of brandy in his hand. I wished for a camera. Never had I seen him so content.

"Want some company?"

He jumped and water sloshed over the rim and onto the marble floor. "Gloriana. Damn it, I can't get used to the fact that my senses aren't worth shit here. I didn't hear or sense you come in."

"How's your eyesight?" I grinned and reached back to unzip my dress. When I let it drop to the floor, I stood there for a moment, enjoying Jerry's eyes widening as he took in my lacy black demi-bra and the scrap of fabric that passed for panties.

"God, woman, you're beautiful." He dropped the lit cigar into the brandy. It hissed as it went out before he set the glass on the deep ledge behind the tub. "Keep going. I'm happy to say that my eyes are working just fine."

I kicked off my high heels and sauntered toward him. But I turned my back to him at the last second to carefully remove the diamond drops from my ears and set them on the dressing table next to the sink. In my usual shape, I never would have stood like this, letting him see me with the lights on, my ass hanging out. But now I took my time, slipping off the matching bracelet. Then I picked up the brush and twisted my hair up, fixing it with a clip on top of my head so it wouldn't get wet.

"You're torturing me. Turn around, Gloriana." Jerry did sound uncomfortable.

I was grinning as I reached back and unfastened my bra. I shimmied out of it and dropped it on the floor before I finally faced him. "Torture? I think you've suffered enough lately because of me."

"Then you'd better come over here and make it up to me. Don't you think?" He widened his legs and I could see he was fully aroused under all those bubbles. "Lose the panties."

I didn't say a word, just slid my fingers under the narrow strips of lace and let the panties fall to the floor as well. Then I walked to the end of the tub and stepped in so that I was facing him. The warm water swirled around us both as I sat then ran my feet up his legs.

"You're pretty far away down there. Come closer." He bent his knees, hooking my legs with his toes. Then I was being dragged toward him. I grabbed the sides of the tub so I wouldn't go under.

"Hmm. I think I'm getting there." I let Jerry settle my thighs over his as his cock rubbed against my sensitive opening. "You're not in a hurry, are you?" I slid my hands down his chest, rubbing his nipples with my fingertips on my way down. "Oops, maybe you are." I laughed as I guided him into me, clamping my legs around his waist as I took him with a groan. "God, Jerry, no man fills me like you do."

"I didn't hear a comparison there, did I?" His growl in my ear, made me freeze. But his hands on my ass didn't give me a chance to move away.

"No, hell no. Make love to me. Please." I turned my head and met his open mouthed kiss. We licked our way into each other's mouth, still unsure how to go on without our fangs to play with. But it was okay, better than okay. I loved him. And I could kiss him forever.

Then he started to move. I braced my feet on the wall of the tub and let him set the rhythm as I stared into his eyes. "Yes!" I moved and the angle got even better. He pushed into me harder and I pulsed around him, feeling the intense pressure that meant I was getting close, closer.

"Not yet, Gloriana." He pulled out then sat up and moved me until one of those jets in the tub hit me just so.

"Oh, my God!" I shivered, so sensitive my toes curled. When he lifted my hips to his mouth, I grabbed the sides of the tub and let my head fall back. To hell with my hair. I was about to come apart and Jerry's clever mouth was the only thing that mattered now. Then, just when I thought I couldn't stand it another moment, he drew me onto him again, emphatically. Like he was claiming me all over again. How many times had he done that? Declared his ownership. And did I care? Not at all. I rode him with the abandon of a Siren who was all about sex and had found her forever lover.

He shouted louder than I did when he finally came. So much for conserving his strength. I felt his last reserves drain from him as I clenched around him, taking everything he had, everything he could give me. Could he give me his child? I could only dream that he had.

I left him dozing on the bed after we moved from the bathroom and made love again. I got dressed in a loose robe and dried my hair, then headed into the sitting room to make sure a fresh meal would be prepared whenever Jerry was ready for it. I was pretty sure the handmaidens could enjoy the food that had grown cold while we'd been doing our thing. Did they have microwaves up here? I had no idea. But I did know that my cheeks burned as I wondered whether they'd heard us through the walls.

"Mistress, the grand sorcerer Cornelius is here to see you." Alesha looked flustered as she stopped me in the doorway. "You might want to change your clothes." She whispered the last. "He is a very important man."

"I know, Alesha. I've met him before." I snapped my fingers and now wore a black pants suit with a white silk blouse tucked in. Pearls were at my neck and ears, black pumps on my bare feet. I followed her into the sitting room. "Cornelius, thank you for honoring us with your presence." I sat on a loveseat and gestured for the sorcerer to sit across from me. He was in a business suit, the opposite of silly throwback Waldo who wore his long purple robes.

"Your handmaiden came to me with a request for an elixir. I thought I should come see about this myself. The sorcerer's world is abuzz with your presence here. And I certainly remember your friend Blade and how he suffered from Waldo's ineptitude the last time we met." He folded his hands in his lap. I noticed his perfect manicure. Which made me remember that Waldo's hands had been less than clean, his nails ragged as if he chewed them off and spit them into his potions. Yuck.

"Um, yes. I hope you know how grateful we both were for your rescue that night. As for now? Well, I thought you were like doctors. That anything that happens in your offices would be confidential." Had Waldo blabbed about my requests from him? And Flo's?

"Oh, it's supposed to be. But I was concerned that you went to that idiot Waldo instead of coming straight to me, Gloriana. You know how incompetent he can be." He leaned forward, his eyes that uncanny shade of orange I remembered from the last time we'd met. "Will you really trust anything you buy from him? After the fiasco that almost killed your lover?"

"What the hell, Gloriana?" Jerry stood in the doorway. He wore the casual clothes Mars had told him were standard in Olympus. Unfortunately, my father was old school so that meant something from before America had been discovered. Not that Jerry looked bad in the short toga, but, seriously, Cornelius was giving him the eye, like what the hell indeed?

"Jer, you remember Cornelius the sorcerer, don't you?" I stood and gestured for Jerry to join me on the loveseat. "Cornelius, Jeremy Blade, my fiancé."

"Of course I do. He saved my life." Jerry strode over and extended his hand.

Cornelius smiled and accepted the handshake then we all settled in our seats. "Yes, I was proud of that. Quite a close call but we managed. I was just reminding Gloriana here of the dangers of working with Waldo. He's the fool who almost killed you, Blade."

"You went to see a sorcerer?" Jerry stared at me. Of course he couldn't read my mind but he still tried. "Why?"

"Birth control." I sighed as if this was embarrassing but a woman's burden.

"Yes, I'd heard that was your mission." Cornelius glanced at Jerry. "It's his specialty here. I must say he seems to manage it fairly well."

"You mean you have to be careful here? About that?" Jerry looked shocked. "Why didn't you tell me? I would have--"

"What? Do you have some condoms in the nightstand I don't know about? You sure haven't bothered to pull one out if you do." I ignored Cornelius or I'd have been embarrassed discussing this in front of him. "What would happen if I got pregnant here? Do you want to take home a baby?"

Jerry picked up my hand. "I wouldn't mind." He squeezed my fingers. "But I'm not sure how that would play with Zeus."

"Really, Gloriana, Blade is right. You were very wise. You don't want to imagine what your grandfather would do if you were to ruin his plans to marry you off to a god with something like an unplanned pregnancy." Cornelius narrowed those pumpkin-colored eyes at me. "But then maybe you don't care about upsetting Zeus."

"Sending Zeus into a meltdown?" I shuddered. "He's scary when he's in a *good* mood."

"Well, you'd be wise to remember who's in charge here." Cornelius pulled a vial of amber liquid from his breast pocket. "I've brought what you requested. I understand, Blade, that you were recently held in the cells. That can take quite a toll on a man's health."

"It was a nightmare. But I'm getting back in shape. Training every day." Jerry kept my hand in his. "I admit I tire easily." He nodded toward the vial. "If that poison is for me, forget it."

"Jerry, please. I asked Cornelius for a tonic. Something to help you get your strength back. Mars recommended it." Tears filled my eyes and I didn't try to hold them back. "I can't take a chance that Kratos will kill you in that fight. You *must* win."

"Kratos is a formidable opponent." Cornelius set the vial on the coffee table between us. "This elixir is fairly harmless. It will give you a boost that will help you be stronger, faster. Consider it similar to the vitamins that mortals take. Why not give it a chance?"

"Because the last sorcerer's potion I took almost made my brain boil?" Jerry dropped my hand and stood. "Thanks for dropping by, Cornelius. I will always be grateful that you saved my life back on Earth. But I'm going to win this fight without performance-enhancing drugs."

"You think Kratos won't take something to increase his strength before the fight?" Cornelius rose gracefully. "He's already put in his order. This will just level the playing field. It's one reason why I came here personally." He frowned and pulled four more vials from his pockets. "Take one every few days until the day of the fight." Then he pulled one last bottle from his pocket. This one was bigger and made of brown glass. "Then on the morning of the fight, swallow this down. It should make you able to do your best."

"Sounds dishonest to me. I'm a Campbell and a Highlander." Jerry hit his chest. "We don't cheat. We win on our own merits."

"Then die on your own merits. This isn't supposed to be a fight to the death but I've heard Kratos has a vendetta against you." Cornelius left all the drugs on the table. "Gloriana, talk to him. And don't worry about payment. I have a score to settle with Kratos myself. Calista is my granddaughter and he has treated her poorly. They were supposed to wed but, when this opportunity to marry you came along, he discarded her without a second's thought. Her heart is broken." Cornelius stalked to the door. "Beat the son of a bitch, Blade. Kill him if you can. I'll be placing my money on you." And with that he left, closing the door behind him.

"That was a surprise." I stared after the sorcerer.

"Good to know someone powerful is on my side." Jerry picked up one of the vials. "But I'm not taking--"

"Listen to me. I will die if you die. Because I'm not marrying Kratos." I wrapped my arms around Jerry's waist. "Those drugs aren't cheating. What was cheating was making you suffer in the cells until you lost weight and strength. Kratos is in the prime of life, in top condition. And still plans to use a drug anyway."

"I'm a warrior, Gloriana." Jerry's jaw was tight.

"Who has spent the past centuries fighting with a vampire's advantages. A vampire's special skills. Where are those now?" I ran my fingertips over that hard jaw, trying to coax it to soften. "Do you even remember how a mortal fights? What it means to stand and battle without the chance to read a man's mind or leap over his back? Tear out his throat?"

"Stop it." He pushed me away but I noticed he didn't fling the vial to the hard marble floor. "You think I'm not haunted by that fact? Mārs puts me up to spar with a servant who is also mortal and I still can't best him." He turned his back on me. "Shit, Gloriana, I am less than a man here. How can you still love me?"

"You are my heart, Jeremiah. I never loved you for the way you swing a sword or use your fists." I slid my hands over his back, feeling how the muscles were taut and yet not as hard as they once were. "I love you for the way you always look out for me, always put me first. You are my hero, my lover, my soul mate."

He whirled to face me. "And you ran to a sorcerer for fear of having my child."

I knew these walls had ears so I said what I had to say. "It's not smart to bring a child into this place, Jerry. Surely you can see that."

"Of course. Because you expect Kratos will kill me. Then where would you be?" He gave me a long look that broke my heart, then set the vial he still held on the table and stormed out the door.

"Jerry!" Where was he going? Would he be safe? I gestured and Alesha came running. "Get a soldier to follow him, no, two soldiers. I want him guarded. Understand?"

"Yes, mistress." She nodded and took off.

I sat down and began gathering up the vials. He'd take the damned stuff or I would slip it into his food. He had to win the fight. Had to.

I'd been walking the floor for more than an hour when Flo burst through the door.

"Glory, you must help me." She wobbled over to the sofa and sat down.

"What is it?" I sat next to her. "Great shoes." I had to comment. They were five inch heels in red leather with open toes. They set off her black and white dress with a red belt perfectly.

"Pah! Torture shoes. I am a disgrace to women everywhere. I hate being a mortal." She kicked them off and rubbed one of her feet. "But that's not why I'm here. It's our men. Jeremiah came by our place just as I was about to make Ricardo very happy if you know what I mean." She added a gesture that made it clear what she meant and I was sorry to have that picture in my head. "Anyway, I think Ricardo was glad to leave me. He claims I am wearing him out." She used air quotes for that. "That birth control." She leaned in to whisper. "It makes me hungry for him all the time."

"Yes, sure. But about the men. Where did they go?" I had no idea if Jerry even knew Olympus well enough to find a place to blow off steam.

"A sleazy bar I think. I bet it's one of those that has naked waitresses or strippers." Flo's eyes filled. "I won't have it, I tell you. If Ricardo wants to drink and look at half naked women, he can do that at home." She hit her own substantial bosom. "What am I? Nothing? I have a nice rack. Ricardo says so."

"You know men, Flo. Sometimes they like to have a drink and just chill." Which made me crazy. "And looking at a new rack makes them happy." And me mad. "Where is this place?" I got up and snapped myself a short leather skirt and red lace bustier that would give a cocktail waitress a run for her money. I gave myself my own pair of red high heels. "We're going to drag them out of this place."

"Now you're talking, girlfriend." Flo jumped up then grabbed her shoes. "Can you make shoes for me? Maybe something with a lower heel?"

"Seriously? You love high heels."

"I can't walk in these things without falling down here." She sighed, looking ashamed. "I know, it is horrible. Maybe I practice."

"No, let me try." I concentrated, picturing some cute espadrilles for Flo in her size and snapped. Nothing. I guess my powers weren't as advanced as my mother's.

"I love it when you realize you need me, darling."

Speak of the devil. "Mother. Can you help Flo? Her feet are killing her." I smiled at my mother. "And we need directions. Our men went to some sleazy bar to drink and look at topless women. Do you know where it is?"

"Of course." She glanced down at Flo's feet and my pal was suddenly wearing some mid-heel espadrilles just like I'd pictured. It was a serious reminder that Mom's mind reading skills were off the charts. "As to the bar, there's one that is known for its strong drinks and loose women. Are you sure you want to go after them? Sometimes men need a chance to cool off."

"Jerry's mad because I told him I'm using birth control." I glanced at Flo. "He took Richard as his wingman I guess. Also I want him to take a strengthening elixir before the big fight. He's being stubborn about it."

"I must say I approve of the birth control." Mother smiled. "The elixir may or may not help but we want to have a fair fight. Zeus does like good entertainment." Mother nodded. "I'll take you there. With an armed guard. It's not in the best part of Olympus and I don't think we should teleport there. We'll take a carriage."

"A carriage? What century are you people stuck in anyway?" I couldn't help it. This whole realm, I guess you'd call it, was so out of touch with modern times. Most of the time the people even talked like they were stuck in a Victorian novel.

"Gloriana, we are above modern ways. This is Zeus's kingdom. We aren't going to bring in a Maserati or a Porsche just because you'd prefer it. Zeus doesn't care for the noise or the pollution. And our beautiful roads would be ruined." Mother sniffed. "Our ways are gentler."

"A Maserati can be gentle. You should feel the leather seats." Flo had quit test driving her new shoes and now came up to us, smiling. "But I understand and respect this, yes? Now let's go before some bimbo gets her claws into my man."

"Relax, Flo. Richard is true to you and madly in love. But maybe he needs a little break from your enthusiasm." I steered her toward the door.

"Hah! He never needed a break before. It is this place. He has nothing to do except help Jeremiah train and make love to me." Flo turned to my mother. "He is bored, Hebe, can you understand that?""

"Too well. It is why we have so much gossip and indulge in

affairs here." She turned when we got outside. "Here's our carriage. If the men are drunk, we can bring them back in this."

I gawked at what seemed straight out of a Cinderella movie. The white carriage had open sides and silk covered plush seats. Everything was trimmed in gold and silver. The horses were white, too, and had silver bridles. I didn't ask what they did about horse poop. Guess that didn't hurt their beautiful roads paved in gold. Soldiers in white uniforms with gold epaulets helped us up the steps and soon we were on our way down one more glittering path.

"When we get there, we'll wait in the carriage. I'll send one of the soldiers in to see if they are there. This may be a fool's errand." Mother leaned back against the silk pillows. She looked beautiful as usual, this time in a green blouse tucked into navy pants. Her navy sandals had silver buckles. There were emeralds in her ears and on her fingers.

"If they aren't here, where could they be?" I couldn't relax.

"Maybe they went back to the training area. Mars has a workout room set up for your lover. He might be lifting weights or hitting one of those bag things." Mother sat up when the carriage stopped. "Elias, go inside and see if two mortals are in there. You know the ones. If they are, come back out before you make contact."

A soldier bowed and took off, pushing inside a large white stone building that looked a lot like most buildings in Olympus. The only way you would know this wasn't a private villa was the discreet sign above the double doors. Bacchanal. Oh, I did not like what that implied. And the music that I heard when the door opened had the kind of throbbing beat that hinted of a mating dance. The insulation must be great because as soon as the door swished closed, all we could hear was the noise of restless horses and the sounds they made as they waited to move on.

"Does Dionysus own this place?" I had to ask.

"Of course. If it involves decadence and a party, he's involved. I have no idea how many such clubs he runs but this is the one most likely to be mentioned in Blade's hearing. It's one of Mars' favorites." Mother frowned. "Maybe we should go in after all. I wouldn't mind taking a look around."

"Now you're talking, girlfriend." Flo's mouth snapped shut at the icy look from my mother. "No disrespect intended."

"I should hope not." Mother gestured and a guard hurried over to let down the steps and give her his arm as she got out of the carriage. "Come on, girls. We might as well enjoy this too. Men and women both come here. My brother does know how to show people a good time." She snapped her fingers and wore a low-cut green cocktail dress. Looking Flo over, she snapped again and put her in black with high heels. I took care of my own dress, a take on the toga look except in gold with shoes to match. Then we strutted into the club.

Well, Mother and I strutted, Flo wobbled and staggered and almost turned an ankle. She hadn't been kidding about not being able to walk in high heels. I hid a grin as I offered her my arm to lean on when we got through the door.

The music was loud, the lights were dim and the place was packed. Scantily dressed women worked the poles set up on the corners of the stage. Actually, they were topless. Eye candy for men. And then there was eye candy for women. Men in G-strings writhed in the middle of the cat walk stage, doing a combination of gymnastics and bump and grind. I admit I had a flash of heat go through me at the sight of their perfect, oiled bodies.

When I could tear my eyes away from the show, I remembered to look for Jerry and Richard. At first I didn't see them. Mother stalked through the crowd, which parted for her like she had a gun in her hand. Not necessary. Daughter of Zeus. You don't mess with the hierarchy. Anyway, I saw where she was headed. Mars had a corner table and had several men with him. Each guy, including Dad, had a beautiful woman draped over him. When he saw Mother coming, he jumped up, dumping his date on the floor. She was on her way to being indignant until she saw who was approaching. Then she scurried away on all fours. It would have been funny except there was a little heat lightning flashing above the table.

I decided to steer clear and grabbed Flo, helping her hobble over to the bar. I ordered two of the drink specials, whatever they were, and then dug for some of my father's coins I'd stuck in my bra. A deep voice spoke from behind me.

"Put it on my tab."

I whirled around, afraid I was going to have to face Kratos again. But it was a man I didn't recognize. "Thank you."

"You *are* Gloriana, aren't you?" He leaned against the bar, his smile charming.

I appreciated the fact that he didn't focus on my cleavage like most men did. Oh. Forgot. I was now a B-cup, not the old double D. I snapped on a pushup bra. Better. His eyes moved there. I was shameless as I smiled.

"'Yes. And you are?" I jerked when Flo grabbed my arm.

"There they are. At the table against the wall. Come on, Glory, help me walk over there."

"Someone who hopes Kratos goes down. Tell your friend from Earth to quit drinking and go back to training. Some of us have money on him." He nodded toward the table Flo was eager to get to. "Welcome to Olympus, Cousin. We will meet again." He nodded and walked away.

"Glory, now! They haven't seen us yet." Flo was strong for such a short woman. "Pick up our drinks. Who was that man?"

"A cousin apparently. Good to know someone else wants Jerry to win his fight." I handed Flo her drink, sure she hadn't heard a word I'd said, and "accidentally" spilled mine. "Okay, let's get over there. Hold on to me."

We made our stumbling way through the crowd to a table that was practically in darkness. But it wasn't all that far from one of the poles where a redhead seemed determined to make our two guys take an interest in her flexibility. Oh, yeah, that had been Kratos' term, hadn't it? I should recommend this woman to him. Whatever, it was clear from the number of empty glasses on the table that our guys had been drowning their sorrows.

"Aren't you a pretty sight, Jeremy Blade?" I couldn't help it. The two men were slumped in their chairs and had almost passed out.

"Glory, glorious, glorified." Jerry threw back his chair, laughing when it hit the floor. "Well, didn't manage that too well, did I? But then what's new? I can't do anything in Olympush." He staggered over to me and slid his hand around my neck. "I'm sorry as hell, lover mine, but I'm going to fuck this fight up. Hope you are happy with that Olympush asshole.'"

Richard suddenly giggled. Yeah, stern always serious Richard actually giggled. "You said 'Olympush'. Twice." He slapped the table and went into a full-fledged guffaw. "Olympush asshole."

"Not funny, sport. She's going to be in his bed. Having his babies. Doesn't want mine." Jerry jerked me to him. "That's what you said, isn't it?"

"Jerry, not here. Please, come home with me." I slid my arm around his waist and tried to turn him toward the door.

"Hey, I was working this table." The redhead dancer closed in and actually tried to hip-butt me out of the way. "That guy was just about to give me gold for a lap dance."

I whirled around and got in her face. I guess my eyes must have told her I wasn't to be messed with and I raised a finger. To my surprise, it glowed white hot. "You want to test me, sweetheart? I can singe your eyebrows with a twitch of this fingertip."

"Uh, never mind." She backed away. "Geez, a girl can't make a living anymore."

I dipped into my cleavage and tossed her a gold coin. "Here. Take a break. I know what it's like to have to dance for drunks. Hit the back room and give yourself five minutes." I didn't wait to see what she did, just slowly turned to face Jerry. He was staring at me with wide eyes. I think some of his buzz was wearing off.

Flo had found a glass of water. She dumped it on Richard's head. "Look at you! Drunk! Looking at boobies of strangers! I am ashamed of you!"

"Baby. You have the only boobies I want." He pressed his face to her chest and kissed each breast through her dress. "But you are wearing me out. All you do is fuck me. Every minute of the day. I can't take it anymore."

Flo looked over his head at me and grinned. "Ah, you should be so lucky, you big cry baby. Come home and I show you what I want. Then we'll see if you have been weared out. Eh?"

"Oh, God." Richard lurched to his feet. "A man's got to do what a man's got to do."

"Don't tell me this is nothing!" My mother's voice was loud enough to be heard over the music and there was a sudden flash of lightning. We all ducked. My mother had decided to cut loose.

"What the hell was that?" Flo shouted to me as we dove under the table.

"Welcome to Olympus, pal." I was lucky that Jerry was so drunk that he'd fallen on the floor next to me. Richard lay next to Flo.

"Just how many women do you need to satisfy you, you oversexed beast!" Thunder roared in the club and one of the women screamed as lightning arced down her pole. She leaped off the stage, her skimpy costume smoking. Amazingly the music never stopped and neither did the other dancers. I guess it was all part of the entertainment.

Flo and I had a good view of my father holding a wooden chair in front of him. It had scorch marks on it but he was grinning like this was great fun. My mother's chest heaved as she picked up a drink from the table and tossed it at one of the scantily clad women who had made the mistake of trying to pick up the pile of gold coins on the table.

"Come on, love, let her have the money. She's earned it." Mars laughed out loud when Hebe screeched and threw the empty glass at him.

"Bastard. Satyr. Don't you ever get enough?" She picked up the table and sent it flying toward him.

He caught it and made it disappear. "Of course I do, Hebe, my love. I was just waiting for you." He leaped over shattered glasses and gold coins, scooped her into his arms, and kissed her quiet. The crowd in the club applauded and whistled. The music changed tempo and the room got darker.

"Time for us to get out of here." I realized my father was carrying my mother out of the room and up some stairs. I had no idea what went on up there and wasn't sure I wanted to know. His hand was inside her dress and I'd just seen too much.

"Yes, we go. Ricardo, you will prove to me you love me. Eh?" Flo hauled Richard to his feet.

I was struggling to get a drunken Jerry out from under the table too. His buzz was back and he'd actually fallen asleep on the floor during all of that.

"What?" He grabbed me and tried to pull me into his arms on the floor.

"No, we're going home." I slapped away his hand.

"If only we were." He kissed me on my chest where my cleavage was exposed.

"Blade, you have to go with Glory. Talk to her." Richard swayed against Flo. "They've got us, dead to rights. Now we have to have makeup sex. That's hot." He smiled drunkenly at his wife. "Isn't it, baby?"

"We talk too much. Blah, blah, blah." Jerry jerked out of my arms and staggered to his feet. "I need action."

"Then come home with me and that's what you'll get." I

couldn't let his words hurt me. So I caught him when he almost fell and got him moving toward the door. Luckily it wasn't far and Mother's carriage was waiting for us. The guards outside helped push the men in, then one of them checked to make sure Mother wasn't coming with us. He emerged in a minute with singed hair and smelling of smoke. Apparently the Mars and Hebe show was still going on upstairs with a Do Not Disturb sign.

"She said to go on without her." He gestured and the carriage headed out. By the time we got back to my place, Jerry was snoring and Richard was trying to talk Flo out of her dress. I left them arguing and, with a soldier's help, got Jerry into bed. Too much talk? I was a goddess, damn it. How would Jerry like it if I showed him some goddess action? When he woke up, maybe I'd do just that.

NINE

"How are you feeling?" I stood over Jerry with a cup of my favorite hot chocolate. His moans had brought me from the sitting room.

"Get that away from me." He covered his head with the silk comforter.

"This?" I waved the steaming chocolate over the bed. "What's the matter, big guy? Hung over? That's what happens when you're a mortal and you drink too much. Morning after regrets." I sat beside him on the bed.

"Quit screaming at me." He pulled a pillow over his face. "Leave me to die. You can marry that god and live happily ever after. Zeus will be beside himself."

"But *I* won't be happy." I jerked the pillow out of his hands and tossed it on the floor. "Want something for your headache?" I whispered this time though I'd never screamed, of course. I tried not to laugh but it wasn't easy. He deserved to suffer. Going to a bar where the women wore next to nothing. I set down my cup on the nightstand with a loud clink and ripped away the comforter.

"My head just exploded. What the hell, Gloriana?" He peered at me through blood shot eyes. "At least dim the lights. Or is this torture my punishment for taking a night off?"

I gestured and the lights went from bright to barely a candle glow. "Is that better?" I stroked his forehead. "Poor baby. Is that what it was? You took a night off?" I pulled on his hair and got an earful of colorful curses. "From *me*?" I stood and glared at him. "Why do you need one, Jeremiah Campbell? Are you so bored with me that you have to escape? Go see other women half naked? Did one crawl into your lap and rub herself all over you before I got there? There was a willing redhead just waiting for you to say the word."

Jerry started to smile then winced. "Are you jealous? Really?" He struggled to sit up. "I went to drink with Richard. He needed a friend. We don't or can't discuss our feelings. So we get drunk. It's what men do when they feel the need to talk."

"Oh, don't I know that. I have to pry your feelings out of you." I sighed and sat down again. "So the drinking and staring at naked women was all for Richard's sake?"

"Well, I didn't say that." Jerry laughed then gasped when I punched his stomach. "Do that again and I may throw up all over you and this bed." He collapsed back on the pillows. "God, I hate being mortal. As a vampire, I could drink the blood with alcohol and rarely got much of a buzz. Last night… Oh, God. Move." He shoved me over and crawled out of bed. "Well, you'd better get out of my way because," he gulped. "Shit. I'm not kidding. I'm about to lose it."

"Go. Hurry." I sat against the padded headboard while he staggered into the bathroom. I gestured and Alesha hurried into the room. "Do you have anything that will cure my lover's stomach problems? He drank too much last night and," we both heard Jerry's retching, "obviously he needs something to fix his hangover."

"I'll run to Cornelius, Lady Gloriana. He will surely have an elixir." Alesha smiled and hustled out of the room.

I debated letting him suffer but didn't have it in me. So I was going to have to go into the bathroom and play nursemaid. Fortunately Jerry had turned on the shower and was standing under a hot spray by the time I got there.

"If you think I'm joining you in the shower, think again. I'm still mad at you." I didn't think he was in the mood anyway. He still looked pale and he hadn't bothered to pick up the soap. He just stood there, hanging his head, one hand braced against the tile wall.

"You *should* be mad. I made a fool of myself. Just go away. I don't want you to see me like this. I am a weakling. Not fit to be your lover." He turned his face toward the wall. "If you hear me fall, leave me on the floor. It's what I deserve. If you can manage it, use your new powers to send me down the drain."

"Oh, stop it. You don't do the pity party thing well. It's not your style." I stripped off my robe and climbed into the huge shower stall. I did love the amenities here in Olympus. The glass tiles were a glowing turquoise and silver and the floor was made of some smooth stone that felt wonderful under my bare feet. I put my arms around Jerry and just held him. The water was a perfect temperature as it pounded against my back.

"You're mad at me, remember?" He rested his chin on the top of my head.

"Oh, yes. I remember. And I'll make you pay later." I picked up a bar of scented soap and ran it over his shoulders. "But I think you're suffering enough for now." There was a tap on the frosted glass door. I slid it open a few inches so Alesha could hand me a glass filled with an orange liquid.

"He's to drink it all. Cornelius said it will work quickly to settle his stomach." Alesha was out of breath and stared at the ceiling, careful not to look into the shower stall. "It smells delicious. Like apricots and peaches."

"Well, then, I'm sure he won't object to drinking it all. Thank you, Alesha." I shut the door and wrapped Jerry's hand around the glass. "Drink. And don't you dare object. The poor girl clearly ran all the way to the sorcerer's lab and back just for you."

"No, she did it for you. The girl thinks you hung the moon." Jerry sniffed at the glass then took a sip. "Not bad. I'm surprised. The elixirs these sorcerers concoct usually taste like frog piss."

"Jerry!" I slapped his chest. "As if you'd know frog piss if you drank it."

He winked then drank every drop. "You'd be surprised. Ma swore it cured boggy foot." He set the glass on a ledge and pushed his face under the water. "Damn, but I think I do feel better. If you don't want to turn this into fun and games, you'd better get out of here now." He moved his hips against me.

"Fun? Games?" Of course I could feel that he was recovering. "No way. I *am* still mad. I never want to have to hunt you down in a strip club again, Jerry." I opened the glass door and jumped out, grabbing a towel and wrapping it around me. I had plans for when he got out. He'd said he wanted action and I was going to show him some, with goddess magic. I dragged a comb through my wet hair, regretting my impulsive climb into the shower. But then I remembered I could *think* a hair style. Oh, yeah, I had dry waves in a snap.

Now for some other miracles. Jerry was going to have a night to remember. And he sure wasn't going to need some sleazy bar for entertainment again. I'd see to that. When there was a knock on the bathroom door, I snapped on a robe then decided I was ready to leave the bathroom anyway.

"Mistress, you have visitors." Alesha handed me a calling card. The name wasn't familiar. Charis.

"Who is she?" I turned the card over. Nothing on the back.

"She's your father's daughter, Lady Gloriana. His other daughter, that is. By the Lady Roxana, your father's wife. Lady Charis has a friend with her. They are calling on you and look friendly." Alesha smiled. "It is a good sign and an honor."

"Hmm. The legitimate daughter is curious about the illegitimate one, I guess." I snapped on a cute outfit—slim skirt and a blue sweater to match my eyes. "How do I look?"

"Perfect, mistress. They are in the sitting room. Shall I bring refreshments?" Alesha was really excited about this.

"Whatever you think is appropriate. Tea and cookies or cocktails and snacks." I looked down and added some Louboutin pumps. Oh, but I loved my goddess powers. Jerry was going to have quite a treat in store later.

"Definitely the cocktails, mistress. I've heard that Lady Charis enjoys her drinks."

"Then we'll do that." I heard the shower go off. "Tell Mr. Blade that I have company, please. I'll be with him later."

"Certainly, mistress." Alesha looked down with a blush.

"Hopefully he won't come out naked." I patted her on the shoulder. "I won't blame you if you look."

Alesha's eyes were twinkling when she glanced up again. "Oh, who could resist, mistress? He is a handsome man in his prime, isn't he?"

"Yes, he is." I headed for the sitting room. I trusted Alesha to look and not touch, of course I did. And Jerry? He would never even think to bother a servant in any way. I glanced back at her. She still stood there, waiting for her peek. "Refreshments, Alesha?"

"Yes, mistress." She hurried out of the room.

The sitting room was just steps away and I could hear two women talking as I opened the door. One girl I recognized instantly. I stopped in my tracks. The other one rushed forward and grabbed me by the shoulders.

"Sister!" She grinned then hugged me. "I have always wanted a sister. Isn't that so, Calista?" She turned to her friend.

"Yes, you have said it often." Calista twisted her hands in her lap. "I shouldn't be here for this meeting." She stood.

"No! I told you. We will work this out." Charis reached out and dragged her friend forward. "Gloriana, this is Calista. I know you haven't met yet, formally, but you may have noticed her at the theater."

"Yes, I saw you dance, Calista. You are wonderfully talented." I smiled at her as I carefully untangled myself from my new sister's arms. "And obviously you are Charis. Mars is your father too."

"Yes. Oh, honestly, I am sorry. I just rushed at you and didn't even introduce myself." She whirled around the room, looking at me from all angles. "You are the image of your mother." She laughed and exchanged glances with Calista. "Won't my mother have a fit when she sees her?" She plopped down on a loveseat. "Mother hates your mother, of course. They are bitter enemies."

"I understand that." I sat in a chair, more than ready when Alesha came in carrying a laden tray. "Drinks! I know I'm ready for one." There was a pitcher of martinis and three glasses as well as an assortment of hors d'oeuvres.

"Yes, let's toast." Charis filled a glass before I could even reach for the pitcher. She handed it to Calista, then filled one for me. Plopping olives in each of ours, she gave herself a full glass then got thoughtful for a moment. "To family. No matter how it comes about."

"I'll drink to that." I clinked my glass against hers and was surprised when Calista made the effort to touch hers to mine. I liked Charis and couldn't help feeling sorry for the shy Calista. I wanted to say something to her about Kratos but wasn't sure how to broach the subject. I shouldn't have worried.

"I bet you're wondering why I dragged Calista here. With the whole Kratos thing going on." Charis had downed half her drink in one long swallow. "May I speak freely? Since we're sisters and all?"

"Well, sure. But let me say this." I sipped my drink. It was icy cold and delicious. "Calista, I'm in love with Jerry, my fiancé from home. I have no intention of marrying Kratos. Jerry has been training like a madman so he can beat Kratos and win my hand. You can have your lover back. I'm fine with that."

Calista's eyes filled with tears. "You are very kind to say that. But it will never happen. You have no idea how much Kratos wants to win a place in Zeus's court. You are his ticket to that. I am just a sorcerer's granddaughter. My father is a mere apprentice to Grandfather. Not important in our world. Marrying me will not raise Kratos' status the way marrying you will." Calista took a gulp of her drink. "This is hopeless."

"Do you love him?" I set down my glass.

"Of course I do. He is good and kind and strong. And a wonderful," her cheeks went pink, "lover."

"There. Gloriana, we must do something. Don't you think?" Charis had polished off her drink and began refilling glasses. "Of course you do. Didn't you just declare your love for this Blade person? Crazy name, isn't it, Calista?" She laughed and fanned her cheeks. "Oh, gods, I must remember to eat before I drink. These cheese puffs look delicious." She stuffed one into her mouth. "Mmm. Tell us about your lover, Gloriana. Does he have a chance at beating Kratos?"

Jerry walked into the room. He was dressed in a short toga like my father wore with a leather belt strapped around his waist. Gladiator sandals were strapped onto his firm calves and he looked every inch the warrior. I wanted to throw myself on him, plant a flag, something, when I saw Charis lick her lips as she looked him over.

"Beat Kratos? Probably not, but I'll do my best." He rested his hand on my shoulder. "Alesha said you were in here, Gloriana. Sorry to interrupt this party but I felt better and decided I'd better go on and train."

"Jerry! Let me introduce you." I covered his hand with mine. "My sister, Charis, has come to visit and this is her friend, Calista. This is Jeremy Blade, my fiancé." I waved my hand at the full table. "Since you're doing better, can I get you something to eat or drink?"

"No, I'm not chancing it." He was still pale as he bowed and smiled. "Ladies, a pleasure. Please excuse me." He headed for the door.

"He's dreamy." Charis watched him until the door closed behind him. "No wonder you don't want to give him up. You should see the man Father wants me to marry." She shuddered. "Lykos has enough hair on his body to knit a thousand sweaters." She and Calista giggled.

"She's not exaggerating." Calista polished off drink two. "But no worries. If you don't want to marry him, Charis, it will not happen." She rolled her eyes. "Mars is wrapped around her finger, Gloriana. He will do whatever his precious Charis asks."

"Perhaps. But Mother likes Lycos as well. I'm not so sure I can wiggle out of this engagement." Charis still stared at the door. "Are all men from your home as handsome, Gloriana? He favors Kratos a little, don't you think, Calista?"

"I suppose. Though I still prefer my man." Calista reached for a refill. "Kratos will beat your man senseless, Gloriana, probably kill him. I know it."

"No, he won't." I leaned forward. "Ladies, we can't let that happen. I won't marry Kratos no matter how the fight goes." I started to pick up my glass then remembered I wasn't drinking now. Shoot. I hoped the one sip I'd taken wasn't enough to hurt anything or anyone I might have going.

"You can't defy Zeus, Gloriana." Charis shook her head. "But we have time to come up with a plan to go around him perhaps. Now I want to hear about your home, sister. I've heard rumors that there are such interesting things there. And clearly the men are special." She winked. "Only the oldest gods and goddesses are allowed to visit Earth. But sometimes they bring back books and magazines. And clothes, thank the gods. Why, if it were up to Zeus, we'd all still be wearing togas."

"So true." Calista ran her hand down her red cotton dress. "I love the clothes we get from there. Mother is a goddess so she creates a new wardrobe for me when she comes back from one of her little trips."

Charis patted her friend's hand. "Someday we'll get to go. I'll see to it." She leaned forward, her silver eyes, so different from our father's, suddenly focused on me. "Father says you live in Texas. I've read stories about it. Tell me all."

"Yes. I live in Austin, the capitol." I settled in for a gabfest. "But if you think Texas is all cowboys and billionaires, think again."

By the time Flo arrived, we were all laughing like old friends. Even Calista, with the help of her fourth martini, had relaxed.

"What is this? A hen party and I wasn't invited?" Flo flounced into the room looking gorgeous in a black sweater over black jeans. She had put on a few pounds and was dressing the way I did on Earth, to look as thin as possible.

I made the introductions then summoned Alesha for another glass, a full pitcher and more snacks.

"Well, I tell you what I miss most about home." Flo was eyeing the stuffed mushrooms but slapped her own hand when she started to reach for one. "Television! How do you survive without it?"

"What do you mean?" Charis shook her head. "They didn't give you a TV? We have it but not as many stations as I hear you have on Earth. Zeus doesn't want us to know too much when we are young." Charis made a face. "We get," she glanced at Calista, "basic cable, I guess you call it. None of the really interesting channels."

"Well. Glory, we need to ask your mother for a TV. Maybe I wouldn't be so bored." Flo had resisted the snacks for a good ten minutes but by her second martini, gave up.

"Flo's addicted to reality shows." I laughed when she nodded and picked up a stuffed mushroom.

"Yes! I missed who the bachelorette picked! Which dancer won the competition! Oh, and the designer who got to show her clothes at fashion week in New York City. It is a tragedy!" She finished off her drink and picked up another mushroom, taking smaller bites this time.

Charis stared at her. "We need to check out these shows, Calista. I'm not sure we get them on our channels."

"Reality shows have contests on television and the audience doesn't know from week to week who will win." I didn't add that my own TV addiction was a singing competition.

"But that is like our own shows in the Rotunda. We do dancing competitions. The judges vote and one dancer must leave until there is only one winner." Calista puffed out her dainty chest. "I won last season. I have the medal to prove it."

"There you go." I smiled at Flo. "Even Olympus has reality shows."

"Do they have a hundred channels? Where are the Real Housewives? The cat fights and hair pulling?"

Charis laughed. "We have those, but they are in our living rooms." She sighed. "Usually about how I am allowed to stay single and won't marry the man they wish for me." She and Calista exchanged looks. "Reality isn't so great, Florence. I can't imagine wanting to see a hundred shows about it."

"You may be right about that." Flo patted her hand then reached for a cheese puff. "But there's nothing to do here, ladies. I am sick, I tell you. If I don't get home soon I die of boredom." Flo waved the puff. "Where's the shopping? The mall? If you have one here, I sure haven't heard of it."

"I can send you home tonight if that is your wish." My mother appeared next to Flo's chair.

"Mother!"

Charis shrieked and dropped her glass. It rolled across the rug, spilling her drink, but didn't shatter. "Hebe! If my mother finds out I was in the same room with you she will lock me in a closet and throw away the key."

"Ah, Roxana. How is the dear woman?" Mother threw back her shoulders and tossed her hair with a smirk. "Still getting your wardrobe at Bella's discount shop, I see."

"As if you care how Mother is." Charis stood and gave her own hair toss. She'd worn a cute designer dress in aqua that did great things for her pale skin. She had dark hair like our father and, with her silver eyes, the combination was stunning. "My clothes are perfectly fine, thank you. Bella has beautiful things. Calista, we will have to take Gloriana and Florence shopping there." She turned to me and I was surprised to see her eyes glittering with unshed tears. "I have to go now, Gloriana. It was great to get to know you. I'll send you a note and arrange for that shopping trip."

"Yes, we'll do it soon." I glanced at Flo. "It will be fun. Charis, I love your dress, by the way. I doubt it would be cool for me to come visit you or I would. You can believe that." I hugged her, happy when she hugged me back, and even kissed my cheek. "I'm so glad to have a sister now."

"Me too. But you're right, don't come to my house. My mother wouldn't like that. You know why." She gave *my* mother a scorching look. "Now, Calista, am I going to have to call a carriage for you or can you walk?" She helped her friend to her feet.

"I'm not that drunk. Though I definitely have a buzz on. Which

I needed. Thanks, Gloriana. I'm glad you're on my side. Too bad we don't have a choice about this. Zeus rules, you know." Tears ran down her cheeks and she sobbed. "Kratos will be very happy with you, I'm sure."

"Oh, gods, here we go." Charis dragged her toward the door.

"Alesha, call a carriage for my guests, please." I walked with them to the door. "I'm sorry Mother interrupted our party." I hugged Charis again.

She held onto me for a minute. "I hope you understand why I can't be friendly to your mother."

"Absolutely." I let go of her. "Hey, I can hardly be friendly with her myself. We have issues, if you know what I mean." I glanced back but Mother was ignoring us. "Take care of Calista. We'll figure out this thing with Kratos. If she still wants him after all this, she can have him." I staggered when Calista flung herself at me.

"Thank you, Glory. Yes, I will call you that. Glory, glory, glory." She danced around me. "You will save me. I know you will and I'll have my lover back. Yes, indeed." She did a twirl then her face went pale. "Oh, I don't feel so well." She leaned over and threw up in the pot plant by the door.

"Gods, what next?" Charis took a wet cloth from Alesha and tugged Calista out the door. "Come on, dear. We're going. Look, there's our carriage." She waved at me. "Bye, Sis."

I turned back and nearly ran into Flo.

"I thought *I* was like a sister to you."

"You are. Sister number one." I hugged her. "Did you hear Charis? We will be going shopping soon."

"Yes, if Hebe doesn't ruin things." Flo shook her head when she glanced back at my mother who was looking over the snack tray. "I'm going. Not home. But back to my rooms. Ask her about getting us a TV. Your mother is staring at me like she will send me back to Austin any minute. You know Ricardo must stay until the fight to stand by Jeremiah and I can't leave my husband. So I go hide." She leaned on me for a minute. "Good luck with her, *amica*." She staggered out the door.

"Way to end a party, Mother." I stalked back to give her a stern look.

"I can't believe you were fraternizing with that twit Charis." Mother settled on the loveseat and filled a glass from the pitcher.

"She's not a twit. I liked her." I shook my head when Mother offered to fill my glass.

"She drinks too much. Mars needs to take her in hand."

"Mars adores her apparently. We were bonding. I think I'll ask her to be my Maid of Honor at my wedding." I said it just to goad her but actually liked the idea. And it would give Charis an excuse to come to Earth and see how I lived. If Mars really was lenient with her, I was sure we could talk him into giving her permission for the visit. If the wedding happened at all.

"Ah, you are teasing. I'm glad to see you realize wedding your vampire is a fantasy that will never come true." She patted the seat next to her. "Come, sit and let me tell you a few things you need to know about Olympus, darling."

I really didn't want to sit close to her. Bad enough that she could read my mind anyway. I sat across from her and popped a stuffed mushroom into my mouth. Crab filling. Delicious. I concentrated on food. Let her read my mind now. All she'd find was an appreciation for cheese puffs and caviar.

"Gloriana, face facts. Your man will never beat Kratos in a fair fight. And if the fight isn't fair?" Mother set down her empty glass. "Zeus will be very displeased. Do I have to remind you how he reacts when he's angry?" She threw up a hand and a sconce on one wall was suddenly a charred remnant of twisted metal and glass that crashed to the tile floor.

"Mother, is that necessary?" I sighed when two handmaidens rushed in to clean up the mess. "I know he has powers far beyond yours or mine."

"Do you? Because I know you're plotting to go home and act as if this little interlude never happened. You want to pretend that your Olympus roots are nothing, mean nothing." Mother stood and loomed over me. "You have no idea how lucky you are. I would have thought the trip to the cells would have convinced you that you would be wise to go along with our plans. I guess not." She waved her hand and we were moving.

I gasped but had no control, no concept of what was happening or where we were going. I had a feeling of flying but the air was silent and cool. Then suddenly we stopped and I could see a pair of men below us. It was as if we were on an invisible balcony, watching them.

"Where are we?" I recognized Jerry and another man stalking each other. They each had a knife and wore nothing but loin cloths. Sweat covered their bodies and they looked like they were breathing hard as they slashed at each other with their knives. I couldn't hear them. Not the sound of their breaths or their shouts when they opened their mouths, clearly exchanging words before they lunged at each other.

"The training field. Of course you know your man. The other is a soldier who volunteered to fight against him. He's a mortal too. Both seem to be well matched. Now watch." Mother hovered next to me. It was as if we sat on a cloud above the men. I wasn't uncomfortable, just felt strange, like I had nothing holding me but needed no support.

The men jabbed and swiped at each other. Jerry drew blood, opening a wound on the man's chest. But the other man didn't seem to notice. Instead he rushed at Jerry and grappled with him, throwing him to the ground. They rolled over until Jerry was on top but the man had his knife to Jerry's throat. They strained against each other, their knives inches from penetrating flesh. I couldn't breathe, terror closing my throat. This was *practice*? I saw a line of blood on Jerry's neck. He was going to be killed!

"We have to stop this!" I tried to reach out, throw myself on them and tear the knives from their hands. I couldn't move.

"Mars will do what needs to be done." Mother leaned back and materialized a pear, biting into the fruit. "Actually, I expected this to be worse. Your man is holding his own fairly well. Mars said at first he had to bring Blade back to life a half dozen times."

"Back to life? What do you mean?" I could finally breathe again when Mars stepped into the circle. The men had rolled off of each other. Jerry tossed his knife aside then lay on the floor as if to catch his breath. The soldier jumped to his feet then offered Jerry his hand, helping him up. I was relieved when Jer stood and seemed no worse for wear.

"Was he dead? Really?" I couldn't take my eyes off of him as he picked up his knife and wiped it on his loin cloth. He clearly wasn't dead now, gesturing and talking as he rehashed the fight that had just ended in a draw.

"Your vampire, who isn't a blood drinker up here of course, was killed during the first few fights he attempted. He was sorely overmatched against Mars' hardened soldiers. So my dear Mars breathed life back into him. We are gods, Gloriana. We can do that. Give life. And take it away." She polished off the pear then made the remains disappear. A basin full of water appeared next so that she could wash her hands. Then a towel fell into her lap. When she was satisfied that she was clean again, she whisked them away with a gesture.

"Mother, I don't believe you. Jerry would have said something." I looked down at him. "He never would have continued if he knew…"

"Oh, your man doesn't remember it that way. Mars felt it would demoralize him. So he planted memories of a fair beginning for your lover." She frowned. "Mars does know how to manage men. But he will not listen to me concerning your future. He should have let your vampire stay dead and you would have no choice now but to marry Kratos."

I barely heard her. "He died." I stared down at the scene where Jerry was wiping himself down with a towel. Mars touched his wounds and they disappeared. Jerry didn't seem to have noticed them. All three men were laughing over something my father said and then Mars clapped Jerry on the back.

"Yes, Gloriana. But Mars can't use his magic on the day of the real fight, not without incurring my father's wrath. Face facts. Your man had too many years of relying on his vampire skills. Then there was the time in the cells that drained his strength. If he stays and fights Kratos, it will end badly. Fatally." Mother picked up my hand. "All you've done is put off the inevitable. For your lover's sake, you must send him home. Do your duty here, darling. Encourage him to find a new woman on Earth. Someone who is like him. Another vampire if that is what he wants. But not you. You are a goddess. Too much for him. Don't you realize that yet?"

I jerked my hand away. I couldn't stand her touching me. She wanted Jerry dead. How easy that would be. I could marry Kratos and be stuck here forever. I wouldn't look at her or I was afraid of what I might say or do. Shoot fire or scream all the obscenities that were on the tip of my tongue.

Instead I watched the man I loved step back into that circle and get ready to spar again. This time with his broadsword. Madness. I couldn't breathe again. And here on Olympus, breathing was recommended. God, I just couldn't make such a choice. Couldn't doom Jerry and couldn't give him up. What now?

"Don't you dare faint." Mother sighed and gestured. "Come. We're going back to your rooms. He will be returning soon and I won't begrudge you some time with him." She lifted my chin and looked into my eyes. "You must tell him good-bye, Gloriana. It will be a kindness. Don't you see that?"

I didn't answer her. I just stayed silent as she whisked us back to my chambers. Just when I thought I couldn't hate Olympus more, she'd twisted the knife. Of course sending Jerry home was the right thing to do. But I knew he'd refuse to go. I couldn't hurt him again by pretending I didn't want him either. There had to be a way to fix this situation. I needed an ally.

When she realized I wasn't speaking to her, my mother invented an excuse and took off. But I hadn't missed her triumphant gaze, as if she knew she'd won. She thought she'd left me with no way out. But she didn't really know me, did she? There had been too many years where I'd been on my own, learning to survive and make decisions without a mother's guidance. With a mother like her, I realized now I had been much better off alone.

As soon as she was out of sight, I had Alesha take a note to the one powerful person who might be persuaded to take my side in this mess. Then all I could do was sit and wait to see if I got the help I needed.

TEN

"Thanks for seeing me, Grandmother." I couldn't help but gawk. I was in the most beautiful room I'd ever seen. Silk hangings on the wall in brilliant turquoise and gold were interspersed with gold framed mirrors. A laden dressing table with a velvet cushioned chair in front of it held at least a dozen of the crystal perfume bottles I adored. I itched to go over and inspect them. They glittered with fine jewels set in silver and gold.

Grandmother was wrapped in an ermine trimmed white velvet robe and reclined on a gilded day bed covered in a striped silk. She sipped something from an exquisite porcelain cup before she sat up and gestured for me to sit across from her.

"It's about time you came to see me, Gloriana." She smiled and waved her hand. "You must try one of these pastries. Your mother says you like chocolate."

I sat on a red lacquered chair. A tray full of chocolate covered strawberries and puff pastries in various shapes and sizes appeared on the table in front of me. The smell made my mouth water.

"Thank you, Grandmother." I picked up a napkin then selected a tiny triangle and popped it into my mouth. Chocolate with a hint of orange made me sigh. "Delicious. Lucky we can't gain weight here." I smiled and sat back, patting my lips with the napkin.

"Yes, indeed. It's wonderful being a goddess, isn't it, child?" She handed her cup to a hovering servant and nodded. In moments we were alone. "But I don't think you agree with me, do you, Gloriana?"

"You're reading my mind. I wish you and my mother wouldn't do that. I'm learning how aggravating it can be to have no secrets." I looked down at my lap where I'd folded the linen napkin into a tiny square.

"Oh, I'm sure you still have secrets, child." Grandmother laughed. "We all do. And I know you don't hesitate to delve into another's thoughts when it suits you. Do you deny it?"

"No." I met her eyes that were so like mine. It really was startling to realize I had so much family after being alone for centuries. Except for Jerry, of course. He'd made sure I was taken care of, even when we were apart, from the day we'd met. That thought made me even more determined to press on. "I admit I'm struggling with the way things are here."

"Tell me what's bothering you, dear. I'll try to stay out of your thoughts since it annoys you." Grandmother stood on the luxurious carpet. It was a deep blue with a design of singing birds. With a snap she changed from her robe to a stylish burgundy dress with matching leather pumps.

"But not here. Zeus has spies everywhere. Come with me." She held out her hand and I jumped to my feet. She had jeweled rings on almost every finger. An emerald on her pointer went to her knuckle. Then there was a huge diamond as well as several rubies. A golden snake twined around her wrist that ended in a ring around her thumb. The serpent had sapphire eyes that seemed to wink at me.

"Where are we going?" I walked beside her. I hadn't even bothered with jewelry except for my engagement ring from Jerry. It was a miracle my mother hadn't taken it from me. My own dress was a plain navy silk wrap with a silver buckle at the waist. I imagined a diamond drop at my neck and was happy when one appeared.

"Somewhere without an audience." Grandmother nodded her approval when she noticed I'd added the necklace. "You have good taste. Your mother has been bragging about your little shop on Earth. She says people like the things you select for them to purchase."

"I have fun treasure hunting." I hid my shock that my mother bragged about me. "It pleases me to help my customers look their best."

"Yes, I can imagine that would be rewarding." She looped her arm through mine.

I glanced around and realized we were in an open field. It was the same place where my brothers had played soccer not long ago. Grandmother led me to the empty bleachers and settled on the bottom row.

"Gloriana, why have you come to me? Is this about the fight between your lover and Kratos?"

I sat next to her. "Of course it is. What am I going to do, Grandmother? Zeus wants me to marry this stranger. I'm sure he's perfectly fine, but I don't know or love him."

"It is our way, Gloriana." She studied her emerald ring. "Arranged marriages help us keep our kingdom in order. I'm sure your mother explained this to you."

"I get that it's your custom." I hoped she really was staying out of my head because I was thinking it was a stupid archaic one. I took a breath. "But look at the result, Grandmother." I touched her arm. "Most marriages here seem unhappy. Infidelity is so common, it's an epidemic. Is there any couple here that doesn't have an illegitimate child or two running around? Men have their mistresses, women their lovers. Frankly, I think it's sickening."

"Well! Don't hold back, Granddaughter." She pulled away from me. "You're exaggerating."

"Am I?" I swallowed, determined to go on even though I could see she was starting to fume. I took another calming breath and gave her time to think about what I'd said. The air was sweet, the grass from the field reminding me of home. How could I get my message across? Desperation could make me reckless if I wasn't careful. No, I had to stay rational, especially around the most powerful woman in Olympus.

"Your own daughter's marriage is a prime example of how arranged marriages don't work. She hates Hercules and rarely sees him. Which is a good thing because he's abusive."

"I admit that union is unfortunate." She was back to staring at her rings, thinking, I hoped.

"And how are marriages arranged anyway? Mother says they are rewards for service. Or to cement an alliance. What about the people you are binding together for life?" I heard my voice rise and held onto the wooden bench. *Calm, Glory.* "Does anyone care if they are a match in personalities or needs?" I leaned closer. "On Earth we have dating services that at least try to find compatible mates. There are questionnaires, a chance for potential mates to communicate before they even decide to meet." I shut up when she glared at me.

"Surely you don't expect us to start an Olympus dotcom, Gloriana."

My mouth dropped open.

"Yes, I am well aware of the insanity raging down on Earth. The high divorce rate and the sexual revolution they called it a few decades ago. An excuse for indiscriminate mating, as I see it. People meet and marry then dissolve the union without a second thought. What of the children? They are left confused, whisked about on alternate weekends to meet the new stepparent of the month. Disgraceful!" Grandmother shook her head. "If you are thinking to make us over in that image, think again, Granddaughter."

"No, not at all. I know you have traditions. But surely there is room for feelings in all this." I couldn't take her stern gaze another second and stared at my own engagement ring. "Jerry and I love each other. It took us a long time to decide to marry. Well, it took me a long time. Jerry has been after me to marry him for a while. I wanted more independence." I looked up and waited until I knew Grandmother was really listening to me. "Surely you can understand my wish to be a strong woman in my own right. In my world women have the power to choose their own destinies. I wanted to be sure I chose the right one."

"Yes." She looked thoughtful. "You seem very strong indeed. And you chose this man after you tried many others." That made her frown.

"I wasn't a slut, Grandmother. I planned to make my marriage vows mean something. I think you feel the same. That they should be binding. And the way the gods here in Olympus seem to scorn them hurts you."

"Child, I've learned to turn a blind eye to things I can't change." She patted my knee. "And you will soon learn that is how it must be here."

I stopped short of knocking her hand off of me. What could I say to make her *do* something? Break down this stupid system and make it better? I put my hand over hers.

"Grandmother, I understand that you ignore what you can't

change. But in this world women are nothing but minions. Little more than the handmaidens who bring you food and sweep your rooms. You may be a powerful goddess, but it seems to me that Zeus calls the shots here. Are you truly satisfied with that? Or am I misunderstanding the hierarchy?"

She stood, energy fairly crackling from her. "I am no one's minion."

"You may shoot lightning at me for this but, Grandmother, if you disagreed with Zeus about something, could you override his decision?" I braced myself. "He's the king here, but you are the queen, aren't you? If you have the powers that I think you do, surely you could decide to change one of his decrees."

"I would never openly defy my husband, Gloriana. It is not how our marriage works." She looked out at the empty field. "You aren't married, yet. But you have been around powerful men, have you not?"

"Sure. I get that men have delicate egos. You have to work around them." Was she thinking about helping me? I was almost afraid to hope. And I hadn't even broached the big question yet.

"Precisely. Zeus has decided that Kratos and your man from Earth will fight for your hand and that is that." She stared at me with a sad smile. "Don't think I haven't been following the progress from that quarter. Kratos will undoubtedly win that fight."

Tears filled my eyes. "Grandmother, I can't marry Kratos. Besides, he loves another. He and Calista had an understanding until this came up. Don't you think it unfair to both of them to make him marry me?"

"He seems eager to do his duty, Gloriana. He is ambitious. Which here in Olympus is a highly regarded trait." Grandmother patted my shoulder. "What would you have me do? The man wants you. He will win you."

"I'm not some damned prize to be won." I threw off her hand.

"Careful, child." Her eyes glowed with blue fire. "You forget who you speak to."

"I'm sorry." I fell to my knees. "Please, Grandmother. I want to go home. To Earth. With Jeremiah. If there is any way you can help me, I would be eternally grateful."

"Get up. Let me think about this." She started walking back toward her rooms. "I admit I don't like being thought of as less than

Zeus."

"Where I live on Earth, women have so many more rights, Grandmother. And it's not just the marriage thing. I don't know how you can stand by and let the handmaidens be treated so horribly here. You have to know they are forced to service the gods whenever they have an urge." I almost bumped into her when she stopped.

"What do you mean?"

"You don't know? My handmaiden Alesha told me that she and the others must pay the sorcerer for birth control or suffer consequences when a god demands they serve him." I saw her frown. "And pity the poor girl who can't afford it. I guess she has bastard children and is sent home in disgrace."

"I certainly don't know about that. *My* handmaidens must stay chaste." Grandmother started to walk again. "You say the gods use the poor girls against their will?"

"Maybe some of them feel honored. I don't know. But most of them wouldn't dare say no. They are merely slaves, aren't they?" I still didn't fully understand where all the servants came from. Earth? Another dimension? Whatever, I knew the girls who worked so hard didn't have any rights.

"It's complicated." She shook her head. "I see by your face that you disapprove. It's a harsh world we live in, Gloriana. Gods are strong creatures and continually fight each other. To prove their power or to gain favor or territory. Our world is not like yours. I can't begin to explain it to you."

"Surely you don't approve of slavery, Grandmother." The thought of it made me sick. I remembered the paintings I'd seen in museums of rapes, pillages. Surely this wasn't how things were still done in Olympus.

"No." She nodded thoughtfully. "But it's considered a necessary part of war. Slaves are part of the spoils, the men call them. Zeus condones it and I have been content to let my husband have his way to avoid confrontations."

I held out my hand and she took it. "He *is* awfully powerful. I can see where you'd rather not--"

"I'm not afraid of him, child." She squeezed my fingers until I had all I could do not to jerk them away with a scream. "He respects me under all his bluster and show."

"Of course he does." I knew better than to keep pushing this.

"Slavery. Yes, it's another tradition that hasn't received much examination." Grandmother stopped at the door to her chambers. "But perhaps it's time it did. Thank you, Gloriana. I've been content to let Zeus wield his power without showing mine for too long. I can change the way things are for women here too and will certainly do so." She raised her hand and a handmaiden rushed out the door to fall at our feet.

"Zora, gather all the female servants into my sitting room. I want to question them. Gloriana, I will see what I can do about your problem. But the fight will go on. I'm sorry, that I cannot change." She kissed my cheek then went inside.

I stared after her, not sure how to feel. Maybe I'd helped the handmaidens but my own situation hadn't changed. I turned toward home, following a golden path. I hoped it was the right one because all of them looked the same to me. I hadn't gone far when a man appeared, blocking my way.

"You must be Gloriana. You are the image of my faithless wife." The man was everything a god should be—tall, handsome, with a beautiful body. He was clutching a spear and had a sword strapped at his waist.

I froze, trying to decide if screaming for my father would help or cause a blood bath.

He narrowed his eyes. "Oh, please call for your father. I'd be happy to meet Mars here and now." He stuck his spear into the ground and pulled out his sword, running a fingertip over it until he drew blood. Another mind reader.

"Hercules!" I sketched a bow. Maybe acting like I respected his power would help diffuse his anger. I peered up at him. Nope. He still looked like he wanted to skewer me.

He stalked closer, until I could almost smell his rage. "How is it you are fully grown?"

"You have to realize I don't have a clue." I backed up a step. "I'm a victim as much as you are. Haven't you heard? Mother threw me in Achelous's Siren harem for a thousand years and hid me there." I knew Hercules as an abusive bully. Hopefully he wasn't so furious he'd risk Zeus's wrath by killing me, a grandchild.

"Yes, the woman can be as cold as Demeter's tit. Her bed certainly was. Tossing aside a child wouldn't give her a second's remorse." He advanced and I retreated when his sword came close to brushing the front of my dress. "Your appearance here has made me a laughing stock. I want you gone."

"Hey, I'd like nothing better than to be back on Earth and out of your hair." I could see though that sending me home wasn't how Hercules thought to make me "gone" as he brushed my skirt with his sword. It was a miracle that it didn't cut the fabric.

"Father! Surely you aren't threatening our sister!" Alex appeared next to me. "She's not to be harmed. Zeus would not be pleased."

"We will protect her, if necessary, Father. Please don't make us call our soldiers." Anni stood on my other side and drew his sword. "You have to know that a melee here would create a stir that would surely come to Zeus's notice."

"What's this? My own sons stand against me?" Hercules face reddened and he looked like he was about to burst a blood vessel. "I won't have it! Not over some bastard child--"

"That's enough, Father." Alex had his sword out too. He and Anni crossed theirs in front of me, a steel barrier that I didn't have much faith in. To my shock, Hercules just stared at us.

"We told you, Gloriana is our sister." Anni, well I was guessing at their names because they were identical, pressed closer to me. "Harm her and you will have to answer to Zeus himself. Surely you wouldn't expect him to take your side over a member of his family."

"We carry Zeus's blood too, Father. You do not. But surely I don't have to remind you of that." Alex stepped forward. He came only to my shoulder but he radiated bravery. I kept my mouth shut, so proud I wanted to cry.

"Zeus put you up to this?" Hercules stomped a sandaled foot and the ground shook. "Why do I doubt that? It's that bitch of a mother who has you running to this whelp's side, isn't it?"

"You want to test that? Ask anyone. Zeus has acknowledged Gloriana as his granddaughter, even arranged an advantageous marriage for her. That's proof enough that she is under his protection and ours." Anni aimed his sword at the stone next to his father's foot. "You may be one of his favorites, but you can't deny that family is very important to *Grandfather*." He emphasized the last word with a raise of his dark eyebrows.

I noticed the boys looked very much like their father. How that must have infuriated Hercules. Two miniature copies of one of the greatest warriors in Olympus. But they never grew up. My thoughts got me a steely gaze from Hercules and I backed up a step. If the god could toss a flame, I was toast.

"Father, the truth has come out." Alex raised his sword and pointed it at his father's chest. It was a bold move and I wondered that Hercules didn't react to it. Maybe he did love his boys. "Now that Zeus knows you've been abusing our mother, I'd advise you to go back to your campaign against whoever you've been fighting and stay there for another century or two. Maybe by then Grandfather will have calmed down. Right now, he's in a temper and thinking he cares not how you've impressed him in the past, hurting his daughter is unforgiveable."

"Who told him such lies?" Hercules tossed a few lightning bolts around and a wooden building went up in flames. A man and woman ran screaming outside, their togas singed.

"Are they lies?" I found my voice. "I know a bully when I see one. Take your son's advice and go, Hercules. I've seen Zeus in action lately and I sure wouldn't want his anger aimed at me." I reached out and put my hands on the boys' shoulders. "My brothers haven't told Zeus a thing, but I'm sure they could add details that would make you a permanent outcast from Olympus. Go now and I'm sure they'll keep your secrets."

Hercules stared at his sons. "Put down your swords. I never want them raised against me again. Do you hear me?" He roared those last four words. I'm sure they heard him three galaxies away.

"Yes, Father." Alex and Anni sheathed their swords.

"You will say no more about my treatment of your mother or anyone else. Swear it." Hercules advanced on the boys and I couldn't help myself. I snatched a knife from a scabbard on the back of Anni's toga and held it in front of me.

"That's far enough." I couldn't believe how determined I sounded.

"What? You're going to stick me?" Hercules laughed, a deep guffaw that made the leaves on nearby trees quiver. "I could take that away from you without--" He snatched the knife, my fingers empty before I realized what he was going to do. "Stupid wench." He tossed it aside. "Anni, guard your weapons, boy. Haven't you learned anything?" He raised his hand as if to strike him, then seemed to think better of it. Oh, yeah. I was a witness. Zeus's granddaughter.

"I think you were leaving? Boys, you were about to promise

your father silence, I believe. Are you willing?" I wouldn't have blamed them if they'd refused and called for their soldiers instead. But I guess "honor thy father" was alive and well in Olympus. When they each nodded, Hercules growled then spun on his heel and strode off down the path.

"Gloriana, you shouldn't be out here alone. Where's your escort?" Alex walked over to pick up his brother's knife as if nothing had happened.

"I didn't think…" I surprised him by hugging him when he reached my side. "Thank you. Both of you." I hugged Anni next. "Your father is one scary dude."

"You don't know the half of it." Anni grinned at his brother. "We pulled it off." He and Alex exchanged chest bumps. "I can't believe he backed down."

"And he didn't hit either one of us." Alex shrugged. "He's bigger, stronger. He can relieve us of our weapons with his powers. But he must have been unsure of *your* powers, Gloriana. I guess he saw you coming out of Grandmother's chambers. That connection is enough to make any god think twice." He finally smiled. "So now he'll leave Olympus and we're in the clear."

"Yes. We're walking you back to your chambers, Gloriana. Don't go out again without soldiers to protect you. Hear me, Sister?" Anni made sure I was looking him in the eye.

"Yes, Brother, I hear and obey." Frankly the run-in with Hercules had convinced me that I would be smart to have an escort everywhere I went. I was pretty sure he wasn't the only enemy I had here in Olympus. From now on, I was playing it safe.

Jerry was waiting for me when I got back to my rooms. He had arranged a dinner for us, complete with candlelight. There were no handmaidens in sight.

"What's this?" I admit I liked where this was going. I strolled over to lift covers from the dishes on the table. Roast beef, potatoes, tiny green peas and hot rolls. I recognized this meal. It was similar to one I'd had right before he'd turned me vampire.

"I hope you'll forgive me for last night. I made a fool of myself." He put his arms around me and dragged me against him. "I can't remember the last time I got so drunk or felt so bad afterwards. And you took care of me. I don't deserve you."

"I won't argue with you about that." I reached up and ran a hand over his smooth cheek. He'd shaved for me and smelled wonderful. He looked great too. I loved him in the snug jeans and soft cotton shirt. I guess one of the handmaidens had found the wardrobe for him.

"Are you hungry?" He kissed me quickly then held out a chair at the table. "I know you like this kind of food. Alesha arranged it for us."

"Yes, it smells delicious." I sat and picked up a napkin. "I went to visit my grandmother." I shook my head when he offered me wine. "I don't think we need alcohol tonight. How about cold water? I want to keep a clear head." There was a pitcher on a sideboard and Jerry filled our glasses.

"You're right. I don't think I'll be drinking wine again anytime soon. So what did your grandmother have to say? You didn't try to stop this fight with Kratos, did you?" He sat across from me. "I'm ready to fight, Gloriana. You will embarrass me if you go around begging for my life like I can't handle things myself."

"Do you blame me?" I reached for his hand but he kept his in his lap. "Jer, come on. These are gods. Zeus may claim he'll make Kratos mortal but I don't trust any of them. I, I can't lose you." I wiggled my fingers and he finally took my hand.

"The fight goes on. Trust *me* to hold my own." He squeezed my fingers then let them go and lifted the lids on the food. "Now allow me to serve you. I have to keep up my strength. We will eat this fine dinner and then I want to take you to bed."

Bed. Huh. Time was flying by and Jer didn't have a clue that he'd probably die fighting for me here. I found I had little appetite but reminded myself that I might be eating for two. So I choked down food that probably was delicious and made small talk while I fought despair over our situation. Finally, as we were eating dessert, a lemon tart, I decided that I had to just enjoy our time together. Every moment. I had vowed to give him a night of goddess pleasure. Well, tonight was as good a time as any. When we pushed back from the table, I encouraged him to go outside to smoke one of his nasty cheroots while I bathed and changed. We'd have a night to remember, one way or another.

"Gloriana, aren't you ready yet?" He lay on the bed where I had told him to wait.

"One moment." I fluffed my hair. The gown I'd chosen was a match for one Flo had given me as a wedding present. We'd never made it to our wedding night so why not use it now? It was the color of the sea with sheer panels of blue drifting down from a lace bodice. It didn't hide much which was the idea. Instead, it made the most of my new, improved figure. But was it improved enough? I looked at myself critically in the mirror.

"Jerry?" I walked into the bedroom. "Are my hips too wide?"

He sat up, bunching some pillows against the carved headboard. "You're kidding. Right?"

"No. Look." I stepped closer. "Look." I patted my hips and turned around. "And my butt. I think I could make it smaller. You know I can do that. Right?"

"Gloriana, I loved you when you were twice the size you are now." He reached for me but I skipped back.

"Twice? You're saying my butt was double this size?" I tried to see behind me. It didn't bear thinking about. How quickly I'd gotten used to this new size. Spoiled. I'd become spoiled by my mother's tricks. I closed my eyes and concentrated. Size twelve. That's what I'd been for centuries. When I opened my eyes again I looked down and gasped.

"There's my woman. Come here, love. I can put my arms around that woman and know I've got my Gloriana." Jerry lunged and pulled me on top of him.

"I'll crush you." I laughed though because this felt familiar and right. My breasts were bigger and Jerry's grin as he ran his mouth over them made me sigh. Oh, but he knew just what to do and say to have me putty in his hands.

"You've never crushed me yet, my girl." He rolled me over until he was gazing down at me. "I love every inch of you. Stick thin isn't for me. Not when there's so much more to love, to taste." He slid a hand over my stomach and down between my thighs, while he kissed each nipple, pushing down the lace to suck one into his mouth. "Mmm. You are perfect, just the way you are. Don't let your mother convince you otherwise."

"She hasn't. But there are so many other, more beautiful women out there. Slender, perfectly proportioned--"

"Hush, Gloriana." He managed to make that happen by kissing

me. His open mouth took mine with a hunger that I answered with everything in me.

After that it was as if we needed to claim each other again. To discover that our passion was alive and well and the fires burned as bright. He pushed my thighs apart and dipped his tongue inside until I pulled his hair and screamed his name. Then I shoved him onto his back and took him into my mouth, squeezing his sacs and holding him hostage until he was almost lost. But I needed his seed inside me and sat astride to take it all. The heat once again shocked me. Mortal. My Jerry was a mortal man, vibrant and full of life. I couldn't let him die. And if he did? Could *I* bring him back to life? It was something I didn't dare test.

I stared down at him with all the love I had to give. Surely it would be enough to save him. Because I couldn't imagine going on without him. And I sure as hell wouldn't stay here.

"You're amazing." He reached up and traced a tear that I hadn't realized had fallen down my cheek. "What's this? You're not still fretting about that fight, are you? Where's the faith? Haven't I proved myself to you in the centuries you've known me?"

I carefully climbed off of him and snuggled into his arms. "I know you can hold your own on the battlefield. Or you could at home, as a vampire. I've seen you fight and felt nothing but pity for the men who met your sword." I kissed his bare chest. "But here you aren't yourself."

"Aren't I?" He glanced down his body. "Guess you're right. Shit. Even my cock knows I'm mortal. It should be ready to take you again, yet it's laying there. Helpless."

I sat up and saw he was right. "Well, I'm sure I can do something about that." I threw my hair back over my shoulders and crawled down to sit between his legs. "Hello there, Mr. Campbell." I ran a fingertip around the tip of his cock. It jerked but didn't come to life. "Oh, being stubborn, are we?"

"Gloriana, don't mock him. He's taking time to recover." Jerry grinned and put his hands behind his head so he could watch me. "Of course if you wish to speed the process along, feel free to take the fellow in hand."

"Oh, you think that would help?" I grasped him gently, leaning down as if to study him. "Oh, are you tired from all that action earlier, big fellow?"

"You think him big, do you?" Jerry spread his legs further apart. "Flattery will get you everywhere."

"I'm sure it will. You are quite an expert at it yourself." I patted myself on the rump. "You go on and on about my curves. Seriously? Then why stare at those females climbing the poles at that club last night?"

"A man has a duty to look over any woman who crosses his path. It's how we assure ourselves that we have the best already." He sat up and pulled me closer with his feet. "I've known that for centuries, my love. And as soon as we get away from this hellish place, I'll stake my claim for all to know that you're mine and mine alone. For the rest of our lives." He held my head as he kissed me, his mouth hot on mine.

When he finally released me I felt a nudge between my thighs. "Well, look who came out to play."

"You're right where he wants you too." Jerry stayed sitting up and lifted me so that my legs straddled his hips. We sat facing each other and, as he slid inside me, I gasped. This position filled me like no other.

"You can't claim me soon enough, Jeremiah. I claim you too. No other woman will ever have you like this." I grabbed his ear and twisted it, just enough to show I meant business. "Do you hear me? You are mine. All mine. Forever. And I won't catch you gawking at another woman's breasts or butt again." I let go and ran my hands over his chest, tweaking his nipples.

"God, Gloriana, don't threaten me. A man sometimes can't help himself." He began to move his hips, wringing moans of pleasure from me. "No self-respecting male can be blinded to the satisfaction of just looking, you know."

"I'm a goddess, remember? I can turn you to stone, set you on fire, hell, I can probably do a dozen other things to you if you make me jealous, Jer." I jerked when he pushed against a particularly sensitive spot. "Oh, do that again."

"What? This?" He thrust at an angle and I had the orgasm of a lifetime.

I shouted his name and held onto him as I quivered from my toes to my nipples. He was suckling one of those, his love bites making me scream as another tsunami broke over me.

"Are you going to keep threatening me?" He worked a finger in between us, touching off a firestorm that blew me apart again. Water, fire, all the sensations that roared through me had me a shuddering mass of sensation that took all control from me.

"No! I'm sorry." I sobbed against his hard shoulder and then bit down, drawing blood. It tasted salty and wasn't unpleasant but lacked the sexy zing that we'd enjoyed as vampires. I traced the bite with my fingertip and watched it heal in an instant. Good to know. Or at least I tried to take note of that as I fell back into my body after one more cataclysmic orgasm.

"I love you, Gloriana." Jerry sank back on the bed, pulling me with him.

"I love you too. But you'd better stop right now." I lay on him, spent. "No more orgasms. I think I may have died a little bit this time." In fact, my insides were quivering so much that if he had planted his seed, I feared for it. So I lay very still, just breathing as I attempted to gather my strength.

"I was just trying to please you." He ran his hand down my back and patted my butt. I quickly adjusted it back down to a size six. Enough of the generous ass. I'm sure he was happy to have less of me on top of him anyway.

"You pleased me a little too much." I finally slid off of him and lay on my own pillow. I definitely felt wrung out. I glanced down at the sheet. No sign of bleeding. Good. I needed to ask Alesha about a pregnancy test before Jerry and I did any more gymnastic lovemaking.

"There's no such thing as too much pleasure. Or at least that's what you used to say." He was up on one elbow. "What's changed?"

"Nothing. I guess it's this place. Mother listens in on our thoughts. Freaks me out." I rubbed the hair low on his stomach. "I forgot her completely just now. Then, after all that shouting and calling for God, I remembered, that's all."

Jerry laughed and captured my hand. "Hebe can listen, even watch, for all I care. You realize she has Mars in her bed now. Since they've had to admit to their affair, Mars is strutting around like he's caught a big fish. Which he has. Zeus's daughter. And stolen her away from Hercules."

"But he's married, Jer. And Hercules is furious. He even confronted me about their affair." I pulled up the sheet.

"What? He threatened you?" Jerry looked around like he wanted his knife.

"Relax. Luckily my brothers told him to back off. He got the message. He's on Zeus's shit list now so he's probably long gone. Back to his wars." I grabbed his hand. "I promised Alex and Anni not to go out anymore without an escort."

"I should hope so." Jerry frowned. "This is a dangerous place, Gloriana. And Hercules may have said he was leaving, but Mars told me that god has powerful friends. Your father isn't taking a threat from him lightly. He certainly never goes out without a half dozen soldiers surrounding him."

"Wow. And my two little brothers faced their father down." I climbed out of bed. "All to protect me." I yawned and stretched. "I'm taking a bath. Are you joining me?" I laughed when Jerry jumped out of bed and picked me up. "Guess so." I leaned against him as he carried me to the bathroom. Yes, I hated Olympus but I would miss getting to know my brothers better. My grandmother too. A family. After craving one for so long, it was a shame I couldn't just enjoy mine, strange though it was.

ELEVEN

"Your sister and your friend Florence are here, mistress. They want to come into your bedroom. Shall I let them in?" Alesha had served me my usual hot chocolate in bed. Now she took the tray, frowning when she noticed it was barely touched. "Or I can send them away if you aren't feeling like company."

"My stomach is upset. But I'll see them." I threw back the covers. The very fact that Flo and Charis were together made me eager to see what they were up to. Flo was right about one thing, it could be boring here in Olympus. When I wasn't worried about the future or dodging irate gods.

"Upset?" Alesha frowned. "I can assure you, Lady Gloriana, that your food hasn't been poisoned. I test everything myself before I serve you." She stepped back from the bed to give me room when I headed for the bathroom.

I stopped next to her. "What? You think that's possible? That someone could do that? I'm immortal. Surely…"

"The sorcerers are very clever. More clever than the gods want them to be." She looked up, her eyes sad. "Oh, what some here wouldn't try if they wanted you gone. And many do. The handmaidens talk you know. Lady Roxana is furious that Lord Mars is favoring you and that Lady Charis has befriended you. Then there is Lord Hercules, of course. He may have left Olympus, but he has allies. Either of them could pay for a person to sneak poison into your food." She straightened her shoulders. "I won't let that happen."

"God, Alesha. I can't let you risk your life for me." I swayed and sat back on the edge of the bed, suddenly dizzy. Was it from the idea that this place could be so deadly? Or was I pregnant? I beckoned her closer and she set the tray on a table.

"It is my choice, mistress. And I take tiny bites and sips. Not enough to kill me. So far nothing has made me ill. But you look pale. Perhaps I haven't been careful enough." She pressed a palm to my forehead. "Your skin is clammy. Should I send for the sorcerer Cornelius? I am sure he would never harm you."

"No. But you can tell me if there is such a thing as a pregnancy test here in Olympus." I whispered, afraid my mother might be listening. The last thing I wanted to do was alert her to my plan. To my shock, Alesha burst into noisy tears and hid her face in her hands.

"What?" I put my hand on her shaking shoulder. "Alesha, talk to me."

She finally looked up with reddened eyes. "Oh, mistress, if you choose to kill me it is only what I deserve. Throw a lightning bolt at me. Please." She bowed her head, like she was waiting for it. "I should suffer for what I've done."

"Why would I want to do that? What have you done?" I was feeling really nauseated now. This was not going to be good. Whatever had her crying was a secret I didn't want to hear.

"I've betrayed you, mistress." She sobbed again, pulling up her long skirt to hide her face. She wore a plain white slip under her simple dress but it was embroidered with pink flowers. Lovely.

I shook my head. I was losing it if I could be distracted by her underwear. "Betrayed? How? Spit it out, Alesha." I was getting mad now. This girl had become like a friend to me. I'd trusted her and now… Why hadn't I bothered to read her mind? I started to then but she began to talk before I could concentrate enough to do it.

"You are not pregnant, Lady Gloriana." She started to hide her face again, then seemed to think better of it. She lifted her chin and took a shuddery breath. "I know that for a fact."

"Oh?" I stood, pretty sure I knew what was coming. "How?"

"Your mother made me put the birth control elixir in your chocolate every day. If you didn't drink chocolate, then I put it in something else you ate or drank." Tears ran down her cheeks. "I'm so very sorry, my lady, but you have been on the potion since the day your lover arrived here."

I was about to shake her silly when I stopped myself. This was a handmaiden, a slave. I knew she probably hadn't had a choice when my mother had ordered her to do this. I just stared at Alesha and her words poured out.

"Mistress, believe me. I didn't want to betray you. Your mother is terrifying. She threatened me and I knew she meant every word. If I didn't do it and you got pregnant?" Alesha sank to the floor, "I would be dead or worse."

"I can't imagine worse, Alesha." Yes, my voice was cold but I was pissed.

"Can't you?" She wiped her eyes and stared up at me. "You know Demos-one-ear, the man who drives your mother's carriage? How do you think he lost that ear? Your mother caught him listening at one of her doors. She sliced it off herself, with a knife she borrowed from a passing soldier. Demos would have bled to death but she cauterized the wound with a hot iron while two other servants held him down. She wanted him to live as an example to the rest of her slaves. His screams were heard throughout the kingdom." Alesha sobbed.

I swallowed, about to throw up. Did I believe her? Unfortunately I knew my mother very capable of such meanness.

"I'm so sorry, mistress." Alesha choked out the words. "I should have refused and taken my punishment."

I looked down at her bowed head. Of course she'd had no choice. Even *I* was afraid of Hebe and she was my mother. A slave would have to do her bidding no matter what other loyalties she felt.

"Get up, Alesha. I don't blame you for this. My mother didn't want me to have Jerry's child and she always gets her way, doesn't she?" I looked around, surprised Mother didn't appear on the spot. No, my mother was too smart for that. She didn't want to land in the middle of her daughter's rage and I was shaking with it. Plus with sick disappointment. "Go tell my guests I'll be out in a few minutes. Serve them something nice."

"Yes, mistress." Alesha straightened her skirt. "Please don't tell your mother I told you about the birth control. It was supposed to stay a secret."

"Oh, I'm sure it was." I looked around the luxurious room. I stalked over to a vase, priceless I was sure, and threw it to the marble floor. It shattered with a satisfying crash. Next came a candy dish, porcelain and very fine. I crammed the chocolate truffle it held into my mouth before I aimed it at the Venetian glass mirror across the room and got a twofer. Then I realized who would have to clean up the mess. Destroying priceless objects wasn't making me feel better anyway. I took a breath and headed for the bathroom. Alesha scurried out of the room to take care of my company.

No baby. Probably just as well. What did I know about being a mother? If I had turned out to be like mine, the kid would have had issues. Not a legacy that needed to be passed on. I stepped into the shower and let a few tears fall. Running a washcloth down my flat stomach made them flow faster. Damn that witch to hell. Why couldn't she have left my dream alone?

Of course she'd sneaked around and read my mind. Figured out I wasn't taking Waldo's elixir and decided to bully Alesha. That was my mother leaving nothing to chance. At least not now. Too bad she hadn't been as vigilant when she'd left me with Achelous a thousand years ago.

I stared at my swollen eyes in the bathroom mirror. A snap and some makeup fixed that and soon I looked good enough to head into the sitting room. Flo and Charis were enjoying a sampler platter of pastries and a pot of coffee. No alcohol so early in the morning though I could have used a stiff drink. Both of them gave me a searching look.

"What's the matter, *amica*? You look upset." Flo stirred sugar into her coffee. She knew me too well.

"Just the usual. It's getting close to the big fight and I've tried everything I could think of to get it cancelled. Looks like it's going on anyway." I sat across from my new sister and poured a cup of coffee, adding cream and sugar. No use denying myself caffeine or anything else from now on. I wasn't pregnant and had to get used to the idea again that I was never going to be. I made a big deal out of tasting my coffee, hoping Charis was too polite to read my mind.

"I'm sorry, Gloriana." Charis set down her own cup. "Calista has been working on Kratos, throwing herself at him. He's still in love with her if that helps." She touched my arm and I realized my cup was rattling in the saucer.

"Not really. He can't call off the fight. Zeus wants it and that's that." I set down the coffee. I didn't have the stomach for it anyway.

"Perhaps he'll lose on purpose. Calista told him she won't be his mistress if he marries you and she means it. She's even tossed around names of men her father can arrange for her to marry instead. Kratos is jealous of course." Charis patted my hand.

I gave my sister a look. A warrior throw a fight? I couldn't imagine it.

"Well, sitting here worrying about it won't help matters, will it, Glory?" Flo jumped up. "Charis tells me there's a store where I can find clothes that fit me. Let's go shopping!"

I couldn't believe I really wasn't in the mood since shopping was usually my go-to when I was depressed. But then Flo started in about her wardrobe and how tight everything was. I knew we were going no matter how I felt. I owed it to my best friend.

"Look at this." Flo pulled up the gathered top she had on. The pants lacked an inch from buttoning and the zipper wouldn't pull all the way up. "If this top wasn't long, I wouldn't be able to go outside at all. And I can't lift my arms." She pulled at the tight armholes and we all heard fabric rip.

"You could always ask my mother for more clothes in a bigger size." I shook my head. "Never mind. I know your answer to that. I don't want to ask her for anything either." I smiled at Charis. My acting ability was coming in handy. They'd never know I was trying not to crawl back into my bed. "Tell us about this shop. Who goes there? Don't the goddesses just make their own wardrobes?"

"Sure. But some of the gods have favorite mistresses, women they brought back from their wars as trophies, I guess you'd call them. The women are mortal so they need to buy their clothes. Some clever handmaidens have earned their freedom and make things to sell. They copy some of the designer fashions the goddesses wear and put them in this shop. All sizes, I think. I've never been, but my handmaidens have told me about it." Charis laughed when Flo ran to the door, clearly eager to get started. "My handmaiden is outside, ready to lead us there."

"Come, Glory. You know I can't go around like this. Or do you wish for me to turn into *un eremita?*"

"What?" Flo and her Italian. Maybe someday I'd learn more than a few words.

"She said a hermit or recluse." Charis laughed. "Poor Florence. Couldn't you find anything in your closet with an elastic waistband?"

"No, or I'd have it on right now." Flo made a face. "I could make a tent out of my purple bedspread and wear that, I guess. Florence the giant eggplant, they'd call me. *Aye*, how did I get so big?" She stuffed the blueberry scone in her left hand into her mouth.

"I think you're eating the answer, pal." I got up and walked to the door. "But we need an escort. I'm not going anywhere without some soldiers."

"There are four posted outside your door." Charis shoved it open and pointed. "See? And they have a list of people allowed entry here. I guess Dad gave it to them. Luckily, I was on it. So was Florence. I bet if my mother showed up, she'd be denied entrance." Charis patted one of the beefy soldiers on his shoulder. "Good luck keeping the goddess Roxana out of any room where she wanted to be, soldier."

The man paled but put his hand on his sword. "We are here to protect the Lady Gloriana. Anyone who tries to harm her has to go through us."

"Hopefully, we won't have to fend off any attacks. Brace yourself, though. We're going shopping. With any luck you'll be stuck carrying shopping bags." I didn't want to think about what would happen if Hercules himself stormed my rooms. These soldiers would be sliced and diced.

Charis dragged a handmaiden away from a handsome soldier. "This is Elena. She's going to take us to the shop." She turned to the girl, who was beautiful in an exotic way with dark skin and a voluptuous figure. The soldiers had certainly noticed.

"It's not far. We can walk. Unless you'd rather call for a carriage." She glanced down at our feet. "You might want to change into more comfortable shoes, except for the little lady. She's good to go."

"I can't help it, Glory." Flo looked insulted. "I told you, I can't walk in high heels. I trip, I fall, and I twist my ankle." She leaned against me. "Look at me. Popping out of my clothes and wearing," she shuddered, "clogs."

"They certainly look comfortable." I laughed when she gave me a gesture that needed no translation. "At least there's no one here who knows you, Flo." I patted her back and was horrified to realize I felt muffin top above her jeans. My buddy had never had extra fat in her life. "Well, no one but me. And I swear that, once we're home, I'll never tell anyone how you've sunk so low." I grinned when she jerked away and swore at me in a spate of Italian.

"Whoa. Do you know what she just called you, Gloriana?" Charis had changed her footgear for some cute flat heeled boots. Which called for designer jeans tucked into them and a different top. I followed her lead and soon had on leggings, ballet flats and a long blue knit top.

"No, but I'm sure I deserve it." I knew using my goddess powers in front of my friend was rubbing salt in her wounds.

"You do!" Flo stared at us, her eyes watering. "Look at you, littler than me now and changing clothes with a snap. I hate both of you." She wiped her cheeks. "Let's go. And I will not eat another bite today. If I so much as look at a scone, you hit me. Swear it, Glory."

"Okay. Charis, you're my witness." I linked arms with Flo and we followed the handmaiden down a path. The soldiers flanked us, keeping a watch over the group. We walked for about ten minutes before we came to a large pink building with picture windows. Manikins were posed in the center of each one and the outfits they wore made Flo sigh. We'd come to the right place.

"Glory." Flo stopped me before we went inside. "I must say something."

"Yes?" I realized she was serious and dragged her over to sit on a bench next to the shop's entrance. "What is it, pal?"

"*Mi dispiace*."She shook her head and grabbed my hand. "I mean to say I'm sorry. I never understood before how you felt. All those years with extra pounds you couldn't lose." She sniffled. "The newspapers were cruel, *amica*, when you were with Israel. They called you a blueberry."

"Yes, the tabloids had a field day with their headlines. Famous rock star Israel Caine engaged to chubby ordinary Gloriana St. Clair." I squeezed her hand. "It hurt. But Ray loved me, curves and all. Jerry's always loved me as I was." I took a moment to appreciate that and my special man. "So I got over it and I'm the first to admit it wasn't easy. But I learned to accept how I look and love myself, no matter what shape I'm in. I hope you can figure out how to do that too, Flo."

"You are brave." Flo wiped her wet cheeks with her free hand.

"Me? What do I have to offer a man besides my beauty, I ask you? Without it I am nothing.'"

"Stop it." I shook her. "This isn't like you. You are smart, strong, independent." I materialized a hanky and gave it to her. "Dry up and stop this pity train right now."

Flo blew her nose. "You are the best friend a woman could have. You are right. I stop whining now."

"Not such a good friend. I dragged you up here. Into my mess." I pulled her up to stand beside me. "But we are going to figure this out and get home better than ever, together. Am I right?"

"That's my line!" She sniffed and actually worked up a smile. "But *naturalmente*." She hugged me for a long moment. "Better than ever."

"Hey, you two. Get in here. They're having a sale." Charis stood in the doorway. "Florence, you'd look great in this red dress." She held up a sheath that was a style Flo loved.

"It *is* my color." Flo smiled and headed inside.

We spent the next couple of hours finding clothes for Flo. When it came time to pay, Charis insisted our father wouldn't mind putting it all on his account. I didn't ask why he had one at this store for mortal mistresses. I was pretty sure my mother wouldn't like to know about it either. I rationalized the expense by remembering that it had been Mars' idea to bring Flo and Richard up here in the first place. After he'd brought Jerry too.

My father and his good intentions. The least he could do was buy a few, okay, a lot of clothes for my best friend. Charis and I were sworn to secrecy as to the size Flo now wore. She was definitely going on a diet.

We arranged for the new wardrobe to be delivered then started back to my rooms. The soldiers kept pace with us, though one of them was busy chatting with Elena. We were laughing and relaxed when a dark cloud in the sky above us made us all stop in our tracks.

"Leave us. I wish to speak to Gloriana." The booming voice could belong to only one man. When lightning cracked next to the soldier beside me, he gestured and the squad saluted and hurried away.

"Glory?" Flo trembled next to me.

"Go with Charis, Flo. I'll be all right." I hoped that was true.

Charis dragged Flo down the path. She darted a few anxious glances toward the sky and then back to me. "Good luck, Sister." Then she whispered in Flo's ear. My pal crossed herself and broke into a run. They were soon out of sight, Charis's handmaiden leading the way.

"Grandfather." I bowed as I'd seen the courtiers do in his presence. You didn't mess around when Zeus sought you out.

He appeared in front of me. Then he looked to his right and a golden throne appeared. He took a seat and nodded. A small bench was suddenly in front of me.

"Sit. We need to have a talk, you and I."

"Yes, sire." I collapsed on the bench and folded my shaking hands in my lap. "How can I serve you?"

"You can stop trying to stir up trouble in my kingdom, Gloriana." His deep voice was deceptively soft, but I couldn't mistake the steel beneath the words.

"Trouble, sire? I don't know what you mean."

Thunder boomed over my head and lightning sizzled mere feet from my bench. "Think, Gloriana. You've been a very busy girl, have you not? Going to your grandmother about the plight of the handmaidens. Poor things. Now Hera is in a froth, determined to stop the gods from having relations with them." He slammed a fist on the arm of his throne and my bench almost toppled over. "Do you have any idea what a problem that will cause here?"

"No." I realized my chin was trembling but I wouldn't look away from his hard gaze. "Sire, how can you condone rape? The girls have no rights. No say in how they are used."

"They are slaves, Gloriana. Spoils of war. Of course they have no rights!" His voice made the leaves on the tree beside me rattle.

"Do you hear yourself?" I covered my mouth. Had I really just called out the lord of all Olympus? "I'm sorry, sire. But slavery is an abomination in my world. I, I can't believe it is still commonplace here. Accepted."

"You may be of my blood, but you are out of bounds, girl. I dictate how things are done in my kingdom. Is that clear?" Zeus raised a hand and I braced myself for a lightning bolt or fire. Instead, he threw a flame at that poor nearby tree and watched it burn down to a pile of ash.

"Yes, sire. I know you dictate everything here. That's why I find it hard to accept that you would wish to let such a practice go on. To make innocent women serve men in such a fashion."

"The slaves are compensated. With pleasure and with coin if the god is feeling generous." He leaned forward. "Have you asked one of them about that?"

"So they can prostitute themselves? Is that the choice they are given?" I leaned forward too. So far he was listening. I couldn't believe it but had to give this opportunity all that I had. "Surely you know that not all men, even gods, care whether a woman gets pleasure as long as he gets his rocks off."

"His rocks. You do speak plainly. But it's true." Zeus sat back. "Coin is given so the women can eventually buy their freedom."

"Can they? Did Grandmother tell you they are charged for birth control by the sorcerer who makes it or must take their chances at bearing a bastard?"

"That's not right. I have no wish for the hierarchy to breed with slaves." Grandfather was so sure of his superiority.

I winced at my grandfather's attitude but kept my mouth shut. Zeus. Yes, I guess he was all that in this world. He'd been frowning and the wind had picked up.

"Sneaking slimy toad. I never liked him. Never was half the wizard Cornelius is. And Waldo is paid well to provide such a service to the handmaidens free of charge. If he is also taking funds from the slaves, then he is going to be punished." Zeus snapped his fingers and a pair of soldiers appeared. "Take the sorcerer Waldo to the cells. I will deal with him later."

"You can't just leave him there. Then what will the poor girls do?" I brushed back my hair, out of control from the gale force winds which were finally dying down.

"You are right, Gloriana. I will have to find another sorcerer to take over his duties. Clearly Waldo was untrustworthy. Cornelius has a son. He has been his apprentice for some time now. Surely he will be able to handle this. It will be a rise in standing for that family as well." Zeus smiled. "See? I am not unreasonable. The handmaidens and my kingdom should not be burdened with unwanted children. I will take care of it."

"But the handmaidens will still be subjected to the whims of your gods and their urges, I assume."

"It is our way. The gods are lusty. And taking slaves from

conquered lands is a time-honored tradition. Surely you don't expect me to deny my men their rights to spoils."

"Women aren't spoils, they're people." I stood which I obviously shouldn't have done because thunder shook the ground so hard that I fell back onto the bench. "Please, Grandfather, reconsider slavery. Where I live on Earth it was abolished centuries ago."

"Enough, child. I cannot and will not remake Olympus just because you don't like the way things are done here. You would do well to hold your tongue. I'm already getting an earful from your grandmother about this fight between your lover and Kratos." He shrugged. "I'm not cancelling it."

"Are you afraid changing your mind will make you seem weak to your subjects?" I fell back as the world went dark and more wind whipped my hair around my head. Cold made me shiver then heat seemed to burn me from the outside in. I tried to speak but had lost my voice. I had an impression of Zeus rising from his throne but couldn't focus. I'd said too much. Again. That was my last thought before the world went dark.

I woke up in my own bed. My mother stood over me.

"I hope you're happy. My father wants you gone from Olympus. As soon as this fight is over. And he's rescheduled it. Ready or not, your lover fights Kratos tomorrow. If Kratos wins, he'll be banished with you, for a time at least. You can imagine how that complicates things."

I sat up and the room swung around me. I gasped and leaned over. Alesha was suddenly there with a basin and I threw up in it. The handmaiden bathed my face with a cloth and cool water then backed away from the bed.

"Go away, Mother. I have nothing to say to you."

"Don't you? Your handmaiden has confessed that you found out about the birth control. I feel sure you wish to speak your mind about my subterfuge." Mother sat in a chair Alesha pulled up next to the bed.

"My mind. Very well." I sat up. "I hate you. You don't care what I want, only what you want *for* me. You are a horrible mother. I realized that you were smart to make sure I didn't pass on these genes we share because I would probably screw up a child. Look at my role model." I gestured toward her then collapsed back against my pillows. "Satisfied?"

"Gloriana, you are being ridiculous. I would love for you to have a child. Just not with that blood sucker. Marry Kratos and I will count the months until you present him with an heir. Once you've done that, I'm sure Zeus will allow you to come back here. I don't doubt you will be a wonderful mother to Kratos' children."

"That will never happen, Mother. Now get out. I can't stand the sight of you." I turned my face away. The fight was tomorrow? Was Jerry ready? Did it matter? The fix was in and he was doomed. A tear slipped down my cheek.

"Lady Gloriana, she's gone."

"Good." I turned my head and saw that Alesha had a glass of water in her hand. "Thanks, I'm so thirsty." I took the glass and sat up to drink. I guess being electrocuted, if that was what Zeus had done to me, had dried me out. "You'll be glad to know Waldo will no longer charge the handmaidens for birth control. He's in the cells."

"I heard. And that you managed it." Alesha straightened the coverlet. "Thank you." She took my empty glass. "Word has come down from Lady Hera that handmaidens may refuse a god if they wish. No consequences will be allowed."

"Really?" I had a feeling Hera and Zeus didn't agree on that decision. Not my problem. At least the handmaidens had the right of refusal for now. "What do the handmaidens think of that?"

"Some of them like the gifts they get when they lie with a god. Others don't care for men at all and prefer," she flushed, "the company of other women. So they will be happy to refuse a god."

"I get that. What do you think?" I was interested in her answer.

"Mistress, I heard your mother. That you might be leaving Olympus soon and going back to your home." Alesha touched the back of my hand. "It would be my greatest wish to go with you. To serve you there. Where there are no gods to tell yay or nay."

"But don't you belong to someone here?" I hated it, but she had to be somebody's slave.

"I am yours, mistress. I have a paper that shows you are my owner now, a gift from Lady Hebe."

"My mother gave you to me?" I swallowed.

"When she set up your rooms here. She knew you'd need a loyal servant. There's no better way to inspire loyalty than by binding us together with ownership." Alesha bowed her head. "I am yours to dispose of as you wish. Of course she still gave me orders and I didn't dare disobey her. She is too highly placed and too powerful."

"Yes, I understand. You were too scared to refuse her when she told you to doctor my food and drink." I kept a leash on my temper. It wouldn't do any good to blame a slave whose mindset was obedience. And my mother was a holy terror, only a step or two under Zeus himself.

"Thank you, mistress." Alesha was almost groveling and I was getting impatient with it. Where was her pride? Her backbone? Probably beaten out of her long ago. "I told your mother you read my mind about the birth control. She was furious but decided the time was right for the truth to come out. So she spared my life. Here on Olympus if she'd killed me there would have been some restitution required since she would have been destroying your property."

"My property." I shook my head. "No. I don't own people. Where are your papers? How can I set you free?"

"Does that mean you won't take me with you?" Alesha didn't look happy. I was shocked. Surely her freedom meant more to her than a trip to Earth.

"If I actually do get to go home and can figure out how to get you there too, you can come. But only if you're free. I don't own people. I mean it. You must be released from slavery. The idea of it makes me sick." I waved my hand. "Bring the basin and hurry." I held my hand over my mouth. I wasn't kidding. When she got close enough I leaned over and threw up again. There wasn't much in my stomach and I ended up with dry heaves.

"Thank you, mistress." Alesha wiped my forehead again. "Of course I'll bring you my papers. But please don't release me until we are away from here. You are very highly placed as a member of the hierarchy. Your family is powerful and that gives me respect among the other slaves. If you free me, then I am nothing. Just another woman without ties. It is not good to be such here in Olympus."

"Well. Okay then. I won't leave you hanging. We'll manage somehow." I dragged my legs over the side of the bed. "I'm going to get up now. This has been a crazy day and I want a long, soaking bath. Help me walk into the bathroom?"

"Certainly, mistress." Alesha put her arm around me and helped me into the dressing area. Weak and not a little dizzy, I sat in front of my vanity while she ran a bath.

Crazy indeed. I'd been zapped by Zeus, betrayed by my mother and now I owned a slave. Next on my agenda? Telling Jerry that he was fighting tomorrow, thanks to me and my interference. I would be excited about going home if I knew he'd be by my side alive and not in a coffin. Somehow I was going to have to make things turn out right.

I was back in bed and dozing when Jerry staggered into the bedroom. He'd clearly had a hard day training.

"What's wrong, Gloriana? Alesha said you were in bed recovering." He set his sword on the carved chest where the vase used to be. If he noticed it was missing, he didn't say anything. "Recovering from what exactly?"

"A meeting with Grandfather." I sat up and noticed he had several cuts and bruises. The room whirled around me before it finally settled again. "You don't look so good yourself. How was practice?"

"Don't ask. I'm going to jump in the shower. Then we can talk." He pulled off his belt and sandals then dropped his short toga before he walked into the bathroom. I couldn't help admiring the flex of his muscles as he strode naked across the marble floor. He looked fit and should have been able to take any man in a fight. Too bad he wasn't fighting a mere man. I heard the shower go on and the glass door slide shut.

I lay back and closed my eyes. This might be our last night together. I'd have to tell him about the fight. Even if I had a way for us to escape Olympus together right now, I knew Jerry had never and would never run from a confrontation. He'd do his best to win tomorrow and go down swinging. I jumped when I realized Alesha had crept into the room.

"Mistress. Cornelius the sorcerer is here. Would you see him?"

"Yes, just a moment. Hand me a robe." I got out of bed. For a goddess, I wasn't bouncing back from my meeting with Zeus like I should have. Maybe that was because I really hadn't eaten all day. I would order dinner as soon as Cornelius left. Jerry needed to eat no matter what. Too bad the thought of food made me queasy again. I leaned on Alesha as I walked into the sitting room.

"Lady Gloriana." Cornelius bowed when he saw me. "I hope I didn't disturb you."

"*I* hope you bring me some good news. Something to help Jerry win tomorrow. Or news that your granddaughter has talked Kratos into calling off the fight."

"He cannot do that, my lady, even if he wished to do it." Cornelius sat at my gesture. We faced each other from matching chairs. "Zeus wants the fight to go on and so it will."

"Grandfather is determined to show who is in charge, isn't he?" I sagged back against the brocade cushion. "I tried to talk to him and all I got for my trouble was a shot of lightning."

"You are very brave, my lady." Cornelius shook his head. "I have an elixir here that should put your lover in top form. It is the best I can do." He pulled a vial out of his pocket and set it on a table. "I am also here to thank you. By calling attention to Waldo's greed, you made it possible for my son, Calista's father, to rise to a powerful position among the sorcerers."

"I was trying to help the handmaidens." I sighed and rubbed my aching head. "I really wanted to gain their freedom but Zeus wouldn't hear of that, of course."

"No, he wouldn't. But now more will be able to eventually buy their freedom. It is a good start." He smiled. "If your friend Blade could win tomorrow, Kratos would be happy to wed Calista now. With her father in a position of power, it would be a good match for him. But I'm afraid Kratos will prevail." Cornelius studied the vial on the table. "Kratos is a god and, even if Zeus takes away his powers, he has advantages here that a mere mortal can't hope to match."

"You aren't making me feel better, sorcerer." I bit back the urge to cry on his shoulder. He had an air about him, solid, inspiring trust. One of the few people I'd met here that I did think I could confide in.

"I'm sorry. You know I want the same outcome you do." He leaned closer. "Are you all right? You are very pale."

"No, of course I'm not all right!" I gestured him even closer and forced myself to whisper. "There's something I want to ask you. If Jerry loses," I heard my voice break and put my hand over my mouth until I knew I could continue without sobbing, "dies," Okay, so I couldn't keep going. I materialized a handkerchief and wiped my eyes.

"Can, can I bring him back to life?" I looked up at the ceiling so I wouldn't see the pity in Cornelius's strange orange eyes. Alesha had left us alone and it was just the two of us. He took my hand. I rushed on before I broke down completely. "I saw Mars do it. My mother showed me when Jerry fell during a practice match. Do I have that power?" I finally looked at him. "What do you think?"

"Mars can do it but few other gods can." Cornelius shook his head. "I don't know if you could, my lady."

"Can you test me somehow?"

He squeezed my fingers. "There is no test unless we killed someone now and tried it." He looked deep into my eyes. "Some would say bring in a slave and do just that."

"God no!" I jerked my hand from his. "This place is barbaric. I can't wait to get away from here."

"Yes, I can see that." He stood. "Get your man to drink the elixir right before the fight. It will give him added strength. I am giving Kratos something too but not as potent. He has paid me for it but I owe it to my granddaughter to try to fix this fight in your lover's favor." He helped me to my feet. "I asked you before. Are you well?"

I sighed. "As well as can be expected after Zeus gave me a dose of his anger." I rubbed my forehead again. "I have a headache and haven't been able to eat today. It's nothing."

"Perhaps. Let me see your bedchamber if you don't mind." He followed me to the bedroom, taking my arm when I staggered. "You are showing symptoms that trouble me."

"I'm not pregnant." I frowned when I said it then sank into a chair.

He stopped beside the bed and gave me a searching look. "No, I don't think so. But there's something here…" He picked up my pillow and sniffed it. "Where's your handmaiden?"

"Alesha." I actually called for her, forgetting that I could just gesture.

Jerry strode into the room from the bathroom, a towel around his lean middle. "What's going on here? Cornelius, I told you I don't want any more of your shit in my system."

"I'm here to help Lady Gloriana. Does she look well to you?" Cornelius had thrown all of our pillows onto the floor.

"Yes, mistress, what is it?" Alesha ran into the room.

"Girl, who brought these pillows into this bedchamber?" Cornelius picked one up, pulled out a knife and ripped open the pillow. A mixture of goose feathers and green leaves poured out. The scent made my eyes water and I suddenly ran to the bathroom and leaned over the sink. I splashed water in my face to keep from throwing up again. I saw Jerry in the mirror, right behind me and felt his arms go around me, holding me up.

"What was it? In the pillows?"

"Cornelius says it's henbane, whatever the hell that is. The sorcerer says it could have eventually caused death. For both of us." Jerry helped me sit on my vanity stool. "He's got an assistant who is taking the pillows out of there. Alesha swears she has the pillows made by the same supplier who serves the royals—Zeus and Hera."

"I know Alesha wouldn't hurt me, us. Let me talk to her." I grabbed a wet washcloth and pressed it to my forehead then peeked in the bedroom to make sure there was none of that smell left. Cornelius sat in a chair next to the bed. He stood when we entered.

"You both could have died. Now we know why you've had such a difficult time getting your strength back, Blade." Cornelius looked grim. "Lady Gloriana, how long have you been feeling unwell?"

"It really just started a day or so ago." Or had it? I'd had symptoms I'd hoped meant I was pregnant. Now I knew they couldn't have been from that. I tried to think. But it wasn't easy when I was still weak from what I'd been through this day.

"Someone tampered with your pillows." Cornelius gestured and we walked into the sitting room. Alesha was there with a stack of fresh pillows.

"I have the replacements for you to inspect, Master Cornelius. I ran to get these myself, from Lady Hera's own stores." Alesha looked at me with glistening eyes. "I swear to you, mistress, that I didn't know your other pillows had been harmed. Lady Hera vows to find out who meant to hurt you. I had to tell her servants why I needed more pillows so soon. Lady Hera is quite upset."

"Oh, boy. Grandmother on the rampage. That should be interesting." I sank down on the loveseat while Cornelius examined each pillow, sniffing them endlessly and even cutting one open.

"You can stitch this back together, I assume." He ordered Alesha.

"Yes, sir. I will do so if you are sure they are safe. And no one will enter the bedchamber to serve my lady Gloriana but me from now on." Alesha frowned. "There are other servants here. Some I do not know so well. I assumed your mother sent them all but perhaps not. It is possible someone sent by an enemy sneaked in among them."

"We will keep the bedchamber locked from now on, Alesha." Jerry sat close, his arm tight around me. "Until we leave this godforsaken place, Gloriana is to be guarded constantly and our rooms served by only one servant." He looked at me. "Are you sure this girl is to be trusted?"

"Yes, I'm sure." I studied her, reading her mind though I didn't need to. I trusted her completely. "Someone wants me dead but it's not Alesha." She straightened when I said that and nodded. "And it won't be long before we're away from here anyway." I sighed and put my hand on Jerry's bare knee. He never had put on any clothes and still wore only that big white towel.

"What do you mean?" He touched my chin so that I was looking at him.

"You fight for your life tomorrow."

TWELVE

"Quit fussing over me, Gloriana." Jerry was strapping on his sword while Mars and Richard watched. I was feeling better, thanks to an elixir provided by Cornelius. But only physically. Mentally I was a wreck. Jerry refused to take any kind of drug no matter how much I begged, cried or softened him up with sexual favors. He didn't cheat in a fight. Period. I was willing to cheat any way I could if it would save his life.

"Do you think we could buy off Kratos?" I whispered to my father.

"You think I didn't already try?" Mars pulled me out of the room. "Don't let Blade hear us. He has more pride than almost any man I've met. A Highlander. I'm sick to death of hearing about the place. I'm beginning to think I may have to pay the famous Castle Campbell a visit, just to see what makes the man so proud."

"You'd like it, I think." Oh, hell, I was going to cry. No, I sucked it up. But the thought of Jerry's parents--the Laird, even his battleax of a wife--never seeing Jerry again made me want to wail then jerk Jerry physically out of Olympus somehow.

"No, Gloriana, you can't take him home. Zeus won't let him escape this. There's too much riding on it." Mars never hesitated to read my mind, damn him.

"What do you mean? Surely Grandfather's not looking forward to the fit I plan to throw when he goes forward with this barbaric thing he has planned. I've told him I won't marry Kratos, no matter--" I blinked back tears. Jerry had warned me not to cry or it would unnerve him completely. Better to get back into the bedroom and make sure all of Jerry's knives were sharp enough, that his armor was strong. Do useful things.

"Zeus will freeze you in your seat before he'll allow you even so much as a squeak in protest and you know it." Mars was very serious. "I must warn you. This day is going to be a circus. Dionysus has planned everything. There's a betting book, of course. Lots of wagering going on, most of it in Kratos favor, though naturally there are those who love a long shot." Mars rested his hand on my shoulder. "Your man is not thought to have a prayer of winning."

"I know." I leaned against my father's massive chest. He hadn't worn his armor today but was dressed as a warrior and would scare most people. Not me. I saw the love in his eyes and sighed when he folded his arms around me. "Jerry will do his best."

"Of course he will. I just doubt it will be enough. Some of the betting is on how many minutes he'll last."

"Bloodthirsty bastards." I pulled back. "You didn't bet against Jerry, did you?"

"I didn't bet at all, Daughter. It wouldn't be seemly." He patted my back. "There will be feasting, plenty to drink and a warm-up match. It amuses Zeus to have some of the slaves fight first. They've been pulled out of the cells to fight for their freedom."

"Oh, no! Do I have to watch that?" I was back in his arms again. "Tell me it isn't to the death."

"No, it's not. Slaves are too valuable and these are strong men, good soldiers. They were in the cells because they have hot heads. Zeus thinks it will be entertaining to see who will win. Then he'll let the crowd bid on the loser." He must have felt me stiffen. "I know you disapprove of slavery. I heard you even went to Hera about it. Blade feels as you do. He's told me his views more than once. But it is our way and you'll not change things here on your first visit."

"First visit?" I stepped away from him. "Zeus wants me gone. I leave as soon as this fight is over. Grandfather commanded it. Mother thinks Kratos will be sent with me if he wins this fight." I shuddered, refusing to imagine it. "I assumed..."

"That you'd never have to come back?" Mars smiled. "No such luck, Daughter. Your grandmother has taken a liking to you and she's more powerful than you know. She'll make sure you'll be called back. When or how remains to be seen."

"You know I hate it here." I smiled sadly. "The place. Not you, of course. Or Charis. Even my brothers would be nice to visit, but--"

"Olympus has not been kind to you. Don't worry, I'll be down to see you. And you know you can't escape your mother." He turned and sighed. "Here she is."

"Gossiping about me. I know I'm on Gloriana's hate list these days." Mother waved her hand, obviously not too concerned. "Just wait, Gloriana. Once you're married and pregnant with your first child, you'll see the wisdom of coming back to Olympus and taking your rightful place here. I'll be very busy making sure my father welcomes you with open arms." She fussed with her skirt, avoiding my eyes. "And you know a man of Kratos' standing certainly won't be happy anywhere else. A houseful of a worthy god's children will make you forget your rebellious notions I'm sure."

"Over my dead body." *Or Jerry's?* I jerked away from Mars and stomped back into my bedroom. The love of my life and Richard were going over strategy. Flo was in my closet trying on a jacket that wouldn't close over her now ample bosom. At least my mother hadn't followed me.

"Can Jerry and I have a moment alone?" I smiled at Richard and gestured at the closet. "Go tell Flo you love her new voluptuous figure."

"I do!" Richard raised an eyebrow. "She doesn't believe me but I like her any way I can get her."

"That's what I always tell Gloriana. I think she finally realizes I mean it." Jerry pulled me into his arms. "Men in love. Let's hope today all that love gives me the extra energy and skill I'll need when I fight. I'll be damned if I let another man have you, Gloriana."

"Oh, Jerry," I said when Richard slipped into the closet and shut the door. "You know you're the only man for me." I lay my head on Jerry's chest. No armor after all. That was one of the rules of this fight. No armor, no headgear, just hand to hand fighting with a sword and two knives. I was terrified that this fight would be bloody and too brief.

"Quit frowning. You make me think you have no confidence in

me." Jerry traced a line between my eyebrows.

"I have faith that in a fair fight you could beat any normal man. I've seen you do it dozens of times." I snuggled closer. We'd made slow and tender love the night before. As if we were saying goodbye. It had broken my heart. But almost being killed by pillow poison had left both of us too weak for wild monkey sex. Jerry had been preoccupied too. I hadn't made a big deal out of it, but it seriously freaked me out. I'd never seen him so worried before a fight.

"Kratos isn't a normal man. I know that. Zeus swears he'll be making him mortal this morning, for what that's worth." Jerry had that worried look again but smiled when he realized I was watching him. "Mars tells me Kratos is a veteran of many wars, a decorated hero. He fought so well that Zeus turned him into a god." Jerry rubbed my back and kissed the top of my head.

"You're good too. Better than good." I wanted him confident going into this. "Come on, Jer. You've had centuries of experience too. Your men would follow you into hell itself if you asked them to. Doesn't that tell you something?"

"That they are idiots?" He laughed when I gasped. "Oh, come on. Where's your sense of humor, my love. I know I'm a leader of good soldiers. A Highlander."

"Just remember all those times you won in battle. That should give you confidence." I ran my thumb over his strong jaw. It had done me good to see him laugh, though I didn't know how he'd managed to find his sense of humor when I was about to become unhinged with nerves.

"And I have an advantage over Kratos. He doesn't know you like I do, Gloriana." Jerry nipped at my thumb with his strong teeth. "He has no idea what a precious prize he could win." He leaned down and kissed me, taking my mouth with a ferocity that startled me. I kissed him back, just as fiercely. My love, the only man I wanted. By the time he pulled back, I had tears running down my cheeks.

"I don't deserve you, Jerry. I'm so sorry you have to go through this."

"I would go through worse to have you, Gloriana. Never doubt it." He grabbed a cloth and wiped away my tears. "Now stop crying or I'll think you don't have faith in me. I'm fighting for our future. I've learned over the centuries that desperation can make a man difficult to beat."

I sniffed and made myself stop the waterworks. Difficult to beat, yes, but not impossible. I didn't say that out loud. I just kissed Jerry again with every bit of love I felt. When we heard Mars clear his throat, we knew it was time to go.

Richard and Flo stepped out of the closet, both of them flushed. At least they seemed to have come to an understanding in there. Flo had on one of her new outfits, the red sheath that did great things for her hair and skin. I guess Richard's love and a long look in my three-way mirror had convinced her. Her shoulders were back like she knew that she looked good.

Mars made sure we were all guarded before he took us to the field where the fights would take place. We teleported, something I wasn't crazy about as it left me a little dizzy. Jerry and Richard seemed unaffected. Flo was more interested in checking out the crowd of people dressed in togas who were milling around the large area. I'd forgotten to tell her it was the uniform of the day. She'd commented on mine but had assumed I wore it because I was related to Zeus and Hera.

"Glory, I look wrong. I see a white tablecloth--" Flo actually started toward a buffet table.

"No, stop, Flo. The people here know you're an outsider. Most of the younger generation, like Charis, would kill for a chance to visit Earth and see what we've seen." I patted her shoulder. "Own it. You're a woman of *our* world. They can only dream of being one."

"Yes, *amica*, you are right." She stuck out her chest and clung to Richard. Her husband wasn't in danger, or shouldn't be. But I could tell she was worried. Mars had explained that a man's second in a fight might have to jump in and try to pull the men apart if things got out of hand. Out of hand. The thought made my stomach roll.

A trumpet blared and Zeus and Hera took seats on their thrones on one end of the field where dancing girls began to whirl in front of them. The music got louder. A runner came up to Mars and whispered in his ear. My father turned to me.

"Lady Hera commands your presence, Gloriana. You'd better go see what she wants. And be careful near your grandfather. Gossip says Zeus is still unhappy with you. Is it true he moved this fight up so he could be rid of you sooner?"

Jerry kept his hand on my waist. "I'm glad to get it over with. I wasn't getting any better with training and you know it, Mars."

"It *is* my fault. I pissed off my grandfather." I looked down at my white toga with the diamond pin. What I'd said to Flo was true for me too. I needed to show my grandfather where I belonged even if it aggravated him even more. I snapped my way into a black silk pants suit. That made me stand out in this crowd of all white and put a smile on Flo's face.

I walked the length of the field, skirting the dancing girls and smiling as the crowd parted. Whispers started when the people noticed what I'd done. Defying the dress code. Just one more nail in my coffin. Since I was a member of the family, I doubted there was much Zeus would do to me. Not in front of all these witnesses. When I got to the thrones, I bowed deeply.

"Grandmother, Grandfather. I hope you are both well."

"Gloriana." My grandmother looked me over with a frown. "I've never been fond of trousers on a woman." She flicked her wrist and my pants became a short skirt. "That's better."

I looked down. I had to admit she'd made it the right length to show off my legs. "Thank you, Grandmother. I don't know what I was thinking."

"That you were in mourning already, Granddaughter? Not very optimistic, are you? I hope your man at least provides us with a good fight." Zeus looked over the field. "Blade looks fit enough."

"Yes, he's ready and willing." I started to beg for Zeus to stop this but his cold gaze warned me not to start with that. "Have you taken care of Kratos? Is he truly mortal now?"

"Yes, indeed. And don't think it wasn't difficult for him. I had him brought to my chambers first thing this morning." Zeus laughed. "I could tell he had enjoyed a late night. The man has a demanding mistress."

"Really, Zeus. I don't think Gloriana needs to hear that." Hera shook her head. "I'm sorry, dear."

"No, it's not news to me. Kratos is in love with Calista, Cornelius's granddaughter. They were promised before this business with me came up." I sighed and looked out over the crowd. "Look at her, Grandmother. There, standing with her father and Cornelius. She can't take her eyes off of Kratos. You can tell she is devastated by this fight." The three were near the area where the fights would take place.

I supposed Cornelius as head sorcerer was available to tend to a wounded fighter. There went my stomach again. No use asking Cornelius for a cure for that. The only way I would feel better would be to see this day through and end up back on Earth with Jerry safe and sound.

"Yes, the poor girl does not look well." Hera glanced at Zeus. "Couldn't you…"

"The fight goes on." Zeus clapped his hands. "Bring on the first match."

"Gloriana, come here. Take your place beside me." Hera produced a low stool and gestured to it. "I want everyone here to see that *I* favor you." She gave Zeus a raised eyebrow.

"I am honored, Grandmother." I hurried to sit next to her. The fact that she had adjusted my clothes but hadn't forced me to wear a toga hadn't gone unnoticed and several women in the crowd now wore colorful outfits. Obviously I was starting a revolution of sorts.

"Careful, Hera. Next Gloriana will have you trading in your toga for pants and serving yourself since all your handmaidens will be free and leaving us for parts unknown." Zeus flicked a wrist and a dancing girl twirled closer to him. She was almost naked and undulated her hips with a suggestive smile.

Hera sniffed. "There's nothing wrong with progress, Zeus. I am certainly rethinking slavery." She raised a finger and the dancer's sheer scarf suddenly caught fire. A soldier ran forward and doused her with a pitcher of water. The fact that he'd had it handy made me think this had happened before.

Zeus turned his back on us. I leaned closer to my grandmother and spoke quietly.

"Thank you, Grandmother, for taking up the cause of the handmaidens. I know they are very grateful." I shut up when Zeus began giving instructions for the coming fight to two slaves who came forward to stand stoically in front of the thrones. The men wore next to nothing and I saw many women in the crowd looking them over appreciatively. They had muscular bodies and seemed well matched in size and attitude. They glared at each other, clearly eager to get to the fight.

A chalk circle had been marked on the grass and the men were ordered to stay inside the line. These two weren't given any weapons but were to wrestle for a certain number of minutes. A referee would determine the winner. There were other rules for the match but I didn't listen because this time Hera leaned closer and started whispering to me.

"I found out who dared tried to hurt you, Gloriana. With the pillows." She glanced at the elegant crowd which was divided between those who were interested in the fight and those who were hitting the buffet tables and drink trays. "Wait and see. Your grandfather and I plan to make an example of her."

"Her?"

"Yes. Of course it is a woman. A man would have been more direct. Would have attacked you on a path and made sure you were dead." Her lips thinned. I was reminded of how much I resembled her. Just this morning I'd looked almost the same when I was staring into my makeup mirror applying waterproof mascara and thinking about how Jerry might not survive this day and it was ALL MY MOTHER'S FAULT.

"Gloriana, don't frown like that. People will think you aren't having a good time." My mother pulled up a stool on my other side.

"Hebe, I didn't invite you to sit." Hera gestured and my mother was suddenly twenty feet away and looking dazed. "She is out of control. I indulged her too much as a child. I'm very sorry for some of the things she has put you through, Gloriana. This coming fight is just one of them, I understand." She placed a hand on my shoulder. "Please believe me when I say I am doing my best to see that you get everything you want."

"Really, Grandmother? Can you stop Jerry's fight before it starts?"

A roar from the crowd made us both turn toward the field. One of the slaves had the other one face down on the grass, his knees on his back. We heard a crack that made my stomach heave. The one underneath went limp and the man on top jumped to his feet to do a victory lap around the circle, strutting with his arms raised over his head as the crowd cheered.

"Too bad. Guess that one was a fight to the death after all." Zeus glanced at us then went back to watching the field. He smiled and handed out a laurel wreath to the victor as if this were the Olympics or something.

I felt my gorge rise and breathed through my nose, refusing to disgrace my grandmother by throwing up in front of her courtiers.

Of course everyone was looking this way, checking to see how I took this turn of events. Fight to the death. Was Jerry's fight going to end like that?

"Zeus, stop this nonsense. Can't you see that Gloriana is truly distressed?" Hera pinched his arm.

"Woman, you forget yourself." He hissed and glanced at the crowd. "If Gloriana is distressed, it is of her own doing."

"She did not make herself a vampire. That came about because of her mother's neglect." Hera wasn't backing down. "Surely the child has suffered enough. If you must punish someone, let's take care of the one who tried to kill our grandchild."

"I'm all for that, but the next fight *will* happen. You won't interfere with my plans." Zeus showed his perfect white teeth in what could only be called a snarl. He stood.

"Hear me, good people of Olympus. It seems that some of you have forgotten to respect the house of Zeus." He folded his arms across his massive chest, his body language shouting "I mean business."

Everyone on the field, courtiers and slaves, suddenly fell to their knees, heads bowed. You could have heard a bird sing except even those were mute. A nervous slave dropped a carafe of wine and everyone gasped.

"First, let me remind you who belongs to the house of Zeus. My dear wife Hera and her family of course. That includes her sisters, brothers and their children, both inside marriage and out of it. Please let yourselves be known." He nodded and about a dozen people rose and bowed.

"Thank you, Zeus." Hera smiled.

"Then there is my side of the family. My sisters and brothers, along with their children both inside and outside of marriage. Stand, if you please." Another two dozen people stood and bowed. "Beloved family, I honor you." Zeus nodded. "But dearest of all are the children of Hera and myself, both inside and outside of our marriage. This includes their children as well. I shouldn't have to mention our newest member Gloriana is in that esteemed grouping." He looked at me while at least twenty other people stood and bowed.

I got to my feet too, though my knees were weak and I wished I had something to hold onto. Hera smiled and took my hand. I felt her power surge into me and I stood straighter.

"I want to make something perfectly clear. If anyone does harm to a member of my family, you are harming me, your exalted leader. I shouldn't have to remind you that my wrath is to be feared. *Do you understand?*" His roar was probably causing a Cat 5 hurricane in the Gulf of Mexico on Earth.

I would have covered my ears if I hadn't been afraid he'd have mocked me for such weakness. He gazed about the field so I did too. At first I thought no one had moved. Then there was a slight ripple in the sea of white togas.

"Seize her!" Zeus thundered. He pointed when a woman stood and darted as if to run from the crowd.

Her scream made the hairs on my arms stand up. When the soldiers dragged the woman out to the center of the field, I heard several cries of shock and horror. Charis reached out but someone dragged her arm down to her side. Oh, no, it couldn't be.

"Lady Roxana," Zeus said after the woman was thrown to the ground in front of him. She laid still, her face on the grass, eyes closed. "Do you deny you meant harm to my granddaughter Gloriana?"

She didn't answer but I could see her shoulders move. Sobs? Breaths? Was she hyperventilating?

"Answer me!" Zeus snapped, lightning sizzling around her prostrate body.

"Sire!" She screamed when the soldiers dragged her to her feet. "Please. Understand. My husband humiliated me. He brought his bastard here and flaunted her. My daughter sought her out and called her friend. What am I? Nothing! Left to pretend it doesn't matter that I am abandoned while Mars is jaunting about with his mistress." Her eyes were wild when she grabbed a spear from a startled soldier. "I won't have it!" She aimed the weapon and launched it straight at Mars who'd come to stand close to the thrones.

"Dad!" I threw myself toward him, knocking the spear off line and into the dirt where I fell too. The soldiers had Roxana in hand now and shoved the weeping woman back to the ground. Mars helped me up and pulled me into his arms.

"Gloriana, are you all right?" He looked me over. "What were you thinking?"

"She tried to kill you." I was out of breath and turned in time to see the soldiers carrying a struggling Roxana away. "What's going to happen to your wife?"

"The cells, I'm sure, and she's lucky that's all she'll get." Mars looked up at Zeus. "Thank you, sire, for not killing her on the spot."

"She's clearly mad. What would be the point?" Zeus studied me. "Impressive, Gloriana. I hope your man has as much courage as you just showed us."

"Grandfather…"

"Don't ask." He looked back at the field. "I see they're ready to start."

Mars helped me back to my stool. Yes, they were ready. Jerry and Kratos were stripped down to loin cloths. They each had a sword in hand with two knives strapped at their waists. I swallowed, not sure I wasn't going to throw up after all. Grandmother took my hand and squeezed it.

"There's nothing you can do now, child. Let them decide your fate. They both look like fine potential mates."

"But, Grandmother, I love Jerry. He's the only man who will make me truly happy." I heard Zeus begin the instructions again. This time he was firm. This was not to be a fight to the death unless an accident happened. There had already been one of those today and he hoped that wouldn't happen again. Then he nodded and the men began to circle each other. I wanted to close my eyes but didn't dare. If I could *will* Jerry to do well, then that's what I had to do.

Swords clanged together and sparks flew. The men were well matched and the courtiers began shouting. Some actually yelled for Blade. But maybe they'd bet for him to last a certain number of minutes. I saw gold coins exchanging hands. I wanted to scream at them to quit betting on my lover's life. I tried to get up but my grandmother's hand was like a vise, holding me in my seat. I didn't doubt she would freeze me in place if I moved again.

Zeus glanced at me and smiled. "He's putting up a good fight. You should be proud."

I didn't answer him. I'd always been proud of Jerry. Of his strength, his integrity, the way he'd loved me all the years we'd been together, even when I didn't deserve his love. I gasped when I saw a red line appear on his chest. First blood. Kratos had managed it and the crowd went wild. A movement at the edge of the throng caught my eye. Calista was struggling in her father's arms. She clearly wanted to do what I was so desperate to do—run into the circle and stop this madness. I knew just how she felt, especially after Kratos took a chunk out Jerry's thigh. Then Jerry managed to slice open a gash on Kratos' arm. I could swear I heard Calista scream. My own mouth was sealed shut. Grandmother's work, of course.

Jerry's sword flew out of the circle. I covered my mouth, ashamed of the mewling sound of fear I managed to make but also afraid he'd hear me and get distracted. All I could do now was pray. Kratos laughed and threw his sword away as well, earning a cheer from the mob that had drawn closer to the circle, almost touching the chalk line. Of course they were careful not to block Zeus's view. Now Kratos and Jerry had drawn their knives and were moving again, sizing each other up, Jerry would say. Oh, God, but I didn't think I could stand to watch. But of course I couldn't look away.

They lunged, going down in a tangle. Jerry was on top. No, Kratos. They strained against each other and the crowd hushed, intent on the play of muscles as the men seemed almost too well matched, trying to best each other. I glanced at Zeus. Could he call it a draw? He looked at me and shook his head. He wanted a winner.

"Please." I stretched across Grandmother, reaching for my grandfather's fist lying on the arm of his throne.

"No. One of them must win." He stood and stalked toward the circle.

I still couldn't move, of course. Grandmother made sure of that. We watched the men struggle, their faces reddened by the pressure of trying to take each other down. Finally Kratos hooked his leg over Jerry's and flipped him, his knife plunging into Jerry when he landed on top of my man. The crowd roared again and Kratos staggered to his feet. Jerry laid still, bright red blood pooling under his body.

My silent scream had to have reached Zeus but he didn't look back. Jerry! Oh, God. He wasn't moving. Cornelius and Richard ran to his side while Zeus strode into the circle and raised Kratos' hand when he tossed his bloody knife away.

"I declare Kratos the winner of this match."

Kratos swayed on his feet and didn't smile. He looked down at Jerry who hadn't moved and shook his head.

"He was a worthy opponent." Then he dropped to his knees and bowed his head. "Thank you, Lord Zeus."

Cornelius was busy pulling things from a leather bag to staunch the flow of blood from Jerry's wound. It seemed as soon as he covered Jerry's chest with a white bandage, it was soaked through.

Cornelius gestured and two soldiers hurried forward, obviously ready to carry Jerry off the field. Richard shooed one of them away, carefully taking Jerry's head and shoulders himself, a tearful Flo beside him. Zeus stopped them with a look.

"How is he?" Zeus's question was easily heard since the crowd had gone silent. Cornelius just shook his head. Flo touched Jerry's chest.

"He is breathing, Glory." She tried for a smile but failed. Then she followed the men as they took Jerry off the field.

"Gloriana, come here." Zeus stretched out his hand.

I stood and walked to my grandfather's side, surprised that I could finally move. I wanted to run to Jerry but Zeus was compelling me. I couldn't cry, scream or pick up Kratos' bloody knife like I wanted to. If I hadn't been under some kind of spell I might have thrown myself at my own grandfather and taken him to the ground in my grief and rage. Instead I was in a haze, a bubble of unreality that turned me into a puppet being controlled by the master.

"Kratos, you have won the hand of my granddaughter by vanquishing her lover fairly. You will be able to join the house of Zeus when you are married to Gloriana and your children will be tied to our family forever."

Kratos was still on his knees. He raised his head. He was dirty, bloody and yet was more handsome than I'd ever seen him as he looked at me. "Gloriana." He smiled. "Please know that any man would be honored to be your husband." Then he took a breath and stared down at my grandfather's sandals again.

I felt like I should say something but couldn't. I was still in that state of shock or whatever it was that my grandfather had done to me. Kratos put one hand on the ground, like he had to steady himself.

"My lord Zeus." He met my grandfather's gaze. "I am honored by the prize you are offering and I did win this victory fairly against a worthy opponent. But I regret I must refuse your granddaughter's hand in marriage."

The crowd as one leaned in, gasps and whispers silenced when everyone realized my grandfather hadn't immediately burned Kratos to a cinder.

"Is this about the lovely Calista?" Grandmother was suddenly there, her hand on Zeus's preferred throwing arm for lightning bolts.

"Yes, Lady Hera." Kratos met her smile with one of his own, though it was strained. "I am in love with her and her with me. I've realized that it wouldn't be fair to Lady Gloriana to marry her when my heart belongs to another."

"Nonsense." Zeus jerked his hand from Hera's. "I took you for a fighting man, Kratos. Making you mortal has obviously muddled your mind." He waved a hand and Kratos straightened from his slouch. "There. You are a god once more. Surely you don't truly wish to turn down a chance to ally yourself with the house of Zeus. Stand and speak to me, god to god."

Kratos did stand, his shoulders back. It was clear he was a proud man. "Sire, I can think of no greater honor than to be part of your family. But how can I marry your granddaughter when I may have just killed her lover? She must hate me." He turned to me. "I am sorry, Lady Gloriana. I knew the rules of course but Blade and I were well matched. My knife slipped. I wasn't aiming for his heart when I struck him and I hope that I missed it."

I still couldn't speak but the fact that Kratos was willing to give me up… I sent my thoughts to my grandmother and she nodded.

"Zeus, the man has made a decent choice here. Calista's father is a well-placed sorcerer and it is a fine match. Gloriana needs to see to Blade's condition and you want her gone anyway. If she marries Kratos, you will either condemn this fine god to an Earthly life he doesn't deserve or she'll be stuck here, getting involved in causes that make you unhappy. Do I need to remind you what they are?" Hera looked around and tapped her foot. "Where is Dionysus? Are Zeus and I to provide the entertainment today?" She glanced around at the avid listeners and the courtiers began to back away from the circle. "Dionysus! To me now! This party is boring me. Where is the music? The dancing? And my wine glass has been empty since I got here."

"So sorry, my dear." Dionysus hurried forward with a tray of full glasses and delicacies. He gestured and music filled the air. A troop of acrobats tumbled across the grass and the circle disappeared. He clapped his hands. "People, what are you staring at? Eat, drink and be merry. Didn't someone say that once?" Excited chatter suddenly filled the air and birds started singing.

"You have made a good point, Hera." Zeus took a glass of red wine. "You always do think ahead." He looked up and saw a woman hovering just feet away. "Calista, come here, child, and bring your father."

Calista came running to Kratos and wept over his wounds. "You are so hurt."

"No, it is nothing. I have had worse wounds out hunting for wild boar." He pulled her into his arms. "Sire, I remain your faithful servant, always. Whatever you decide, I will do. I hope you know I mean no disrespect. I will remain loyal to the house of Zeus forever."

"Yes, you have proven yourself to me time and time again." Zeus spoke to Calista's father. When he was sure the sorcerer approved of the match with Kratos, he turned to me. "Enough. Your frantic thoughts are getting on my nerves, Gloriana. I know you are worried about your lover and will hold you no longer." He shook his head. "Yes, the wound did look grave but Cornelius can work wonders, you know. Go, see to your man. If he is dead, I am sorry. Take him or his body home with you. And be sure to drag your friends there with you as well. All of you need to go back to Earth immediately and stay there."

"Yes, Grandfather." I would have run off the field but he hadn't released me yet.

He smiled. "When your grandmother wants you, you may come back, but not for a while. You have caused me nothing but trouble. But that is because you are so like me, I think. With a strong will and spirit." He kissed my forehead. "Call me if you need anything, Gloriana. And never forget that you are from the house of Zeus. If anyone tries to hurt you, I will end them."

"Thank you, Grandfather." Finally I could move. Even though I was desperate to check on Jerry, I paused long enough to hug Grandmother then even dared hug Zeus. He didn't seem to mind it. "Kratos, thank you too for choosing love. Calista, have a happy life."

That done, I turned to her father. "Where would I find Cornelius and Jerry?"

He took my hand and nodded gravely. "Hold on and I'll take you there." In a blink we were teleporting. I had no idea where we were going and I didn't care as long as Jerry was at the end of the journey and he was alive.

THIRTEEN

We landed in what must have been Cornelius's rooms. There was a table with the kind of equipment I'd seen at Waldo's and various bottles containing elixirs. But I wasn't interested in that. I could only focus on Jerry. He lay on a wide bed. His eyes were closed and he wasn't moving. Richard and Flo hovered nearby while Cornelius listened to Jerry's heart with what looked like a modern stethoscope.

"I think that's the first thing from this century I've seen you use." My voice was raspy with suppressed tears. "He's alive?"

"Barely. Your father healed his wounds but he's lost a lot of blood. He's in a coma." Cornelius stepped back so I could run to Jerry's side.

I picked up my lover's limp hand and held onto it. "Jerry, can you hear me? Wake up. I'm not marrying Kratos and we can go home now."

"That's wonderful, *amica*!" Flo clung to Richard. "Once he's there we can help Jeremiah *our* way. Isn't that right, Ricardo?"

"That depends." Richard looked over his shoulder. "Mars, how do we get home and what are we going to be like when we get there? Will we be vampire again?"

My father must have been standing in the shadows. I'd been so intent on Jerry I hadn't even noticed him.

"Dad! You healed his wounds. Thank you!" I threw myself into Mars' arms and cried. "Answer Richard. I have to get Jerry back. All the way back."

"You really want to be a vampire again? Even you, Gloriana?" Mars held me away from him and stared into my eyes. "Surely you realize that's not any way to live."

"It's the only way for us to save Jerry." I turned and laid my hand on Jerry's chest. His heart was beating but barely. You didn't have to be a goddess to realize that. He was so pale, so still, his breathing shallow.

"He needs blood, Lord Mars." Cornelius stood beside me now. "I can't give it to him here. We are ill equipped. I have told Zeus time and time again that we should upgrade but he is stubborn about certain alterations to Olympus. He clings to the old ways and won't allow me to materialize what I need. It would be my death if I went against his wishes." The sorcerer didn't need to add that he wasn't about to risk his life for Jerry.

I could snap on clothes but had no idea how to make anything else magically appear. Certainly not medical supplies. I leaned over Jerry. If I could have breathed life into him, I would have.

"Dad, isn't there anything else you can do? You brought Jerry back to life before, I saw you do it." I stood, ready to beg if it would do any good.

"He's not dead, Gloriana. And I am grateful for that." Mars put his arm around me. "I did what I could, but this deep sleep of his is because he *does* need blood. Giving him that is beyond my capability."

"But not mine. When we are vampire, we give and take blood all the time. Send us home, Dad. Restore us like Flo said and we can give him our ancient blood. It will make him whole again in no time." I leaned against him, my arm tight around him. "Please. I know you and Mother don't approve of my lifestyle but I've had centuries to get used to being a vampire."

"Used to never seeing daylight again?" Of course my mother had to make an appearance. "Drinking blood instead of your favorite chocolate or eating the food you love?" She stepped back when I whirled, my fingers held out like claws.

"You have nothing to say to me, Mother, that I want to hear." I strode toward her. "Jerry wouldn't be in this fix if you hadn't meddled in my life, dragged me up here against my will. I told you before that I don't want to see or speak to you again. I meant it."

"Gloriana, she is your mother. Treat her with respect." Mars said it quietly and I couldn't have been more surprised than if he'd sprouted horns.

"What?" That was all I could say.

"I know she is headstrong and sometimes acts without thinking things through, but Hebe loves you and wants only the best for you." Mars took my mother in his arms. "She needs to know you will give her a chance to earn your forgiveness and love."

"Never. I am done with her." I ran back to Jerry's side and held my hand over his heart. Was it still beating? I couldn't tell. "We are wasting time. Please take us back to Earth, Dad. I can almost feel Jerry's life slipping away."

"You will go back as you wish on one condition." He studied me solemnly and I braced myself. I knew I wasn't going to like this.

"What condition?" I froze when I sensed a change in Jerry under my fingertips. "Cornelius! Do something!"

"My lord, he has given up life again." Cornelius checked Jerry from the other side of the bed.

Mars stalked over and laid his hand on Jerry's heart, over my own. "I can bring him back once, even twice, Gloriana. Then it won't work again. This is number two." He nodded and Jerry jerked, breathing again. I'd felt the jolt go through my hand and stared down at my lover. He was still unconscious and barely breathing. No significant improvement but at least he lived again.

"Tell me! What do you want me to do so that we can take him home and give him blood?" I was desperate and grabbed my father's toga, about to shake him when I realized that probably wouldn't be smart when I needed his help.

"You will give your mother a chance to win your love again. Speak to her. Include her in your wedding if Blade makes it through this crisis and you actually have one. I want your promise, Gloriana." Mars was clearly reading my mind so I knew this was going to have to happen if I made this bargain. I glanced at my mother. A bargain with the devil.

"Yes, I'll do it. She can buy her damned mother of the bride dress. Whatever she wants. Come to my shop and make a nuisance of herself. I don't care." I choked on a sob. "Just please, please, take us home, Mars. Make us all vampires, as we were when we left Earth.

And hurry!" I dropped to my knees and clasped his sturdy legs.

Flo and Richard stared at me. Cornelius took Jerry's pulse then lifted an eyelid and shook his head. I took some comfort in the fact that my mother had seemed as surprised by Mars' request as I was. At least this wasn't one of her manipulations. Damn, that meant he really did love her, didn't he? I couldn't believe she'd inspired such devotion from a worthy man.

That was the last thing I knew before I landed in my apartment. Mars had taken me literally. Jerry was lying on our new king-sized bed, pale and still in a coma. Flo and Richard staggered up from the other side, holding on to each other. Flo's red dress was huge on her because she was back to her usual size six. Richard still wore his warrior's toga, the correct dress as Jerry's second.

I looked down and realized I'd burst out of my black suit. Buttons had popped open, the bra was strangling me and my skirt's seams had ripped down each side. Did I care? Not at all. I inhaled and all the scents I'd missed as a mortal goddess came flooding in, some of them not so great. Actually, every one of my senses came alive. I smelled Jerry's blood, heard his barely beating heart and even realized the air conditioning was purring in the background. There was traffic outside the window below us on Sixth Street. Texas, no matter the season, was probably hot and the street busy. Of course I had no idea how long we'd been gone, the date or time.

I reached up to check my mouth and Flo sighed. "I see your fangs, *amica*. Now let's get to work."

"Yes." I held my hand out to Richard. "I know what to do. Will you help me?"

"Of course if you're sure." He looked grim.

"Yes, I've done it before. Once when Ray was out of it from alcohol poisoning. But…" I couldn't speak for a moment. This was *Jerry* so close to death.

"Just bite into your wrist, Gloriana. Let's hope the smell of your blood will make his instincts kick in. If not, we'll force feed him. Trickle it down his throat." He gently raised Jerry's head. "Come on, you can do it." He smiled to encourage me. "My blood is older than yours but I think at first he'd respond better to yours, don't you?"

"Yes, sure." I shook my head to clear the cobwebs or shock or whatever my problem was then wiped away a tear. It was easy to bite into my own wrist. The pain was nothing. As soon as the blood welled up, I waved it under Jerry's nose. No reaction. Richard and I exchanged glances. We both realized Jerry's heart was slowing even more. "Pry open his mouth."

"Here, *amica.* You are shivering." Flo set a robe over my shoulders. "What can I do?"

"Get her some synthetic blood out of the fridge, darling. I'm sure they have some. She'll need it after she's done here. Bring a sharp knife too. In case we have to cut a bigger vein." Richard pushed his fingers into Jerry's mouth and forced it open. "All right, Gloriana. Squeeze your wrist to increase the blood flow then rub some on his lips and tongue. If he doesn't start drinking soon, we'll all cut ourselves and bleed into a glass then pour it into him."

"Oh, God, this has to work." I looked up when Richard started to mumble. "Don't you dare say some kind of last rites over him!" Richard had once been a priest.

"I wasn't, I wouldn't." He frowned and shook his head. "Am I allowed to at least say a prayer for this to work?"

"Sure. Sorry. I'm just so--" I sobbed, completely losing it. Flo ran in and put her arms around me. Then I felt a sharp stab when Jerry's fangs came down on my wrist. "Wait! He's responding. He just bit me!"

"*Dio sia Iodato*!" Flo crossed herself. "Ricardo's prayer has been answered."

"He's drinking. I can feel the pull." I bowed my head, thanking God myself. Flo shoved a bottle of synthetic blood into my free hand and I took a swallow. When Jerry swallowed feebly too, I wanted to sob again.

No, I had to stay calm. So I took a moment to look around my bedroom, the one Jerry had decorated to please me. Strange. I was back where I belonged and it was as if I'd never left. Did I miss my sweet hot chocolate? Maybe. But the surge of energy from the A-Negative synthetic was welcome. I wondered how much we had left in the kitchen…

"Oh, no! I promised I'd bring Alesha down here with me."

"Your handmaiden?" Flo squeezed my shoulders. "How will that work here, Glory? She is a slave, isn't she? And used to Olympus."

"I, I own her." I saw Jerry's cheeks were beginning to get color and handed Flo my empty bottle to stroke his dear face. He had to come back to me. I didn't want to stay here in this lavish apartment without him.

"You own a slave?" Richard had pulled a chair up to the other side of the bed. "That's not even legal here."

"I intend to set her free of course." I brushed Jerry's hair back from his face. He was filthy from rolling around in the dirt, fighting. I should clean him up. But he was still drinking, though not very fast and his pull on my vein was weak.

"The handmaiden will understand." Flo stood behind me. "We were busy when we left. You were worried about Jeremiah."

I sighed. "I sure don't want to leave Alesha there to serve someone else. Someone who might not be kind to her."

"Someone like me, Gloriana?" My mother appeared at the foot of the bed. "I know you think I'm horrible. But I'm working on it." She stepped aside with a gesture. "See? I brought you your little handmaiden. She can help you clean up this place and take care of your man." A startled Alesha appeared next to her.

"Mistress!" Alesha stared around the room then shrieked when she focused on the bed. "It is true! Mr. Blade is gravely wounded."

"And, don't look now, you nitwit, but he's biting our dear Gloriana and sucking her blood." Mother smiled. "Just wait until you find out just what you've been dying to see here on Earth, handmaiden." She laughed. "I won't overstay my welcome. Oh, yes, Daughter, I'm trying." She vanished.

"Mistress." Alesha couldn't look away from my wrist at Jerry's mouth. "He *is* biting you." She stared at Richard, then Flo. "Why aren't you helping her?"

"We're all helping Mr. Blade, Alesha, giving him blood. He lost so much on the field that he almost died." I glanced at Richard. "Why isn't he waking up?"

"I don't know, but you need to let him go. Or I guess it's the other way around. He's taken enough blood for now and you're looking pale, Gloriana." Richard reached into Jerry's mouth and with an effort pried his fangs out of my wrist. "Let's watch him for a while. Give the blood a chance to take effect. If he doesn't rouse soon, I'll give him some of mine."

I sat back on the bed, suddenly dizzy. Alesha hurried to my side. "I would bring you a wet cloth, Mistress, to wipe away the blood from your wrist, if you would show me where to fetch one. Then, with your permission, I would like to help clean Mr. Blade. He still lies in the dirt he got from the fight with Kratos. I heard it was a terrible battle."

"Yes, it was. We are lucky he wasn't killed right there." Flo took charge and grabbed Alesha's arm. "Now I'll show you where to get water and a cloth." She steered her to the door. "Good for you, Alesha. No questions, but eager to serve Glory. I'm going to like having you here, I think."

"Thank you, Mrs. Mainwaring." Alesha gave me one last look then went docilely with Flo.

"See here. That door leads to one bathroom and there's another powder room next to the front door. I'll show you the kitchen too, but you won't have to cook for these two. They only drink a special brew. It's in bottles in the refrigerator." Flo looked over her shoulder and winked. "I'm sure Jeremiah will wake up any minute. My Ricardo's prayers are *molto potente*."

I stared after them, too tired to say anything. It was a familiar feeling, as if sunrise was pulling at me. I glanced at the clock next to the bed. Five-thirty. I got up and jerked the curtain back on the window behind the bed. Yes, the sky was just beginning to lighten. No wonder Jerry wasn't waking up.

"You and Flo had better stay in the guest room, Richard. I'd say we're about ten minutes from the sun coming up." I yawned and looked down. "Hopefully at sunset Jerry will wake up good as new."

"He looks better anyway." Richard caught Flo coming back in the door. "Come, my love. We have a few minutes before we fall dead at sunrise. You just gave Alesha the tour. Now show me to the guest room."

"No time for a shower then, Ricardo?" Flo frowned then walked over and gave me a hug. "He hasn't waked up yet?"

"No." I took the wet cloth from Alesha who had followed Flo. She'd also filled a glass bowl with warm water. "Good night, both of you. Thank you for everything. Keep those prayers coming, Richard. Flo's right. Yours are powerful." I sat next to Jerry and began to tenderly clean off his face.

"I am feeling strange, you know?" Flo stopped next to Richard at the door. "I admit I liked being awake during the day for a change when we were in Olympus. Now I can't control myself. I am crashing." She frowned at Alesha. "Listen to me, handmaiden. You are not to bother us in our bedroom until the sun sets. Do you hear me?"

"Yes, Mrs. Mainwaring." Alesha even curtsied. I think she was a little afraid of Flo.

"Don't worry, Glory. I explained to our new helper what we are. She has seen plenty of unusual things in Olympus so vampires? Yes, we are new to her, but she will be free soon and can run for her life if she wants to." Flo showed her fangs as a tease and I saw Alesha stiffen. "Oh, really, girl. I told you. We will not hurt you. No one in this room anyway. And we will make sure none of our friends touch you either. Am I right, Glory?"

"Yes, of course." I realized Flo was actually freaking out a little, chattering nonstop and tossing her hair like she was fine. But I could see her hands shaking and one foot tapping the floor almost like a nervous tic. I stopped cleaning off Jerry's chest to look at her. "You're safe here too, pal. Jerry has a state-of-the-art security system." I smiled when Richard put his arm around her and whispered comforting words in his wife's ears. "Richard, maybe you could stop by the front door and make sure it's armed before you 'crash'."

"Consider it done." He pulled Flo out of the room. "Come on, darling. I've got you."

"But you will be dead too, Ricardo." Flo sagged against him.

"And we've survived centuries that way. Relax, my love. This apartment is just like our home. Blade used the same security company I did. No one's going to bother us while we sleep." He kissed her cheek and looked back at me over her shoulder. "Good night, Gloriana."

I nodded and went back to taking care of Jerry. Mars really had healed his knife wound and there wasn't even a scar. Jer was breathing easier now and I was optimistic as I wrung out the cloth and finished washing him down to his loin cloth. When I looked up, I saw that Alesha stood waiting by the door.

"He seems to be sleeping now, mistress." She hurried over to take the basin when I dropped the dirty cloth into the water and set it on the nightstand.

"Yes. I guess Flo explained that at sunrise we're as good as dead. In a few minutes I'll lie down next to Jerry and we'll both be out of it until sunset." I stood and pulled off my ruined jacket.

"You look different here." Alesha helped me out of my skirt and underwear and I slipped on the robe Flo had brought me. I'd gotten used to Alesha taking care of me in Olympus and wasn't shy around her anymore. She had a way of being nonjudgmental that worked for me.

"Yes, back to my bloated self." I smiled. "Oh. Where will you sleep?" I yawned, almost ready to collapse.

"I saw a comfortable couch in one of the rooms, mistress. And Mrs. Mainwaring showed me where the linens are kept. I will be fine." Alesha gathered up my ruined clothes.

"We'll go shopping for clothes for you as soon as," I took a breath and looked down at Jerry, "well, as soon as I'm sure Jerry will be okay. You can't go around in that outfit here."

"I have no wish to embarrass you, mistress." Alesha looked down at her simple shift and sandals. She could have come straight from a rehearsal for a Biblical play.

I didn't bother to explain. "Food. Are you hungry? Don't drink that red stuff in the bottles. That's our synthetic blood. I have some snacks in the pantry for my shape-shifter friends. Check the kitchen cabinets." I sank down on the bed, too exhausted to say more.

"I will manage, Lady Gloriana. I can see you are tired. Rest now." Alesha pulled back the covers and helped me slip beneath them. Then she walked around and made sure Jerry was covered as well. I didn't have the strength to explain that vampires didn't care whether we were hot or cold when we died at sunrise. I opened my mouth to thank her when it was lights out for me.

I woke to the sound of the television. It probably wasn't that loud, but I couldn't believe Alesha would just turn it on and enjoy the run of the place that way. I rolled over to look at Jerry first. His eyes were still closed and I ran my hand over his bare chest, hoping he'd wake at my touch. No such luck. He was breathing easily though and I could hear his heart beating, not that it was easy over that damned TV.

I got up, cinched my robe and opened the bedroom door. The noise was coming from Jerry's man cave. She'd obviously taken it over and the big screen TV there with the surround sound. No wonder I could hear it in my bedroom with both doors shut. I opened the door to the small room with the comfortable leather sofa and then stopped to take in the sight.

Mars sat in the recliner that had become Jerry's favorite chair and Charis sprawled on the couch. She was the first to notice me and sat up quickly.

"Uh, Father, she's awake." Charis gave me a finger wave. "Hi, Glory."

Mars hit the mute button on the remote. "Good evening, Gloriana. I'd forgotten you sleep the damned day away."

"Yes, it's a vampire thing." Apparently a state-of-the-art security system didn't work on visitors from Olympus. That thought made me frown until I realized Charis looked concerned. Did she think I was going to kick them out? Tempting. The last thing I needed right now was company.

I finally found a smile for Charis. "I see you got your trip to Earth. How are you doing, Sis?" I didn't add, *"Since your mother was dragged screaming off to the cells for the insane."*

"I had to get out of there, Glory. Everyone was talking about my family and the scene Mother made." Tears welled in her eyes and she suddenly threw herself at me. "Please tell me I can stay. Until the wedding at least. You did say I could be a bridesmaid, didn't you?"

Mars pried her off of me. "Charis, we don't even know if there's to be a wedding yet. The groom was gravely wounded. Remember? How *is* Blade?"

"I'm sorry, Glory. Of course. How is he?" Charis wiped her eyes on her sleeve. She wore a blue sweater and skinny jeans and looked pretty much like a typical teenager today. She was younger than I'd realized. Good to know since she was way too fond of dirty martinis. I was glad to have a sister and was happy for a chance to get to know her better. But the timing sucked.

"He's still not awake. I need to check on him. Give me a few minutes? And I need a shower. Clothes." I gestured at the TV. "I see you made yourselves at home."

"We're watching the best show. It's about brides, picking wedding dresses." Charis seemed oblivious to the fact that my groom was in a coma.

I tried not to show my aggravation but seriously? "Okay, then. Where's Alesha?"

"I'm here, mistress." She appeared behind me with a tray. "This is what I could find for your guests." Her tray was loaded with bowls of Cheetos and Twinkies. They were Rafe's favorite snacks that I kept for my shape-shifter friend. "I hope they are adequate."

"You don't even know where the grocery store is yet, so I guess they'll have to be." I turned to my father. "We need to talk. But later. I'll go get dressed and see to Jerry. Alesha, you just take care of our guests. Which it looks like you're handling perfectly." I patted her shoulder. "Don't worry. I'm used to doing without help here anyway."

"If you're sure, mistress. I'm here to serve you of course." Alesha set the tray on the coffee table and Charis fell on the Cheetos with delight. She also grabbed a bottle of water I hadn't realized I had stocked.

"Call me Glory, Alesha. Down here mistress and Lady Gloriana will sound strange to most people you meet." I saw her frown. "You'll get the hang of it." I smiled and headed back to the bedroom. Richard was there, checking Jerry's vital signs. I think Richard had been a doctor once in his long, long past. He certainly seemed to know what he was doing when he dropped Jerry's wrist and nodded.

"I have a feeling he's going to wake up soon. His pulse is strong. Go ahead and get dressed. I plan to give him some of my blood while you do." Richard's hair was wet and he'd obviously showered. He had on a shirt and pants that must belong to Jerry. Guess he'd raided Jerry's closet which was in the guest room. I'd taken over all of the generous closet space in the master bedroom. Jerry had insisted. The reminder of how thoughtful he'd been made me tear up but I wouldn't allow myself to cry again.

"He's really better? I thought he looked like it, but was afraid it was wishful thinking." I sat on the bed next to Jerry and pried open his mouth. Richard used the knife Flo had brought in the night before and cut his wrist then slid it inside Jerry's lips.

"Good. His fangs came down right away this time." Richard smiled. "An excellent sign, I'd say." He nodded toward the bathroom. "Go on, you'll feel better once you've showered. Florence is making use of your guest bath so I don't expect her out for another half hour."

"I'm sure you're right. I wish I had something for her to wear." I glanced at my bedside table. Where was my cell phone? Where was Jerry's? We'd obviously need new ones. But we had a land line, Jerry had insisted on it for the high speed Internet. So I picked up the phone and called my shop.

"Vintage Vamp's Emporium, best vintage clothing store in Austin, Lacy speaking. How may I help you?"

"Lacy, it's Glory."

"Oh, my God! Where have you been? Where are you now?" She burst into noisy tears. "Sorry. But we've been so worried."

"I know. If I could have contacted you, I would have." I really felt bad about that. It was my shop and I'd left people in charge who I didn't pay nearly enough. I needed to get down there and see what was happening.

"Are you all right?" Lacy had calmed down.

"Sort of. Jerry's been hurt and I'm taking care of him. But that's not why I called."

"What can I do? Anything. Just lay it on me." Lacy called to someone and I could hear excited chatter. "You have no idea how frantic we've been, Glory."

"What's the date, anyway? How long have I been gone?"

"Months! It's October 15, girl. Don't you know? Were you hit on the head? A prisoner? Oh, God! I knew it had to be something bad for you not to reach out to us." Lacy's voice went shaky again.

That long. I'd been gone almost a year. Ten months anyway. I really, really had a bone to pick with my mother.

"Are you there? What do you need?"

"Something for Flo to wear. She's here in my apartment with me and needs an outfit in a size six to wear home. We arrived in the middle of the night last night and her clothes were ruined. You know nothing of mine will fit her. Can you pick out something cute and have someone bring it up? Quickly?"

"Arrived from where?" Lacy wasn't the kind of person to let little details slip past her. Of course her boss disappearing wasn't exactly a little detail.

"It's a long story. I'll catch you up later. Promise." But would I? This goddess thing wasn't going to play well among most paranormals. Lacy was a proud were-cat and wouldn't like the news of my Zeus connections and that I had the powers to go with it. And who would blame her if she was skeptical about tales of Olympus? I'd had to see it to believe it myself.

"So, about those clothes, Lacy."

"Sure. On it. I'll bring them myself." Lacy started issuing orders to someone with her. "And, Glory? I hope Jerry is okay. I'll say prayers for him. We all will. Are you sure you're all right?"

"Yes, I'm fine. Just worried sick about him, you know?"

"Yes, I do." She thanked someone. "Got an outfit. I'm on my way up now."

"That was nice of you, Glory. You know Flo didn't want to put on that big dress again. Bad memories, she said." Richard was patiently sitting beside Jerry on the bed, his wrist in Jerry's mouth.

"It's the least I can do for my best friend. When I think of how you two came up there to help…" My voice quavered.

"We both love you, Gloriana." Richard held out his extra hand. "Would go through hell for either one of you."

"I think you just did." I squeezed his fingers. "I love you too. Thanks for being Jerry's friend and mine." I studied Jerry's face, so still. "How's he doing?"

"He's drinking strongly. I'm going to pull him off soon." Richard tilted his head toward the door. "There's the doorbell. I wonder if Alesha will answer it. She's dressed a little strangely for a housekeeper."

"True. I'd better go." I gave Richard's hand one more squeeze then headed to the living room. Sure enough, Alesha had shown Lacy in and was taking some skinny jeans and a sweater from her arms.

"Mistress, uh, Glory, I will take these to Mrs. Mainwaring." Alesha smiled and hurried toward the guest room.

"Wow, who was that?" Lacy asked before she threw herself into my arms. "I'm so glad to see you, girlfriend."

"My housekeeper." I hugged her and realized she had changed in a big way. "Um, glad to see you too. Is this a baby bump I'm feeling?"

"Yes." She grinned and twirled around in front of me. "Can you believe it? Rafe and I are having a baby." She got serious. "I hope you're okay with that. I know you two are close."

"Close. Yes, really good friends. I'm happy if you two are." I read her mind. She was happy but worried about her family and his. Smart. Were-cats and shape-shifters mating wasn't accepted by either clan.

"We have some issues to work out but we love each other. That's the important thing." Lacy paced in front of me. "How's Jerry? Is it life-threatening?"

"He's getting better. He's in a coma but we expect him to wake up any minute. Keep your fingers crossed and your prayers going." I could hear the TV blasting again. "I have company on top of everything else. I'll tell you all about it when I come down to the shop. As soon as Jerry wakes up, I promise."

"I'll hold you to that." Lacy hugged me again. "There have been changes. I had to hire someone new. I hope you like her. She's a shifter. Rafe knew her from back in the day." She made a face. "Pretty sure they hooked up but what are you gonna do? We were desperate for help and she fit in."

"If you're okay with her, I trust your judgment, Lacy." I was anxious to get back to Jerry and was afraid it showed.

Lacy nodded. "Thanks. She can be a little rough, but customers get her. Kira is steady so far. That's what we need, especially if I take time off when the baby comes."

"Yes, you'll have to, won't you?" I'd taken her for granted. That had to stop. "Thank you! For holding things together at the shop. I am so lucky to have you. Don't think I don't realize that. I do."

"I'll let you get back to Jerry." Lacy sniffed. "I know if Rafe was hurt… Well, hang in there, boss." She hugged me again and headed for the door.

"I'm trying. See you soon." I shut the door on her and leaned against it.

"Glory! He's waking up." Richard yelled from the bedroom.

I ran to see what was happening. It was true. Jerry was tossing and turning. Muttering in his sleep. A nightmare? When I tried to take him in my arms, he lashed out. Richard and I each grabbed one of his hands and held him down.

"Jerry, you're home and you're safe. It's Glory. Wake up, love. Wake up and talk to me." I kept talking, trying to penetrate whatever dream world had him locked away. He finally quieted and lay still.

"Glory?" He opened his eyes. "Where are we?"

"Safe. Home. Away from Olympus." I scooted next to him and touched his cheek.

"Thank God." He closed his eyes again.

"Please don't go back to sleep." I laid my head on his bare chest. At least I could hear his heart beating strongly.

"Let him rest, Gloriana. It's a healing sleep." Richard walked to the door. "I'm going to check on Florence. She's having a hard time getting used to Earth again. I'm surprised at that. My strong Italian woman is showing me a vulnerable side." He smiled. "It just makes me love her more."

"Yes, take care of her, Richard. Flo acts tough, but she needs you." I couldn't let go. "Just like I need Jerry."

"He's on the mend. I'll be back in a few minutes to check. Are you all right?" Richard leaned against the door frame. He probably needed blood after giving Jerry so much.

"Sure. Why wouldn't I be? It's Jerry I'm worried about." I sighed and closed my eyes when I heard the door shut. Why wouldn't I be? Because Jerry should be blaming me for everything that had happened, starting with his trip to Olympus. Then there was being mortally wounded. Not to mention all his suffering in the cells and the humiliation of finding out that his skills weren't good enough to win one of the most important fights of his life. I couldn't stop the tears that trickled down my cheeks to fall on his skin.

"What's this?" His hand landed on my hair. "Crying with joy, I hope. I seemed to have lived after all."

"Jerry!" I sat up and saw he'd opened his eyes again. "How are you feeling?"

"Like I've been dragged behind a running horse over a mountain or two." He took my hand. "This is our bedroom. Finally."

"Yes, Mars got us home. And we're vampire again."

"Everything back to normal."

"I hope so." I was almost afraid to ask. But, being me, I had to know. "Do you still want to marry me?"

"After what I went through to have you how can you ask that?" He looked away. "But I lost the fight. Kratos won you fairly."

"He chose someone else." I laid my hand over Jerry's heart, just to check. It beat strongly.

"You can't be serious." Jerry covered my hand.

"Oh, yes. He risked Zeus's wrath to be with the woman he loves. Sound familiar?" I smiled, pretty sure we were going to be all right.

"I knew he was a brave man. Didn't know he was crazy. Did he live?"

"Yes. My grandmother talked some sense into Zeus. Seems my grandfather was tired of my interference in certain matters anyway. You know I'm anti-slavery. And big on the rights of the handmaidens."

"Yes, those are just two of the things I love about you." Jerry smiled. "Guess Zeus wasn't a fan."

"No, he wanted me gone anyway. If I married Kratos I would have been a constant thorn in his side. Now I'm safely home and will only have to go up there once in a while to see Grandmother. Hopefully it will be once a century." I leaned down to kiss Jerry. "I love you. I never saw such bravery as when you fought Kratos for me."

"I lost."

"I think he cheated." I smiled against his lips. "You are much more the man than he is. Put him on Earth on your turf and he wouldn't have lasted five minutes."

"You are very loyal, Gloriana." He pulled me down to kiss me deeply and I realized he was well down the road to recovery. I finally pushed him away.

"Jerry, you need rest and I need a shower. Stay here. Sleep some more. No nonsense now." I said it sternly. I meant it. Of course he followed me into the bathroom anyway. Vampires have such miraculous abilities to recover. I have a feeling Richard knocked on our bedroom door a few minutes later but realized he wasn't needed. Not at all.

FOURTEEN

"Good news. Jerry's awake and the wedding is on." When I walked into Jerry's man cave, I knew I probably still had the glow of a woman who had been well-loved. Did I care? Not at all.

Mars looked me over but didn't say anything. Charis jumped up and hugged me.

"Does that mean I can be your Maid of Honor?" She pulled me down to the leather couch. "I have some ideas about the dresses. Flo will be the Matron of Honor, won't she?"

"Slow down, Charis." I laughed, still giddy at the thought of my man even now talking to Richard about wedding plans. "I think Jerry should have time to recover first."

"Yes, of course." Charis nodded to Mars. "Find that show on the recorder, Father, and let Glory see it. We need to take her dress shopping."

"I have a dress, Charis. It's in my closet."

"Indulge the girl, Gloriana." Mars clicked the remote. "I've learned it is the father of the bride's responsibility to pay for the wedding. Whatever dress you bought on your budget surely won't compare to these."

I stared at the TV screen and realized immediately what show my sister had found. It was set in a high-end bridal boutique. Brides and their friends, with their mothers too, tried on a variety of dresses, each costing thousands of dollars. Then, when they found the right one, they said, "Yes!" Every once in a while, they didn't pick anything but usually the choice was a gorgeous confection of lace and satin that made my mouth water. Dad was right. My off-the-rack choice which had been on sale didn't compare.

"Glory, what is going on here?" Flo was at the door and had her hands on her hips. "Are you changing your wedding plans? Without me?"

"I haven't agreed to anything, Flo." I patted the seat next to me. "Look. It's that program. The one you tried to get me to watch before we went dress shopping."

"You refused to even consider it." Flo flounced across the room and sat. "You already picked a red dress. It looks good on you."

"I've offered to pay for a new one." Mars smiled like he was anxious to indulge me. I couldn't say a thing. "No budget. If you girls want to fly to New York, I'll take care of everything. What do you say?"

"Hold it." Of course this was like a dream come true. Or would be if the very mention of New York City didn't make my stomach churn. "I can't just take off again. I have a shop to run. I've neglected it for way too long." Yes, that was a good, legitimate excuse. I really wasn't *afraid* to go back to New York. No, I couldn't be.

"Surely another week or so won't make a difference." Mars frowned. "And your mother is anxious to help you with this."

"Oh, now I see where this is going." I stood. "Payback for getting us home. How much are you going to make me suffer for getting Jerry back here?"

"Glory, calm down. Since when is dress shopping suffering?" Flo jerked on my pants until I was down on the couch again. "Your father is trying to make you happy. So we have to take Hebe along. She's trying to win your favor now. Remember? So she should be on her best behavior."

"Great. How lucky can we get?" I couldn't imagine my mother on her best behavior. That would last about five seconds. New York and my mother doing her level best to drive me crazy. Could this get any worse?

"Glory, Father's willing to shell out big bucks for bridesmaids' dresses too. Flo and I can pick out whatever we want." Charis and Flo smiled at each other. Both of them were tiny, though Flo was the smaller of the two. I really didn't want to think about following them down the aisle with me in white, a color I never wore because it made me look like a snowball.

The program was still going, but on mute, as we debated the issue. I didn't have time for this. Flo thought I should get my priorities straight. I knew it could take months to get the right dress ordered and into the store. Flo pointed out that they already had some in stock. In *my* size? Charis admitted she'd done research on the Internet, her new favorite toy once her father had explained it. She was sure she could find the right dress in the right size once I picked it out.

Why was I arguing? Because I hadn't been back to New York City in decades and there was a reason why. I had a history there but with gaping holes in my memory of that time. My boyfriend back then had somehow managed to erase my memories. How? I had no idea. But I did remember how helpless I'd been back then, refusing to use my powers and letting Greg Kaplan run all over me. Yeah, the Glory years in the Big Apple hadn't been good ones.

"Glory, are you even listening to us? We could have fun in New York. A girls' only road trip, *amica*. You should be all over this." Flo was looking at me strangely.

I was beginning to feel outnumbered and bullied when Jerry appeared in the doorway. He was dressed in jeans and a white dress shirt and had never looked so good to me.

"What the hell is going on here?" He held out his hand and I ran to him. "Glory, you look like you're about to cry or hit someone."

"Wedding plans. I guess I'm afraid we'll never get to the altar, Jer." I wrapped my arms around him.

"We will. I'll see to it. Remember, we had it all figured out before. Richard and I were just discussing it. But that booking fell through since you disappeared." He glanced at Mars. "Now I find out from Richard that we are expected to be civil to your mother. Not sure I can do that. Considering how she interfered before."

"Gloriana made a promise." Mars stood and faced us.

"But *I* didn't." Jerry didn't back down. "As far as I'm concerned, this wedding can be anywhere anytime. But I don't want Hebe near it."

"I did promise, Jer." I rubbed his back, trying to calm him. I still couldn't believe he was standing here, strong and whole, himself again. "It was necessary to get you home, love. She has to come to the wedding and be part of the festivities."

"Damn it, Gloriana, she almost got me killed. You wouldn't have had to bargain for my life if it wasn't for her interference in our lives in the first place." He pulled away from me. "I have work to do. Make whatever plans you wish. But I am telling you now, Gloriana, that if she is there, I won't be." He turned on his heel and strode away. I heard the front door slam and sagged against the door frame.

"Has a temper, doesn't he?" Mars settled back into the recliner. "But he certainly seems fully recovered." He smiled like he didn't care that I was almost in tears. "Relax, Gloriana. He'll come around. If he loves you."

"He has proven he loves me more than any man should have to, Dad." I wanted to scream. "How far are we going to push Jerry before we push him away?" I left them then, sick of the whole wedding discussion. Flo followed me to the living room.

"I'm surprised you and Richard are still here, Flo."

"We are going soon." Flo touched my shoulder. "*Amica*, Mars is right. Jeremiah will calm down and see that he must put up with your mother one more time." She sighed. "Don't look so worried. It was only last night that he was close to death. Am I right?"

"Yes, of course." I collapsed on the couch. "He looked well, didn't he?"

"*Sí.* But he is still recovering from a terrible accident. *Mentalmente.* In his head, you would say. All that time in Olympus. The fight that he lost. He will want to prove his *virilità.* Understand? That he is still the man you need. Can you blame him if he's touchy now?"

"No." I rubbed my forehead, getting a headache. "And the first thing we do is try to shove my mother down his throat. Take over his wedding."

"It's your wedding too, *amica.*" Flo sat beside me and gave me a hug. "Just give him some space."

"I know. I just feel all this pressure."

Richard walked in and stopped next to the front door. "Darling, can we go home now? I have business to attend to." He grunted when Flo ran up and threw her arms around him.

"Yes! We go home now." She pulled his head down to kiss him thoroughly. "I feel like we've been gone forever."

"What happened with Jerry, Gloriana? Why did he run off like that? He should stick close to home for a day or two. The man came close to death not twenty-four hours ago."

"First, he's mad about the wedding. My father's taking over." I sighed and leaned back. "Second, Jer likes his mortal donors. He's probably trolling Sixth Street right now for a live one."

"Oh, right. Sorry. Should have remembered that." Richard was clearly anxious to leave. "About the wedding. We can probably still get the venue you wanted. The Tuscan villa on the hilltop. If you have the wedding after midnight. The owner told me that it's rare that they can't fit us in at that time. It costs extra, of course. But they will manage it."

"Money is no object now. My father is paying for everything. Which will probably also put Jerry's tail in a knot." I sighed, then noticed Alesha hovering in the kitchen doorway. "Yes, Alesha?"

"May I bring you something, mistress? I mean, Glory?"

"A bottle from the fridge. One marked A-negative. Thanks, Alesha." I waved at Flo and Richard. "Go, you two. I love you both and can't thank you enough for everything you did. Up there and down here." I was feeling teary again and sucked it up. "As soon as I drink this, I'm taking Alesha and going down to the shop. Hopefully Jerry will catch up with me there. My guests here can fend for themselves."

"Thanks for the clothes." Flo looked down at her jeans and sweater. "Now I am my size and feel like myself again." She checked me out. "Sorry you couldn't--" She must have decided there was nothing to say that wouldn't offend me. "Well, you are back to your usual self. It is good everything in your closet still fits."

"Exactly, pal. I tried a while ago to snap on an outfit like I did up there. It was a no go. Guess turning vampire again killed that power."

"Hah! It made me crazy jealous anyway." Flo pretended to pout.

"Let's forget what happened in Olympus, shall we?" I laughed. "No one has to know that Florence da Vinci was ever anything but a perfect size six."

"Thank you, my friend." Flo dragged Richard out the front door. "Come, *mio caro*. I want to soak in my own bathtub with the many jets. Bubbles too. And you in there with me. How does that sound?"

Richard rolled his eyes at me. "Did you hear me say I have business, darling? You can enjoy your bubbles but I am getting on the computer when we get home. My investments may have gone to hell for all I know. We've been gone for months."

"Months?" Flo pulled on his arm. "*Impossibile.*"

"That's what I thought. Just wait till you get a look at a calendar." Richard gave me a rueful smile as he was dragged out the door.

I took the cold glass from Alesha as the front door closed behind them. "Thank you. Some vampires like their synthetic warmed, others straight out of the bottle. I spent a lot of time in Las Vegas, a part of Earth that is in the desert, so I learned to enjoy the drink cold. Always ask a vampire how he or she prefers it."

"That is good to know, Glory. I will remember that." Alesha stood next to the door. "You told them we were going downstairs. To your shop? I'm sorry if my clothes embarrass you."

"You see how I dress. And now Charis is here and dressing in a similar fashion. I want you to fit in so *you'll* feel more comfortable." I drank quickly then handed her the empty glass. I would never admit to her that her mortal blood had started to smell a little too good to me. "My shop is a vintage clothing store. It will be fun for me to find some things for you to wear." I looked her over. "You're about a size ten, I think. And with your brown hair and eyes, you'd look good in greens, blues, many colors. You can pick what you like, of course."

"But the expense! How can I repay you?" Alesha hurried into the kitchen and rinsed out my glass. I was right behind her.

"This will be my treat. Then we have to discuss salary of course. I won't toss you out on the street to make your own way. Did you bring your papers? The ones that say you belong to me?" I couldn't imagine how they would look or what they would say.

"Yes, mistress." Alesha dug into the deep pocket of her shapeless dress and pulled out a folded packet of parchment paper. They looked very official with a seal on the bottom of page three. "Here they are. Your mother insisted I bring them with me. I wasn't allowed to pick up anything else when she came to get me. All I have are these clothes I am wearing."

"Oh." I saw her face work, like she was holding back tears. "What or who did you leave behind, Alesha?" She *had* begged to come with me.

"A few trifles, nothing more." She bit her lip. "Before I was taken, I managed to save a scrap of embroidered cloth that my mother had made for me in my home country. It is still in my room on Olympus. I hope my friends there will keep it for me. When we go back..."

"Yes, I'll make sure you get it. But I don't plan to return for a long time." I fumed. Seriously? My mother didn't even allow the girl to pack a bag? I could see this new relationship with Hebe was going to take some work. "Anything else you want? I can get it sent here. I'm pretty sure my connections are good enough for that to happen." If my mother wanted my favor, she could damn well arrange it.

"I can make a list, if it pleases you." Her face brightened. "There are just a few things. All of them are in a box beside my bed."

"It pleases me. But what about home? Would you like to go back there? Once you are free?"

"Oh, no, Glory. There is nothing for me there now. I had word my parents are dead and the wars have destroyed much of what I remember." Alesha rubbed her eyes. "You are too kind to even mention it. I am very happy to be here in this new place. To work for you. Everything is so new and clean."

"I know. Jerry tore out two old apartments to make this giant new one. I still can't believe it." I took a few minutes to show Alesha around the kitchen. The microwave amazed her. I nuked a cup of water as a demo. The dishwasher scared her with the noise it made when I turned it on. She claimed she would never use it when she could wash the few glasses we needed by hand. I reminded her that if Charis stayed, she'd probably have to cook for my goddess sister and for herself, of course.

"We'll go to the grocery store later." I sighed. "I guess I'd better invite my sister to come along with us down to the shop. She'll probably get a kick out of seeing it."

"Here you are. Father had to leave, Olympus business." Charis appeared in the kitchen door. "We're out of these orange things, Alesha. I love them. So crunchy. What are they called, Glory? Or do you know since all you drink is blood?"

"Cheetos." I made a face. "I wish I could eat them too. But, you're right. I'm back on the liquid diet."

"That's tough. Will you show me your fangs?" Charis moved closer. "Vampire. I can't believe you chose that over being a goddess."

"I'm a little of both, I guess. I still have a few of my Olympus powers." I gave her a fanged smile and laughed when she backed up a foot.

"I can get more Cheetos for you, Lady Charis." Alesha hurried to the pantry and pulled out a new bag. She was surprisingly cool with having a vampire close to her. I had a lot of respect for the woman and deliberately stayed out of her mind. It wasn't the nicest aspect of being a goddess or a vampire and I'd had way too much mind-reading done to me recently.

"Instead of eating, why don't you come with us down to my shop, Charis? I'm taking Alesha to shop for some clothes."

"Seriously? Am I dressed right for it?" She looked me over then snapped on leather pants and a long white shirt. "That's better." She grinned. "You look cute, Glory. Red is definitely your color."

Of course I'd put on the red sweater with Jerry in mind. He loved me in red. My black leather pants were some of my favorites. I missed my big closet in Olympus, but I had some great clothes here, collected over the years. My boots were vintage and fit perfectly. Charis added some boots to her outfit and we were ready to go.

"Will I have to wear leather clothing, Glory? In my religion it is frowned upon." Alesha looked worried.

"Religion?" Frankly, I'd been guilty of treating Alesha like a servant and had never considered she might have issues like religion to think about.

"Never mind. I shouldn't have spoken." Alesha glanced at Charis and bowed her head.

"Really. I am shocked you did so." Charis sniffed. "Can we go now?"

"Not yet. Hand me your papers, Alesha." I took them from Alesha's shaking hand. Looking them over quickly, I spotted the place where I could sign to free her, pulled open a drawer, and found a pen. I laid the page on the granite countertop and, with quick strokes, signed the document then gave the pen to Charis.

"Witness my signature please."

"What did you just do?" Charis looked horrified.

"I don't own people. Our father knows that. Now you do. Sign or you're going right back home to face the gossip you just ran away from." I wasn't going to cut her any slack and glared at her.

"Hey, Alesha knows how things are up there. Don't you?" Charis aimed her own glare at Alesha.

"Yes, mistress." Alesha wasn't about to get in the middle of this but I could see her mouth quivering on the edge of a smile.

"Sign, Sister." I slapped the pen into Charis's hand. "Then we can go shopping. Or not."

"Fine. But you're giving away a valuable piece of property. Alesha is worth--"

"Shut. Up." I was close to throttling my father's child. She got it and quickly signed where I pointed.

"There you go. Congratulations, Alesha. You're a free woman." Charis threw down the pen and spun toward the door. "Can we go now? I can't wait to see more of Earth."

"I can't wait either, Glory." Alesha surprised me with a strong hug. "You are the most wonderful of women, lady. I will live with you and serve you until the day I die."

"No, you won't." I laughed. "I hope we find you a handsome husband to live with. Or if you don't want one, maybe a career that will help you be independent, making good money so you can take charge of your own life."

Alesha did a little dance. "All of that sounds fine to me. But first I get new clothes. I want some of those cotton pants, jeans you call them. They look pretty and comfortable. Would they be appropriate for your housekeeper to wear, Glory?"

"Yes, indeed." I grinned at Charis.

"Are you done yet?" My sister dragged me toward the door. "Honestly, you act like you've never had a servant before, Glory. Buying her clothes. What's next? Adopt her? Set her up on a blind date with a hot guy?"

"If I knew a single one I thought she'd like, I might." I ignored the words Charis muttered as she stalked to the door. Of course I'd never had a servant before. Independent Glory worked and scraped by. Living with Jerry now had changed all that. It wasn't the worst thing that had ever happened to me.

"You're insane." Charis reached for the doorknob.

"Stop. The alarm is set, I saw Richard arm it again when he left. Both of you watch me punch in the code." I gave them a quick lecture on the importance of keeping the security system set, especially during the day if they went out. Once I was sure they had the code memorized, we stepped into the hall.

"Well, that was interesting. I guess vampires do have to be security conscious." Charis tapped her foot while I locked the door. "Father told me something about your, um, lifestyle."

"Yes, we're immortal unless we're caught during our death sleep by someone with a stake." I shivered, thinking about that vulnerability. Flo had been right about one thing, coming back to the death sleep was a little unnerving. "The very fact that both of you will be awake in our apartment when we are dead to the world means we are trusting you with our lives."

"Don't worry, Glory, I will guard you with my life." Alesha looked very serious. "Give me a weapon and I will lie across your bedroom door each day if you wish it."

"Honestly, could you be more melodramatic? Like you could hold off anyone with your pathetic skills." Charis stomped down the stairs. "You did say the shop was down here, didn't you?"

"Yes." I waited at the top. "Don't you have something to say to me, Sister?"

She stopped at the first landing and looked back with what I was beginning to think was an evil smile. "Sure. You can trust me, Glory. I want you to live. Or Father would make me go back to Olympus. But die for you like little miss handmaiden here? Don't count on it." She turned and tromped on down the stairs.

I shrugged. What did I expect? She was young and selfish, raised by a woman who was nuttier than a Christmas fruitcake. And, yes, her father had neglected her to run around with his mistress. I jumped when Alesha touched my shoulder.

"Are you all right, Glory? That was unkind."

"I'm fine." I stuck my cell phone and keys in my pants pockets. It was a tight squeeze. "Let's go. I have a business to check on and shopping always cheers me up."

As soon as we got downstairs, Charis and Alesha headed to the racks. I rushed to the cash register and the stack of sales slips next to it. I wanted to see the day's receipts.

"Hold it right there, Goldilocks. You touch my register and you'll be drawing back a nub." The voice meant business and I actually felt my stomach plummet to my toes before I turned to confront whoever thought they could boss *me* around.

The tall black woman wore skinny jeans like they'd been invented just for her. She strutted toward me, not bothered at all by the balancing act it must have taken to be so confident in the platform heels that added an extra five inches to her six feet. Amazon. That's the word that came to my mind. Then I was pinned to the checkout counter by her hand on my chest.

"Kira?" I glanced around and saw at least three mortal customers watching us warily. "I'm Gloriana St. Clair, the owner here."

"Prove it." She kept her hand on me, sharp painted black nails making it obvious that moving might draw blood. Then she inhaled. "Oh, shit. Guess you are. Either that or another of your kind has the guts to waltz in here and go for the receipts." She finally released me and stepped back. "Guess Lacy told you I'm the new girl."

"She mentioned you." I rearranged my sweater and relaxed, smiling at the mortals who looked afraid to move. "Nothing to see here, folks. Just a little misunderstanding. I'm Glory, the owner. Welcome to my shop."

"She's right. It's the head honcho herself. Laura, go try that dress on, girl. You're going to have Eli panting for you when he sees how it shows off your tatas." Kira walked over to take a cocktail dress from one of the women. "Let me set you up in a dressing room. These your friends? You all going to the same party?" She smiled at them. "Where are your picks? You telling me we've got nothing you want to try?" She led them to a rack and started pulling looks that would flatter them. Before she was done they each had a half a dozen outfits and were excited to try things.

"Good work." I had the day's total figured out and was happy about it. So far the shop looked good. Merchandise was in order and the shelves were well-stocked. I assumed Lacy had left for the night since she usually worked days anyway.

"So where have you been all this time?" Kira leaned against the counter. "Lacy's been frantic, you know. And in her condition, it isn't good for her to be under stress. You couldn't drop her a text? A quick email? Something to let her know you weren't dead in a ditch somewhere?"

"No, I couldn't." I set down the paperwork and decided I needed to get some things straight right now. "I don't have to explain myself to you, Kira. I appreciate the fact that you're protective of

Lacy. She tells me you're a friend of Rafe's. So am I."

"He told me." Kira turned and watched Charis throw a stack of clothes on a chair. "She came in with you. You want me to tell her we don't treat the merchandise that way? She's got a five hundred dollar Chanel jacket on the floor."

"I'll handle her. She's my sister." I could see Charis was going to take some work. She was used to snapping on outfits with her goddess magic. What the hell was she doing messing with the clothes from here?

"She's a pig. Look at that." Kira stalked over and rescued a silk scarf before Charis stepped on it. "Lady, please respect the clothing here. Most of it is old and well-loved. It would be a shame for you to ruin it for someone else."

"Excuse me? Glory, are you going to let this clerk talk to me that way?" Charis hung a silver chain around her neck. "Father will pay for anything I want, you know."

"How? Did he leave you a credit card?" I walked over to stand beside Kira. "Honestly, Charis, Kira's right." I smiled at my clerk. "I couldn't have said it better myself. Respect the clothes. Until I see the color of Dad's money, you can't take anything upstairs with you."

"Well, what's the fun of bringing me down here then?" Charis looked mulish, especially when she saw that Alesha had a pair of jeans and a white shirt in her hands. "But you'll dress the hired help?"

"You bet I will. Kira, this is Alesha. She can have whatever she wants and put it on my tab." I led Alesha to an empty fitting room. "Try those on and let's see how they fit." I glanced at the tags then pulled her dress tight around her. "You may need a smaller size. I had no idea you were so tiny under that baggy dress."

"I was looking for ten, you said, Glory." Alesha was obviously excited. "I will put these on then come show you. If you approve, then I want them."

"Boring. Jeans and a white shirt. At least pick a color." Charis plucked a blue cotton blouse from the rack. "Take this in there. It's a medium. Should fit. Glory will want you to have more than one top anyway. Right, Sis?"

"Of course." I was surprised that Charis was willing to help but then maybe she was like me and got off to shopping, even if it was for someone else. "Charis, go ahead and pick something for yourself. I'm sure Dad will be good for it. I'll have to talk to him about billing options anyway. If we go to New York."

Kira grabbed my arm. "What's this? You're leaving again? You sure you own this place? You have any idea what we've been through without you here? The complications it caused?"

"I'm sorry but it looks like you dealt very well with my absence. Thank you for your part in it." I lifted her hand off of me. At least she'd retracted her claws this time. "Oh, look. Your customers have made selections. Why don't you write them up?" I showed the tip of my fangs, making it clear that was all she was getting from me. "Now."

"Sure, play the 'v' card. Meet me in the alley later and I'll show you how a proud black woman turns into a panther." She had leaned in and I was sure no one heard her but me. With a hint of a snarl, she stalked over to the register. Then she turned on the charm for the customers, laughing and taking the clothes from the women who had emerged from the dressing rooms.

"Wow. I heard that." Charis was wide-eyed. "Shape-shifter."

"Say that louder. I'm not sure the mortals heard you." I frowned. "And, no, not the Chanel jacket. Not until I'm sure Dad's going to be that generous. Pick something under a hundred dollars."

"I doubt he'll deny me anything, since he's just driven my mother insane, but go ahead, be a bitch." Charis pouted. She thrust the jacket into my hands and flounced around the store. "Forget it. I can make my own jacket." To my horror, she snapped one on.

I looked around and sighed in relief when I realized the mortals were too busy signing credit card receipts and laughing about their purchases to have noticed. I snatched Charis by the arm and dragged her back toward the dressing rooms.

"This bitch can send you home you know. Behave in front of the mortals."

"Sorry." Her eyes filled with tears. "Guess I can't do anything right." She sank down in the chair I kept for the people who waited while a friend or loved one tried on clothes.

"Glory, what do you think?" Alesha stepped out of the dressing room.

"You're getting there. Comfortable?" She nodded, looking shy and a little overwhelmed. Pretty too. The white shirt fit perfectly but I could tell she needed a good bra. Olympus was behind in a lot of ways, including outfitting the handmaidens. The servants were mortal and didn't have any magical powers. I assumed what they wore was provided by whoever owned them. The jeans were baggy in the butt and I found a pair in a size eight for her to try. "Back you go. I want to see you in the blue shirt next." In a few moments she was out again.

"I like this look but do you think I am too bold?" She twirled in front of the mirror. Then she gasped. "Oh! You are standing behind me, but…" She glanced around. "Does your kind not reflect?"

"No, we don't. It makes it hard to do makeup but I manage. I've had years of practice." I saw Charis was up again and had slipped the silver necklace she'd liked into her pocket. Brat. Now she was shoplifting. I was tempted to call her on it, but the bells on the door signaled we had more customers coming in.

"Glory, I told my guy you were home and he insisted we come by." Lacy was followed closely by Rafe.

"Blondie, where the hell have you been?" Rafael Valdez, my one-time bodyguard and one of my best friends, pulled me into his arms. "You have any idea how worried we were?"

"I'm getting the picture." I felt a push when Kira brushed past me as she escorted her customers out the door. "I'm sorry. I was basically a prisoner." I inhaled and knew we were finally alone in the shop. No more mortal customers except for Alesha. "Kira, put up the closed sign."

"Really?" She raised an eyebrow. "We never close except on Sundays and Mondays."

"I am still the boss, last I checked."

"Yes. Was that December? January?" Kira locked the door and turned the sign.

Rafe said something to Kira in a foreign language and she flushed then answered him in the same language. They were soon practically yelling at each other and I was beginning to think they were going to exchange blows when Rafe grabbed her by the neck and gave her a quick hug.

"Ignore them. They do that all the time. Whatever the language is, I don't know it." Lacy bit her lip. "Both of them have a temper. Kira's is the worst. But I don't know what I would have done without her the last few months. We needed the help."

"Yes, I'm sure you did. I just saw how great she is with customers." I smiled at Rafe. "Congratulations, Papa. A baby on the way. That's huge."

His grin said it all. He wrapped his arms around Lacy. "Isn't it? I never thought I'd have a family but now I can't wait."

Lacy snuggled into him. "He'll be a fantastic father. But his hours are ridiculous. I'm trying to get him to sell the club or at least hire a competent manager. With me working days and him working nights, we hardly see each other."

"Seems like you saw each other enough." Kira patted Lacy's rounded stomach. Then she laughed. "Just wait till Rafael's grandfather meets you and sees that."

"Don't start, Kira." Rafe muttered something in that language of theirs and she gestured at him in a way that I had no trouble interpreting.

"When is the baby due?" I sighed, thinking about a baby. My dreams of having my own had been ruined so recently. Damn my mother. And I was supposed to get into wedding plans with her by my side?

"This spring." Lacy hummed when Rafe stroked her stomach. "I'm so big already. I'm afraid it's more than one. Which wouldn't be unusual in my family."

"We're thinking of asking Ian MacDonald to do an ultrasound. I know he did one once when you were possessed by that demon." Rafe couldn't seem to keep his hands off of Lacy.

"Yes, he has the equipment or maybe he rented it. You should ask him. You'll need a good doctor when the time comes anyway and he's the closest thing we've got to one for paranormals here." I liked the way Rafe was holding onto Lacy. He looked happy.

"Wait a minute. Aren't you going to introduce me to these people, Glory?" Charis came up beside me. She'd been busy trying to stuff small pieces of jewelry into her jacket pocket. She'd even had the nerve to put a purse strap over her shoulder. Had she snapped it on? No, I saw one of my price tags tucked into the side pocket. Little thief.

"Rafe, Lacy, Kira, this is my sister Charis. Charis, you heard that Kira is a shape-shifter, well, so is Rafe. Lacy is a were-cat." I waited for my sister's reaction.

"Cool. Can you do some shifting? Now? I'd love to see that." She sat on the stool next to the counter. "Does it hurt? Tingle? I heard Kira say she was a panther. Black I guess. Rafe, what do you turn into?"

"Charis, you are being politically incorrect." I jerked the purse off her shoulder and reached into her pocket. "If you don't want to be sent back upstairs, and I mean *way* upstairs, you'll shut up."

"Oh, let the girl ask her questions." Kira seemed amused. "Come out back, light fingers. I'll show you my panther. Can't do it here. We've got picture windows. Wouldn't want the people walking by on Sixth Street to get scared, now would we?" Her smile would make most people shiver.

"No, that's okay. I'm good." Charis lost her attitude.

"Kira's right. We can't shift here." Rafe shook his head. "I can be whatever I want, Charis. It doesn't exactly hurt, though I'll admit to a tingle or two." He laughed. "Glory, where and when did you pick up a sister?"

"Olympus. You can all come upstairs after I have a few days to get settled and I'll tell you about it." I turned when I felt Alesha behind me. I introduced her then sent her back to pick out more things.

"You're getting carried away, Glory. It's like you forget she's a servant." Charis was pouting.

"Make that a sweater, a jacket, a scarf and three pairs of shoes, Alesha." I stared at my sister. "Say another word and she'll own that necklace in your pocket."

Charis clamped her lips shut.

"I can see you have your hands full. We'll leave you to it." Rafe pulled Lacy toward the door. "Is Blade all right? Lacy said he was hurt somehow."

"He's fine now. You know vampires. Once we finally arrived home and he got some blood, he was soon back to normal. I expect he'll show up here any minute." I looked out the plate glass window. Of course there was no sign of him. "He's not too happy about some things that happened up there. It didn't help that my mother instigated the entire thing right before the wedding. He still doesn't know we have Charis staying with us either."

Charis grabbed my arm, her look of distress one of the first genuine emotions I'd seen her display. "Will he make me leave?"

"We'll talk about it later." I walked Rafe and Lacy to the door and unlocked it, turning the sign to show we were open again.

Rafe kissed my cheek. "I'm glad you're back." He looked over my head. "Kira, quit giving her a hard time. She can fire your butt, you know. You seem to like this job."

"I know." Kira waved. "Look, there's someone trying to get in. Would you two lovebirds go home now? Lacy worked all day. She's exhausted. Take care of her, Rafael."

"I plan to." He smiled down at Lacy. "Foot rub?"

"Oh, you do know how to get to me, don't you?" Lacy sighed. "Good night, Glory. Glad you're back."

I waved them off, a little surprised that seeing Rafe happy with someone else didn't give me even a twinge, then I turned to Kira. "Can you handle things by yourself while I help Alesha and Charis?"

"No problem, boss." She saluted then greeted a new customer. "I've been doing it for months."

I ignored the jab and pointed to my back room. "Come on, Charis. Talk to me."

"Answer me. Do you think Jerry will want me to leave?" Charis jumped off her stool and followed close behind me. "I'll behave, I promise. Just don't make me leave, Glory. Olympus will be unbearable. The gossip…"

"What about your fiancé? Surely he will want you to come back." I closed the door so that we couldn't be heard by the customers who'd come into the shop.

"His family called off the match." She leaned against the door. "They didn't like the gossip my mother caused and then there's the worry that," She bit her lip. "Well, I just hope insanity isn't hereditary."

"Charis!" I started toward her but she wasn't about to let me hug her.

"I'm dealing with it. But maybe not like I should." She shrugged. "I know I can be a bitch. But what do you expect? This place is strange. So far I've been cooped up in your apartment with bloodsuckers and a handmaiden who doesn't know her place."

Well, that had been honest anyway. I sat on the wooden table and stared at her. "Here's the deal. I won't make you leave if you get your act together. But I might have to put you somewhere else for a while." I sighed. *Where* was the question. "Don't worry. I know how Olympus is. I'm not that mean unless you push the wrong buttons."

"But pushing buttons is how I amuse myself." Charis grinned. Incorrigible.

I ignored the attitude and jerked open the door. I went to help my overwhelmed housekeeper who couldn't seem to make a decision. Charis decided to get involved, probably to earn points with me, and tried to talk Alesha into high-heeled boots. The thought of Alesha scrubbing toilets in five inch platforms put a smile on my face.

Too bad I lost it when a man walked in who was about to ruin my night.

FIFTEEN

"Miguel." I nodded and left the shoe section to greet him. We were friends, sort of.

"I overheard your clerk tell Rafael at the club that you were back. I trust the shop meets with your approval." Miguel looked around. "We had an agreement before you disappeared. I have kept my end of it."

"Agreement?" I had to think for a moment. "Oh, yes, you were going to provide security if I needed it. Lacy didn't mention…"

"She didn't have a clue. There was an incident while you were gone."

"What kind of incident?" I dragged him into my back room. Miguel was a former hit man. For him an incident could be anything from a full on gang war to a minor skirmish with a homeless man in the park across the street. When we were alone, I looked at his amused smile.

"Don't just stand there like you think it's funny. Spill." I collapsed on a chair.

"A couple of rogue vampires looking to make a name for themselves had heard the gossip that one of us owned this shop. They had plans to make trouble." Miguel shrugged, like running off rogue vampires was all in a night's work for him. Actually, I knew it probably was.

"They won't be back?" I pressed a hand to my queasy stomach. What might have happened while I was gone? And I hadn't given the shop a second's thought. Lacy, my other clerks, any of them might have been hurt or killed.

"You can count on it. They are spreading the word that this store is protected. No one will bother your place again." His dark eyes had hardened and he looked dangerous. I was glad he was on my side now.

"Thanks, Miguel. I guess I owe you." As soon as I said it, I regretted it. His slow smile made me shiver.

"Of course you do. That's why I'm here. I want answers, Gloriana. Where have you been? Olympus? Did you find out anything?" He took my arm and I was standing in front of him before I knew it. "Do my powers come from there?"

"I was a little busy. Didn't have time to bring up your name." I knew I needed to get out into the shop and pulled away to open the door in time to see Charis dump some items on the checkout counter. She leaned against it and gave Miguel a look of interest when he came out to stand beside me.

"You expect me to believe that?" He scanned the room, clearly dismissing Charis as of little importance. Then he focused on Alesha who smiled shyly at him.

"You have no idea what happened to me up there." I faced him, poking him in the chest with a fingertip. "Seriously, I went through hell, Jerry too."

"Calm down. I'm sorry if it wasn't a pleasure trip but I still need answers." He took my finger and flung it away from him. "You understand that, don't you?"

"Yes. You just might not like them. That's all." I sighed and looked around. Mortals in the shop were either in the dressing rooms or too far away to hear us. "Listen. You know that's where your special powers must come from, just like mine do. Let me introduce you to some people."

"You can't put me off. We aren't done." He did follow me though.

"I know. Humor me for a minute." I stopped in front of Charis.. "This is my friend," I almost stumbled over that word, "Miguel Cisneros. Miguel, Charis is my sister and behind her is my housekeeper, Alesha. We'll have to work on last names for them."

"How do you do?" Charis held out her hand, running her eyes up and down Miguel like she'd inspect a fine race horse. "Last name? I've never had to bother with one before. In Olympus it is enough to state your father's name. Charis, daughter of Mars."

Miguel took her hand briefly, his eyebrows lifting before he released it. Knowing Charis, she'd probably zapped him with some power just to show off.

"Alesha Melanos." Alesha nodded her head. "I have always had a last name though no one on Olympus bothered to learn it." She smiled at me. "It is one I am proud of."

"Good to know. Jerry will have to get you both identification. Charis, while you're here, you'll have to pick a last name to use. Think about it."

"St. Clair, I guess. Like you, Glory. Charis St. Clair. Sisters should share the same last name." She smiled. "Will you take Blade's last name when you marry?"

I felt all eyes land on me. Good question. "No. But don't tell him. We haven't exactly discussed it yet."

"Ah." Charis had the avid look of a woman with a valuable secret.

I wished I'd never started this. "If you're done shopping, let me add this up and we need to get back upstairs. I'd hoped Jerry would show up by now. But he hasn't, so let's go."

"You and I aren't done, Gloriana." Miguel wasn't going to be dismissed. "I've been waiting for almost a year for you to get back with answers. My patience is shot."

"Then we'll get some answers for you. Come up with us and we'll call my father down and ask him." I stepped behind the counter. Kira had kept the mortal customers on the other side of the shop but she was giving me a strange look. Of course the shifter had heard us. Not only had Charis thrown around the "O" word like it was no big deal, but there was the name thing. I quickly pulled tags from Alesha's pile of purchases and left them together. I gave Charis the evil eye until she dragged the necklace from her pocket and I got the tag from that too.

"Kira, I'm leaving these tags here. I'll figure out the damage and take them off inventory later." I smiled at the pair of women looking over a set of porcelains then turned to Alesha. She had already carefully folded her selections and put them into bags.

"This is so much, Glory. I can never repay you." She started when Miguel took the bags out of her hands.

"Gloriana is generous. Just accept and say thank you." He strode to the door. "Can we get going now?"

"I guess so." I looked around for Charis. "Where's my sister?"

"She's out on the street. When you said we were on our way upstairs, you didn't see her face. She's probably halfway down the block by now. She wants to see more of Austin." Miguel pulled open the door with his free hand. "Let her go. What's the worst that can happen?"

"Are you kidding me? She's never been away from her home before. She looks like a teenaged girl, alone on the street." I had picked up one of Alesha's bags, now I thrust it into her arms. "I'll see you upstairs after I find her. Alesha, do you remember the codes to get into the apartment?"

"Of course, Glory. Do you want me to let Miguel in? To wait for you?" She glanced at him, like she wasn't sure what she should do in this new world. "Should I offer him refreshments?"

"Yes, but this shouldn't take long. He's, um, like me." I gave Miguel a look, warning him to be nice to my housekeeper. His smile wasn't reassuring. I was about to take off when Miguel stopped me with a hand on my arm.

"If she's got the same powers we have, I don't think you have to worry, Glory." He really wanted those answers. "Surely you can let her have a little fun."

"She has more than we have down here. Different ones." I plucked his hand off my arm. "And maybe it's not her I'm worried about." I glanced around to make sure we weren't attracting attention. "What do you think is going to happen if she starts using her, um, *abilities* where just anyone can see them? The girl's a loose cannon, Miguel."

"Fine. Go. We'll be waiting." He turned his attention to Alesha. "Tell me about Olympus."

Damn it, was I the only one worried about being overheard? Luckily no one on the street seemed interested in us so I just took off. I kept imagining Charis getting mad and shooting fire at someone before I could catch up with her. Sixth Street was famous for its late night bar action and the girl did love her alcohol. Would I have to mesmerize a crowd of strangers to forget whatever the hell stunt she pulled? It made me tired just thinking about it. As I strode toward the bright lights of the clubs, I kept looking for her. Rafe's nightclub was one of the busiest and I had a feeling Charis would notice and want to get in. The bouncer at the door surely would turn her away, looking like she did without I.D.

"Hey, Glory. Long time, no see." The bouncer, Ed, hugged me and waved me in. "We've missed you. Afraid you missed Rafe. Boss is gone for the night."

"I know. I saw him earlier. I'm looking for someone else. A little blond. She's my sister, actually."

"You must mean Charis. She's inside. Once she told me who she was, I let her in. I know how it is. Can't tell age by looking." Ed winked. "Not with our kind of crowd."

"Sure." Ed was a shifter and looked thirty but had a few hundred years under his belt. He was almost seven feet tall and just the kind of intimidating presence that Rafe liked to have man the door. He and I both knew vampires that would forever look like teenagers because of when they were turned. Obviously Charis had implied that she had the same excuse and weaseled her way inside. But what was she using for money? I thanked Ed and moved into the club.

No worries about money for my beautiful sister. She had two men buying her drinks at the bar. As I walked toward her, she spotted me and pulled one guy onto the dance floor. Obviously she wasn't ready to leave. I decided one dance couldn't hurt her and sagged onto her empty bar stool.

"Dance?" The man she'd left at the bar held out his hand.

"Thanks, but I'll wait here." I flashed my engagement ring at him so he'd know why I wasn't interested. "That's my sister dancing with your friend. She needs to come home now. Our father is arriving for a visit and she needs to be there."

"Too bad. We were having fun." He looked out to where Charis was showing that she knew how to make her body rock. The way her butt moved suggestively, it didn't take a mind reader to know any male seeing her would want to tap that.

"I'm sure she'll be back." I was glad when the song ended. I waved Charis down. She shook her head. When I slid off the bar stool like I was going to come drag her off the floor, she shrugged and walked toward me.

"Already? We just got acquainted." She smiled up at her dance partner. "This is Tony and I guess you met Lance."

"Not formally." I smiled at both of them. "We have to go. Dad is going to meet us at the apartment."

"Why?" She got a mulish expression and picked up her martini, throwing it back in a long swallow. "I just got down here and now…"

"I'm calling him and it's not about you. So come on. We haven't had time to go over some rules." I smiled. "She's under age. Did she tell you that?" I waved at the bartender, an old friend. "I need to have a talk with all the people here. But you two had better be careful. Wouldn't want you to get in trouble buying alcohol for a minor."

"Glory, just shut the hell up." Charis stomped her foot when the two men backed away, hands up in surrender. "No, she's lying. I'm way older than I look. I'll be back tomorrow night and I'll have documents to prove it." She turned so fast she broke one of her high heels. "Shit. Look what you made me do."

I did look her over. Somewhere between the shop and the bar she'd snapped on a low-cut top and a mini skirt that barely covered her butt. With the high-heeled shoes she seemed closer to twenty-five than sixteen. She'd added makeup too—smoky eyes and red lips. I just hoped she'd stepped into an alley to do it. Now she snapped and her heel was back on. Had anyone noticed? I pulled on her arm and got the hell out of there.

"Charis, you must stop doing that. The snap thing when mortals are around." I was hissing like a furious cat but what could I do? She kept bumping into me and trying to jerk out of my grasp. I wasn't about to let go and was glad I had my vamp strength back.

"And *you* must stop treating me like a child. Under age? What the fuck is the right age? Can you tell me that? I'm over a hundred, Glory. Want me to start telling people that?" She knocked me against a brick wall and I finally stopped.

"Okay. Thanks for not sharing that with the men and the bouncer at the club." I leaned against the cool brick and took a breath. Vampire. I looked around and saw Jerry grinning at me from a few feet away.

"Would you hate me if I said that was pretty funny?" He stepped closer and put his arm around me. "Glory? Are we going to have a house guest?"

"If it's okay with you." I gave Charis a warning look. "She'd like to stay until the wedding. Be my Maid of Honor. Or at least that was the plan until she started making me crazy."

"Glory, I--" Charis stopped when I held up my hand.

Jerry examined Charis and didn't seem impressed. "You heard her, Charis. You want to stay, you're going to have to do what your sister says. Can you handle that?"

"Blade." Charis nodded, as close to a bow as she'd get to a mere vampire. "Thank you for allowing me into your home. I know it is yours too."

"Yes, it is. But this is Gloriana's decision." He looked down at me and smiled. "She has always wanted a family. I wish she'd found one that was more… loving."

"Jerry." I kissed his cheek. How well he understood me. "Charis, he's right. I *have* always wanted a family. Jerry is my family, of course. And my friends are also part of it. You and Mars can be a big part of it, but not if all you do is cause me grief. It will hurt me to have to send you back. I will miss the chance to know a true sister. But I do have to live here. Austin is our home. We can't be constantly looking over our shoulders, worrying about what stunt you might pull or trouble you might bring down on us."

"I get it. You pretend to be mortal here." Charis sighed. "It's a drag to have to hide my powers. I'm proud of them, you know. But I can do it if those are the terms. I want a sister too."

"Okay, then. Please go on upstairs and wait for us there. I need to talk to Jerry for a minute. See if you can get Mars to come down. I do need to talk to him and not about you. Do you remember the security code?"

"I remember." She smiled at Jerry. "I'm sorry about the fight with Kratos. You should have won. But my best friend loved Kratos and has him now so it all worked out." She waved a hand and started down the sidewalk.

"Interesting woman." Jerry watched her walk away. "That's a very short skirt."

I pinched his side. "You're not supposed to notice."

"I'd have to be dead not to notice." He grinned. "You'd look good in a skirt that short. No underwear. And when you bent over I'd…" He whispered the rest in my ear.

I was sure my face went pink. But I liked the idea and planned to surprise him one night in our bedroom with an outfit just like that.

"Now let me tell you what's coming upstairs." I leaned against him. "Miguel is waiting for us."

"Cisneros? Why?" Jerry wasn't a fan. He couldn't forget that Miguel had spent a long time killing for a living.

"He has many of the same powers that I have. We think he's related to someone in Olympus, Jer. And, it's crazy, but it may be Mars too." I leaned back to look at Jerry's face.

"He might be your brother?" Yes, Jer was incredulous. "After all these years alone, you could have even more family?"

"I know. Seems impossible but I noticed a similarity when I saw them together Halloween. Mars was part of the Mayan religion back in the day and that's Miguel's background. Let's go up and find out." I took Jerry's hand and headed for the apartment.

"You can just call Mars and he'll come?" Jerry punched in the security code for the building when we got there.

"He promised he would." I trudged up the stairs in front of Jerry, sure he was watching my butt. When he squeezed it, I wasn't surprised. I turned around at the top and threw my arms around his neck. "I love you. Have I said that lately?"

"Can't remember." He kissed me deeply, making me want to drag him into a storage closet somewhere and take advantage of him. He pulled back and smiled. "I love you too, just not all of your family. Your mother--"

"Can we table that discussion for later? I really do need to deal with this Miguel thing now." I pressed a finger over his lips, not unhappy when he dragged a fang over it.

"But we *will* have that discussion, Gloriana." He reached past me, frowning when he realized the door was unlocked. "So much for security."

"When I am here, there is no need for any other security, Blade." Miguel stood on the other side of the door, ready to take on whoever had pushed the door open.

"So you say." Jerry shouldered past him. "But these women need to get in the habit of coming in and arming the system."

"You are right." Miguel nodded. "It is the wise thing to do."

"Is he here?" I stepped between them. "Where's Charis?"

"In what you call the man cave, Glory." Alesha had changed

clothes and was in the blue shirt and jeans. She looked beautiful and I noticed Miguel watching her. "She is looking at that bride's show again."

"Oh, good grief. Please go get her. I'm calling Dad myself. He promised to come if I needed him." I gestured to the living room. "Miguel, please have a seat. Jerry, you want to be in on this?"

"Might as well. Your family will become my family after the wedding." He gave Miguel a look like he'd rather suck a rat dry.

"Do you think we might be related, Gloriana?" Miguel looked delighted. "Wouldn't that be interesting? You and me brothers-in-law, Blade." Miguel laughed, one of the few times I'd heard him do it. "Glory is more than you bargained for, isn't she?"

"I can take it." Jerry settled on the couch and pulled me down beside him.

"I don't know, Miguel. Let's wait and see what Mars says." I was suddenly nervous.

Alesha came in with Charis on her heels. The housekeeper handed me the remote for the TV. "It was the only way I could get her to come."

"The handmaiden has gotten completely out of control." Charis flounced over to a chair and fell into it. "Can I have it back after this?"

"No." Jerry took it from me. "There's a TV in the spare bedroom, Charis. That's yours. Leave my man cave to me and Gloriana. If we invite you to join us for a movie, then you can come. Otherwise, it's off limits." He smiled. "Got it?"

I waited while Charis swung a high heel from one foot and fidgeted with her hands. Yes, she could shoot fire with her fingers upstairs. Could she do it here? I had no idea. But it would get her a one-way ticket back to Olympus and she finally figured that out. Maybe she read my mind. I hoped not.

"Fine. Any other house rules, Blade?" She remembered to smile after she said that.

"I'll let you know." Jerry just kept smiling and toying with the remote. "And call me Jerry or Jeremy. Blade is too formal if we are to be family."

"Thank you, Jerry." She nodded but still looked like she wanted to grind a stiletto into someone's instep.

I was proud of myself for not laughing as I looked at the ceiling.

"Mars, can you come down here? We need you."

Mars winked into view on the other side of the wooden coffee table. "Is this a surprise? Did you remember that October fifteenth is my fête day? In Rome they used to celebrate my day with chariot races."

"No, um, sorry." I gestured for him to have a seat in the remaining upholstered chair.

"Tell me you at least sacrificed a horse." He plopped down with a frown, glancing back when Alesha gasped. "What? They picked one that was on its last legs. A good soldier doesn't waste a decent steed." Mars smiled at me and took note of everyone else in the room before frowning at Alesha again. She stood wringing her hands. If I knew my housekeeper she was trying to decide whether to offer my father refreshments or not. "Still there? Go clean something, girl. Or sit. Don't just stand there gaping at me."

"Alesha, why don't you go outside and look around? This would be a good time to see what's on Sixth Street." I felt sorry for her. She didn't even have a bedroom here. I was going to have to do something about that. Had I brought her to a life no better than slavery?

"Thank you, Glory." She nervously smoothed down the front of her blouse.

Jerry got up and dug in his pocket. "Here. Take some money. There's a convenience store a block down. Maybe you'd like to buy some personal items while you're out. Take your time."

"Thank you, Mr. Blade." She flushed and stuck the money in her jeans pocket, then hurried to the door. We heard her set the alarm before she shut the front door.

"She's learned about security anyway." Jerry slung his arm across my shoulders.

"Can we get on with whatever brought me here?" Mars was eyeing Miguel. "Is it about him? I've seen him before. At that club. Last Halloween."

"Yes. I remember. You were dressed much as you are now." Miguel's look was disapproving. "Don't you have clothes more appropriate for a visit to Earth?"

"Yes. But I wasn't planning to stroll the streets. And who the hell are you to ask me such a question?" Mars' eyes were as hard as Miguel's.

"I think we may be related." Miguel stood and walked over to Mars' chair. Of course the god wasn't about to let someone stand over him so he got up to face Miguel. I couldn't help noticing a resemblance again. Now, with them so close, it was like Miguel was a harder, sharper version of Mars, but with the darker coloring of his Mayan ancestors.

"Related? How is that?" Mars was looking Miguel over good.

"You ever spend any time with the Mayans?" Miguel leaned against the wall, which gave Mars enough space and he decided to sit down again.

"Of course. One of my titles was Kukulcan. Who do think has his picture in the center of that calendar the Mayans carved?"

"Kukulcan?" I leaned forward.

"The feathered serpent. The priestesses would make sacrifices to him." Miguel straightened from the wall. "My mother was one of those priestesses."

"Ah. That explains something." Mars was up again and walked around the room. "You see, it was considered an honor if Kukulcan came to a priestess when she was praying in a retreat at a certain time of year."

"Some honor." Miguel sneered. "Those priestesses were virgins before they shut themselves away in a cave, praying and fasting. By the time this so-called god came calling they were high on incense and weak from hunger. Of course they couldn't resist--"

"Resist? You think they wanted to resist?" Mars laughed. "Son, if one of them bore my child, they were considered the most blessed of all. If your mother was one of my women, then she lived the rest of her life in luxury, honored and showered with gifts as the favored of Kukulcan." He grunted when Miguel screamed some words in a language I sure didn't recognize then threw himself at Mars. "What the hell?" With little effort he tossed Miguel to the floor and froze him in place.

"Dad, I think Miguel needs to tell you something." I got up to kneel next to Miguel. "Would you let him talk? You can keep him pinned to the floor if that makes you feel safer."

"Watch your mouth, Daughter." Mars paced the floor. "As if a mere vampire is any danger to me. I am Mars, god of war!" He slapped his chest with one hand. Yes, he had on the full regalia, the breastplate and short toga. At least he'd left off the helmet. "Talk!"

He pointed to Miguel.

"Yes, you left my mother pregnant. But she loved another man before she went into her cave. That man would not accept me or the fact that my mother had willingly given herself to you. All the gold and honor my mother's pregnancy brought her did nothing to heal her broken heart. After I was born, my mother threw herself into a volcano. That left me without a mother or father. I was raised by the other priestesses. Yes, I was a son of Kukulcan, but so what?" Miguel was clearly frustrated that he couldn't move. "There were at least a dozen of us and I had no obvious powers at first. Eventually I discovered that I could freeze people in place and read minds, but I was growing older. I knew I was not immortal."

"How was I to know all this?" Mars paced the small living room. "I visited hundreds of priestesses. Kukulcan is just one of my guises. I am Loa to some and I could name other places where the god of war is worshipped by different names. It is impossible to keep track of--"

"Your children?" Miguel was suddenly free and on his feet. I didn't know if Mars had released him or if he was just that strong. "Stupid me, wanting to know my father. I should have known it would be a waste of time when that man is so careless about his own flesh and blood."

"Now who is foolish? I am a god, boy. Gods make their own rules." Mars watched Miguel carefully. "So when you realized you were not immortal, you took matters into your own hands."

"Yes. By seeking out a vampire and becoming one. I had a mission, you see. To discover if the stories were true. If Kukulcan was really my father. If the Mayans were right."

"Not right about everything. The world didn't end, did it?" Jerry had to get in on this.

"That wasn't the meaning of the calendar." Mars looked impatient. "I'm not about to explain such deep thinking to vampires. But take a close look at it sometime. I am telling you, that's my likeness in the center of it."

"What now? Are you saying Miguel is your son?" I looked from Mars to Miguel. "Is he my brother?"

"We could do DNA to verify it but I don't think that's necessary." Miguel looked at me. "Smell him, Glory, his blood. Then smell me. Compare it to yours. Even to Charis. It should be obvious."

"Vampire mumbo jumbo?" Mars sat down and glanced at Jerry. "What next? One of you want to drink at my vein? Do a little taste test?" He leaned forward, elbows on his knees, and raked me, Jerry and Miguel with a hard stare. "You even so much as show me a fang and I'll burn this place down around your ears." He nodded. "I see you understand me. Now I admit, I've been careless. I like women and they offer themselves to me. But it's no treat when they lie there like they're making a big sacrifice." He paused when Miguel growled. "No, I don't remember your mother. In a cast of thousands, and that's no exaggeration, it would be impossible. And you must be ancient yourself. What name do you go by?"

"Miguel Cisneros now but I was first named Ahkal." He sat on the couch on my other side. "I'm eighteen hundred years old. Not that you give a damn."

Charis leaned forward. She'd been quiet through all this. "A new brother. Cool. I wondered why I wasn't getting the sex vibe off of you. Thought maybe you were gay. Now I know you just weren't into me. Thank God."

"Glory, you are claiming this female as a sister?" Miguel rolled his eyes.

"She's a pain, but, remember, I was desperate for family." I laughed but reached out to squeeze Miguel's hand.

"Obviously." Miguel glanced at Charis. "I am not gay."

"You want to come up to Olympus? Look around." Mars had apparently decided to accept Miguel. He knew a macho man when he saw one and wouldn't mind showing this son off to the other Neanderthal gods up there.

"No, thanks. Glory just got back and it took her almost a year to make it." Miguel smiled at me. "I just needed to know. But if you want to visit here and tell me what skills I might have, I'd appreciate that. I'm pissed at you. But I can see that you do what you do without thinking about consequences. That's pretty much the way I've lived my life too, until now. If you don't have anyone that you care about, that's okay." He stood. "A while back I decided I've been alone too long. So I came to Austin, looking for answers. Now that I've got them, I need to think about what to do with them."

"Miguel, we're family now." I stood and followed him to the door.

"Here we go."

I ignored Jerry's remark. "I'm here if you need to talk. To help you figure things out. And you'll come to my, *our* wedding." I looked back at Jer, hoping he'd say something encouraging. He just raised an eyebrow. Okay, so he'd need some work. "I'll send you an invitation when we get the date and details set."

"Not necessary, Glory." He had also seen and heard Jerry's reaction. "But I appreciate it."

"Hey, you have two sisters. Or hundreds." Charis stood and sauntered over. She patted Mars on his shoulder. "Daddy's been a busy boy. If Mom wasn't already in the cells for the insane, this would push her right over the edge." She leaned against me. "Glory, don't you want to come into my room and watch some Bride Wars? It's this great movie. I think we can get it on Netflix." The girl had learned fast.

"Not now, Charis. Go ahead. Maybe Alesha will watch with you when she gets back." I punched in the code and let Miguel out. I didn't bother to cover my hand and knew he'd seen the code. "Do you mind watching for Alesha out there? I don't want her to get lost on the street."

"My pleasure." He grinned.

"I thought so." I watched him walk down the stairs.

"He has an edge to him, Gloriana." Mars was right behind me. "A dark side."

"Yes, he's done some very bad things. To survive, to hear him tell it." I sat beside Jerry again. "He was right. It was irresponsible to just scatter your seed everywhere. You probably have bastards all over the world."

"I'm sure I do. But that was mostly in ancient times. As the world grew more sophisticated, the practice of worshipping gods like me became rare." Mars grimaced. "It's tough now to find an available priestess, though there are some voodoo women who will do anything for Loa."

"Haven't you learned your lesson?" I admit his attitude appalled me.

"What? That I make great children?" He came over to pull me up and into his arms. "I'm sorry that you were left to become vampires to find your immortality. Yes, for that I am truly ashamed. If I had followed my children as I should have, I might have been able to give them immortality another way." He gave me a hard hug. "No guarantees though. I'm a god, not a magician. Or a sorcerer."

"Well, it's done now. I hope you and Miguel can work out a decent relationship. He is a strong man, maybe not a good one, but he's trying."

"I hope you're right, since you're determined to drag him into our lives." Jerry got up and walked to the door. "I'm setting the alarm now. Mars, I assume you're leaving through the ceiling. Sorry we can't offer you a dead horse or a chariot race, but that's the way it goes."

"Happy fête day anyway, whatever that is." I hugged Mars one more time. "I hope Mother hasn't been listening in. All this talk about doing priestesses wouldn't go over too well."

"Hush, Gloriana. Even speaking her name will put her on alert. As to my fête day? It's sort of like a birthday. Not that we have them." Mars smiled. "Call if you need me." Then he disappeared.

"Hush, Gloriana. Even speaking her name will put her on alert. As to my fête day? It's sort of like a birthday. Not that we have them." Mars smiled. "Call if you need me." Then he disappeared.

"About my family." I turned to Jerry but he'd disappeared. I found him in my closet, rummaging through my skirts.

"Don't you have any that are really short?" He turned when he felt my arms go around his waist.

"You really are a mind reader. Yes, I have one. Give me five minutes. Lock the bedroom door then I'm coming out." I kissed his smile then swatted his bottom in his snug jeans when he almost ran to take care of that lock. We'd discuss my family later. Much later. I looked at the ceiling. My mother knew she was on probation with me so showing up in my bedroom would be a very bad idea. I threw off my clothes, slipped on the tiny black skirt, no panties and a low cut white blouse, no bra. Then I found my highest heels. If this were Halloween, I'd be perfect as a hooker on the corner. I slapped on a smile and strutted out to meet my lover. His groan of appreciation told me I had met expectations

SIXTEEN

Wedding plans were coming along thanks to Richard. He was a demon when it came to organization. We had the venue and we had the date. But I needed a dress. My father had miraculously produced a credit card for me and for Charis, no limit. We were to go to New York City and pick out a fabulous dress, on him. Just like that show Charis loved. He also arranged plane tickets and hotel reservations for us and for Flo. I wasn't sure Charis could take the excitement. She might not be a real teenager, but she was sure acting like one.

"He does know vampires have to fly at night, doesn't he?" Jerry wasn't happy with my trip. He wanted me to stay close. I didn't blame him. After I'd disappeared for months, he was right to be leery of my Olympus connections.

"He did it right. We take off after dark and land before sunrise." I was leaving on Friday. This was Monday and the shop was closed. Good thing because I needed to go down there and take a hard look at the books. I trusted Lacy but couldn't believe all had gone as smoothly as she claimed without me around to supervise.

"What about the stores you want to visit? Are they open at night?" Jerry had the TV on mute and was mindlessly flipping through channels. Once he'd moved in, he'd had a satellite dish installed on the roof. Now we got channels I'd never heard of before, most of them showing sports. I didn't think he was really watching the TV until he stopped on a UK soccer match. Scotland versus somebody. Good. That would keep him occupied while I went downstairs.

"Charis called them and hinted we had a big budget. They'll stay open for us. She has three appointments lined up." I'd also done my own research. Charis would be surprised by some of the stops we made. Now I sat in Jerry's lap and ran my hands through his soft hair. "Will you relax? We'll be fine. Or you could come with us. I won't let you go to the actual appointments though. Bad luck to see me in my dress before the wedding. But I'd love to have you in New York."

"No, I can see you're excited for this girls' weekend." He ran his hand up and down my back. "Just be careful. You know your mother is going to be there. Your father has made it clear he wants her involved. I don't trust her, Gloriana. I wouldn't put it past her to take you back up to Olympus." Jerry hadn't agreed she could come to the wedding yet. Which was a worry. I leaned against his chest.

"Mars won't let her do that again." I hoped not anyway. "But refusing to let her come to the wedding? I'll just have to try to keep it our secret for now and hope she doesn't read my mind." I touched his lips when I saw he was about to argue. "I know. It's reasonable for you to ask her to give us our wedding in peace. She knows I'll never forgive her either." I kissed his cheek. "She almost got you killed, Jer." No, that was wrong. She *had* gotten him killed. We'd just been lucky enough to bring him back.

"I wish you didn't have to deal with her at all." He squeezed my bottom. "If you're going downstairs, run along. This game is getting good and I know you don't want to watch it with me."

"You were paying attention to the TV instead of me?" I tried for indignation but couldn't pull it off. Hey, we were a couple who'd been together a long while. I was glad we were this comfortable.

"I can focus on two things at the same time. Later, when you hit the bedroom with me, I promise to give you my undivided attention." His smile was wicked and his hands even more so when they traveled under my skirt. "Is it a date?"

"Always." I gave him a kiss as a down payment then slid out of his lap and headed for the door. "Oh. I have an idea that I want to run by you. Lacy says she's living at Rafe's now. That means her apartment upstairs is empty. What do you think about letting Alesha have it?"

"Rent free, I suppose." Jerry actually looked away from the TV. I glanced at it. Commercial of course.

"Yes. It would be a perk. And Alesha does need a place to live. She's been sleeping on the living room couch." I sighed. "The poor girl has no place to call her own. She's keeping her clothes on a shelf in our kitchen pantry."

"There's certainly plenty of space in there." Jerry grinned. "You own the building, my love. If you can do without the extra rent, have at it. You should put a pencil to it though. To make sure you can still pay for utilities, taxes and insurance on this place. They aren't cheap."

"Oh. I forgot you gave it to me." Which was ridiculous since it was the most extravagant engagement gift ever. "No wonder we were showing a profit while I was gone. Lacy didn't have to pay rent for the shop." I really wasn't crazy about all the math and figuring that I'd have to do to get to my bottom line. Numbers started whirling through my brain—overhead, inventory, maintenance. I closed my eyes but statistics kept multiplying and dividing, adding and subtracting, until I wanted to scream.

Jerry jumped to his feet and grabbed my shoulders. "Okay, calm down. I can see you're about to freak out. You need an accountant."

"Someone I'd have to pay?" Now I was hyperventilating. "When did I get to be such a big deal entrepreneur that I needed that?"

"When you agreed to marry me, love. Relax. I'll find someone who is cheap and honest. I actually know a guy. The shifter who does the books for your pal Valdez. How does that sound?"

"Perfect." I kissed his chin.

"Is that all I get?" He tipped up *my* chin and gave me the right kind of kiss. "Now I'm going to call him and see if he can meet you downstairs tonight."

"I knew I was right to agree to marry you." I pulled his head down for another kiss. "But I have a confession to make."

"What?" He pushed me back. "You look guilty. What now, Gloriana?"

"No biggie. Just that when we marry I want to keep my last name." I braced myself. How would my stubborn Scot take that?

"You'd still be Gloriana St. Clair?" He stepped away and fell back on the couch. "Not Blade or Campbell?"

"You see the problem, don't you?" I realized I was wringing my hands and forced myself to stop it. "We change names all the time. It would be easier…"

"You change names too, Gloriana. I've known you by at least a dozen." He stared at the TV but I knew he wasn't seeing the game. He was thinking, running the pros and cons through his mind.

"Yes, that's true." I sat beside him again and picked up his hand. "The whole name thing for us is complicated. I guess I'm staking a claim to mine for now. As a symbol of my independence. You know how I feel about that, Jerry."

"God, yes. You're close to paranoid about it." He gripped my hand. "I do not want to take away your individuality, sweetheart. I love the fact that you've found yourself these past few years. That you've grown into a strong, assertive female who knows who she is." He stared directly into my eyes, willing me to believe him. "I couldn't be prouder of what you've accomplished with your business and the powers you've discovered in yourself. Even better is that you're no longer afraid to use them." He pulled my hand to his lips and brushed it gently with his fangs. "I feel that our marriage will be a partnership now. Two vampires who will promise to take on the world together, come what may. Do you agree?"

I blinked at the rush of tears blinding me for a moment. "Yes! God, yes, Jerry! You said it perfectly. I want that for us. To be side by side, facing everything that comes at us together." I jerked his hand to me and bit into his wrist, his blood flooding my mouth. I drew hard, relishing the way his taste seeped into my very soul. After I swallowed, I licked the punctures closed then leaned in to offer him my own wrist,

"Gloriana." He groaned and bit into it, pulling so that he had a good taste of me as well. When that wound was also sealed, we crashed together, devouring each other with our mouths, teeth, and tongues.

Before I knew it we were tearing at our clothes, desperate to be closer. He dragged aside my panties under my long wool skirt. I shoved down his zipper and pulled him free so he could plunge inside me. He hauled my legs up around his waist and rode me, muffling my screams of pleasure with his mouth. We knocked over the heavy brass and wood coffee table and rolled off the couch to hit the floor. I ended up on top, pushing up his shirt so I could rake his chest with my fangs while he opened my blouse and held onto my breasts through my bra.

"Jerry!" I couldn't hold back a sob as an orgasm shook me before I could lick away the traces of his blood. "Now!" He knew what I meant and pulled my head down to sink his fangs into my jugular. The suction was too much and I seized again, digging my nails into his biceps. I almost tore my own skin from his fangs, my reaction was so strong, so wild and out of control. I was coming apart. Could I hold onto even one piece of myself? Why bother? Not when Jerry released me, growled my name, and offered his own vein. I took it, drinking deep. This man was my mate. My forever lover.

When we finally lay speechless and breathless, all we could do was stare at each other and grin. Names? What did they matter when we had this between us? Jerry stood and helped me up with one hand. He glanced at the TV and shrugged when he saw the score. Scotland had lost and now some other teams were on the field.

"You'd better change before you go downstairs. There's blood on your blouse." He pulled the edges of my top together. "And a button or two missing." His grin was one of pure male pride.

"Hmm. You call that accountant. Then I think I'd better shower first. I wouldn't want him to smell sex on me." I trailed a finger down to where Jerry's cock lay vulnerable outside of his zipper. "We are terrible. You could have at least taken off your pants."

He gave me a wicked smile, moving closer and pressing his thumbs to my aching nipples through my sheer white bra. "Next time I'll definitely take off my pants. And you'll take off your bra."

"Yes, indeed." I gave his cock a squeeze. "I love you, Jeremiah Campbell. You want me to take your name, you've got it."

"No, I see your point. Stick with what you've earned." He sighed when I slipped a finger inside, to tease his balls. "And it will keep my mother from starting in on you."

I stepped back abruptly. "Thanks for that reminder. Of course they'll be here. Mother Campbell in black, no doubt." She'd never liked me. "I hope the Laird is happy about the wedding."

"He knew it was inevitable and he likes you. My mother?" Jerry pursued me to the door. "Gloriana, sweetheart. We both have difficult mothers. Can we help it?"

"No, you are right. So they will both be at our wedding. I will deal with yours and you will deal with mine." I faced him, waiting for him to try to wiggle out of that.

"Well, you know when to pounce, don't you, love?" He looked frustrated but knew that he'd been had. "Fine. I won't speak to Hebe or even look at her. You'd best warn her not to get close to me or try to press the issue."

"I could say the same to you. Your mother has said some very hateful things to me, Jer, and you know it. I won't have her ruin my big night." I stayed stiff in his arms when he tried to hug me. "Are we clear?"

"Yes, I guess we are." He kissed my cheek. "Go. You do smell like sex. Which I find very stimulating. If you have to do business tonight, get out of here. I'll make that call. You shower."

"Fine." I relented and kissed him too. "Thanks for giving in on the name thing. It's important to me."

"Yes, I know." He headed back to the couch, picking up the coffee table on his way. "I can't believe your sister or Alesha didn't bother us after we made all that noise in here."

I opened the door and almost knocked down both of them. "I think they were getting an earful." They both had pink cheeks. "Ladies? Did you have some questions? Alesha, if you want to clean Mr. Blade's room you should do it during the day. Otherwise you have no need to be in here. Charis, I doubt you want to watch soccer, so go away." I brushed past them, closing the door behind me. "He has ID for you both. Look in the living room, on the coffee table. Charis, you're twenty-one on the passport. That's the oldest he could make you with the way you look and it will allow you to drink those dirty martinis you love."

"Thanks, Glory." Charis followed me to my room. "I checked on the Internet and saw I'd need a photo ID to get on the plane. Where'd he get a picture of me?"

"He pulled one from our surveillance cameras in the shop. Go see." I turned to Alesha. "He made you twenty-five. I hope that's all right. I forgot to ask your age."

"I'm twenty-seven. That's close enough. I guess you got my picture from the same place." She winced when we both heard a screech and curses coming from the living room.

"Could this be any worse?" Charis came in holding her fake U.S. passport.

I hid my grin. Yes, I'd picked a pretty bad photo. Maybe it was mean of me but she'd been a handful since she'd arrived a week ago, disappearing when she felt like it, usually to Rafe's club at night. Then Alesha had told me Charis also took off during the day. At least now she had a credit card, courtesy of our father. But that didn't mean she'd stopped shoplifting for the thrill of it. She'd threatened to try her hand at driving my car too. I had the keys locked up now, afraid I'd wake up some night and find my pretty convertible totaled.

"It's not that bad." Alesha had run to get hers. It included a flattering picture, taken when she'd come out of the dressing room in her blue shirt and new jeans.

"I look like I just got out of the cells." Charis glared at me. "Make me a new one. Don't you have a camera on your new phone? Take a picture now. Then Jerry can get another passport made for me before our trip."

"No, he can't. Those things are expensive and take time. Or you'd have had it sooner." I did have a nice new iPhone which took excellent pictures. But I was telling the truth about the passports. "No one looks at those things. Maybe after the wedding, if you're still here, I'll teach you to drive. When you get your license, they'll take a new picture. It will be better." Or not. Mine made me look like a demented serial killer.

"Really? You'll teach me to drive a car?" As I knew it would, this got Charis off on a new subject. "Then I could get Dad to buy me one. I love your little convertible." I'd taken her and Alesha to Wal-Mart to buy some things a few nights ago. She'd insisted we ride with the top down though it was forty degrees outside.

"I'll teach you too, Alesha. It will be handy for you to be able to drive. So you can go to the grocery store and Wal-Mart on your own, during the day."

"I'd like that, Glory." Alesha kept staring at her passport. "This says I was born in a place called Michigan. Where is that?"

"It's north of here. Jerry didn't think we should all come from Texas. Especially since none of us has a Texas accent. Charis, why don't you show Alesha where it is on a map? Use my computer." I was more than ready for my shower and hadn't missed Charis checking out my blouse with the missing buttons and blood stains. Did I really want company for the long haul? How many empty apartments did I have? Would Dad pay rent for one for Charis?

"Now I've got to go. I have work to do in the shop."

"Can I come?" Charis obviously wasn't excited about spending time with a handmaiden. She'd never gotten over her superiority complex.

"I'm just going down there to look over the books. The shop is closed. It will be boring."

"I have a credit card. Maybe I'll buy something." She actually batted her eyelashes at me.

"Whatever. Give me a few minutes to clean up." I opened my bedroom door.

"Yeah. You and Jerry were really hitting it hot and heavy in the man cave." Charis nudged Alesha with an elbow. "The handmaiden here was ready to barge in to save you. She was afraid you were being hurt. I told her that was just you having a very, very good time." She winked.

"I'm sorry, Glory. I didn't mean to invade your privacy." Alesha's cheeks were pink again and she stared down at her new shoes. "From now on, I will stay in the kitchen unless you call me."

"Listen, you two." I tapped my foot. What could I say? Ignore all screams? But what if I really needed help someday? Who was I kidding? I sure wouldn't ask either of these women for help. "Jerry and I enjoy an active sex life. I'm noisy. Deal with it. I will never scream for help and expect either of you to come running. Got it?"

"Well, thanks a lot. I do have skills, you know." To prove it, Charis shot a flame at the wall and incinerated a picture of bluebonnets. Luckily, I'd never liked it.

"Hey, you could have just told me you could do that here." I grabbed a vase and jerked out the fresh flowers. I tossed the water at the smoking spot on the wall just as Alesha ran in from the kitchen with a fire extinguisher.

"Glory will make you leave if you keep doing things like that." Alesha squirted the spot again for good measure. "But we both could help you if attacked, Glory. If you are alone and need help, scream. We will come. If you are with Mr. Blade, we will assume you are having… fun."

"What the hell can you do to help Glory, chickadee?" Charis had her hands on her hips and looked Alesha over. "Hit a bad man with a mop?"

"I have skills too. My mop can be lethal." Alesha held the fire extinguisher over her head like a weapon. "And a good blast with this in the face won't be soon forgotten either."

Charis laughed. "Yeah, I can see you're fearless." She patted Alesha on the back. "Come on, I'll show you Michigan. Or was it Minnesota? I get all those M- states mixed up." She glanced at me. "Will you get a move on? You already wasted half the night in the *man* cave."

"Not a waste at all, Sister." I grinned as they headed for my laptop in the living room. Okay, so maybe they were starting to get along. Alesha was showing Charis her passport as they walked away. Shower. Oh, yeah. I had work to do.

As predicted, Charis was soon bored in the shop and waved her credit card at me before she headed down Sixth Street and toward Rafe's club. I shouted a warning at her to limit her drinks then sat down with the books again. Not having to pay rent had made a big difference on our bottom line in the shop. Lacy had great connections among the shifter community too. She had taken in a lot of inventory at rock bottom prices. If I could afford it, I was going to give her a raise.

I'd no sooner had that thought than there was a knock on the front glass door. I got up to see if my new accountant had arrived. Surprise, surprise. It was the shifter who guarded Rafe's door some nights.

"Don't tell me you're also an accountant?" I said as soon as I got the door unlocked.

"Bouncer slash accountant, that's me." Ed was intimidating, but there was certainly a gleam of intelligence in his dark eyes. "I have always had an affinity for numbers, Glory. So I do Rafe's books. If you want to call him for a reference, be my guest."

"I'll take your word for it." I led him to my back room where I had spread out my bills and ledger. It was a bit of a mess. "I hate this kind of paperwork. I got into this business because I love to shop. Hunting for the vintage clothes and collectibles is addictive. I get a rush from finding a great piece at a bargain price and then hooking up a customer with something they always wanted."

"Sounds like the perfect job for you. But these numbers are important." He started rattling off information about profit and loss until my head hurt.

"Hey, hey, just tell me what it'll cost to have you handle all of this from now on. What made a big difference in profitability here is that my fiancé gave me this building as a wedding present."

Ed whistled. "Now that is a man in love."

"Yes, well. I kept him dangling for a century or two before I said yes." I was blushing. It sounded pretty bad when I put it that way. "Can you take a quick look and see if I can afford to keep one of the apartments for my housekeeper? I wouldn't charge her rent, of course. I'd consider it part of her pay."

"Let me look things over." He began going through my stacks of papers. "Is there anything on this laptop? A spreadsheet?"

"My inventory but not my bills. I never got around to it. I had a friend who put the inventory on the computer but Derek moved to Paris with his partner so that's as far as we got."

"Well, I'll be taking care of that too." He quoted a price and I realized the number wasn't bad in the overall scheme of things.

"Okay, just do it. I'll be in the shop, rearranging things for the coming holiday rush. Call me when you have the answer about the apartment." I patted his bulky arm. "I consider that a priority so if we have to cut something somewhere else, do that."

"Wait." Ed walked with me into the shop. "I have a question." He walked over and picked up a pair of gold pumps in a size eleven. "Would you consider an employee discount?"

"Uh." I was temporarily speechless. I glanced down at his feet in tennis shoes. Size elevens?

"Okay, Glory, you can shut your mouth now." Ed laughed. "Let me tell you about my other gig." He sat on a chair, stripped off his shoes and slid his feet into those heels. Then he stood, strutted over the cash register and began to sing "Chain of Fools".

"Aretha Franklin?" I hadn't shut my mouth yet. "Are you serious?"

"You should see me in my wig and sparkly clothes." Ed laughed and hooked my elbow with his. "Come on, you know you know this song. 'Chain, chain, chain…'" Before I knew it we were singing and strutting around the empty store together, our hips in sync.

"Oh, wow. You are awesome. I totally believe you." I was laughing when we finished. I looked down at his feet. "Employee discount. Of course. I bet they're killing you though. Most shoes like that end up here because they're uncomfortable."

"No pain, no gain." Ed laughed and pulled them off with a sigh. "It's a hobby of mine. Singing and doing the cross dressing. You okay with it?"

"Love it." I dropped the shoes in a sack and wrote down the total. "I'll just put these on your tab. We can deduct it from your pay at the end of the month if that's all right."

Ed looked up from tying his shoes. "Thanks, Glory. Not everyone I meet understands the stuff I'm into."

"I'm older than dirt, Ed. I've seen and done more than I want to remember. You enjoy it and you're not hurting anyone, so have at it." I found myself humming another Aretha song. "Now you've done it. I've got her music in my head."

"Not a bad thing. Give me an hour or so and I'll have an answer for you about that apartment." Ed sat in front of my bills and the laptop, already deep into numbers mode, rearranging the stacks of papers.

I sighed just thinking about those papers. Yes, I loved the shopping but this business was getting complicated. And I'd promised Jerry we'd have a two week honeymoon after the wedding. How would the staff take that? After I'd been gone for almost a year? I wandered around, picking out a scarf to go with the sweater I had on.

The shop was already in good shape for the holidays. I wasn't needed here after all. So I spent the time thinking about a going away dress. Nothing on the racks spoke to me and I figured I could look while we were in New York. I felt that twinge in the pit of my stomach again, thinking about the trip. Stupid. Whatever had happened there had been decades ago. It was ridiculous to worry about those lost memories now.

When my mother materialized in front of me, I jumped. "Mother. Could you at least rattle a hanger to warn me when you're about to show up? You scared me." I collapsed on the stool in front of the register.

"Sorry, darling. You look worried. Trouble in paradise?" She plucked off the scarf I'd draped around my neck and threw it on the counter. "That color does nothing for you. Gray? Seriously? How about a shot of red with that cream?" She snapped her fingers and a lovely red and cream scarf floated down from the ceiling and landed on my shoulders. "There. Much better. It makes your cheeks look flushed."

"No, that's from frustration. Why can you snap and materialize a scarf and I can't snap so much as a hanky?" I did stroke the silk. Exquisite.

"Because you became a blood sucker again, Gloriana." Her mouth thinned. It was not a good look on her. "You made your choice. Deal with it." She waved her hand and the scarf vanished. "Now about New York."

"I know. I expect you'll be there. By my side to help pick out my wedding dress. Dad insisted." I didn't bother to hide my distaste.

"It had better be a lovely bonding moment for us, Gloriana. I would hate to disappoint your father when he is going to all this expense." Mother pretended to examine an earring display but I knew she was totally focused on me.

"I didn't ask for this, Mother. I already had a dress, plans. Remember?" I studied my nails. Manicure before we headed to New York. I would definitely book one.

"Look at me, Gloriana." Mother grabbed my hand. "I'm not going to keep begging for forgiveness. It's not my nature."

"Fine. I'll see you in New York, not before. I can't forget that you almost got the man I love killed." I couldn't look at her, couldn't stand to be in the same room with her. "Get out of here."

"Gloriana." Mother's voice was close but I refused to face her. "Your lover is upstairs even now, as alive as he'll ever be. So get over it, Daughter. Or bear the consequences."

I stared blindly at the clothes on the table next to me, sorted neatly into piles—pink sweaters, blue, purple. So pretty. I wanted to shred them with my nails and fangs. Stomp them with my high heeled boots. I was supposed to just get over it? Over that impossible dream of giving Jerry a child too of course.

I sank down on a stool and knew I was being a fool. Coming home pregnant would have been a disaster. The only way to have made it work was if I'd remained mortal. But Jerry would have still been vampire. Could we have been happy in such a situation? I jumped up, all my pent up frustration needing somewhere to go. Luckily for my mother, she'd run back to where she'd come from after making what I knew was a threat.

"Are you okay, Gloriana?" Ed was standing in the storeroom door.

"No." I shook my head. "I guess you heard that."

"Just some yelling. Don't worry. Nothing I hear or see here will go anywhere else. Accountant/client privilege." He gave me a little smile then glanced at the computer and piles of bills. "You can afford the apartment for your housekeeper. But you need to rent out the other vacant place. Put an ad on the bulletin board at Rafe's club. It should go fast. If you don't charge too much."

"Good idea. Or I may rent it to my sister. Charis? You met her." I glanced out at the sidewalk. A few people walked past. I pulled my phone from my jeans pocket and saw it was still early enough for the club to be open. "I need a drink. Think I'll walk down to the club anyway. I could at least take a look at that board and see what places are renting for. Anything else you need to tell me before I go?"

"It's about Kira." He leaned against the doorway. "Hot shifter that works here?"

"Yes, the panther. Lacy hired her while I was gone. I like her." I sat again and leaned against the counter. My meeting with my mother had drained me. "What about her?"

"She's one reason your shop is in the black. The woman spends more than she makes here each month." He grinned. "I noticed she dresses well. Now I know why." He glanced around the shop. "She likes the kind of stuff you sell. Old things and buys a ton of it."

"We call it vintage. And I give the clerks twenty percent off. Which you'll get now too." I grinned. "No kidding. She basically works for free?"

"Yeah. It's been months since Lacy has had to write her a paycheck."

"Good to know." I got up and headed for the door. "Thanks, Ed. Leave me a bill and I'll write *you* a check when I get back. I won't be long."

"Sure. Thanks, Glory." He started to go back into the storeroom. "Oh, and I'm sorry about your mother. My own is great. Can't say I relate to what you're going through but I have a big shoulder if you ever need one to lean or cry on."

I stared at him and looked into his kind eyes. "I appreciate that, Ed. I really do. I've discovered you can never have too many friends in our world."

"Know what you mean. Rafe and I go way back. It was a lucky day when I hit Austin and ran into him again." He shrugged. "I know you and he are friends. I'm giving you what we call the 'family discount' for my services."

"Wow. Thanks." I blew him a kiss then headed out the door. That encounter had gone a long way toward lifting my mood. I walked down toward Rafe's club, N-V, wondering if I'd run into Charis there or if she'd tried one of the other bars still open on the busy street. Another bouncer was at the door when I got to the club, a vampire I knew who was happy to let me in.

"Rafe's here, in his office, if you want to see him." The man obviously remembered when I'd been first on Rafe's speed dial.

"I think I'll just hit the bar. You're really crowded tonight." I was going to have to push my way through a lot of people to place a drink order.

"You must not have seen the sign out front. Israel Caine is on at midnight. Special performance. He has a new album coming out soon so he worked out a deal with Rafe to do a short set of the new songs, as a preview."

"Oh, wow. Glad I stopped by." I looked up at the balcony. This was where the vampires usually congregated and I was glad to see a few of them there, including Flo's brother Damian. He waved at me to come up and I hurried toward the stairs.

"Glory! Where are you going?" Charis intercepted me before I made it up the first step.

"Upstairs. Some friends are there. I'm going to join them."

She looked up and of course Damian was checking her out. "Oh. Is that great looking guy..?"

"He's like me." I glanced around, surprised some of her men weren't flanking her. "You know what I mean. Not sure you want to get involved."

"You don't think I could handle one?" Charis grinned. "Introduce me." She gave me a shove between my shoulder blades. "Dare ya."

"Oh, hell." I didn't want to do this, but she was right. Of course my sister could handle a vampire. I smiled, thinking of her whipping out a blazing finger if Damian got too fast, too soon. So I stomped up the stairs, still pretending that this was against my will.

"Gloriana, it's been too long." Damian was on his feet at the top of the stairs. "Who is this lovely lady with you? She looks like you, but is not, how you say, one of us."

"I'm Glory's long lost sister." Charis held out her hand.

"Charis, this is Florence's brother, Damian Sabatini." I kissed Damian's cheek. "Damian, Charis St. Clair."

Damian kissed Charis's hand in his Italian way and began to charm her. We were introduced to his party, a group of visiting vampires from Houston. Apparently they were in town to study the way he ran the local Vampire Council.

"I know Florence. We met when Glory was visiting my home." Charis had claimed the chair next to Damian's. "Flo is such fun."

"Yes, my sister can be." Damian obviously had questions about that home but his manners were too impeccable for him to ask in front of these guests. "Glory, have you talked to Ray since you got back from your, um, visit?"

"No. I need to. I was gone much longer than I expected." Not that I expected to be gone at all. I turned my chair to face the stage when the lights dimmed and it became obvious the show was about to start. "Ray must have been worried."

"Charis, this Ray we are talking about is Israel Caine. He and Glory used to be a couple." Damian smiled.

"Really. You and a rock star, Glory?" Charis leaned forward. "Good for you. I saw the posters. This guy is hot and obviously very famous."

"Yes, he is. He took Glory to the Grammy awards once." Damian had managed to rest his hand on Charis's shoulder. "They were engaged at the time. He was frantic when she disappeared. He was sure you had been kidnapped, Glory."

"Engaged!" Charis sat back. "Is he..?"

"We don't need to talk about it here, Charis." I was determined to end this conversation. "Love the dress." Tonight she wore a slinky cocktail dress in electric blue made of a stretchy fabric that showed off her perfect figure. It was cut low in front and high on one thigh. Damian was certainly noticing.

"Thanks." Charis shrugged off the compliment. "Damian, Glory *was* kidnapped. Her mother dragged her away against her will." Charis had a martini in front of her already. How, I had no idea.

No one had even asked me what I wanted. Now the lights dimmed completely and I gave up hope on a drink. At least that had ended the conversation that was going in a direction where it had no business going.

"Ladies and gentlemen, Israel Caine!" The crowd roared. Then there was silence as a throbbing beat came out of the darkness. Finally a single spotlight hit a man dressed in black. Ray. He stood there, looking out at the room, but I knew he couldn't see us. He looked good, dark hair a little long, curling at his shoulders. He wore a black silk shirt and snug black leather pants. The shirt was open over his chest. I knew what every part of him looked like and didn't blame Charis when she sighed and tapped me on the shoulder.

"Girl, I can't believe you had that and chose Blade."

I reached back and pinched her knee. Damned mind reader.

"She's gone. The woman I loved. Gone. Where did she go? She took my heart and left me wanting her." He sang as if his heart were broken. The lyrics went on. How he'd searched. Tried to substitute others for that woman, but they weren't the same. Couldn't fill the hole where his heart had been.

Damn him for making me feel guilty. We'd had this out before I left. But that was Ray, pouring his emotions into his music. It was cathartic for him, I knew that. By the last note, when he bowed his head and the audience went crazy, I had to wipe away a tear.

The lights went up and so did the beat. He grinned and talked to the crowd.

"Bet you thought I was done. I know I sounded like the sorriest son of a bitch you ever heard, pining for a woman." He walked the stage, leaning down to shake a hand, making a girl giggle and sigh. "But I'm moving on. Sometimes you have to wallow a little before you suck it up and say, to hell with that, to hell with *her*." He gestured and girls squealed.

"Now I'm no monk. I have needs. You feel me, guys? Do I hear a 'Hell, yeah.'?" There was a resounding answer from the men in the crowd. "So I picked myself up, which wasn't easy since I quit drinking, and found a new woman. And this is what she did for me."

The beat that had been gradually picking up steam behind him got louder and faster. The drummer, a man I knew well, started really rocking. The rest of the band picked up the tempo and Ray launched into a song about hot nights, good times and easy love. No strings and no worries. It was a good dance song and the crowd got into it. I know my toes were tapping.

Charis jumped up and dragged Damian down the stairs with her. They were soon in the middle of the crowd, bumping up against each other and laughing about it, hands in the air. The music swiftly segued into an up-tempo song, another new one. This tune had an island feel and I knew Ray must have gone back to the Caribbean, where he had loved to play before he'd been turned vampire and was robbed of sunlight. I was glad he'd done that. He sang of hot island nights. It was perfect.

Finally he ended the set with one of his greatest hits. It was a slow song that had the crowd dancing body to body. Damian had Charis draped over him and that made me worry. I was halfway down the stairs before I realized what I was doing. I stopped and looked at the stage when the song stumbled. Ray was staring right at me. Oh. Maybe he hadn't heard that I was back. Shit. I waved at him, not daring to smile, then I plunged into the crowd, working my way toward the stage. I stopped next to Damian first, hissing in his ear that he'd better be careful with my sister, then kept going.

Ray had kept going too, quickly regaining his composure and finishing the song to thundering applause. There were cries for an encore and stomping feet, but he just dropped the microphone, shook his head, and walked off the stage. I knew where he was heading and followed him to the dressing room area. Would he speak to me? There was only one way to find out.

SEVENTEEN

"Ray? Can I come in?" I knocked on his door. No answer.

"You mean you just walked in here and surprised him?" Rafe came up behind me. "Shit, Glory. The guy was a basket case when you went missing."

"I'm sorry. It's not like I did that on purpose. Am I supposed to apologize for being abducted?" I knew I sounded defensive but this wasn't fair. "Ray, I know you can hear us through the door. Come out here. Please talk to me."

"Maybe you'd better go. He's probably embarrassed. You heard his song. He pretty well laid his heart out there for anyone to see." Rafe winked at me. Yes, he was goading Ray. The men were old rivals and never had liked each other. The fact that Ray performed here was strictly business.

"Fuck off, Valdez." Ray pushed open the door. "Get in here, Glory." He grabbed me, hauled me inside then slammed the door in Rafe's face. "I'm never embarrassed about my music."

"Of course not." I looked down at where he gripped my arm. "You really want me to go home to Jerry with your fingerprints on me?"

"I'm not afraid of that asshole." But he did let go. "Sorry. I don't want to hurt you." He threw himself into a chair. "Where the hell have you been for almost a year? Are you okay?"

"Olympus. My mother kidnapped me. Yes, I'm all right. Now." I sat across from him, making it clear the subject was closed. I wasn't about to tell him all the gory details of my visit up there. "Loved the songs. New album almost ready to drop?"

"Yes. I got my groove back. I know that first one seemed pretty bleak but I was in a dark place for a while. Then I snapped out of it." He took my hand. "I could finally hear my music again, Glory girl. I know who I have to thank for that." He kissed my fingers. "Can you blame me for freaking when you just disappeared?"

"You got *yourself* clean, Ray." I gently eased my hand from his. "I love seeing you like this. Loved the songs too. Tell me more."

He leaned forward and started talking. His eyes were shining and he looked better than he had when I'd left. He'd obviously come to terms with the vampire lifestyle.

"What about Sienna?" I asked when he finally ran down.

"The great Sienna Star. Kicked me to the curb as soon as she felt like she had a handle on the vampire thing." Ray ran his hands through his hair. He opened his mini-fridge. "Drink?" He pulled out two bottles of premium synthetic blood.

"Thanks. So where is she now?"

"Touring. Management set her up with a team that understands her special schedule. She'll be okay. No thanks to me." Ray took a deep swallow of his synthetic. "She'll never forgive me. Not that I blame her."

"Lesson learned?" I would never forget how Ray had almost drained Sienna dry when he'd been drunk. To save Sienna's life, I'd had to turn her vampire. Since he'd also been turned against his will, it was an accident that haunted him.

"Definitely. I won't touch the stuff again."

"Good to know. Since you're turning out amazing music, sober."

"Which is helping me stay on the wagon." Ray stood and pulled me to my feet. "But I almost fell off when you just disappeared, Glo. Seriously. Kidnapped? By your own mother? Can I help your old man get revenge?"

"My old man. Jerry?" I laughed. "Okay, I'll give you that. He's got a few centuries on you. But then so do I." I touched Ray's cheek. Such a beautiful man. He'd been my crush long before I'd met him in person and we'd had a brief fling. "No revenge, unfortunately. I'm stuck with my family. I have to swallow my feelings and deal with it. At least the wedding is back on." I told him the date.

"You want me to sing? I'll do it. Just to show Blade that I can. He may have won you now, but we have forever for you to get tired of the son of a bitch." He grinned then pulled me close, setting our bottles on top of the fridge before he pressed one hand on my butt.

"Ray." I rested my hands on his chest. "Stop it."

"I'll be here for you. Waiting." He tipped my chin up then kissed me hungrily.

Call me a slut but I allowed it. Even enjoyed it.

"Just a little reminder, Glory girl. You know we have it. That chemistry. Sizzling still."

"You have chemistry with every woman you meet, unfortunately. But it's not enough, Ray." I pushed gently and he let me go. "I just listened to your new songs. You can't wait more than a nano-second before you have another woman in your bed. I get that. It's all about your 'needs'." I grinned at him. "Man whore."

"If I were with you, my needs would be satisfied, Glory girl. Every night." His eyes burned, the blue so bright I had to look away.

"Never going to happen. Move on, Ray." I made myself face him again. "I love you, I do. As a friend. I'll always value our friendship."

"Fuck friendship." He picked up his bottle and drained it. "You want me to sing at this wedding or not?" He tossed the empty into a trash can.

"Of course I do. You've always been my favorite singer and that *is* forever." I managed a smile. "Have to keep Jerry on his toes, don't we?"

"Now that's my Glory." He gave me one more hug before I walked to the door. "Text me your song selection."

"Will do. And thanks. I'm sorry I made you worry." I stopped with my hand on the doorknob.

"You sure we can't make your mother pay? I'm up for it." He was the picture of cocky male. My heart turned over. He was probably right about one thing--I'd always have a little thing for him.

"You don't want to know what she could do to you, pal. The world she's from…" I shook my head. "Well, Jerry found out how things are up there and it almost killed him."

"Too bad." Ray picked up my bottle this time and drank out of it. "Mmm. I can taste you on this. Shit. I may have to write another sappy love song."

"Do that. They're my favorites." I had to fight to keep from touching him again. He was very appealing, standing there and pretending to wallow in his disappointment but more bad boy than any woman would ever be able to tie down. He'd move on and quickly too. But he'd always draw me in a very physical way. I could resist him because I knew who was waiting for me down the street and I would never betray him now.

He'd moved close again, bright blue eyes intense, trying to read me. I shut him out. "You need me, Glory girl, call. I mean it."

"I'll remember that. Thanks." I gave in and ran my hand down the scruff on his lean cheek before I whirled and bolted out of his dressing room. I hadn't gone more than five feet when I met Rafe.

"He okay now?" He took my arm and walked me toward the dance floor.

"Yes. How about you? This thing with Lacy moved kind of fast, didn't it?" I breathed in the reek of a hundred mortals to get the smell of Ray out of my system. They were still dancing to Ray's hits, blasting from the sound system. No sign of Charis and Damian. But I couldn't worry about that now. I was still trying to show Rafe how not affected by Ray I was. Yeah, right.

"You were gone a long time. It just seems fast to you." He kept his voice even, not giving anything away, but I knew him. Was he happy, trapped? I couldn't tell for once.

"Come on, Rafe. We're still friends, aren't we?" I stopped and nodded toward his office. "You want to talk about it?"

"Not really. It is what it is. I stepped up. The baby's mine and I love Lacy. We'll make it work." He pulled me along, steering me around the crowd. "Our families are going to be a problem. But you know what that's like."

"Yes, I do." I finally saw Charis heading for the door with Damian. "Look who my sister is leaving with."

"Casanova." Rafe laughed. "You think I should go run interference?"

I told him about Charis's powers. "I have a vision of Damian making her mad and running away with his pants on fire."

Rafe stopped next to the outside door that led to the sidewalk. "I'd love to see that." He kissed my cheek. "You want me to walk you home?"

"No, I'm okay. I have Ed at the shop. He's doing my books. He said you were his reference. Should I be hiring him?" I moved over when a couple came out who couldn't keep their hands off of each other.

"He's great. Especially at tax time. You'll save money in the long run. And he makes a hell of an Aretha Franklin too." Rafe looked away when the couple stopped a few feet away and kissed. "The wedding back on?"

"Yes. You'll get your invitation." I gave him a hug. "We're okay, aren't we?"

"Yes. Moving on." He rubbed my back. "But you know I'm here if you ever need me, Blondie. I feel like I let you down. I hate to think that you were taken away like that and I wasn't around to stop it."

"Rafe, no one can stop my mother or father when they decide to do something." The truth of that made my stomach squeeze. "You're not my bodyguard anymore. Besides, you could be standing right beside me and if Hebe wanted to suck me back up into her world, I'd be gone and there's not a thing you could do about it."

"Well, that's a pisser." He put me away from him and looked me in the eyes. "I'm damned sorry about that."

"Me too, buddy. Me too." I sighed. "Sometimes I miss the old days, me in the Suburban, you in dog form, howling to drown out my singing. I had no idea back then that I had these Olympus connections."

"They aren't all bad. Now you can sing better than most people, thanks to your mother." He squeezed my shoulder. "We had good times, that's true. But I'm damned glad to be out of the fleas and fur, if you want to know the truth."

"I guess so." I looked down the block where the crowd had thinned to a trickle. "I'd better go. Must be closing time for you."

"It is. Take care, Glory." Rafe turned when one of his employees called his name.

"You too." I was strangely reluctant to go back to my shop or apartment. I breathed in the cold night air. Freedom. It was the first time I'd been alone in a long time. I walked across the street to the small park and stepped behind a bush. For years I'd been afraid to shape-shift. Now I effortlessly turned into a bird and flew up to sit in a branch where I could see the activities on the street. Same old thing. I flew farther and saw Austin's state capitol building, brightly lit at night. It was beautiful and there were plenty of trees to sit in. I flew from branch to branch for a while, just enjoying the peace and quiet. No people to talk to, no noisy television or demands on my time.

Finally I flew back to Sixth Street, then to the hill at the end where Damian lived in a castle, yes, a castle on top of that hill. His sports car was parked behind the house and I heard Charis's laughter coming from the terrace out back. It was a great place to host parties, including the Winter Solstice Ball in December. He'd offered to host my wedding there but Flo and Richard had been married there and I didn't want to copy my best friend.

Now Damian and Charis were sipping drinks at a table where they could enjoy the panoramic view of the city. I decided I didn't need to be spying on my sister who was an adult anyway and flew back toward my home. I landed in the alley behind the shop, the one we had nicknamed Death Alley because of all the problems we'd had back there.

A man stepped out of the shadows. "About time you got here."

"Ian!" My heart pounded and I realized I'd grown careless. Ian MacDonald had caught me in the act of shifting. I knew better than to just do that without checking for observers. But then Ian was clever when it came to lurking.

"Did I scare you? Sorry." He didn't sound like he meant it. "I've been talking to Cornelius. The sorcerer told me you were finally allowed to come home. You've got some interesting relatives, haven't you?"

"Seems like Cornelius has a big mouth." I pulled my key from my pocket. "What else did he tell you?"

"Not nearly enough." Ian grabbed my arm then put himself between me and the door. "Wait. There's someone inside. I smelled shifter."

I shoved him aside. The look on his face was priceless. "Relax, Ian. It's just my accountant." I opened the back door into the shop. Ed *was* still there and jumped to his feet. I turned and smiled at Ian. "Do you know Ed, Ian?"

"You need help, Glory?" Ed looked ready to defend me. "MacDonald." He nodded but didn't smile. Ian wasn't a fan of shape-shifters and didn't hide that fact, which made them hate him too. Vampires either loved him or loathed him, depending on whether they could afford the outrageous prices Ian charged for the premium synthetic blood he sold.

"Ian and I go back a long way. I think he's here in peace." I waited. "Is that right, Ian?"

"Sure. Just checking in on you." Ian looked Ed over then smiled. "But if the shifter wants to go a few rounds, I'm up for it."

"You want a piece of me, dude? It's on." Ed seemed to stretch before my eyes. Uh oh, he was going gorilla. And it was a huge one. Papers flew everywhere and my one chair got crushed against the wall.

"Stop! My computer is about to hit the floor!" I lunged for it. Those words did the trick. And since Ian hadn't made a move toward either me or Ed, the shifter settled back into his human form.

Ed looked around and frowned. "Shit. It'll take me hours to get this back together."

"Maybe next time you'll take it out back." I patted Ed on the arm and picked up a handful of papers, shoving them into his hands before I slid past him. "Come on, Ian. And quit looking like you want to say something that will start trouble."

Ian bit his lip, then just shook his head as he followed me into the shop. Once the door closed, Ian started laughing and couldn't stop.

"What?" I stumbled when he leaned against me and wiped his eyes, gradually subsiding into chuckles.

"Christ. Didn't you notice? I've seen gorillas before but," he lost it again, "holy shit, never King Kong in gold high heels."

Okay, that got me going too. I finally had to grab a tissue and wipe mascara from under my eyes. "Stop it."

Ian finally pulled himself together. "Interesting friends you collect, Glory. Where'd you find a cross-dressing shape-shifter?"

"Not your business. What's up with you and Cornelius?" I stopped grinning and unlocked a drawer, then pulled out my checkbook to write a check for Ed.

"He's helping me work on some new formulas. You know how I am about chemistry. It's an interest I share with the sorcerer." He was reading over my shoulder. "You sure the shifter is your accountant? Except for the shoes, he looks more like a bodyguard.

Are you in danger again?"

"No. He's good with numbers." I locked the checkbook away again. "I don't use bodyguards any more. I can protect myself."

"And you'll soon have the intrepid Campbell as husband to do it for you as well." Ian raised an eyebrow. "Will I be invited to the wedding?"

"A MacDonald at a Campbell wedding? I don't think so, Ian." I walked around the counter. "You and the Laird in the same room is a recipe for disaster."

"But think what fun it would be." Ian put his arm around me. "Come on, Gloriana. Talk to the old man about it. Every vampire who is anyone in Austin is on your guest list and you know it. I want to be included. You owe it to me. Didn't I save Jeremiah's life once?"

I couldn't deny that. Ian had actually called Cornelius down from Olympus to do it. I sighed, just thinking about broaching the subject to Jerry. My old man. That was two people who'd called him that tonight. What did that make me? Jer's old lady? The thought made me smile.

"I knew you'd do it. Are there going to be bagpipes?" He almost looked nostalgic. "There's nothing like a Highland wedding, with the pipes playing. I had one once, more centuries ago than I like to admit. 'Twas a beautiful thing." He squeezed my shoulders.

"You've been married?" I eased away from him. Ian was a difficult man and I couldn't imagine him with a wife.

"Hasn't everyone? Even your dear Jeremiah." He smirked. "Oh, I forgot. Not you. Amazing really, that you've managed to stay single all these years. One would almost think you were commitment phobic. Is that it, Glory? Will you get to the altar and bolt at the last minute, scared Jeremiah will make you into his little woman?" He stared at me like he was trying to read my mind.

I threw up a block he'd never be able to get through. "I'm marrying Jerry this time, Ian. Maybe I'll send you that invitation just so you can witness our vows."

"Excellent." He laughed and rubbed his hands together. Manipulative bastard. "And wait till you see my wedding present! I've just about perfected it. The formula that will allow you to eat. How would you like to take a bite of wedding cake?"

"Now you're just teasing me." I couldn't imagine anything more wonderful. There would be a cake of course, a work of art from a famous cake designer. My father had already ordered one he'd seen on the Internet. He and Charis had been having a ball with my computer during the day while Jerry and I died. The shifters and the guests from Olympus would enjoy it.

"I'm telling the truth. I know the Energy Vampires will have their paltry treats there for the vampires to enjoy." Ian was disdainful. "But they can't compare to a layered wedding cake."

"There's nothing wrong with the EV's chocolate covered strawberries." I'd made sure those were ordered and looked forward to them.

"Just wait. I'm in the final testing stages. I may want you to try it before the big night. Just to be sure your goddess genes don't go haywire like they've done before. But with Cornelius working on it too, we think we've solved that kink in the chemistry." Now Ian's pale blue eyes were shining. With his blond hair, if you didn't hear just the trace of a Scottish accent when he got excited, you'd think Ian was a Viking instead of being second in line to being laird of his own clan in the Highlands.

"That would be wonderful, Ian. But I've regretted trying your stuff before. I don't know if I want to take a chance again." I escorted him to the door. "I need to get back upstairs and it's close to dawn. We both have that deadline."

"You're right. I'm not giving up on this, Gloriana." He kissed my cheek. "Don't worry, I'll be civilized when I see the Campbells. I wonder if they can be the same." He stepped out into the night. "See you soon." Then he looked both ways, shrugged, shifted into a hawk and flew away.

"Interesting character. Don't trust him, Glory." Ed stood behind me.

"I don't." I handed him the check. "Sorry about what happened earlier. I hope we didn't add to your work."

"My own fault for over-reacting. I'm going to take these papers home with me." He showed me a shopping bag full of those papers. "I downloaded everything else I need onto a flash drive. I can work on it in my spare time."

"Great." I saw him glance at the check.

He bumped the shopping bag with his hip and I saw the gold shoes were in there too. "I'm taking the shoes. Did you forget to subtract for those?"

"Consider them a bonus for the hassle of dealing with Ian and my horrible record keeping this first time." I turned off the lights and made sure the shop was locked up before we stepped outside. "Thanks, Ed. I know my accounts are in good hands. And maybe you'll turn out like Kira and spend more than you make here." Wouldn't that be a bonus for me?

He looked around the shop. "Give me a ring when you get something in my size. That's my problem. There's not much here that is big enough. Of course beating Kira to the shoes is an issue too. I'm surprised she hadn't jumped on these gold pumps." He was humming Aretha as he walked off down the sidewalk.

I went upstairs, concerned with figuring out how I was going to break the news to Jerry that I'd invited Ian to our wedding. I decided to check out bagpipers on the Internet first. A Highland wedding theme. Jerry could wear his kilt instead of a tux. Yes, I'd lead with that. Maybe if he knew Ian had thought of it that would soften the blow of having an ancient enemy witness our vows.

Oh, who was I kidding? Jerry was going to hate having Ian anywhere near our wedding. But then with our mothers there too, the night was shaping up to be a fiasco anyway. Adding Ian and bagpipes would just be the icing on my cake. Which I might even be able to taste. How about that?

New York City. I loved the place or did I? Walking around Times Square brought some memories back. I had tried to get parts in the chorus of Broadway shows but vampires' schedules just don't allow for daytime rehearsals. So I'd ended up waitressing, a job I'd held all over the world. I was glad that part of my life was behind me. It was really hard on my feet because of my love of cute shoes. I remembered spending time with Greg Kaplan, my lover back then, but not why I'd left. The holes in my memories were maddening. So was the dress shopping.

"We're running out of options, Glory. If you don't pick a dress at this last place, I don't know what you're going to do." Charis was getting impatient. She and Flo had found what they liked for bridesmaid dresses at the first shop. They were wearing red this time and had picked dresses that flattered both of them. Of course they looked good in everything.

"This is a once-in-a-lifetime decision. I'm going to take my time." I never thought I could get sick of shopping but this had been a frustrating evening.

"Gloriana, you are absolutely right. Don't let them push you into making a hasty decision." My mother was enjoying every moment of the trip. She had ordered a limousine and at each stop let the clerks at the bridal shops assume she was footing the bills.

One look at our group and we were treated royally everywhere we went. I had on my big diamond engagement ring, Charis wore Chanel, Flo sported her good jewelry and my mother did her best to make the clerks feel like dirt under her Prada pumps. So out came the champagne. Mother sipped and commented as I was stuck in a dressing room then trotted out to be examined like a puffed up Barbie doll. My size was discussed, figure defects analyzed and styles selected and discarded regardless of what I thought.

Flo wanted sparkles.

Charis was all for ruffles.

Mother voted for satin and lace.

I finally couldn't take it any more after shop number three.

"Would you all just stop it?" My head was spinning. I wanted to be alone. Look at dresses by myself. But I knew that wouldn't happen. "Let's skip this last shop, go back to the hotel and lie down. Can we do that? Start again tomorrow night."

"No!" All three of them looked horrified.

"We only have one more night and the dress might need alterations. You must use every minute you're awake, Gloriana." My mother grabbed my arm. "It would be different if you could use the daylight hours, but--"

"Don't start, Mother." I gently removed her hand from my arm. "Here's what we're going to do then. I emailed a place that carries vintage clothing. You all know I love vintage."

"You're kidding, right?" Charis had been watching a cute guy walk past us but now I had her full attention. "You'd seriously wear someone else's wedding dress? What if it was a bad marriage? One that ended in divorce?"

"She's right, Glory. It could be *sfortuna.* What you call bad luck." Flo frowned.

"Don't be silly." Mother was on my side for once. "If I had an appropriate dress to hand down to my daughter, it would be wonderful for her to wear it. Happens all the time in families. Isn't that right, Gloriana?"

"Yes. And sometimes a woman doesn't have a daughter so she sells her wedding dress. She could have had a perfectly wonderful marriage." I wasn't about to get into the pros and cons of a dress being lucky. I'd had customers who wouldn't buy an antique for fear of a "bad vibe." I had no patience for such thinking.

"So where is this place? Did you see a picture of some of these dresses? Are they by famous designers?" Flo, at least, was showing an interest.

"Yes! Many famous designers. Beautiful, handmade gowns that you just can't get any more. Come with me and see. Get in the limo." I got in first and pushed the button to talk to the driver. I gave him the address of the shop that had seemed to have the best selection. "We can go now. I told her it would be late and she had no problem with it. The woman lives above her shop and told me to just ring the doorbell and she would come down and open for us."

"Sounds a little strange to me. And cheap. Used clothing. Like in your shop. I don't like it." Charis wasn't happy but she reached for the limo's built-in bar as soon as we started moving. "Drink, Hebe? Since the vampires can't indulge, there's more for us." She expertly opened a bottle of champagne, laughing when the cork popped.

"I suppose so." Mother took a flute and held it out to be filled. "I'm sure this place won't be cheap, will it, Gloriana? I expect you to spend plenty of your father's money. He has centuries to make up for. Since you were struggling on your own all that time."

I held back the snarky comment I wanted to make. Whose fault was that? On my own. Yes indeed. Except for Jerry. I smiled at Flo. She knew what I was thinking and reached out to pat my hand.

"I wonder where we could find a vampire shop here in New York." She looked longingly at the champagne.

"I'm sure there's more than one, but I don't know where. I haven't lived here in decades and back then we survived the old-fashioned way." I glanced at my mother and Charis.

"Really, Gloriana. Just thinking about you biting into someone's vein makes me ill." Mother drained her glass and held it out to Charis to refill.

I ignored her. "Flo, you want me to call Jerry and have him send us some of the Energy Vampires special champagne? He could overnight it to the hotel." It was torture to sit here while my mother and Charis were getting tipsy. As a demi-goddess, I could drink, but didn't think it would be nice to flaunt that ability in front of Flo.

"Don't bother. We'll be home soon enough." Flo sighed. "I just want you to find a beautiful dress."

The car pulled to a stop in front of a small building in a sketchy neighborhood. The sign in front, "Vintage Beauty," was simple. We couldn't see into the windows because iron shutters were closed over them. I got out and pushed the doorbell under an intercom.

"Hello! It's Gloriana St. Clair. I contacted you from Texas?"

"Yes. I'll be right down." The voice sounded far away.

I gestured to the rest of the gang to get out of the car and they did, muttering about the trash in the gutters and the bars we could see on the windows of other buildings nearby.

"I don't know about this, Glory." Charis was determined to be a wet blanket. "The other places were much nicer."

A buzzer sounded and the door clicked open. "Come in!" A short woman with wild gray hair waved us in. She wore a wonderful caftan made of purple silk and her feet were bare. "I wasn't sure when you were coming so I was watching a DVD upstairs and fell asleep. Sorry I look a fright."

"Thanks for having us this late." I stepped inside and sucked in my breath. Clothes. Everywhere. They were beautiful and from all my favorite decades—the fifties, forties, even the roaring twenties. There were cocktail dresses, suits, blouses made of silks and satins and, against one wall, ball gowns and wedding dresses. I lunged for them.

"Gloriana! Look at this!" My mother had stopped next to a black velvet cocktail dress that looked straight from the fifties. "I had one like this that I wore in Paris. The men would follow me, hoping for a look down my décolleté. Naughty boys." She laughed and moved on to the jewelry. "Oh, I love these earrings. Give me your father's credit card."

"Mother, can't you, uh, you know," I snapped my fingers.

"Of course. But sometimes one enjoys owning a thing. And taking this home and showing it off will be worth the trouble." She was slipping off her own diamond earrings and tried one on in front of the mirror. "Gold filigree with pink diamonds. Aren't they exquisite? You just don't see this anymore."

"No, you don't. They are Tiffany, of course." The clerk zeroed in on her. "I am Matilde." She held out her hand. "Did you say

Paris?" She said something in French and my mother answered her in that language.

I tuned them out. I was carefully going through the rack of wedding dresses. Would any of them fit me? I was afraid to hope.

"Glory, this place is a gold mine." Flo came up next to me. "I'm with your mother. The jewels! Ricardo may scold me but I can't resist. Even if it has been worn before." She stopped and pointed at a wedding dress. "That one. You must try. It will fit. I know it."

"You think?" I had my hand on a cream gown heavy with appliqued lace. The vee neck would show off my assets and the satin came in at the waist to flatter even my figure. If I could get it to button at the low back, I had a feeling it was *the* dress. A sprinkling of seed pearls and crystals made it sparkle under the lights.

"Oh, it's beautiful," Charis said as I pulled it off the rack. "Try it on!"

"That color of cream is perfect for you. Those are Swarovski crystals, hand sewn on the dress. It is exquisite work." Matilde took it from me and led the way to a drapery covered alcove. "Here is the dressing room. If you need help with the buttons, call me." She hung it on a hook and left me alone.

I quickly undressed and stepped into it. Heavy. Flo slipped inside before I could ask for help and began working on the buttons.

"The back is very beautiful. It is low and very pretty with lacy edges. And it fits perfectly." She sniffed. "I think you will be the most beautiful bride. This dress feels lucky to me." She turned me. "Let me look before you go out there."

"It feels good." I looked down. My breasts swelled above the low neckline and built-in bra. She was right, the lacy scalloped edge was beautiful.

"It is *perfetto*." She pulled out the skirt. "Not too much. You will be able to dance without tripping over it. I think you must have it."

"Come out, will you?" Charis was impatient.

I threw back the curtain and walked into the shop.

"Oh, Gloriana. You look radiant." My mother beamed. "It's the one. Don't you agree?"

"It's a designer original. An elderly woman brought it in just last week. She and her mother both wore it for their weddings but now there are no more children or grandchildren to pass it on to. They each had long happy marriages, if that makes a difference to you."

Matilde handed me a swatch of antique lace that matched perfectly. "She said this veil was handed down with it. If you pull your hair back, it will frame your face without hiding it." She got busy with a few hair pins and soon had it fixed to her satisfaction. "The mirror is right over here."

"No, I just want to stand here and feel it on me." I wasn't about to let this woman know I didn't reflect. "Seriously? Mother, Charis, should I get it?"

"It's lovely, dear." Mother actually pretended to wipe away a tear.

"You look great, Glory. Didn't you say you also needed a going away dress?" Charis had a couple of things over her arm. For once, she'd thought of someone besides herself. "Try these on. I wasn't sure if you wanted cocktail or simpler so I picked one of each."

"Thanks, Sis." I smiled. "Flo? You sure this is it?"

"*Sí, amica.* You must have. The veil too. Like I said. *Perfetto.*"

"Okay then." I tugged her into the dressing room with me. "Now help me get this off." I tried on the other dresses and ended up getting both of them. Charis had great taste and obviously was more observant than I'd given her credit for. She'd nailed my size and preferences.

Mother insisted I needed to select earrings and a necklace to go with the wedding dress too. By the time I handed Matilde my father's credit card, I was afraid to look at the total. It had to be enormous from the way the shop owner was beaming. What the heck. I couldn't stop smiling either. For the first time in my life I hadn't looked at a single price tag.

"I hope you will be very happy, Gloriana." Matilde certainly was. She carefully placed the wedding dress in a garment bag of its own. It would need to be hemmed, but we could have that done by my own alteration person at home.

"Thanks, Matilde, for staying open late for us. I will tell everyone I know that this is the place to come in New York City for vintage clothing." I wanted to rush right back to Austin. Of course our plane didn't leave until Sunday. We had another night to spend in the Big Apple.

"Vintage jewelry too." Flo had a tiny bag that had cost a big price. So did my mother. Surprisingly Charis hadn't bought anything and I hadn't caught her shoplifting either. We settled into the limo and I hoped we were headed back to the hotel.

"All right. Our work is done. Now it's time to play." Charis had finished off the bottle of champagne. Now she pressed the button to call the driver. "Take us to a club. One that has good music and a lively crowd."

"Charis, no! I'm tired. I want to go back and rest." I got a look that made me squirm.

"Excuse me? Who just spent two solid hours in a shop full of old clothes just so you could find the dress of your dreams? And before that how many hours did I spend on you? It's all Glory all the time. Right, ladies?" Charis dared anyone to disagree with her. No one seemed inclined to argue. In fact, Flo was busy adding her new bracelet to her outfit.

"I know. You were all great. Seriously, thanks for being there for me. I needed the help making a decision." Not. "Anyway, if you want to go out. Go. Drop me back at the hotel. Flo, you'll watch Charis for me, won't you?"

"I don't need a watch dog, Glory." Charis leaned forward, ready to fight about it.

"Don't you? And I'm not taking responsibility for you." Flo was studying Charis. "Glory, I think she took something from that last shop. What's in your pocket, Olympus girl? Show me."

Charis stuck out her lower lip. "What did Glory tell you? That I might do that? Slip things in my pocket from time to time? Gee thanks, Glory."

"I didn't tell her a thing. You didn't do as Flo asked, Charis. What the hell is in your pocket?" I was going to die if she'd stolen something from that nice Matilde.

"Oh, give me a break." Charis pulled out a tiny chain with the letter C on it.

"A Chanel ankle bracelet!" Flo slapped Charis's hand. "Little thief! You know what that costs?"

"Oh, get over yourself. You telling me you never picked up something without paying?" Charis still didn't look ashamed. I wanted to slap her.

"What I might or might not have done when I was hungry, centuries ago, is not the thing here, is it, Glory?" Flo's face was red. "I liked Matilde. She works for her money. Which you never do, do you, *ladro*?"

"She will pay for it. Tell me how much it costs and I will see that it is paid for." My mother finally spoke. "And her father is going to hear about this." She plucked the anklet from Charis's hand. "Don't be surprised if this is your ticket home, girl."

"No, please don't tell him. I can't go home. Not now." Charis teared up.

"Why shouldn't I tell him?" My mother wasn't smiling but she looked like she was enjoying this. "You've been acting like a spoiled brat since you got to Earth. You think I don't monitor what goes on around my daughter? Oh, yes, I've heard your excuses. Mama's in the cells and my fiancé dumped me. Poor Charis." She twirled the thin chain on her finger. "Well, none of that excuses theft. Grow up or go home. What's it going to be, Charis?"

"I'll change. I promise. Is that what you want to hear?" She stared down at her lap.

"No, I want to *see* the change. You're on probation, as of now. I'll be watching. If I see even one more thing that makes Gloriana uncomfortable around you, your father gets the whole story." Mother smiled. Obviously she was trying to mend fences with me by helping with this.

"Thank you, Mother." This was one favor I'd take. "Can we go back to the hotel now?" The limo had stopped in front of a club that was clearly popular if you could believe the line snaking around the block and the loud music blasting from the doorway.

"Sure. Whatever you want." Charis slumped in her seat.

"Tomorrow night we must go out, though, Glory." Flo admired her bracelet in the dim light. "We can't be in New York City and not visit the most famous vampire club in the world."

"Seriously? And you'd take me with you?" That got Charis up again.

"Doubtful." I punched the button and told the driver to head to the hotel. I hoped Flo knew what she was doing. Of course I'd been to the club before. And had vowed to never go back. Damn it.

EIGHTEEN

When we got back to the hotel, we went our separate ways. As luck would have it, we had rooms on different floors. Flo and I were on sixteen, Charis and my mother were on twelve. They stepped off the elevator first, then Flo and I rode up in silence. There were two mortals in the car with us and I saw Flo's nose quivering.

"Thirsty?" I said this casually. The mortals didn't have a clue that they were in danger.

"God, yes." Flo glanced up at the ceiling. "Great security in this hotel."

"Yes. Cameras everywhere." We both sighed and stepped off on our floor. The mortals stayed on and the doors closed.

Flo giggled. "You weren't really thinking of drinking from those two men, were you?" She'd already checked to see that we were alone in the hallway.

"One of them was kind of cute and smelled delicious." I slung an arm around her. "But, like you said, security. It's almost Halloween. Think going vampire on hotel guests would be seen as a prank we could talk our way out of? A little mind wiping and we'd be home free."

"Stop. I know how you are about sticking to synthetics." Flo stopped at her door. "But what are we supposed to do? Starve ourselves?"

"There will be plenty to drink at Red tomorrow night. I think you can hold out until then." I was across the hall and dug into my purse for my key card so Flo couldn't see my face. I dreaded going. Wished I could think of an excuse to skip the whole thing.

"Do you know the owner of Red?" Flo paused with her door open. "I've been hearing about that club for decades and I know you lived in New York for a while."

"Oh, yes, I know her." And she knew me, or at least she'd known the wimpy Glory who'd been afraid to use her powers back then. "Red might not even remember me, Flo. Maybe I can find us another vampire club to go to." I pushed my door open and almost tripped over a package. "Hey, I got a care package. Come here and let's see what Jerry sent me." I'd spotted the return address immediately and was glad for the change of subject. I picked it up. "It's heavy and says 'Fragile.'"

Flo let her door slam and came inside with me. "He's so thoughtful. What is it?" She sat on the bed while I ripped off the brown paper. Inside were an insulated box and a note.

"He says he knows I won't sample New Yorkers so here's a little something from home to tide me over." I grinned. "That's my man." I pulled out six bottles, two of the EV champagne, two of my favorite A-B Negative and two of Flo's favorite flavor. "There's a note inside from Richard for you too." I handed the folded paper to her and opened the champagne then grabbed two glasses from the bar.

"Ah, Ricardo is thoughtful too." She pressed the note to her bosom. "*Mio amante*." She took the glass of blood with the champagne kick and we clinked glasses. "To our men."

"Yes. To our men." I took a drink and we grinned at each other. "Guess we won't have to go trolling the streets of Manhattan for blood donors after all."

"I'm almost disappointed." Flo laughed. "It's been a long time since I let my fangs out on a stranger."

"Me too." I sat next to her. "But you'll have another chance if you really want to go native. Red runs a pretty wild place. Plenty of donors, if you feel the urge. Red calls them drones. There's a fee to use one, of course. You can even charge it on your credit card. It's not a nice place."

"Really. Are there both sexes? And exactly what kind of services can you get from these drones?" Flo refilled both of our glasses until the bottle was empty. "Not that I'm interested since I'm true to Ricardo. But it's a matter of curiosity, *capisci*?"

"Oh, yes, I get it." I was feeling pleasantly buzzed. Some things I hadn't forgotten. "Back in the day, you could buy anything you wanted. You know how some mortals are about vampires. Silly drones think it's an honor to have sex with a pair of fangs in their neck."

"It isn't?" Flo laughed. "How do you think I became vampire myself? I was dazzled by a man who honored me that way." She fanned her cheeks. "So handsome, and one of the best lovers I ever had." She flushed. "Don't you dare tell Ricardo this but that vampire made me beg to be turned."

"You think I don't get that?" I sighed. "That's how I was with Jerry." I missed him desperately just then.

"I'm getting the feeling that you don't like this club or Red." Flo stared at me. "Is there something you're not telling me?"

Something? There were a lot of things I wouldn't share with Flo. But then I knew little about her life before she'd come to Austin either.

"New York wasn't the best time in my life, pal. I'd run from Jerry, thinking I could make it on my own. When I couldn't, I let the first vampire who came along with a good line and nice body take over." I jumped when Flo sat beside me and squeezed my shoulders.

"I understand, *amica*. I hope he was at least rich."

"No! He was also a bully and I let him get away with it. We both had to work to pay rent." I leaned against her. "He worked for Red so I spent a lot of time in the club. The vampires who hung out there did whatever they wanted and things would get pretty rough." I drained my glass. "You could get high by taking blood from a drone on drugs. It didn't always end well for the drone. I hope Red has things more under control now."

"She's stayed in business a long time. So she must be doing something right." Flo shook her head. "You sure there's not more to it?"

"I did a stint there as a cocktail waitress until Red decided using mortal waitresses was better for business." I decided we might as well finish off the champagne and opened the other bottle so we could refill our glasses.

"I'll just bet she did. So the waitresses could give blood too." Flo studied me. "You don't have to go if you don't want to, Glory. We can find other things to do."

"No, I need to see Red. Because not only was my boyfriend then a bully, he did something to me that made me forget whole chunks of my New York years." I got up and paced the floor. "I ran into him in Austin, Flo. He worked for the Energy Vampires."

"Really? Strange. But then the vampire world is not so big, I think." Flo watched me walk the floor. "What did he say?"

"He taunted me. Said we'd done things here when we were together that I couldn't remember." I sat beside her again. "It's driving me crazy, Flo. How could Greg have erased *my* memory? And what have I forgotten? I need to know and maybe Red can help me fill in some blanks."

"Yes, we must go." Flo finished her drink, got up and stretched. Then she gathered up her two extra bottles. "I'm sorry this happened to you, Glory. Tomorrow night I will help you. Now I go call Ricardo and thank him." She faked a smile. I could tell she was trying to cheer me up. "What will you do with the rest of your night? Will you call Jeremiah?"

"Yes, but I won't tell him about my dress. Just that I found one. Let's keep this trip to Red our secret, Flo." I walked her to the door. "I'm sure the guys have both heard of the club and wouldn't approve of our going there without them."

"Fine. I like keeping a little secret from time to time." She played with her new bracelet. "It is enough that Ricardo will notice I bought another expensive piece of jewelry and fuss at me." Flo shook her head. "Pah. I say enjoy your money. I have always managed to find more, have I not?"

"Yes, but that was because you always moved on to a new man before." I hugged her. "This time you plan to stick."

"You're right. But Ricardo makes no sense." Flo stepped across the hall. "If I had bought one of his religious relics for him? Hah! No limit then. I say we rob a grave, then tell Ricardo we'd found old bones of saints. And look at the pretty bracelet the saint was wearing!" Flo wobbled a little, obviously feeling her champagne, before she slammed the door.

I was smiling as I put my bottles into the mini-bar fridge then called Jerry. He wanted to hear about the dress shopping and I laughed about my night and the struggles with the entourage and their "help."

"But did you get the dress *you* wanted, Gloriana?" He sounded concerned.

"Of course. I can't tell you the details, but it's vintage and I love it." I went on to thank him for the synthetic blood. Then I said good night with the excuse that I was tired and longing for a long soak in the bathtub. But I wasn't headed for the tub. Instead I got on the elevator again and went down to the floor where Charis had her room. I needed to have it out with her again about her stealing.

I was relieved when she answered my knock.

"Checking up on me?" She was in pajamas and the TV was on pay per view. It was a movie that included nudity. I had to remind myself that she was an adult. "I'm here, as ordered."

"Can you pause that thing so we can talk?" I sat where I didn't have to see the threesome on the screen.

"Sure. Or you could take the stick out of your butt and watch it with me." Charis flounced over to pick up the remote to hit pause.

"I'm not a prude, Charis. I've seen and done plenty of things. Though I have no idea if they match up to your experience." I crossed my legs and waited until she was settled on her bed. She'd poured herself a drink but didn't offer me one. Which was okay. I'd had enough for one night. Clearly she watched a lot of TV. She talked more like a twenty-first century girl now than I did.

"In Olympus I'm still considered something of a child, sheltered until I'm married. Not that I'm a virgin. We're given sexual freedom. But we live at home with our parents and you know first-hand that marriages are arranged. Ridiculous conventions." She made a face. "You saw that, despite your grandmother's preferences, staying true to your mate is no big deal in Olympus. Most of us are adventurous." She glanced at the TV to make her point.

"Yes, Hera would like it to be like the old days. But immortals don't seem to be built for monogamy." I knew that from dealing with vampires too.

"No kidding." Charis leaned forward. "I knew about Earth before I came here but the way Zeus keeps everything kind of old fashioned up there didn't really prepare me for this reality. Fast cars, so many good looking men and then all the paranormals!"

"You're seeing those paranormals because you're traveling in my circles, Charis. Most mortals don't have a clue that there are werewolves, shape-shifters, and vampires living among them. We keep a low profile deliberately and what you've been doing since you got here is jeopardizing that way of life. That's why I have to come down hard on you." I tried to see it from her point of view. Okay, so she'd been pampered, spoiled, and kept in an archaic world where she was part of the pampered hierarchy. Then she'd come down here and she'd been just one of the crowd.

"I see what you're thinking, Glory. You're right. I hate not standing out." Charis rattled an ice cube in her glass. "I know I have my looks but there are so many other pretty girls in Austin. I'm learning that most of them go to the University of Texas. They're smart and know so much! I know nothing!"

"Would you like to go to school? Enroll in the university and be part of that scene?" I had no idea what kind of schooling Charis had finished. I'd seen no signs of a teaching program there but then I hadn't been looking.

"Glory, you are so easy to read." Charis smiled. "We have tutors and I am well-educated in a way. My last tutor was quite handsome." She waved a hand over her face as if to cool her cheeks. "He taught me things my mother would be horrified to discover."

I was horrified too, but figured that saying so would brand me a prude again. Instead I tried to imagine Charis as part of the University crowd. Yes, she could fit in and, with her bubbly personality and great wardrobe, would be a hit with the sorority girls. We'd have to invent a background for her that would work, but it could be done.

"Are you serious about wanting to go to the University?" I looked at her lolling on her bed, ready to open yet another bottle from the mini-bar.

"I don't know. Do you think I'm smart enough?" She bit her lip.

"Don't be ridiculous. Of course you are. But you'd have to really work if you plan to actually enroll and take classes. What would your major be?"

She grinned. "Classical studies, of course. I think I could nail anything about the ancient Greeks or Romans, don't you?"

I had to laugh. "Wouldn't that be cheating?" I shook my head. "But then that wouldn't bother you, would it?" And now we were down to why I'd come here. "What's with the stealing, Charis? I thought you were done with that."

"I don't know. I get bored. Tonight it was Glory this, Glory that. Oh, look at Glory in the gorgeous designer dress. The wedding will be so wonderful. Now let's pick out earrings for Glory. I'd had it up to here with the Glory night." Her hand was at her eyebrows. "What about me?" She slumped and let her glass fall to the comforter, ice cubes going everywhere.

"Can't I have one night to be the center of attention, Charis?" I gathered up the ice and threw it in the bathroom sink. Then I took the glass and filled it with water, handing it to her. "Drink. You've had enough booze tonight. It's making you maudlin."

"You think this is just self-pity?" She sniffed then took a swallow. "Add some vodka to that and it would taste better."

"No vodka. And, yes, you're wallowing in it. Come on. I know you have legitimate gripes. But you have a rich and powerful father who's let you run wild until now. He's feeling so guilty about your mother that he's willing to give you an apartment of your own here." It was true. I'd talked to Mars about it already.

"Seriously? An apartment of my own?" She perked up.

"You think I want to go to bat for you now? After what you pulled tonight?" I sat across from the bed. "I'm sick of this, Charis. The stealing has to stop. You have a credit card now. All you had to do was whip it out to buy what you wanted."

"Stealing gives me a rush, Glory. Sometimes I don't even know I'm doing it until I leave the store and stick my hand in my pocket. Then, oops, there it is. A little something shiny to make me feel better." She finished off the water. "It does, for a little while. I like getting away with taking something right from under someone's nose. Making a fool of a mortal, if you want to know the truth. Surely you can relate."

I realized I was looking at a woman with no moral compass whatsoever. With an absentee father and an unstable mother, she'd obviously been raising herself in Olympus. Well, now she had a sister who wasn't going to let her get away with a damned thing. Charis was going to learn right from wrong even if it was painful for both of us.

"No, I can't relate. I don't steal. It's wrong and illegal. And you have to face the consequences of your actions. Tomorrow you and Mother will go back to Matilde's shop and pay for the Chanel anklet. You will apologize for taking it. Right to Matilde's face. No excuses."

I took her glass away from her and shook her hand. "Do you hear me?"

"That would be embarrassing." She tried to squirm away from me.

"That's the point, Charis. I'm going to Mother now to make sure you do it." I let her go. "Mother wants to get on my good side. Do you really think it would bother her if you hate her? You can be sure she'll drag you kicking and screaming to that shop if she has to. Understand?"

"Yes." Charis hung her head. "No need to be a bitch about it."

"Oh, there's every need. She'll call you and let you know when to be ready tomorrow." I walked to the door. "If you don't do this, you'll be on your way back to Olympus right after the wedding. Before the wedding if you embarrass me again. That's a promise. Clean up your act and we can talk about that apartment and the future. That's a promise too." With that I left her and headed to my mother's room. It didn't take five minutes to tell her the plan. She was all over it. I think she saw it as progress in her campaign to get on my good side.

"Thank you, darling, for trusting me with this important task. I won't let you down." She hugged me until I squirmed away from her.

"It's a start, Mother." I looked into her eyes. "Just remember that if you want to have a relationship with me, you'll let this wedding go on as planned. Are we clear?"

"Certainly, Gloriana. I told you. I'm ready to let you have your way now. You have chosen your man and I realize there is nothing else to be done about it." She followed me down the hall toward the elevators. "About tomorrow night. I have no desire to go to this vampire club you mentioned."

"Good. I don't want Charis there either. Why don't you pick up tickets to a Broadway play for the two of you? Use Dad's credit card." I pushed the up button then dug the card out of my pocket. "Just leave it in an envelope at the front desk when you're through with it, please."

"You could go with us. I'm sure there's a show you'd like to see. I know you love musicals." She took the card.

"Yes, I do." And how freaky was it that my mother knew that? Did her spying on me know no limits? "But I need to go to the club because Flo wants it and she's been a very good friend to me."

"I understand." But Mother was frowning. "If you insist, that's what we'll do. Are you sure it's safe? Two women alone in a club like that?"

"We're not just women, Mother." I smiled as the elevator opened. "The better question would be is New York safe from us. Remember what we are." I enjoyed the look on her face as the doors closed. Yes, I gave her a glimpse of my fangs. How could I resist?

I never thought I'd arrive at Red in a limo. We'd dropped Mother and Charis at their play, then I'd given the driver directions to the club. I'd used my phone to look it up and saw that it was still at the same address. On Google it was listed under private clubs, membership only. I knew that was Red's way of insuring that mortals wouldn't wander in, not unless she *wanted* them to drop by. A burly shape-shifter stood at the red lacquered door. It only took a flash of our fangs for us to be allowed inside. That was Red's problem. She had never learned to discriminate between decent vampires and the kind of low-life blood suckers out to cause trouble.

"Oh, this is a nice place." Flo had dressed to impress in a low-cut leather sheath dress of bright red. For some reason she thought there was a color theme going on here. I'd dressed in my favorite black but had the girls out tonight in my own vee-neck top cut low enough to make a bra impossible. Jerry would have been pulling out his knives at the looks I was getting. That made me smile.

Two men approached us immediately and offered to buy us drinks.

"Why thank you." Flo wasn't about to turn down a freebie. She held out her hand. "I'm Flo and this is my friend Gl-"

"Gloria! What the hell are you doing back in town?" The husky voice cleared a path in front of us. I knew it instantly.

"Red." I nodded and grabbed Flo's arm. "How are you?" I looked Red over, determined to keep my cool. "This is my friend Flo."

Red scanned Flo and shooed her away with a flick of her wrist. "Run along, sidekick. Troy, go buy her that drink. Gloria and I are going to be catching up in the office."

"Wait!" Flo was being maneuvered toward the long black bar against one wall by Troy, one of the men who'd approached us. "Glory? Do you need me?" She glanced at Red and frowned, digging in her heels. "I am not leaving you unless you say the word."

"It's fine. Go." I gave Troy a hard look. He seemed decent but you couldn't always tell. The lights were dim, the music was loud and I couldn't read his thoughts. Not a recipe for trust. "Any harm comes to my friend while I'm gone and I'll tear off your balls and shove them down your throat. *Capisci?*"

"Yeah, sure." He swallowed and dropped Flo's arm.

"Well, well. Look who's grown her own pair." Red strode toward her office, leaving me to follow her. Since she stood about six feet tall even without her five inch heels, it took me a while to catch up. Of course the crowd on the dance floor cleared a path for us. No one messed with Red. By the time we arrived in her office, I was out of breath from almost running in my own high heels.

The door shut behind me and we were in silence. She had great soundproofing.

"You look good, Red." I strolled over and sat in one of her black leather chairs, not waiting for an invitation. If she liked my new confidence, I wasn't going to let my nerves show now. "I see you decided to go with a brighter shade this century."

"Sure. Why not?" She ran her hand over her brush cut. It was a fire engine red instead of the burgundy it had been when I'd known her before. "I'm also into women this century. I don't suppose…"

"No, but I'm flattered. I'm engaged." I held out my left hand. "Getting married soon. To my sire. He's been after me for a long time. I finally decided to take the plunge."

"Another ballsy move." She sat on the edge of her desk. "What happened to you, Gloria? You've changed."

"I'm going by Gloriana now." I leaned forward, relieved that she was being friendly. As far as I could remember she hadn't really liked me. "Will you tell me something?"

"What? You looking for Greg Kaplan? I didn't like the way he treated you back then. Pissed me off. But then you let him bully you. That pissed me off too. If you're ready to make him pay for that, I'll help you." She smiled, full fang. "He was a real asshole."

"I know where he was a few months ago, but have lost track of him again. Thanks for the offer though." I sat back. I was glad I hadn't seen him in a while.

"Then what do you need?" She walked around her desk and sat behind it.

"Somehow Greg erased most of my memories of my time here. How did he do that? The Greg I met in Austin didn't have that kind of power."

"No, he didn't." Red steepled her fingers. "But he did have access to the drugs I ran through here then. I still do as a matter of fact." She slammed her hands on the desk. "That stupid bastard. Obviously he helped himself to one of them." She studied me. "Lost your memory? Oh, yeah. That one. I don't sell it anymore. Too much blow back from dissatisfied customers. It's like a roofie for vampires. The date rape drug?"

"But why would he need that for me? We were together." I glanced around the room to keep from meeting her intense stare. Red had the light blue eyes a lot of redheads seemed to have and freckles. Maybe I could look at her if I concentrated on the light dusting of freckles across her nose. I tried and found my eyes filling.

"Aw, Glo, don't start. He just wasn't worth it." Red was up and by my side in a flash. She put her arm around me.

"I'm not crying about him." I dashed away a tear. "But that I was so stupid. And I hate that I can't remember things from that time. There are blanks. It's driving me crazy."

"Sure it is. Damned bastard." Red handed me a tissue. "I never could figure out how you got hooked up with him in the first place. He was a loser who liked playing the field. You caught him a time or two and made a scene. Then he'd talk his way out of it. I thought you were crazy for putting up with him. Obviously he decided to get rid of you but didn't have the guts to end things like a gentleman." Red's frown was fierce. "One day you were just gone. I didn't know how he did it at the time. He spread the story that you'd reunited with your sire. Bullshit, obviously. He must have drugged you and dumped you somewhere else."

"Yeah." I faced her. "Tell me more about this drug."

"For vampires that roofie shit not only wipes out the memory of the night but of days, weeks, sometimes months." She wiped my cheeks with her fingers and I realized I'd been crying again. "If I'd known what he was up to, I'd have staked him myself."

"All I know is that I woke up one night and found a note. He said we were done and it was my fault for being a nag." I took a breath. "I was in Chicago. In a hotel with about forty bucks and no idea what to do next."

"What about your dog? You always had a guard dog with you, a shifter. That's why I had to fire you. Couldn't have a dog in here, running his mouth at the customers who tried to come on to you. Remember? Oh, maybe you don't." Red paced the room.

"He was there when I woke up. Didn't say much. Just that he was glad Greg was gone." I blew my nose. "Valdez always hated Greg. He obviously didn't know I'd been drugged. Greg wasn't stupid enough to do it in front of the shifter. Valdez would have torn Greg apart."

"That chicken shit son of a bitch. I've seen the way the drug works. People walk and talk like they're fine. But later, they can't remember jack." She sat next to me again. "The dog was right. You were lucky to be away from that creep. And now look at you. You survived. Got a rock on your finger and a man who loves you enough to commit forever. Tell me more. How'd you get strong enough to stand up for yourself?"

I started to tell her about Jerry and Olympus when there was a noise outside her door. Then a man burst in and began talking rapidly in another language. His gestures made it clear there was trouble in the club.

"Shit. One of my rivals is here and starting trouble. He took a drone into one of the private rooms and decided to scare her." Red glanced at me. "You want to wait here?"

"No, I'll come with you." I followed her to the stairs that led to the private rooms. We could hear screams coming from behind one of the doors.

"Liam, I've warned you before. Leave my people alone," Red shouted through the door then nodded. Her employee unlocked the door then shoved it open. Inside a vampire had taken off his shirt and had a woman pinned down on a couch. She wore next to nothing, and that had been ripped open. His fangs were in her throat and he gripped her arms with long nails that were making bloody furrows in her skin.

"Let her go!" Red grabbed his shoulders and tried to shake him off of her. He didn't budge. He sent her a mental message that I caught as well. Then he shoved the woman's legs apart and fumbled with his zipper. "Don't you dare!"

"I've got this." I touched his back and he was frozen. Red and her guard stared at me as soon as it became clear that the vampire couldn't move. "Now let's get this girl out from under him." I peeled his hands off of her arms then jerked his mouth away from her neck. She sobbed gratefully.

"Max, grab Liam and throw him on the floor." Red pulled the girl up and helped her out of the room. "I don't know how you did that, Glory, but you just saved Amy's life."

Amy swayed and Red told Max to take her down to her office where he could find a blanket and a protein bar for her.

"Does this kind of thing happen often?" I stared down at the vampire. He was handsome, but had a cruel look to him. The long nails and greasy hair along with the dark clothes were probably supposed to make him look dangerous. It was working.

"No or I'd have closed my doors long ago. Vampires around here know I won't tolerate this kind of behavior." Red snarled. "Liam has a tribe of followers across town, assholes like him who seem to have forgotten what it means to be human."

I nudged Liam with my foot. "Listen to me, asshole. Right now you're at my mercy. Red could cut off your package and you couldn't lift a finger to stop her. Are you hearing me?" I got his mental message. "Oh, I wouldn't talk to me like that if I were you." I aimed a kick at his zipper and put enough into it to make sure he knew I wasn't playing around. Tears leaked from his eyes but he stared at me with hatred. "Now are you taking me seriously?"

Red nodded. "Oh, yeah, he heard you, Glory. And he's dying to hold onto that teeny wienie cause it hurts like hell. Doesn't it, you son of a bitch?" She walked over and slammed her stiletto into his thigh. Red turned to me with her hands on her hips. "That has got to be the coolest power I've ever seen. Can you teach it to me?" Red backed up, casually stepping on Liam's fingers.

"No, it's inherited." I shook my head when Red decided a stiletto heel on his other hand was called for. "I didn't know about it until recently. My parents just found me. Long story. What are you going to do about this piece of trash?" I nodded at Liam.

"I can't kill him, damn it. That would start a war that I can't afford. So here's the deal, Liam. You can't come back here. Ever. If you do, I'll send for my pal Glo here and she'll do this again. But next time she'll leave you outside when she's done. That's where you'll meet the sun. Do you hear me?"

We both heard him in our heads. He was furious but knew when he was beaten.

I got down in front of him and stared into his eyes. "And, Liam, no retribution on Red for this. You knew the rules here and chose to ignore them. I don't think Amy signed on for being raped and drained dry. Did she, Red?" I glanced at her.

"No, she sure as hell didn't." Red kicked Liam's head, just to make that point. "In fact, you only paid for a drink, not a fuck. So you're not only a sleaze, you're a cheap bastard." She shook her head. "When Glo here lets you go, you are to head straight for the door and out of here. You will not tell anyone about what happened tonight or I will make sure every vampire that crosses my path knows that you cried like a little girl when Glo beat you tonight. Are we clear?"

Liam's curses were colorful but somewhere in there was an agreement. Then I released the freeze. He got slowly to his feet, cradling his hands against his body. He glared at both of us, obviously thinking about making a move before he shrugged and headed for the door. Max followed him until he was outside and staggering down the sidewalk.

"Well, that was something. You ever want to come back to New York to live, you can work for me. I can always use another strong enforcer." Red slung her arm around me. "Come on. I'll buy you a drink." She walked me to the bar. "Looks like your friend Flo is having a good time."

Flo was surrounded by men and had several drinks in front of her. I noticed for the first time that she wasn't wearing her wedding band or engagement ring. Bad Flo. I wasn't about to say anything to her though. As far as I could tell all she was doing was a little harmless flirting.

"We have the real deal on tap if you want it." Red nodded toward a row of blood bags lined up behind the bar then signaled the bartender. "What's your favorite?"

I told her. "How do you get it on tap?"

"My drones donate. I pay them well for it and feed them to keep up their strength. There's a steak house around the corner and we have an arrangement." She grinned when a handsome mortal sidled up to the bar. "But if you'd prefer to drink straight from the source, Ben would be happy to take you to a private room."

I was almost tempted. Jerry took blood from strangers' veins all the time. But that seemed too intimate to me. Ben was friendly and cute. I'd be lying to myself if I said it was a necessity, a meaningless way to get nourishment. I shook my head. "AB Negative, if you have it. If not, whatever is on tap. But thanks, Ben. I'm sure it would have been a pleasure." He shrugged and moved on down the bar. He'd never said a word.

"He's not drugged, is he?" I took the glass the bartender handed me and sipped. Oh, it *was* fresh.

"No, but some are. If you want to get high, I can arrange it. Coke, meth, whatever is your pleasure. Some vamps still do that. Get high vicariously. No need for the alcohol thing now that we can get blood with alcohol. You remember how we used to have drones for the alcoholics?" Red started reminiscing about the old days. I just listened, only remembering some of it. Damn Greg Kaplan. If I could find him, I was going to make him pay for what he'd done to me. It was long overdue.

Two hours later, Flo and I piled into our limo. We were tired and not a little tipsy because we'd switched to the blood with alcohol. Red had given us whatever we wanted on the house and we'd taken full advantage. I'd danced with her and a few of the men who were everywhere. It had been fun.

"You were having a pretty good time, pal." I leaned against one door and Flo against the opposite one.

"Are you mad at me? Will you tell Ricardo?" Flo had even disappeared into a private room with a drone.

"No. You can do what you want." I was pretty sure I was drunk. "How far did you go? With Ben."

"You think I'd betray my Ricardo?" A big tear ran down her cheek. "How can you say that?"

"So you didn't, uh, you know?" I could have sworn she'd come downstairs with her dress on crooked.

"I was tempted. You know how it is. He was handsome. I was feeling, um, hot." She giggled. "He touched me a little when I was taking his blood which was really delicious, by the way." She sighed. "But then I remembered that Ricardo is my love. I cannot betray him." She blinked and frowned. "Do you think I am bad? That I wanted to see how it would be with another man? I liked that Ben seemed to want me." She wailed. "Oh, what have I done?"

"Nothing!" I patted her shoulder. "It was a little experiment, that's all, *am, amica.* Yeah, that's what you call me. We don't want to turn into old married women who become invisible to men." My head was too heavy for my body and I finally just let it fall back on the leather seat. "What would we do if no other man ever gave us 'the look'?"

"I know!" Flo sat up straight. "So I thank you for taking me there tonight. I feel renewed. I still got it, as they say. Yes. Florence da Vinci can still make a man want her. Hah!" And with that she fell over on the seat and started snoring.

I didn't point out that Ben had been paid to want her as I stared at the night passing by the limo's windows. I hoped I still had it too. A few male vampires had approached me and offered to buy me drinks. I hadn't been tempted even once. Good to know. All I could think about was getting home to Jerry. I'd had enough alcohol that I wanted to go to bed and make love with my man and no other man would do. I closed my eyes and didn't open them again until the driver shook me awake at the hotel.

"It must have been a good trip. You brought back an extra suitcase." Jerry greeted me at the airport with a big smile. I had thrown myself into his arms when I saw him. Now we were at baggage claim and I was relieved to see that extra suitcase with my wedding dress come around the carrousel. Richard had already met Flo and they'd hurried away with her bags, eager to be alone.

"It was fine. I got everything I needed." I stood back while he effortlessly carried both bags.

"Well, who is going to carry mine?" Mother complained behind me.

"And mine?" Charis managed to tug hers off the revolving platform and stood with her hands on her hips.

"You can pay for a rolling cart and fit both of them on it. Then drag it out to the curb." I loved being able to give both women a dose of reality. "Jerry, why don't you sit my bags down out there and we'll wait for you to bring the car from the parking lot?"

"Fine." He kissed my cheek, led me outside and planted the bags where I could wait with them. Then he strode off without a backward glance.

"He's really not going to help us?" Charis wasn't getting the picture as she followed me outside.

"You want to stay and act like a normal person, get with the program." I pointed to the sign with the rules for the rolling carts. "Need change for the cart?"

"No problem, Gloriana." My mother snapped her fingers and her bags disappeared.

"Mother!" I glanced around. Several people were rubbing their eyes like they might have had a hallucination. Well, yeah.

"This is what you get when you try to play hardball with me, darling." Mother raised an eyebrow. "There was nothing there I can't recreate with a snap."

"Cool. I can do that." Charis raised her hand.

"Don't you dare!" I ran over and grabbed her hand. "Your bridesmaid dress is in one of those."

"True." She grinned. "What are you going to do about it?"

I looked around and saw an abandoned cart then hurried to get it. "Why didn't you get luggage with wheels?"

"It wasn't as cute as this." She hefted her bag onto the cart.

"Now push it outside. Damn you both." I was over this whole trip.

"No need to be rude, Gloriana." Mother smiled. "Which is what you were when you wouldn't help your elderly mother with her bags."

"Elderly?" I laughed. "Oh, right. Next you'll be whipping out a Medicare card and asking for a senior discount at MacDonald's."

"Oh, do they give one?" Mother winked. "I do love their big hamburgers and the French fries!"

"Now who's being rude?" I winced when Charis ran over my toes with her cart. "Watch it!"

"You'd better go stand by your suitcases. What if someone steals your wedding dress?" She pushed through the automatic doors. "Where's Jerry anyway?"

The idea that I'd left my suitcases unattended galvanized me. I raced outside, breathing a sigh of relief that they were still where I'd left them. Of course they were. Because standing guard was a man who looked like he'd escaped from a gladiator movie.

"Dad! I didn't expect you to be here." I gave him a hug. "You really need to dress more appropriately for the place, you know."

"It's almost Halloween. I told the policeman a minute ago that I was going to an early costume party." He kissed my cheek then turned to my mother. "Hebe, you're looking beautiful as always. Love the earrings."

"Thank you, love. You paid for them. We gave your credit card quite a workout in New York." She kissed him on the mouth for a long time until Charis finally gave her father an elbow.

"Dad, I'm here too, you know."

"Of course. Did you have a good time?" Mars hugged Charis.

"It was okay. I saw a play. A musical about shoes. It could have been worse." She glanced at me.

"You do like shoes." He turned. "There's Blade with the car. Let me get all these bags. You girls get in the vehicle. I had to run off a character who tried to take your two bags, Gloriana. That's why I'm here. Lucky for you I was paying attention tonight. I knew you were riding in one of those airplanes. Hate the things. So I was tuned in and here comes this man about to grab your bags." He began stuffing suitcases in the back of Jerry's SUV while I stared at him.

"What?" I counted my bags. Yes, they were both there.

"Lucky I interfered in time. That man won't be walking right for some time, I tell you. The policeman liked the way I used the suitcase as a battering ram. He took the fellow into custody." Mars slammed the hatchback closed and walked around the car.

"Dad! Thank you! If I'd lost my wedding dress…" I broke into tears. Stupid, careless…

"Glory, relax. He saved the day. Get in the car and quit making a scene." Charis grabbed my arm.

"Gloriana, sweetheart, it's okay." Jerry ran around the car and pulled me into his arms. "Don't cry. Mars took care of it."

"I know. But I almost lost it." I sobbed against his chest. What the hell was wrong with me? I didn't fall apart like this over small things.

"You didn't, did you? Now come on, get in the car. We'll be home soon." Jerry tenderly helped me into the front seat, daring anyone to object to the seating arrangement. Charis had a tendency to call "shotgun", something she'd learned on TV. My mother also wanted to ride up front, claiming car sickness in the back. Now they both meekly got in the backseat, making a tight fit with Mars.

I buckled my seatbelt and pulled a tissue from my purse. It had been a near miss. I had to get over this kind of emotional reaction and concentrate on moving forward with wedding plans. It wouldn't be long now and I would be Jerry's forever. Uh oh. Fresh tears. Of happiness. We should have eloped. Because we'd tried to do this before and hadn't made it to the altar. What else could go wrong? I knew better than to ask a question like that.

NINETEEN

"I have some bad news." Richard looked solemn to go along with his statement.

"Just spit it out." Jerry held my hand.

"I got a call from the venue for your wedding. They had a fire last night. Seems a drunken guest knocked over a candle and the whole place went up." Richard had his laptop open and spun it around. There was a picture of the Tuscan villa we'd chosen for our wedding. It was on a hilltop, miles from the nearest small town. A beautiful setting and unusual in Texas. But the villa was now a smoldering ruin.

Richard slammed the computer closed. "I'm sorry."

I couldn't say a word. Jerry's arms came around me.

"*Oh, mio Dio!* I can't believe it. I am beginning to think your marriage is cursed." Flo crossed herself.

"Shut up, darling. You're not helping." Richard glared at Flo. "But I have a solution. I was on the phone to Damian earlier and he is perfectly willing to let you have his home. Like he did for Flo and me. I thought it made a beautiful setting for a wedding."

"It did! Glory, it will be *perfetto*." Flo wiped away a tear. "You tell me to shut up?" She whispered a spate of Italian at Richard that promised retribution. "If you don't mind, Glory, Jeremiah, why not move the date to the Winter Solstice? Damian will have the decorations ordered already and he always does a beautiful job, doesn't he?" She wouldn't look at Richard.

I turned to Jerry. "At this point I don't care where we get married. I just want to get this over with."

"You make it sound like having a tooth drawn." Jerry grinned. "I know what you mean though. Why give the fates or Olympus another chance at us? If you're okay with it, I'm okay with it." He pulled me closer and kissed me. "I love you. I want to marry you. Whenever and wherever you say."

"Shall I call Damian back?" Richard wanted this nailed down. As best man he took his job seriously.

"Flo, are you sure you don't mind? That we're having our wedding in the same place?" Maybe *I* minded a little.

Flo had put a foot between herself and Richard. "We will make your wedding unique. It is you, not me who is the bride this time." She stepped forward and hugged me. "I don't want you to worry. I love you." She glared at Richard. "Glory, *you* would never tell me to shut up. We have a month to make this wedding amazing. Am I right?"

"Thanks, pal. I don't know what I'd do without you." I smiled at Richard over her shoulder. "And give Richard a break. He's stressed. I'm sure he's sorry he snapped at you. Aren't you, Richard?"

His slight nod wasn't exactly an abject apology then he pulled out his phone and hit speed dial. "Damian, Richard. The wedding is on. Can we come over and look at the house? Gloriana has an idea about bagpipes." He smiled at me. "Yes, a Highland wedding. That should be different from mine, don't you think?" He walked out of the room, still talking.

"Flo, forgive him. You know a man doesn't like to be bossed around." I whispered this in her ear.

"She's right, Florence." Jerry patted Flo on the back. "Glory has led me a merry chase for centuries. I know you have Richard well-trained but you are usually more subtle than this."

"Stop it." She glanced over her shoulder. "Can't I be mad at him for at least five minutes?" She sighed. "Ricardo makes me *pazzo*. You would say crazy. Since I got back from New York I feel guilty. I did nothing I tell you. Maybe a *little* something but he keeps looking at me like I was *indecente* while I was there. So I block my thoughts. That just makes him more suspicious."

"Then tell him what you did at Red, Flo. Clear your conscience. It'll make you feel better." I glanced at Jerry. "I told Jer all about going to the nightclub. He's put out feelers to see if Greg Kaplan is still around Austin. No sign of him." I'd told Flo all about my history with Greg and what Red had told me.

"Too bad. I'll take him apart with my bare hands if he comes around Gloriana again." Jerry couldn't keep *his* hands off of me. Which made me very happy.

"Hah. You didn't do anything to be ashamed of, Glory. I, I feel like I was *cattivo*, not so nice at Red. With that drone."

"What's this? You went to Red. In New York?" Richard walked back into the room. "We're going home, now." He issued an order and Flo didn't take it well.

"Maybe I'm not ready to go home. Glory and I have plans to make." Flo spun around and put her hands on her hips, ready to do battle.

"That's okay, Flo. I'll get with you tomorrow night. I need time to think about this. Okay?" I wanted them out of here. I really didn't want to be in the middle of their fight.

"Don't order me around, Ricardo." Flo stalked to the door. With her hands fisted, she looked like a mini-warrior in her high-heeled boots, black jeans and black leather vest over her sweater. All she needed was a weapon. Of course the way she moved her hips, I'd say she had weapons and knew how to use them. "I will tell you everything but only if you are kind to me."

"When the hell have I ever been anything but kind to you, darling?" Richard looked back at Jerry like a lost man.

"You told me to shut up." Flo jerked open our front door.

"It was an emergency. I'm sorry." He was right behind her, his eyes on those hips. "Now about Red. I've been there. You had no business going to that club without me. Someone could have hurt you. Is that what happened? Do I have to go there and kill someone?" Richard could be heard haranguing Flo all the way up the stairs. They'd shift on the roof and fly home. I was glad to see them go.

Jerry laughed as he walked over to lock the door. "You sure I know everything that happened at Red?"

"Everything that happened to *me*. I'm not spilling Flo's secrets." I walked up to him and slid my arms around his waist. "Now let's talk about this Highland wedding. I can't wait to see you in a kilt again. Did you tell your father to bring his? And the other relatives arriving from Scotland?"

"Of course. Now I'll have to tell them we've changed the date, and the place. I'll call them later." He began nibbling on my neck. "But I doubt that will be a problem. My mother will complain of course."

"She would complain if we were marrying in your home church at the Campbell Castle with the Queen's blessing. Because of who your bride will be." I ran my hands up under his shirt, enjoying the way his muscles flexed beneath my fingertips.

"She'll just have to deal with it." Jerry swung me up into his arms. "We're alone for a change. It's Alesha's night off, Charis is settled into her new apartment, and there's no sign of your parents."

"Well then. It seems like it's time to christen another room in this new place." I unbuttoned my blouse then unhooked the front of my bra. "We haven't made love in the guest room yet."

"No, we haven't. That's because we've had one guest after another since this apartment was finished." Jerry leaned down to kiss the spot where my underwire had left a mark then strode toward that bedroom. "Time to check that off our to-do list."

"I do love a man who is well-organized." I laughed when he tossed me on the bed.

Jerry landed next to me. "Are you very disappointed about the wedding?" He stared down at me.

"I meant what I said. I just want to marry you, Jer. Any time, any place." I pulled up his shirt and he got the message, wrenching it off over his head and throwing it aside. "What about you? Is this wedding what you want?"

"I want you, Gloriana. I meant it when I said the when and where makes no difference to me." He leaned down to lick a delicious path across my breasts. "I promise one thing. I'll never tell you to shut up."

"Can I have that in writing?" I held him by the ears and smiled into his eyes.

"Later." He unbuttoned my jeans and helped me wrestle them off. "Will you make *me* a promise?"

I froze with my jeans stuck around my thighs. "What?"

"That you won't keep secrets from me." He dragged my jeans

down and threw them to the floor, then settled next to me, one leg sliding between mine.

"Secrets." That had been an issue between us before and I still had a big one I'd kept from him. Did I dare tell him the truth now? How would he take it?

"Obviously I just struck a nerve. What is it, Gloriana? What big secret are you holding back?" He levered himself on top of me, his body adjusting until we fit the way we always did. I shifted, happy to derail this conversation with love play. He wasn't having it. "No, come on. Are we to start our married life with something between us?"

"Well, this is between us." I nudged his erection with my knee.

"Stop it." He rolled off of me and stared at the ceiling. "I thought we had this settled. What are you hiding that you feel I can't handle?" He turned his head toward me. "Is it another man?"

"I'm marrying *you*, Jerry. There has been no other man since I made that commitment." I reached out to stroke his cheek.

"You worded that very carefully." He grabbed my hand. "So it is about another man." He tried to read my mind and hit the blank wall I set up. "Shit. Are you really going to ruin things between us over an old affair?"

"Not so old." I jerked my hand from his. "You want all my secrets? What about yours? I know you've had plenty of women when we were on breaks. Probably hundreds. It's okay. I understood. You're a virile man who needed someone."

"So this secret you're keeping happened when we weren't on a break." Jerry wouldn't look at me. "You say you've been true to me since you took my ring. Fine. I've been the same. And once we say our vows, I intend to be with you and only you." He sat up then, his eyes searching mine. "What about you?"

"Yes! I want no other man now or ever!" I sat up until we were face to face. I was at a disadvantage with my blouse and bra hanging open and naked from the waist down. Jerry still wore his jeans, even his boots. I'd lost my high heels in the living room. But the way he let his gaze travel over me, maybe I wasn't at such a disadvantage after all.

"Prove it. Tell me this secret. I can take it. Maybe I'll get mad. Maybe jealous. But I won't kick you out of bed and out of my life, Gloriana. I swear it. Because you are mine and always will be. Do you trust me enough to believe that?" He pulled me to him. Our chests hit and I gasped, flooded with the lust we always felt for each other. His belt buckle dug into my stomach when he stood and hauled me against him. I made quick work of the offending metal and ripped open the button on his jeans.

"Come on, Jerry. No more talk." I pushed down his zipper. "I want action."

"No way in hell." He stared into my eyes. "The truth, Gloriana. What's the big secret?" He groaned when I ran my hand inside and squeezed his sacs.

"You don't want to know."

"Yes, I do." He backed up and kicked off his jeans then came to me again, his hands on me everywhere. I was fully naked now, my blouse and bra somewhere on the floor. He pressed close but wouldn't enter me. "Say it."

"I slept with Israel Caine."

"Shit." He froze for a long minute. "How many times?" He ground it out. He was so hard that it could have been a stake pressed close to my most private place.

"I don't remember." I reached for him again but he wouldn't let me pull him inside.

"Yes, you do. Say it." He slid a hand down my side and squeezed my butt. "You would never forget fucking Israel Caine."

"Twice. You were in Scotland. I thought you weren't coming back." I held onto him, terrified he'd shove me away and out of his life, despite his promise. "I'm sorry, Jerry. I told him it would never happen again. It was a...mistake."

"Damn right, it was." Jerry gritted his teeth as he dragged my legs around his waist and pushed into me. I gasped, eager to take all he had to give. God, he felt good. Amazing. And when he sank his teeth into my vein, I called his name, tremors of satisfaction shivering through me. He drew hard then let me go. We slid down the wall to hold each other, breathing hard in a way vampires seldom do.

"I knew it," Jerry finally said as he licked the punctures closed. "You can tell when a man has had your woman."

"No! Surely he didn't say--" I didn't even mind the "his woman" comment. I *was* his and he was mine. Thank God.

"He knew better. He's afraid of my knives. But there was a look in his eyes when he was around you. I know that look. He'd had a taste and wanted more." Jerry stood then picked me up. He carried me into our master bedroom and laid me on the bed. Then he just looked at me.

I shivered, waiting. "He's never getting more. He knows that." Did Jerry believe me?

"Doesn't stop him from wanting you." Jerry sat on the bed and I reached for his hand.

I almost sobbed in relief when he let me wrap my fingers around his. Callouses. He'd spent too many years working with those knives. Was he thinking about taking one to Ray? To me?

"Jerry…" I knew I should stay quiet but couldn't.

"Relax, Gloriana. You always wanted the man. Played his music endlessly even before you met him."

"It never should have happened. I love *you*, Jeremiah." I suddenly couldn't look at him. I didn't deserve his forgiveness. I'd let my lust for a shiny toy of a man get the best of me.

"Then I guess I should feel sorry for the stupid bastard." Jerry lay beside me and turned my face to his. "Because I won you and he lost." He smiled and kissed my lips. "Dawn is close and I need a shower. Join me?"

"Of course." I slid out of bed. "You won't hurt Ray, will you?"

"How can you ask me that?" He strode into the bathroom, his shoulders rigid. My beautiful warrior, scars and all.

"You didn't answer me, Jer." I ran after him. "I don't love him. But he's my friend."

"And if I decide to put a bit of hurt on the *buthaidir duine?"* Jerry started the water in the shower, adjusting the temperature as if he hadn't just made a threat. "What will you do then? Call off the wedding?" He stepped into the shower, giving none of his thoughts away.

"Nothing will make me cancel our wedding." I stepped in behind him. "But I was looking forward to having Ray sing there. If you're going to be a jealous jerk about it, I guess I could call him and cancel."

"A jealous jerk?" That got his attention. He whipped around, a bar of soap in his hand. "What do I have to be jealous of, I ask you?" As usual, when Jer was upset, his Scottish roots showed. "Is he a better lover? Is that it? Are you *pining* for him? Wishing you could have him again?"

"Oh, please." I trailed a fingertip across his chest, flicking a nipple with my nail. "I'd never say that. You've had centuries to prove you can outperform a mere fledgling vampire, Jeremiah Campbell. And centuries to learn how to please me." I took the soap from Jerry and ran it over his chest. "He did have a piercing though. Here." I ran the soap around Jerry's cock. "A novelty. Can't say it added much to the experience."

"By God!" Jerry slammed a fist into the glass shower door. By some miracle, it didn't shatter.

I gave in and pushed him against the tile wall, my hands on his shoulders. "Would you stop this? Israel Caine is nothing next to you, Jeremiah Campbell. Are you always comparing me to the other women you've bedded? Are you?" I rubbed my breasts against his soapy chest. "Say yes and I'll use one of my Olympus powers on you. I guarantee you won't like it."

"No, of course not. You are all I think about when we make love, lass." His eyes softened when he slid his hands around me. "Do you blame me for being jealous? The man is handsome, talented, and sings like an angel."

"Now who sounds like he has a crush on Israel Caine?" I kissed Jerry's chin. "None of that matters, Jerry. Ray is an alley cat. He uses women and throws them away. I can't be with a man like that. You are my forever guy." I dropped to my knees. "You're the one who I want to please." I kissed a path down his stomach then took him into my mouth. Yes, I was manipulating him with sex. It was an ancient tradition with women and I wasn't above it. His groans of pleasure and his gentle hands in my hair reassured me that he was on his way to forgiving my confession.

He let me hold him in thrall for a few minutes before he reached for the spigots with a shaking hand and turned off the water. He picked me up and carried me to our bed where he gently laid me down.

"You drive me mad. You know that, don't you?" He leaned down to begin an erotic exploration of my inner thighs.

"It's my duty." I sighed when he pushed my legs farther apart and rested them on his shoulders. "I don't want you to get bored."

"No chance of that." He dipped his tongue inside.

"God, Jerry." I grabbed his hair and hung on as the pleasure surged in waves.

He teased with tongue and fangs until I screamed and bucked against his mouth. It was too much. I tried to drag him up and over me, needing him inside. He wasn't having it. He reached down to squeeze one of my breasts and I broke, sobbing his name. Was he punishing me? Making me pay for sleeping with Ray? I realized I wasn't the only one who knew how to use sex in our relationship.

I went limp as my orgasm finally subsided and he let me go. He wiped his mouth, streaked with my blood, with the back of his hand then smoothed that hand over my stomach.

"You're giving me an evil look. Didn't you enjoy that?" He kissed my inner thigh then gently pressed his cock inside me. I shuddered, so sensitive I came again instantly.

"Enjoy?" I panted, raking my nails over his back. "Not sure about that. It was more like torture, I think. But then perhaps I'm perverted enough to like a bit of that kind of torment." I moved against him. God, yes, I needed this. Wanted this. No one filled me like Jerry.

"You screamed my name." He kissed me deeply, his tongue raking my fangs so I could taste his blood. Then he leaned back. "You always scream my name when you come." He smiled and teased one of my nipples then bent to take it into his mouth, sucking hard. It popped, rosy and wet when he released it. "Say it again. Look at me and say my name, Gloriana. Say you will always be mine." He was moving now, stroking inside me, bringing me close again as he pulled my legs tight around his hips. "You and I together forever and no others. That is the promise we will make on our wedding night."

"Jeremiah. Yes! You and I together forever and no others." I found the strength to flip him so I was on top now, riding him. I gazed down into his dear face, the man who had been the one for me for centuries. I pulled his hands up to my breasts and left them there, then leaned down to take his vein. His blood, warm, salty and perfect, filled my mouth. Tears stung my eyes by the time I sat up again.

We stared at each other, no words needed as we moved faster, our bodies thrusting against each other as we strove to keep the sensations climbing. When we reached the pinnacle I did shout his name again, I couldn't seem to help myself. Trembling with satisfaction, I dropped to his chest and lay there, listening to the slow thud of his heartbeat. Not dead but not alive. But forever mine. I smiled and let the dawn suck me under.

We'd been invaded. Campbell brothers, Campbell cousins, even the Campbell pipers had come to town for the wedding. If I thought too much about it, I might have run away. As it was, I watched Jerry turn into a Scottish prince, the host to all and happier than I'd ever seen him. Laird and Lady Campbell declined to stay in our guest room, thank God, and had booked a suite in a hotel an enterprising vampire had set up in town. In fact, the entire hotel was full of the Campbell clan.

"Rehearsal dinner? Isn't that strange, considering vampires can't eat?" Lacy sat on a stool in the shop, rubbing her expansive tummy.

"It's a ritual, according to the wedding magazines Flo has had me studying. And there are plenty of guests who can eat and should be included. My side of the family for instance." I was going through our new stock of shoes, trying to find something to wear with the dress I'd bought in New York.

"So you said the groom's family is responsible for it. Where's it going to be?" Lacy got up and shuffled into the back room. "Try these. They came in yesterday and I haven't had time to price them yet. They're your size." She handed me a pair of Alexander McQueen shoes. I knew instantly that they were perfect.

"The Campbells are taking over N-V. I'm surprised Rafe didn't tell you. They've hired a caterer to provide food." I sat down and kicked off my shoes.

"I come home so tired these days, Rafe and I don't talk much. What about those shoes?" Lacy was back on her stool.

"Love them. You have such a great eye." I strapped them on and stood. "There's nothing like a designer shoe to make a woman feel sexy."

"I know." Lacy kicked off her own shoes. "My feet are so swollen, I'm down to moccasins. This pregnancy is killing me."

"Did you have the ultrasound?" I'd been so busy getting ready for this wedding that I'd totally neglected the shop. Luckily it could run without me and very well too.

"Yes." She reached in a drawer. "Look. This is the picture Ian took." She flushed. "You're not going to believe it."

I walked over, only wobbling a little on the high heels, and grabbed the black and white. "Uh, I think I'm seeing more than one baby in there."

"You are! Triplets." Lacy laughed. "My mother is beside herself. It may have helped a little with the rift between us. You know she's not a fan of shape-shifters."

"Were-cats are shape-shifters too. Right?" I was fascinated by the blurry black and gray picture that looked like an x-ray.

"Were-cats are were-cats. We don't shift into anything else." Lacy reached for the photo. "These precious babies could turn out to be either cats or just shifters. It's driving my family crazy. Rafe hasn't told his yet. When he does, all hell will break loose. You know Rafe is from a powerful shifter family. He left home because they wanted choose his mate. He's not great with being told what to do." Lacy sighed.

"I'm sure they'll love you when they meet you, Lace." What else could I say?

"Who knows when that'll be? I think Rafe wants to wait to see what we get. If the babies are shifters, then he'll have to approach his family. If they're cats," Her eyes filled with tears. "Well, he may never tell them."

"No! He would never just deny them, Lace." I put my arm around her. "You have talked about this, haven't you?"

"I'm scared to bring it up." She held the photo against her swollen breasts. "I love Rafe but this pregnancy was an accident. He never said he wanted a family before this happened. I feel like I trapped him."

"Stop it. He loves you. He told me that himself. He's excited to have a family." I patted her shoulder. "It sounds like you two need to talk this out." I sat down and took off those shoes. The heels were awfully high and they weren't terribly comfortable. I was taking them anyway, of course. Sexy trumped comfort. "Communicate. Jerry and I are finally talking and I couldn't be happier. It took us long enough. Secrets will kill a relationship."

"Glory is right." Flo walked in from the back room. "I let myself in from the alley."

I found a bag and dropped the shoes inside. "I'm glad you and Richard are speaking again, Flo."

"I had to make him suffer a little. No one tells me to shut up and gets away with it." She held out her right hand. "How do you like my new ring? I always wanted a heart-shaped diamond."

"Wow." Lacy got off her stool to look. "I can't even get a proposal out of my man." She looked at her watch. "Kira is late. I should be leaving now."

"Go. I'll stay until she gets here." I noticed Lacy's ankles *were* swollen as she struggled to put her moccasins back on. "Is Rafe picking you up?"

"I'm taking a cab home. It should be here any minute. He has a big band playing tonight. He said some of your out-of-town company booked the upstairs to see them perform. I'm surprised you're not there." She pulled on a coat that didn't meet over her stomach. It was cold outside.

Three days from the wedding. Our outdoor wedding. Jerry had laughed at my worries. Vampires don't feel the cold and Scots? A Highlander thought nothing of our puny Texas cold fronts. Men. Why couldn't he get stressed like I did?

"Wait a minute." I realized I'd spaced about the wedding and totally missed the point of Lacy's comment. "All the Campbells are at N-V? Including Jerry? Without me?" I thrust my feet back into the boots I'd worn down to the shop. "What the hell?" Not that I was surprised that Mag Campbell would want to see her son without me around to dampen her spirits. But I wasn't letting her get away with it.

"That's why I'm here, Glory. Ricardo sent me. He said Jeremiah has been trying to call you." Flo shook her head. "Didn't Lady Campbell invite you? I told him you must not know about the party or you would be there."

"Of course not." I pulled my phone out of my pocket. I'd put it on vibrate but realized my battery had died. I'd been so busy doing wedding things I'd forgotten to charge it. "I guess I could give Mag the benefit of the doubt but you want to take bets on whether she tried to call or not?"

"Well, come on. Or do you want to change?" Flo looked me over.

"Oh, I'm going to change." I wasn't wearing the plain jeans and top I had on. "Come upstairs with me and help me pick an outfit to wow Mother Campbell."

"But you said I could leave now." Lacy sagged back to her stool.

"No, you're right." I turned to my best friend. "Will you…"

Flo held out her hand and I gave her my key. "I'll find

something for you." She helped Lacy to her feet. "I talked to Rafael at the club. He is telling everyone that he is having three babies! How are you feeling?"

"Really? He's telling everyone? Was he bragging or bitching about it?" Lacy walked outside with Flo.

"Bragging, of course. You know men. He is powerful. He can make three babies at once. So macho, this shifter! Bang, bang, bang." Flo moved her hips in a parody of a man putting it to a woman, then laughed. Lacy was laughing too as they parted.

I smiled, glad Flo had said the right thing. I had just started straightening stock when the door opened. Kira walked in, smiling when she saw me.

"Boss lady. Good to see you here. Finally. Are you going to be working with me tonight?" She threw her purse under the counter and went to the stock room to hang up her coat.

"No, I'll be leaving in a few minutes." I hated to admit that. Was I going to get a lecture about how I was abandoning the shop again?

"Well, can we talk?" Kira came back and leaned against the counter. "About Ed or Edwina or whatever the hell he wants to be called."

"He's my accountant now, Kira. You have a problem with that?" I looked her over. She'd been buying in the shop again. I recognized the vintage shirt.

"My problem is that gorilla beat me to a pair of gold pumps I'd had my eye on. Now I find out he's getting the same discount I get." She cocked one hip and leaned closer. "If he starts trying to beat me out on the cocktail wear, then I'm going to have to put my foot down."

"Well." I didn't know what to say. Kira was as tall as Ed, but not nearly as wide. "You're stressing over nothing. You know Ed must wear about a twenty-two and you can't be more than a twelve."

She smiled and straightened. "You're right. That hulk could never squeeze his shoulders into the kinds of things I wear." She sighed. "But those gold pumps! Glory, they were perfect!"

"I'm sure they hurt like hell." I grinned and she laughed. "You ever go out with him?" I had to say it. It wasn't like me to play matchmaker but those two would be perfect for each other. "Ed seems straight to me."

"Oh, he is. Just because he likes his cross-dressing doesn't make him gay. He's gone out with some women I know." Kira looked thoughtful. "We've had words though, about the shoes. It pissed me off. He had to know I would want them."

"Maybe you could offer to watch for things he'd like. In his size. And take turns on the shoes. I can't fire him. He's done amazing things with the books. And he did say you were hot." I patted her shoulder.

"Oh, he did." She stuck out her chest. "Man wants to take me out, he'd better not show up in those gold shoes, that's all I'm saying."

I nodded, hiding a grin when I heard the front door open. "Here comes Flo. I'm going to change then I've got a party to go to. Will you be okay by yourself?"

"Aren't I always?" She raised an eyebrow and turned to Flo. "Hey, short stuff. Did you see that we got in a vintage Chanel bag last week? I know you don't like old things, but this one is a beaut."

Flo practically threw my clothes at me and followed Kira to a locked case. "*Davvero*? Vintage Chanel? You know they make fakes, Kira."

"Honey, I'm an expert on this stuff. I would never show you a fake." Kira unlocked the case then turned to wink at me. "Party? Go change. I got this."

I shook my head and walked to the dressing room. Flo had brought a pair of brown velvet jeans, a purple and gold satin blouse and a gold chain belt. With a gold leather jacket I was definitely going to be noticed. By the time I got out of the dressing room, Flo was moving her credit card, compact, lipstick and phone into the small gold quilted Chanel bag.

Flo slung the chain over her shoulder. "What do you think, Glory?"

"It looks perfect." I smiled at my clerk then looked around the shop to make sure we didn't have any customers. With the all clear I glanced skyward then braced myself and did something I wasn't sure was wise.

"Mother, Dad, if you're listening, I'd like to invite you to meet the Campbells."

"Darling, I thought you'd never ask." My mother appeared in front of me. She was dressed in her usual perfection in a black dress that could have come from a Paris designer's showroom. Dad appeared a moment later and he was in a business suit and tie for a change.

"No, Mars. Too dressy." Mother flicked a fingertip and he was in slacks and a silk shirt with a velvet sports coat over that.

"Really, Hebe. You could have just told me what to wear. I can dress myself." To prove he could, he changed the coat from black to navy blue and added a pocket square in bright red. "Gloriana, do you approve?" He kissed me on the cheek.

"You both look perfect." I turned to Kira who was standing next to the register with her mouth hanging open. "These are my parents, Kira. They are Hebe and Mars, from Olympus. If you tell anyone who they are or where they come from, they can make you very sorry."

"Yes, indeed. You can't imagine the tricks we have up our sleeves." My mother's smile was so evil that even I shivered. "Florence, I see you are here as usual."

"Yes. The Campbell family is down the street, at a club called N-V. I came to get Glory. Her phone wasn't working and she almost missed the party." Flo looked nervous now and I didn't blame her. My mother was examining her like she would a cockroach that had crawled out from under a dress rack.

"Mother, Flo is my best friend. My matron of honor. Be nice." I grabbed Flo's hand.

"I am always nice." Mother took Mars' arm.

He laughed. "Nice? Dear, I love you but I'd never say you were nice." He patted her hand. "I am not fond of nice anyway. You are much more exciting than a bland nice woman."

I rolled my eyes when Mother practically melted into his arms. "Let's go, please. We're going to walk down Sixth Street. Like normal people. It's only a few blocks. Can you act like a mortal for a little while?" I directed this at both my parents but mostly at my mother. "I don't want anything to disappear or any unusual weather patterns to happen around us. If you need a coat, Mother, snap it on now, before we step outside."

"Yes, I suppose it is chilly." She snapped on a chinchilla shrug.

"Not that. Austin isn't friendly to people who wear furs." I ignored her pithy opinion of the barbarians in Texas then sighed in relief when she snapped on a pretty blue cashmere coat.

"Is this better?" She also added leather gloves.

"Perfect. Thank you. This is a big deal to me. I want you to get along with Jerry's parents. So please make this a nice evening." I ran my sweaty palms down my velvet pants.

"Hmm. Nice again. Well, Hebe, clearly our daughter is ashamed of us." Mars nodded. "But I should remind you, Gloriana, that, as mortals and blood suckers, these Campbells are our inferiors. I hope they remember that."

"Oh, boy," I said to Flo as I pulled her along with me.

"Tell us about these people, Gloriana." Mars opened the door to the sidewalk. Then he looked back. "Kira, is it? We will not hurt you. But Gloriana is right. Keep your mouth shut about what you saw tonight. I am Mars, god of war." He smiled and thunder clapped, making the room shake just a little. "I don't play around when I'm betrayed."

"Yes, sir." Kira sank down on the stool, her lips trembling. "Good night."

I wanted to go back and give her a hug but figured that would spoil Dad's warning. So out we went. I gave my parents a quick summary of the Campbells. The fact that the entire clan was vampire got a reaction.

"How can they change their own children into blood suckers?" Mother looked at Mars. "I can't wait to meet these people. Do they still live in caves and carry clubs, Gloriana?" She shuddered. "You must rethink this alliance."

"The wedding goes on, Mother. The Campbells have a castle in Scotland. Dad, the Laird is a famous warrior over there. I think you'll like him." But then I felt I had to warn them that Mag, Jerry's mother, had never thought I was good enough for her son because I'd been an actress back in the day. I wouldn't be surprised if Mag didn't show some of her negative attitude, even in front of my parents.

"Not good enough, Gloriana? Well, we'll soon straighten out that woman." Mother's lips were firm.

"No, you won't. I'm not turning this night into a free-for-all with thunder and lightning." Though that would be fun to watch. "Jerry and I are marrying and I'm stuck with his family. You can't hurt them."

"What about his father, this warrior? Does he also disrespect you, Gloriana?" Mars looked ready to take on the entire clan and teach them a lesson.

"The Laird likes me. He's never been the problem." I stopped and pulled them both into an alley. "Listen to me. It's like when I announced I was marrying a vampire. You were instantly prejudiced. Even without meeting Jerry. But, Mars, you came to admire him as a fellow warrior once you got to know him. Right?" I noticed Flo sidling away toward the club. I let her go.

"Yes. He was very brave in Olympus. But he wasn't a blood sucker there." Mars kept looking toward the street. People walked past, ignoring us.

"Well, just try to forget your prejudices when you meet the Campbells. They have their own biases. But I'm betting they will be impressed when they see how important my parents are. Remember, when they first met me I was nothing, a poor widow with no background. Now look at the pedigree I have." I put my arms around both of them.

"Do you hear that, Mars?" Mother kissed my cheek. "Gloriana is proud of us."

"So she says now." Mars stepped back. "But if I hear that Campbell woman say an unkind word to our daughter, I'll not stand for it." He patted his jacket pocket. "You think I came unarmed to meet a potential enemy, Daughter? Not on your life." He nodded toward the street. "Let's go. If your man is still the warrior he was on Olympus, he won't allow his mother to disrespect you either."

"Dad, please. Calm down. This is supposed to be a party. I want both of you on your best behavior and I'm sure Jerry has told his parents the same thing." What had Dad put in his pocket? He was not only the god of war but had that voodoo following as well. I didn't trust him or his temper. I hoped Jerry had his parents under control. If only my phone worked so I could warn him. At least Flo had a head start so maybe she'd give Jerry a heads up. I didn't want to imagine the consequences if Mag attacked me like she usually did.

Mars dragged me toward the bright lights of N-V. A wedding celebration. Whoopee.

TWENTY

The music was loud and the crowd was thick. Ed was at the door so we had no trouble moving past the line and into the club.

"The Campbell party is upstairs. Band starts in thirty minutes." Ed didn't look anything like Aretha Franklin tonight. He was in a black N-V sweatshirt and jeans. "Have fun." He nodded to my parents.

"Mother, Dad, this is Ed Halloran, my accountant. And part of the security here." I stopped, not sure if I should use their real names.

"Max and Helen St. Clair. Happy to meet you." My father shook hands with Ed then winked at me. "We just got into town for our girl's wedding. Glad to know she has an accountant now. You a C.P.A.?"

"Dad, Ed's on the clock here. Maybe you can quiz him later." I hustled them through the doorway and into an empty spot against the wall. "What the hell was that? Max and Helen?" I whispered in my father's ear.

"What were you going to say, Gloriana? Our names from upstairs? I don't think so. Your mother and I discussed this and came up with these names. Don't you like them?" Mars patted Mother's hand. "Helen chose hers because of that thing in Troy. My lady could certainly launch more than a thousand ships with her beautiful face."

"Oh, Max!" Mother kissed him on the cheek. "Gloriana, answer your father. Isn't this what you want when we are in public? Two mortal parents with nice names and ordinary backgrounds? Your father is in the military supply business. Isn't that right, Max?" She was holding onto his arm like she'd never let go. "No one knows war like my man."

"Yes, indeed. I make modern weapons for, um, I guess I should say the Americans. Is that correct, Gloriana?" Mars puffed out his chest. "Where are these Scottish freaks? Let's get this over with."

"Oh, God." I had a feeling my father had been watching bad television. "Stop it. The Campbells aren't freaks. That would make *me* one. The names are good. The rest? I don't know. Just go back to being yourself, only not." I had no idea what I was saying. Luckily I saw Jerry coming. But then I noticed who was hot on his heels. Laird and Lady Campbell.

I prayed the mortals nearby were too into the music or eager to get to the bar for a drink to pay much attention to these people with me who were dressed way better than they were. It was mostly a college crowd and I spied the poster advertising the band tonight. Alternative rock. We probably should take these introductions somewhere else. If my father didn't throttle back his attitude about vampires, I was afraid things could turn ugly.

"Gloriana, you finally got here. I expected you an hour ago." Jerry kissed me and pulled me to his side.

"My phone died so I didn't get your message. Or Lady Campbell's?" I looked at Mag but she just smiled. Of course she hadn't called me. "But I'm here now." I knew my smile looked strained. "Can we go somewhere quiet for the introductions?" I saw Rafe next to the bar and waved him over.

"Welcome to N-V. Who is this, Glory?" He nodded at my parents. I blurted out an introduction which made Rafe look like he wanted to ask some questions. Too bad.

"Hey, congrats on the triplets." I was desperate to change the subject.

"Thanks." He just kept staring at my parents. "I didn't know--"

"My folks just arrived in town. To meet Jerry's parents before the wedding. Could I use your office for a little while?" I gave Rafe a look that said *Help!* "We could use some privacy."

"Sure, go ahead. It's empty." He nodded to Blade. "Looking forward to the big night?"

"Of course." Jerry's grip on my arm tightened. "See you there?"

"Wouldn't miss it." Rafe grinned and winked at me. "Good luck. Both of you."

I couldn't stand all this cordiality. "Come on. Let's go where it's not so noisy." I led the way, not even looking back to make sure they were following me. I dreaded the whole thing. Dad kept fiddling with his pocket square. And then there was my mother, who hadn't stopped assessing Jerry's mother since she'd walked up. I ushered them into Rafe's office and slammed the door.

"Well now." Mars nodded. "Guess these are your folks, Blade." He stuck out his hand. "We were incognito out there. Max and Helen, not our real names of course." He did one of those artificial laughs then focused on the laird. "I'm Mars, God of War. This is my, ahem, fiancée, Hebe, daughter of Zeus." Mars wore a smile, but he might as well have had a sign around his neck that said, "Mess with me or my family and I'll strike you dead on the spot."

"My parents," Jerry was doing all he could to keep from reaching for a knife, I could tell. He hadn't missed my father's hostility or obvious condescension. "Angus, Laird of Clan Campbell, and Magdalena, Lady Campbell." The two fathers shook hands and sized each other up. The mothers studied each other with narrowed eyes.

The women each wore expensive designer outfits head to toe, complete with jewelry that cost a fortune. I noticed my mother now sported a huge pink diamond on her engagement finger. I didn't dare comment on the fiancé statement. Since both my mother and father had living spouses on Olympus, I was sure it was merely a convenient lie. For my sake? As if I cared that I was the result of their affair.

"Well, this is going well." I kept my arm around Jerry, determined to make this a happy occasion. "Mother and Dad took on those mortal names so we can use them in public. Isn't that nice? It will make it so much easier to introduce them around to people outside this room."

"Yes. Jeremiah warned us, of course. About you people." The Laird looked like he'd caught a whiff of bad fish. "Couldn't figure out how to explain the entire thing to the rest of the family and my friends, Gloriana. Olympus, gods and goddesses. It defies logic."

"Da, ease up now." Jerry stepped closer to his father. "We know there are many things on Earth that defy logic, vampires included. I think it is quite remarkable that Gloriana is related to royalty."

"Royalty?" Mag Campbell sniffed. "Is that what it is called? This Olympus is some place in the ether, I ken. Where is it exactly? And, Hebe, you claim Zeus, like in mythology, is the king? He's your father?"

"I *claim* nothing. It is a fact that my father is very powerful. And where we live is not your business." My mother stepped closer. Her fire-throwing finger was twitching. "Can your queen make the earth shake, mountains crumble and the skies rain fire?"

"Let's not get into politics now. Please?" I laid my hand on Mother's. Yes, that finger was hot. Damn it. "Mother, isn't Lady Campbell's dress beautiful? St. Laurent, I believe. Did you go shopping in Paris, Mag?"

"Yes, I did. My son doesn't get married every century." She looked fondly at Jerry. "Thank the good Lord."

"Now just a minute." Mars reached for his pocket square. I was afraid of what it could do. Make someone vanish? Set fire to the room?

"Dad, I'm sure Mag meant that she is glad Jerry hasn't been one of those men who treat marriage lightly." I shut up when both of my parents glared at me. Oh, yes. Their own wedding vows had been little more than a joke.

"Ma, I'm glad you admit this is a special occasion. I'm marrying the woman I love." Jerry kissed me on the cheek. "The band is starting soon. Shouldn't we go up and let the, um, St. Clairs meet the rest of the family?" He pulled open the door and loud music hit us hard.

"Good idea. No need to stay in here." I hustled my parents out and into the crowd.

"Gloriana, I'm not sure we should stay. This music…" Mother looked toward where the band was setting up. What we were hearing was courtesy of a disc jockey but probably just a sample of things to come. "It is very loud."

"Are you saying you're too old to appreciate a rock band, Mother?" I teased her as I steered her around the crowd and toward the stairs. "Come on. Be as gracious as I know you can be. Apparently some of Jerry's relatives are fans. You don't have to stay for the entire show, but you can at least come up and meet the rest of the Campbells."

"We are young enough to appreciate all kinds of music." My father was right behind me. He'd been careful to make the Campbells go up the stairs first. He obviously didn't want vampires following him. "Maybe we'll dance, Helen." He emphasized her new name.

Upstairs we made quick introductions and got everyone seated before the band started. To my relief it wasn't a loud band but one that did a lot of ballads, some of them with a Scottish sound. The Campbells were happy and had glasses of blood with alcohol in front of them, keeping the waitresses busy running up and down the stairs. My parents ordered a bottle of expensive champagne and toasted each other like *they* were the couple about to be married.

"It's going well, I think." Jerry whispered in my ear when we saw my parents head down the stairs to dance to a slow song.

"So far. Your parents and mine are sitting on opposite ends of the balcony. But I was worried there at first." I leaned against him. "Dance?"

"Sure. Oh, now my parents are getting up too. Guess they couldn't be outdone by your folks." It was true. Laird and Lady Campbell were headed for the dance floor.

I put my hand on Jerry's and we stopped at the top of the stairs. It was like there was a Dancing with the Stars competition going on. If my father dipped my mother, then the Laird twirled Mag until she was dizzy. They bumped into each other and Jerry was down the stairs so fast I was afraid the mortals below might notice.

Jerry stepped between the simmering males. I had a feeling he'd said something that diffused the situation when he clapped his father on the back then laughed. I hurried down the stairs to join him when the couples started dancing again.

"What did you say?" I whispered to Jerry as I moved into his arms.

"That it was a tie. I told them they'd have to quit doing a dance battle or I'd take both men outside and we'd settle it there." He pulled me close. "They were eager to do that, of course. But your mother and mine insisted they keep dancing. So they calmed down." He laughed. "Max and Helen?"

"I know!" I rested my head on his cashmere sweater. "I am actually proud of them. They're trying to fit in."

"Yes, they are." He leaned his cheek on my hair. "What a relief. I had visions of lightning bolts tonight."

"Don't rule it out." I closed my eyes and let Jerry lead me as we moved to the music. Two more nights and we'd be married and could go on with our lives. I couldn't wait.

#

If what they say about bad rehearsals making great weddings was true, then tomorrow night would be amazing. Jerry's parents had brought the Campbell family priest over on their chartered jet to marry us. Now he was balking because we hadn't had premarital counseling. Seriously? After four hundred plus years together?

"Father, if you won't marry us, my best man, Richard Mainwaring, will." Jerry wasn't going to put up with a delay.

"I'm familiar with Mainwaring." Father Tim, as they called him, sniffed. "He's no longer accepted in the church. Would you want to be married by such as that, son?"

"Frankly, I don't care who marries us tomorrow. Just so long as it's done." Jerry held my hand, his strength keeping me from saying something I'd regret or bursting into tears.

We'd been pulled into Damian's study for this talk and I knew both sets of parents weren't far away. I was itching to check on them. The priest was staring at me. Had he asked a question?

"I'm sorry, Father. I'm a little distracted. What did you say?" I smiled for him. Yes, he was a vampire. Everyone Campbell was. But he was a comfortable looking man who did inspire trust.

"Gloriana, I asked if you belonged to the Church." He reached out his hand and I let go of Jerry's to take it. "I've heard you and Jeremiah are from very different backgrounds. Seems like caution is called for here."

"Not your church. I go to the Moonlight Church of Eternal Light and Joy." I lost my smile when Father Tim's face fell. "It's nondenominational." I squeezed his fingers. "You know how difficult it is for vampires to find a, um, church family."

"Of course. I'm sure it's just fine but not the answer I was hoping for." Father Tim sighed. "Are you two very sure you are suited? Marriage is forever, you ken. I want your assurances that you intend to keep your vows." The priest looked at me when he said that.

"Of course we intend to stay married." I dropped his hand and jumped to my feet. "It took me hundreds of years to commit to Jeremiah. Now that I am ready to marry him, I expect it to last forever." I reached for Jerry's hand. "Do you doubt that, Jerry?"

"Not for a moment. Father, does that satisfy you? Can we get out of here now?" Jerry was frowning. Obviously he was unhappy with how this had gone.

"Yes, of course. I'll marry you two, Jeremiah, but it won't be with the Church's full blessing." Father Tim sighed.

"That's fine with me, Father. I'm sure you know that I'm doing this for my parents. Gloriana and I would be perfectly happy going to a Justice of the Peace." Jerry drew me back against him when Father Tim crossed himself and muttered something. "But thank you for doing it instead." Jerry clapped the priest on the back with his free hand as the door burst open.

"Gloriana, you must get out here. The Campbells are insisting that they wear native dress tomorrow." My mother smiled at the priest. "Oh, is that a clerical collar? Gloriana, are you having a *Catholic* wedding?" She said it like I'd agreed to bring Beelzebub up from Hell to perform the ceremony.

"Mother, this is Father Timothy Campbell." I hurried to her side. "Let it go. What other kind of wedding would we have? Would one of the sorcerers toss incense at us and recite something in Greek?" I whispered this in her ear.

"A pleasure." Father Tim approached my mother with his hand outstretched.

My mother looked like she'd rather touch a snake but gritted her teeth and let him take her fingertips. "Helen St. Clair. Father, I hope you understand that Gloriana comes from a different background than the Campbells."

"Yes, we discussed that." The priest was solemn. "We can only hope that love will help them overcome any differences they have. Now Gloriana was telling me about her church. Do you go there too?" Father Tim smiled. He was relieved that Jerry was marrying a church-goer no matter the religion.

"You go to church?" My mother stepped back from the priest and grabbed my arm. "Gloriana, it is obvious we have much to discuss."

"About the 'native dress', Mother." I grinned at Jerry. "That's the Campbell plaid. The Campbell men are wearing their kilts, including Jerry. You should see Jerry in one. He looks amazing." As I knew it would, it got Mother's mind off of the religious debate.

"Kilts? Men's skirts?" Mother turned around when Mars entered the room behind her. "Did you hear that, M-Max? The Campbell men are wearing their kilts to the wedding."

"Then I think I should wear my usual formal dress, Gloriana." Mars slipped his arm around my mother's waist. "What do you think, Helen? We could both wear our court dress."

"No!" I looked at Jerry for backup.

"And what would that be?" Father Tim was eager to meet my father and had his hand out again, introducing himself. The men shook hands. "Your wife was just discussing the religious differences as well." He looked at Jerry fondly. "I've known this lad for centuries. All I want is his happiness. As I'm sure you want for your daughter. It won't be easy for them with so many differences between them."

"Oh, we've been against this marriage from the start. Religion is just a small part of it." My mother was warming up to the priest. "Tried everything we could to get Gloriana to change her mind. Even gave them time apart." She sighed heavily. "But she claims he is the only man she can love."

"She not only claims it, she knows it." I had to put a stop to this. "The wedding is on."

"It certainly is." Jerry gave the priest a searching look. "I don't know where this is coming from but Gloriana and I don't have any differences now. We've worked them out." Jerry began ushering the group toward the door. He looked at Mars. "Last I heard you were wearing a tux and walking your daughter down the aisle. I doubt Gloriana wants you sporting your court dress tomorrow, do you, my love?"

"Absolutely not. I'll get my brother to escort me if you show up wearing anything but a tuxedo, Dad." Miguel was around and had told everyone he met that he was my half-brother. Jerry wasn't thrilled but he was dealing with it.

"You wouldn't do that." Mars looked like he had thunder and lightning on his mind.

"Yes, I would." I put my hand on his arm. "Remember, Max and Helen St. Clair don't have court dress. And that's who you are, right?" I ignored the priest's puzzled look.

"I suppose." Mother smiled. "Let it go, Max. I do have the most amazing dress, the one we bought in New York. I'm sure Mag Campbell won't have anything half as beautiful." She ignored Jerry's groan. "Now about these flowers…" she took my arm and dragged me toward the courtyard.

"There they are!" Angus Campbell, the Laird, came bustling toward me. "I see Father Tim got time to bend your ear. Ignore him. He's been fussing ever since we pulled him onto the plane."

"Da, why would Father Tim have a problem with this marriage?" Jerry was too close to his father.

"Your mother might have said a few things." Angus gestured toward where Mag was surrounded by a group of Campbells. I heard her say my name.

"About Gloriana?" Jerry marched straight to his mother and made excuses to the group then strong-armed her over to me. Of course my mother was still by my side, not about to miss a moment if there was a confrontation in the works.

"Gloriana, Helen." Mag was all graciousness as her eyes swept over both of us.

I dared her to find fault with either our clothes or our manners. Of course I held my mother's arm in a grip that telegraphed caution. This was my future mother-in-law and frying her with a flaming finger was not going to happen, no matter how she provoked us.

"Magdalena, lovely dress you're wearing. I saw something like it in New York." My mother smirked. "Didn't buy it. I thought that shade of yellow a bit too…"

"Oh, yes. It would look horrid with brassy blonde hair." Mag countered.

"Ma, I just got through with Father Tim. Clearly you have been spreading your poison about Gloriana." Jerry took her by the shoulders. "This has been going on since I first brought her home to the Castle. I was a fool for thinking you would come to love her as I do." He tightened his grip and I saw the Laird step closer. "Obviously you are too damned stubborn to change. So be it." He let her go and pulled me to his side.

"Jeremiah." Mag reached out to him.

"No, say nothing. You have one choice. Accept Gloriana and be kind to her or I'm done with you. I love her and am wedding her. She will come first with me. Above all others. If you say one more hurtful thing to her or about her, you will never see me again. Is that clear?"

"Jeremiah Campbell, you'll not speak to your mother so!" The Laird pushed in between Mag and her son. "Apologize at once!

Poison indeed."

"Da, this is between Ma and me." Jerry put his shoulder against his father's. "But if you want to make it your fight too, I can cut you out of my life as well. Gloriana's my choice. Am I clear?"

Muttering what were probably Gaelic curses, Angus stepped aside. "Mag, the boy has loved her these many centuries, *luaidh*. If you persist in this campaign to discredit the lass, you'll only drive him away. Your hatred is uncalled for. The girl has done nothing to earn it."

"She is not worthy to bear the Campbell name. You know that. Who was she when Jeremiah brought her home? Nothing. Nobody. A common--"

"You are singing an old tune, woman. Look at the girl now. She is not that widow who had to make her own way in the world on the stage, Mag." Angus took his wife's hands in his and forced her to look at him. "The very fact that our boy still loves her after all this time should be enough to convince you that the lass is worthy. Is hanging onto old ways worth losing him? Truly? Is being right so important to you, *mnaoi*?"

Mag looked at me with what could only be described as loathing. The courtyard had grown very quiet.

"Listen to me, woman." My mother hadn't moved but her voice rang out and I wanted to slap a hand over her mouth. I couldn't move. The old freeze trick at work. Shit.

"Do you think her father and I are happy that our daughter is marrying a vampire?" A glass shattered nearby. Surprise, surprise. "Where we come from bloodsuckers are despised. My father only spared your son because our daughter loved him and Jeremiah proved his bravery." She looked at me. "Oh, yes, Gloriana, your grandfather knows this wedding is happening. He won't send his blessing, but he is allowing it. You know he could stop it with one gesture."

"I don't believe you." Mag raised her chin. "Who in the hell are you? I didn't swallow that nonsense about Olympus for one minute."

Mother looked around. She was in her element here, showing her roots as the daughter of the most powerful god in Olympus. She raised a hand and thunder shook the clear night sky then lightning flashed.

Mars came up behind her and decided to join the party. He

glanced at a nearby tree and I wished I could move. Did he remember I was supposed to be married here tomorrow night? Burning down the landscaping wouldn't add to the ambience. He smiled at me then pointed to a shed at the house next door. He flicked a wrist and the wooden building burst into flames. That caused a gasp from the crowd. Another gesture and rain hit just that one spot, drowning out the fire. We could all smell the wet, charred wood.

Father Tim crossed himself. The crowd was restless and muttering but looking at me with new respect. Flo, Richard and Damian had come running out of the house at the first sound of thunder.

"*Mio Dio*, are your parents going to bring the skies down around us, Glory?" Flo grabbed my arm but soon realized I couldn't answer her. "Oh, you are frozen. That is too bad of them."

"Please stop this." Jerry was still in front of his mother. "Who or what Glory's parents are isn't your concern. Helen is right. She and Max are powerful. She's told you who they are. Believe it or suffer the consequences." He glanced meaningfully at the smoldering ruin next door.

"Gloriana hates us." Mag just didn't know when to quit.

"Ma, I know first-hand that vampires aren't accepted where they come from." Jerry stepped to my side. He glared at my parents when he realized I couldn't move. "When Gloriana was in their homeland, she was mortal again. No, not mortal, more than mortal." He looked into my eyes and I'd have given anything if I could have smiled back with the same look of love. "She gave up a life that offered her a chance to have children, a normal family and power. For me."

Mag was now leaning against Angus and they both looked shocked to their toes. Finally Mag drew herself up.

"We are not ashamed of being vampire." But her voice shook and she flinched when my mother aimed a finger at her.

"And *I'm* not ashamed of my daughter." Mother had a way of smiling that made you want to beg for mercy. "Our children have made their choices. Now we must live with them. Agreed?"

"I don't know about that, um, Helen. This woman has obviously made Gloriana's life hell for a long time." Mars strutted around Mag and Angus, looking for a fight. "You, sir, what do you say? Is your woman doing all the talking here?"

"By God!" Angus reached for his sword but of course we hadn't allowed any weapons onto the property. In fact, Damian had employed security to check everyone at the door and they had confiscated a huge array of knives and other hidden weapons. "I'll have you know I always liked Gloriana. You seem a man of the world. Are you telling me you control this fiancé of yours?" He nodded toward my mother.

I would have laughed if I'd been able. Mother's eyebrow was up as she waited for Mars to answer that.

"Point taken." Mars nodded. "Jeremiah, is it true that your father has been on Gloriana's side in all this?"

"Yes. Da has been fair to her." Jerry ran his hand through his hair, suddenly tired of the whole thing. Who could blame him? "Now would one of you release Gloriana from the spell you have her under? She's about to lose it, trapped as she is." He held my hand. "Anyone who can't allow this wedding to go on without objection, should leave now and not come back tomorrow night. Is that clear?"

Mother turned and waved her hand so that I was suddenly free.

"Thanks, Jerry." I threw myself into his arms. "I agree with everything he said. If anyone," I turned to face my parents, "Anyone, tries to stop this wedding again, we will make him or her very, very sorry. We tie the knot tomorrow night and that's that."

"Good news." The voice from the sliding glass door made everyone turn at once. "Dad, I'm glad you are finally marrying the woman you love. You need help keeping away the naysayers, I'm here for you."

"Lily. I thought you were on the other side of the world." Jerry walked over to hug his daughter. "Come meet Gloriana's parents."

"Are you sure it's safe? I saw quite a display from the living room." She smiled though and came out to get introductions. "Glory, I think I want to hear the story of how you suddenly got parents and such powerful ones."

"When we're alone. Sure." I was happy to see her. Jerry had been texting her, but had been disappointed when she hadn't responded. "If you have a red dress, I'll put you in as another bridesmaid."

"I'd love that." She was suddenly surrounded by Campbells. "Well, look who else is here." They took her off to catch up. I noticed she avoided Mag as she greeted her cousins.

"Glory, another bridesmaid? We will not match." Flo wasn't happy.

"I'll say. And I didn't like the attitude of those Campbells." Charis was by Flo's side and they both pulled me as far away from Mag and Angus as the space allowed. "Jerry's mother seems like a real bitch."

"Welcome to my world. I've been putting up with her for hundreds of years." I glanced at the huddle of Campbells around Lily. "Excuse me, ladies. If you get a chance, talk to Lily about your dresses." I left Flo and Charis griping about changes while I went over to Mars.

"Yes, the wine and champagne came earlier in the week and is chilling now." Damian looked a little badgered. "The caterer has called me six times to confirm the food. Really, Max, it will all work out. I promise you. I have held many Winter Solstice Balls here. The wedding will go off without a hitch."

"It had better. I want everything perfect for my daughter's wedding. Where the hell is the band?" Mars sounded like a general, ready to lay into a new recruit. "I want to see the setup."

"Dad, please trust Damian to know how to do this." I smiled at Damian then kissed his cheek. "Damian's parties are legendary. We are so lucky he's letting us use his home." I pulled Mars away from our host. "Come here. Let me talk to you."

"I'm sorry if starting that fire upset you, Gloriana. But I'll not be pushed around by the likes of those Scots." He looked over at the vampires, now taking glasses of synthetic blood with alcohol from a circulating waiter. Good call by Damian. Maybe it would mellow them out. Or not. "Notice, Daughter, that I did not call them by a name you could object to."

"Yes, you're trying. I appreciate that. And the fire was necessary, I think. To prove to Mag that I come from extraordinary people." I kissed his cheek. "You are really being wonderful about this wedding when I know you don't approve of Jerry."

"I don't dislike the man. Just what he is. If you love him and he makes you happy, then you'll have him. At least he's a warrior." Mars couldn't take his eyes off of Mag and Angus. "Wish we could dispose of the family. You know Zeus could arrange a little something. An earthquake or a rock slide at their castle. No one would have to know who it came from. I mean where, of course." He smiled and rubbed his hands together. "Yes, I need to have a little talk with your grandfather."

"Don't you dare. If any harm comes to my in-laws, I'll never forgive you." I held onto his arm. "In fact, it would be wise of you to get one of your sorcerers to put a protective spell on the entire family."

"Now Gloriana, that's a little extreme, don't you think?" Mars patted my hand. "I'd better go see to your mother. She's into the champagne and looks ready to take on that Campbell woman again."

"Yes, please keep them apart." I had my own worries now. The band was arriving and, of course, Ray. I saw Jerry turn as if he had Israel Caine radar. Ray held some sheet music and walked over to the baby grand piano which had been wheeled out to the terrace a few hours before. Uh oh. Jerry had a determined look on his face. He was going to confront Ray about my confession.

I had to practically fly across the stone floor to beat Jerry there. "Ray, thanks for coming. Did you get my text? About the songs?"

"Sure, babe. Good choices. I've got a new song I'd like to sing for you tonight. See if it will work for your first dance." Ray kissed me on the cheek then looked over my shoulder. "Blade."

"Caine. We need to talk." Jerry nodded toward the house. "Inside."

"No, you don't." I slid my arm around Jerry's waist. "Jer, Ray has things to do. And you two have absolutely nothing to say to each other."

"Oh, don't we?" Jerry stepped away from me. "I said inside, Caine."

"What's this about?" Ray looked at me. "Glory?"

"I told him. About us." I had sworn I'd never freeze Jerry again and I wouldn't now. So I just stepped between the two men. "Jer, it was nothing. Really. I love *you*."

"I won't do this here. Every vampire can hear us." Jerry gently moved me out of the way. "Are you coming in, Caine? Or do I have to force you to move your ass?"

"You could try." Ray grinned like he was looking forward to a fight. "But this is Glory's party. I don't want to upset her, so let's go." He strolled toward the house, hands in his pockets, like he didn't have a worry in the world. The fact that those hands pulled his already snug jeans taut over his butt was just unfair.

Jerry noticed me watching Ray walk and snarled. "Will you ever quit?"

"What? I like eye candy. So do you. Are you telling me you don't notice good looking women? Ever?" I teased his cheek with a fingertip. "And if you think I'm letting you two go in there without me, think again." I sashayed after Ray, putting a twitch in my hips that I hoped would distract Jerry from thoughts of murder.

"You could at least pretend to be over him." Jerry grabbed my elbow and jerked me to a stop.

"Ow! I am over him. I just like to watch. There are some Campbell cousins with great butts I've looked over tonight too. You mad about that?" I glanced at the way he gripped my arm. "Let go."

"Sorry." Jerry marched into the house. "You know I want to kill the son of a bitch. I keep seeing him with you. Fucking you. It's making me crazy." He finally stopped at the same door where we'd met with the priest, Damian's study. Ray was staring into the fireplace but whirled when he heard what Jerry said.

"Yeah, that *would* bug the hell out of you." Ray didn't smile. "You won, man. You gonna begrudge me the few times I got to live my dream?"

"Shit. You talk like one of your sappy songs, *aesheʊl*." Jerry had his hands fisted but was holding himself back. I was proud of him.

"She chose *you*. Made it clear to me. So let it go." Ray strode past Jerry and out of the room, his face unreadable. He stopped and turned around, his fist raised. "But the next time you insult my music, *I* won't let it go." Then he was gone.

"Thanks, Jerry." I leaned against him, so relieved I was weak in the knees. "You want me to tell Ray to forget singing at the wedding?"

"No, I can take it." Jerry lifted my chin and kissed me hungrily. "He said it himself. I won." He cocked his head. "Did you just hear thunder? Either the weather report was wrong or your parents are tuning up for a showdown."

I ran for the terrace, determined to keep things calm. Twenty-four more hours. Then I was escaping with Jerry to an island somewhere and a magical honeymoon. If we could prevent the war sure to come, that is.

#

My wedding day. Technically speaking, it was night, of course. I was getting dressed in one of Damian's bedrooms. Flo was on hand to help me with all those buttons. She looked great in her red bridesmaid dress. To my surprise, she, Charis and Lily had decided to add a sash of Campbell plaid to the dresses.

"The hem is perfect. You can just see the toes of your shoes." Flo fluffed out my skirt.

"I was lucky to find these shoes. You sure they look all right?" I was unbelievably nervous. I kept worrying something would go wrong. Since the showdown between the parents the night before, things had settled down. The rehearsal dinner had been a lively affair at N-V with an impromptu performance of the sword dance by Jerry and his cousins. They'd been accompanied by the bagpipers brought in for the wedding. I would never forget Jer's face as he'd laughed and jumped over his sword. My man.

"Earth to Glory." Flo laughed and hugged me. "We have company." She nodded toward the door. "The mothers are here."

The mothers indeed. Mag and my own mother stood side by side in the hallway. I could tell it was a test to see which one I would invite in first. I compromised, stepping outside the door.

"How do I look?" I twirled in front of them.

"Lovely." "Perfect." They looked at each other in surprise, for once agreeing on something.

"We came by to help you put the finishing touches on your costume." Mag held out a coin. "In Scotland a bride puts a sixpence in her shoe for luck."

"Oh, Glory, we almost forgot." Flo exclaimed. "Something old, something new, something borrowed, something blue and a sixpence for your shoe." She handed me the heart shaped diamond ring from her finger. "Wear this on your right hand. You can borrow it."

"Oh, Flo. I couldn't. What if it slips off?" I shoved it on my ring finger anyway. No chance of that. The real question was how I was ever going to get it off.

"I trust you." Flo looked at my mother. "Do you have something for Glory, Helen?"

My mother looked like she'd swallowed a porcupine. I was sure it was because Flo had addressed her so casually. "Yes. I brought something very old for you, Gloriana." She handed me a delicate piece of lace, the trim like a spider's web. "This handkerchief belongs to my mother. She wishes she could be here but never comes to

Earth." Mother glanced at Mag. "My mother doesn't like to fly."

"So many elderly people feel that way." Mag said. We all looked skyward when thunder boomed. "Oh, dear. I hope it doesn't rain."

"It won't." My mother said decisively as I carefully tucked the handkerchief between my breasts. "Now, Gloriana, you need something blue and something new."

"Well, the new is covered. Jerry gave me this last night." I held out my wrist and showed them the diamond bracelet Jerry had surprised me with. It was covered by my long sleeve but I wouldn't have taken it off for anything.

"My son is so thoughtful." Mag preened.

"Here's something blue, Glory." Charis rushed in with a small box. "I hit the Internet and found out you should have a garter. To toss to the single girls in the crowd." She pulled off the lid and showed us a blue satin and lace garter. "You put it on under the dress." She winked. "And, yes, I paid for it. At that little boutique down the street from you, Girly Things."

"Thanks, Charis." I hugged her then held up my dress and set my foot on a chair so she could help me put it on. "I toss the bouquet to the girls though and the garter to the single guys. I did some research too."

"Oh, right." She laughed. "I knew I had a chance somehow."

"Very nice of you, Charis." Mother smiled. "You see, Magdalena, our family is thoughtful too." Now it was Jerry's mother's turn to look like she'd swallowed something unpleasant.

"I think it's time to head downstairs." Flo shooed everyone out. "Give Glory a minute to breathe. I remember my wedding. I was going crazy, so surrounded by people." She walked outside and shut the door.

I stared at the door, listening to the noises of the crowd as everyone went to get ready. I walked over to the window that looked down at the terrace. The moon was brilliant in the night sky and it was cool tonight but not too cold. The longest night of the year, always a great night to celebrate for vampires. There was a good crowd. Ian had been right—just about every vampire in town was here, plus a few shape-shifters, of course. Add the Campbells and the terrace was full.

Ray's band was playing quietly. As I watched, Damian began moving among the guests, urging them to take their seats. This was really happening. I was going to get married. My heart was pounding and my palms were sweating. I found a linen hand towel to blot them with. I couldn't believe this could go off without a hitch. I saw Jerry, Richard and Jerry's brothers move to the front of the aisle where Father Tim waited. Jerry looked solemn and so handsome my stomach twisted with hunger. Would it always be so? Hundreds of years from now? I hoped so.

Ray's voice soared above the crowd. He sang of love, of waiting for your one true love. When Flo opened the door and whispered that they were starting down, I felt like I was floating on a cloud of that love. She handed me my bouquet then left. I headed back to the window to watch. Lily moved away from the door first. She was a beautiful copy of her father. She did the Campbell plaid proud and the spray of heather pinned on her shoulder looked perfect.

Next Charis walked out onto the terrace. She'd pinned her plaid with a symbol from Olympus. Not many in the crowd would recognize the lightning bolt for what it was but my mother smiled and reached out to brush her hand when she got close to the altar.

Then Flo stepped outside. She was the tiniest of the bridesmaids but you would never discount my best friend. She walked regally down the aisle. Her plaid was pinned with a beautiful jeweled brooch that must have set Richard back a pretty penny. Her smile at him surely was full of the memory of their wedding here not so long ago.

Then the bagpipes began to play a traditional wedding song as I'd requested. I tore myself from my window and walked down the stairs to my father's side.

"You are beautiful, Gloriana. I couldn't be prouder." Dad kissed my cheek then tucked my left hand in the crook of his arm.

We walked out onto the terrace and everyone stood. All eyes were on us but I couldn't look at anyone but Jerry. He smiled and my heart turned over. He loved me. He was giving me *his* heart. When Dad placed my hand in Jerry's, I never looked back. This was where I belonged. Forever.

ABOUT THE AUTHOR

Gerry Bartlett is a native Texan and lives halfway between Houston and Galveston. When she's not writing her bestselling ***Real Vampires*** series, she is treasure hunting for her antiques business on the historic Strand in Galveston. You can read more about Gerry and her series at gerrybartlett.com, friend her on Facebook, follow her on twitter @gerrybartlett or Instagram.

CPSIA information can be obtained at www.ICGtesting.com
Printed in the USA
LVOW04s0650140415

434402LV00037B/2461/P